Resurrected Light

Resurrected Light

Savanna Macphee

ISBN:	Softcover	978-1-5245-0759-6
	eBook	978-1-5245-0758-9

Print information available on the last page.

Rev. date: 05/02/2015

To order additional copies of this book, contact:
Xlibris
1-888-795-4274
www.Xlibris.com
Orders@Xlibris.com

743332

CONTENTS

Preface

400 years ago, a great battle started in the town of Spirit-villa, and now the times have come again for another great battle between a white spirit name Anilea, and a dark spirit name Donovan.

Will they battle for the last time, after years of fighting? Their fought during the dark ages, taking a long break and now will them going at it again.

Donovan, a 1614-year-old dark spirit, wanting to rule over the human kind to make their pity lives a living hell. His dark spirits followers Desdemona, Eris, Ryu, and Crevan, listen to every word Donovan say to him. They do nothing but cause trouble and terror to the human lives. The only thing Donovan wants is to kill Anilea for good and her friends too.

Anilea, a 1314-year-old white spirit, wanting to protect the human kind from the dark spirits, try to live a normal life. Her friends Roselyn, Tiffany, Andrew, and Aaron, all white spirits and follow Anilea every word. They protect the humans from the darkness, and live out a normal life the best they can too. Anilea only goal is to put an end to Donovan evil ways for good, so she can finally rest forever.

Anilea and her friends come back to Spirit-villa again, a year before the battle began. Anilea live a longer spirit life then her friends, and trying to put the pain of her human past life behind her for good. She knows that she must carry out her mission to end Donovan evil ways for good, but the entire human live that are lost during this battle plays out in her mind. Anilea try to force on her mission, but the pain of losing her only human family, friends, and lover fill her heart with pain. Anilea, human name is Sanna so no one will know that she a white spirit. She had that name for a long time, since she was reborn into her spirit form.

Anilea meets Adam, a normal 26-year-old human. Adam helps Anilea out, but does not know that she a spirit for a long time. They started to fell in love with each other, but Anilea has a feeling that something about Adam. What is it?

A battle will beak out in the town and things will happen.

Will lives be lost again or not?

Who will win the fight?

Will love save a life or not?

"I can hear their shrieks, the howling of help, and the sounds of torment in the wind blowing around me. Cries of babies, screams of the children, men, and women. I can see the people running through the streets of the town screaming in terror at the top of their lungs. The fire blazing through the town, through out the builds and homes, people died bodies lying all over the roads, blood all over the place... Their blood is on my hands."

~Anilea Thoughts.

CHAPTER ONE

Coming Home!

Young woman wearing a long white flowing thin strap dress, stood solemnly in front of a huge wall of fire with a sword clinch in her right hand, blood drizzling to the ground from a cut across her upper right arm. She lowers her head, and speaking in a whisper, "The deal is done. It is over... Finally," her long blonde ponytail glow by the light of the fire as the moon glistening off the lake. She drops her sword from her hand to the ground, looking at the fire with sigh as she turns her back to the fire.

Dark male shadows appear in the fire-blazing wall, eyes glowing from the fire light. His right hand reaches out of the fire, and grabbing the back of her dress in his hand. Fear hit her eyes with the hand still on her back of her dress. "It can not be," she spoke in a stun voice, turning her head to the shadow with her fear eyes looking at the shadow standing there in the firewall. The shadow started to drag her back into the fire, she let out aloud scream in the air, as she was being drag into the fire.

~~*~*~*~*~*~*~*~*~*

"Sanna, Sanna wake up!" Roselyn say rubbing Sanna shoulders with her hands. Roselyn, a brown straight shoulder length hair, 5 ft 3 in tall with blue eye, and look like a 28-year-old human woman, but really is 655-year-old white spirit. Roselyn like wearing blue jeans, long sleeves shirts, and flat shoes. Sanna was sleeping in the backseat of the car, "Sanna wake up!" Roselyn keep on rubbing Sanna shoulders with her hands, but Sanna just grumble a bit under her breath. "Anilea wake up!" Roselyn slapping Sanna face with her right hand.

Sanna eyes shot open quickly, and started to breathe heavily. Sanna a.k.a Anilea is a 1314 year-old white spirit, but looking like a 25 year-old woman, 5 ft tall even with hazel eyes, and a scare across her upper right arm from the first battle with Donovan after a long break. "Where are we?" Sanna spoke to Roselyn, looking at Rosalyn and Tiffany standing outside the car, and calming down a bit to know that her friends were the one with her.

"We stop here, because you were screaming in your sleep, and you're bleeding from your right upper arm again," say Tiffany to Sanna, standing by the car back passenger door, and lending against the door. Tiffany is Roselyn twin sister with medium length straight brown hair with a few white highlights, 5 ft 3 in tall with blue eyes, and like 28 year-old but is 655-year-old white spirit. Tiffany like wearing jeans, t-shirt, and running shoes.

Sanna look over at her right upper arm, and seeing the blood bleeding from under her light grey hoodie jacket. "I did it again. I reopen an old wound again," Sanna see the blood through her hoodie jacket, and giving a small chuckled at her seeing the blood on the hoodie jacket.

"Yes, you did," Roselyn say to Sanna, looking at Sanna to know Sanna will be okay, "Take off your hoodie and I will fix the wound for you." Sanna took off her hoodie jacket showing her tank-top underneath. Sanna looks at the wound, taking her left hand, touching the wound with her fingers tips, and looking at the blood on fingers. Sanna had a flashback to her past on the day she got that wound. Sanna curled her left hand into a fist, and trying to stay calm. "Don't worry Sanna. It will heal," Roselyn told Sanna, touching the wound with her hand, and looking it over closely. "Tiffany goes get the first-aid kit from the trunk of the car for me please," Roselyn ask Tiffany nicely.

"Okay Roselyn," Tiffany says to Roselyn going to get the first aid from the trunk of the car, grabbing the kit, and handing the kit to Roselyn.

"Thank-you Tiffany," Roselyn thanks Tiffany, holding the kit in her hands. Roselyn open the kit, looking through the first-aid kit, trying to find the first-aid spray, and could not find it. "Tiffany, I need some herds to heal this wound, and you know what ones too," Roselyn ask Tiffany. Tiffany nodded her head to Roselyn, running into the forest for a bit, and coming back in a few minute with herd in her hands. Tiffany handed the herds to Roselyn, "Thanks Tiffany." Roselyn put the herds into a bowel and started to grind the herds up, "Tiffany takes Sanna hoodie and cleans the blood out of it."

"Sure sister," Tiffany grab Sanna jacket from the ground, and walking to the creek in the forest to clean the blood out of it.

Roselyn put the ground up herbs on a glazed pad. "I'm going to blow it," Sanna softly told Roselyn looking down at the car floor, and thinking about all the times she fought with Donovan.

Roselyn put the glazed pad on Sanna right upper arm, and looking at Sanna for a moment. "You're not going to blow it," Roselyn told Sanna making sure the wound was cover up by the glazed pad, and starting to wrap the arm up with a bandage wrap.

"I am sorry; I did not mean to reopen the wound again. It's just..." Sanna started to say still looking down at the car floor, and rethinking over things in her mind.

"It's alright, I was watching you sleeping. I saw you grab the right arm, and ripping opening the wound, that why we stop here at this rest stop," Roselyn finish wrapping Sanna right arm, and cleaning up now.

"I see," Sanna looking up and around at the area, the birds was crippling in the tree, the sound of the running cheek in the trees, and the sight of empty of campgrounds.

Tiffany came back with Sanna hoodie jacket in her hands. "Here you are Sanna, all clean," Tiffany says to Sanna handing the jacket to Sanna.

Sanna reach out of her jacket, feeling something was not right with her jacket, and ask Tiffany, "You use your powers to remove the blood and dry it." Sanna grabbing her jacket from Tiffany hands, hold the jacket in her own hands, and looking it over at the sleeve of the jacket.

"Maybe, I did," Tiffany told Sanna looking at Sanna in the face, and knowing what she did to Sanna jacket by using her powers to remove the blood from it.

"YOU'RE AN IDIOT, TIFFANY!" Sanna yelled punching the back of the front passenger seat with her right fist.

"Hey easy, I am not going to heal this wound if you going to hurt it more," Roselyn yelled at Sanna getting off the ground and looking at Sanna, who was still in the backseat of the car.

"What if someone saw Tiffany using her powers?" Sanna was piss-off at Tiffany actions, and worrying that someone saw Tiffany using her powers on her jacket.

"Don't worry no one saw me. We are the only ones here, and no they are not here at all," Tiffany tells Sanna as she sat down in the front passenger seat of the car.

"Don't worry Sanna; we are three hours away from home," Roselyn tell Sanna walking a few steps from the car, and letting Sanna exit the car for a moment. Sanna exit the car to breathe, putting on her jacket on her body, walks up to an old death three standing on the edge of the tree line. Sanna placing her hands on the tree, and blast the tree into pieces with her powers. Sanna turn around, walk to back to the car, sitting back down in the back seat, and closing the car door. Roselyn sat down in the driving seat, starting the car up, and Roselyn look in the rear-view mirror at Sanna. "Feel better?" Roselyn ask Sanna with a smile on her face. Sanna sigh and look out of the window. Roselyn drive along the road, "We are almost home." Roselyn say to everyone in the car, turning onto the small road.

Sanna was thinking to herself, '*What is a home? Is it a wooden structure or in your heart? I have no real home anymore... Why do we come to this town? Is it to finish what we started almost 400 year ago or to destroy the town every time? Why can I relax and finger out where I belong for once?*'

Roselyn pull into the small town called Spirit-villa, and to the house. The car pulls into the driveway in front of the house. Sanna look out the window at the house. "Welcome home," Sanna whisper to her quietly. Sanna pulling her baseball hat down almost covering her eyes a bit, exit the car with her jacket on, and hands in the pockets. Spirit-villa is a small town in the mountains with a large lake within the town. On the lake is a large inland with forest life, and looks so lovely. The town made small, but has the big caring heart ever to any new comers.

Roselyn and Tiffany exited the car first with Sanna not far behind them. Two men were unloading the moving truck, "Boys, we're here, did you miss us?" Tiffany says to the two men with boxes in their hands.

"Of course, I miss you," say Aaron kissing Tiffany on the lips with a box in his arms. Aaron is 6 ft tall, short brown hair with brown eyes, wearing jeans, t-shirt, and running shoes. Look like a 29-year-old male, but is 655-year-old white spirit, and Aaron married to Tiffany for along time.

"Me too," say Andrew kissing Roselyn on the lips with a box in his arms. Andrew is 6 ft tall, long brown hair passes the shoulders a bit, with brown eyes, wearing jeans, long sleeves shirt, and running shoes. Look like a 29 year-old man, but is a 655-year-old white spirit, marry to Roselyn for along time, and is twins to Aaron. Andrew, Roselyn, Aaron, and Tiffany walk up to the steps to the house. Sanna stop in front of the house, just look up at the house, shaking her head slowly, walking up the steps, and into the house.

The house is a three-story height with a walkout basement facing the backyard, six bedrooms, and six bathrooms in every bedroom in the house. The house is an old style with a lot of class, and not far from the lake in the west with a lot of trees and flowers around the house. A two-car garage off the North side of the house with a long driveway and two cars park on the driveway.

Main level has a cover deck in the front of the house; you enter the house through the front double doors facing the east to a small entryway with a small hallway down the right side of the stairs, and the dark wooden stairs along the left wall. Office was on the south side of the house, with a large wrap around corner computer desk in the east corner. The computer sat on the desk in the corner of the desk, computer chair sat in front of the desk, and papers on the desk. Windows were along east wall and south wall that let in the sunlight every morning, a couple of tall bookshelves along the west wall with a chair beside the shelves.

Living room and dinning room on the north side of the house in an opened area. Living room was on the east side of the long opened room, two big windows along the east and north walls with a big couch under the window, with three end tables, one end table in-between the couches, and other two at the end of the couches. The coffee table was in front of the couches with a large rug unearth the table. Two comfort chairs in front of the couches facing the east wall. A love seat couch was in front of the fireplace that in the middle of the long room on the north wall.

Dinning room was on the west side of the room with two big windows along the north and west walls. A long wooden table was in the middle of the area with six wooden chairs around the table, and a huge rug under the table. There are two glass corner cabinets with glass fingerings in each other it in the west wall corners. Hardwood flooring was through out the living room, dinning room, office, hallway, and entryway. The walls color is a warm natural color through out the main level of the house.

Kitchen is in the back of the house on the south-west area of the house, stairs going to the basement under the main staircase. Stove and fridge along the east wall with a small countertop between them. Windows were located along the big one on west wall and small one on south wall, the door the sunroom along the south wall closer to the west wall. The sink was under the south window, the cupboards and countertop was wooden and along the east and south walls. A small wooden inland was in the middle on the kitchen. Small breakfast nook was along the west wall with a long table with two benches under. The floor and wall was white, and the floor was white tile flooring.

Sunroom was off from the kitchen on the south side with couple of chairs and couches along the walls, and a door on the west wall lend out to the deck to the backyard. Larges windows along the west wall, south wall and east wall of the room. The floor a crème color and the walls were white.

Basement has hardwood flooring and the walls are light tan color. Storage room and laundry room was locate in the east side of the house beside each other. Wooden stairs was in the middle of the basement, glass door in the middle of the west wall lend out to the backyard, and two big windows beside the door. The entertainment system was along the south wall with a couple of couches in front of the system. A 50" T.V. with surround sound, DVD player, and ton of movies in the large case. Pool table was in the middle on the room, and a wet bar along the south wall.

Second level of the house had hardwood-flooring hallway, stairs lending up to the third level beside the staircase, four bedrooms and bathrooms on the second level. Every room had their only bathroom, walk-in closet, and balcony offs the room. One bedroom along the north side of the house is Tiffany and Aaron, having a double bed in the middle on the north wall under a large window with a couple of nightstand on each side of the bed. Along the east, wall a walk-in closet, the bathroom along the south wall close to the west wall, and the French doors to the balcony along the west wall. The four-piece bathroom had the tub along the west wall, toilet along the east wall, and the sink beside the toilet the bathroom was white all around. The bedroom belong to Tiffany and Aaron, the color of the walls was white with a soft yellow bottom with a whit trim a few feet from the floor, and the floor was hardwood.

The bedroom across from them was Roselyn and Andrew bedroom with the double bed along the south wall under a larger window, with a couple of nightstands on each side of the bed. Along the east, wall a walk-in closet, and the bathroom along the north wall close to the balcony French doors along the west wall. Bathroom had the tub along the west wall, toilet along the east wall with the sink side it and the color white around the room. The bedroom flooring was hardwood, walls was a light green color.

Two bedrooms along the east side of the house, one in the north and the other in the south, was empty. Both had bathrooms along the east walls, balconies along the east wall beside the bathroom. Walk-in closets along the west wall, two large windows, one facing north and the other facing south. The bedrooms colors were white walls, and hardwood flooring.

The third level has a small hallway that around the staircase, two bedrooms and two bathrooms with walk-in closets and balconies. South bedroom was empty with the walk-in closet along the north wall. Along the east wall, the bathroom with the tub along the east wall, toilet and sink along the west wall. The ceiling was slop halfway down along the south wall. The balcony with French doors was along the east wall, a window sitting area along the west wall, and build-in desk in the north wall a bit by the window sitting. The floor was hardwood, and white walls colors.

North bedroom is Sanna room; the walls are a light blue and hardwood flooring. The ceiling slops halfway down the north wall and the wall color go up the ceiling. Bathroom along the west wall with the tub along the west wall, toilet and sink along the east wall, and walk-in shower stall beside the tub beside the bathroom door. Walk-in closet beside the bathroom, and the French doors along the west wall to the balcony, window sitting area along the east wall, and a built-in desk along the south wall a bit by the window sitting area. Along the north wall, a double bed with no headboard in the middle of the room with a white lace canopy around the bed, two nightstands on each side of the bed with lamps and stuff on them. A make-up table along the South wall and a hope chest at the end of the bed makes the room complete.

Sanna walk into the house with her hat almost over her eyes, looking up around the house with a trouble look on her face. Roselyn was unpacking the dishes in the kitchen, when Sanna came walking in, "Hey Sanna, how it's going?" Roselyn ask Sanna unpacking the dishes from a box.

"It's going alright now, sorry about reopening the wound," Sanna say to Roselyn walking up to the inland, and lending against the front of the inland.

"Those okay it will heal here soon, why don't you go up stairs to your room, unpack your stuff, and rest up. You look like you have not slept in 300 years," Roselyn say to Sanna looking at Sanna tired face, and getting a bit worry about Sanna health.

"Thanks for making me feel better," Sanna say to Roselyn in a mild tone voice, running her fingers through her hair, kicking off her hat to the floor, and turning around with her back to Roselyn.

"Anilea just go relax upstairs in your room, you need it," Roselyn told Sanna, keeping on unpacking the dishes from the box, and setting the dishes in the cupboards.

Sanna look over her right shoulder at Roselyn with two baggy eyes. "Okay, I will see you later for dinner," Sanna say to Roselyn, picking up her hat from the floor with her right hand without missing a step, leaving the kitchen, and heading to her room to unpack.

Sanna walk by the office, where Andrew was setting up the computer. "Hey sport,"

Andrew called out to Sanna as he saw Sanna walking pass by the office.

Sanna poke her head into the office, and looking at Andrew. "Hey," Sanna greeted Andrew standing in the doorway of the office.

"What are you up to now?" Andrew says to Sanna plugging in the computer into the wall.

"Just going to unpack my stuff in my bedroom," Sanna told Andrew, put her hat back on her head, and straighten her hat out.

"Okay then sport," Andrew agrees with Sanna. "There a surprise in your room that Aaron and I did for you," Andrew says to Sanna turning on the computer to see if it is working right.

"See you later," Sanna wave to Andrew with her right hand, heading upstairs to the second level.

Sanna hit the second level, she look to the right to see Tiffany and Aaron making their bed together. Sanna saw the love between them, Sanna let out a sigh, turning to the third staircase, and walking up to the third level. Sanna hit the third level, turning to the left from the stairs, walking to her bedroom, opening the bedroom door. Sanna enter her bedroom, closing the door behind her, and looking around her room to see that Andrew and Aaron put up her curtains and canopy over bed. Sanna walk up to the canopy, pulling the white lace curtains back from the bed, and tying them with a light blue ribbon. Sanna took off her jacket, throwing the jacket onto the chair in front of the make-up table. Sanna took off her hat, taking her hair out of the ponytail, and running her fingers through her hair. Sanna look at herself in the big mirror on the make-up table, her long wavy-curly hair down her back, the sunshine through the window hitting her sunshine blonde hair with light brown highlights. Sanna look at the wrap on her right upper arm, and touching it with her left hand. Sanna stood there in her blue jeans, white tank top, and blue-white running shoes with white ankle shoes. Sanna sat down in the chair in front of the make-up table and take off her running shoes. Sanna stood up from the chair, walking over to big box the have 'Pillows and Blanket' write on it, and a small one that had 'Bed sheets'on it. Sanna opened the boxes, grabbing the stuff inside the boxes, and started to make her bed.

Sanna finishes making her bed, Sanna unpack the clothes in the closet, hanging up the sweaters and nice shirts, and folding her jeans up, putting them on the shelves. Sanna reach down in the last clothes box and pulling out a long white flowing with thin straps also stitch-work along the top of the dress. Sanna look at the dress for a moment as a tear fell onto the dress, "Why do I keep this?" Sanna whisper back to her in an upset voice, hang the dress in the back of the closet. Seeing a large rip along the bottom of the dress, "I need to sew that," Sanna whisper to herself looking at the dress, Sanna shook her head, walking away from the dress, and out of the closet.

Sanna was unpacking a few things, when she looks out of the window at a group of people walking to the house. "What are they doing here? Who are they?" Sanna say to herself looking out the window. Sanna saw a 6 ft tall even,

26 year-old, young man with blonde shaggy hair, wearing blue jeans, t-shirt, and running shoes, and walking from the north with his friends. Sanna lend closer to the window, placing her hands on the window sitting, a pain shock hit her right upper arm. "Ouch, that hurt," Sanna jump back a bit, and grabbing her right arm with her left hand. Sanna remove her left hand to check if there any blood, but there was not on her left hand. Sanna breathe a sigh of relief, walking out her room and downstairs a bit.

Downstairs the doorbell rang and Tiffany answer the door. "Hello," Tiffany says nicely seeing the group of people standing on the front deck.

"Welcome to the neighbourhood," say an old man with his wife beside him, and happy grin on his face.

"Thank-you, come in, and I will introduction you guy to the rest of the family," Tiffany greeted the group, moving the side of the door, and the group enter the house.

Tiffany shows the group to the living room, and Sanna watch from the third staircase through the railing, sitting close to the bottom step. Sanna saw the young man entering the house with his three friends behind him. The young man look up at Sanna with his blue eyes, Sanna quickly move to the other side of the stairs. *'I wonder if he saw me,'* Sanna thought to herself breathing heavily. Sanna running her fingers through hair with both hands, and trying to calm down of the feeling she was having now.

In the living room Andrew, Aaron, and Roselyn was trying to hang some pictures on the wall. "Andrew, sweetie, that picture is crocked," Roselyn say to Andrew pointing to the small picture on the wall.

"How this Roselyn straight effect for you?" Andrew say to Roselyn straighten the picture in front of him.

"That prefect Andrew, the picture looks straight," Roselyn gave Andrew the thumb-up. Roselyn saw the group of people walking into the living room. "Hello," Roselyn greeted the group of people.

"Greetings, and welcome to the neighbourhood," say the old man walking into the living room.

"Why thank-you, come in and sit for a while," Roselyn told the group of people, pointing to the couches under the windows.

"So are you guys and girls related?" ask the old man sitting down on the east wall with his wife sitting beside him, and the four people sat down on the couch along the north wall.

"Yes, my name is Roselyn and this is husband Andrew. Tiffany is my twin sister, and Aaron is Andrew twin brother," Roselyn introduction Andrew and she, sit down in one of the chairs in front of the coffee table with Andrew behind her.

"I'm Roselyn twin sister Tiffany, and this Andrew twin brother Aaron, my hubby," Tiffany introduction Aaron and herself, sit down in the other chair with Aaron behind her.

"Nice to meet you all, I am Mr. Williston and my wife Mrs. Williston," say Mr. Williston looking at his wife for a second.

"Nice to meet you two both," Roselyn say to Mr. and Mrs. Williston, there turning her head to the group of boys.

"I'm Mike; this is Dave, and Jay," Mike a 25-year-old man introduction his two 25-year-old friends sitting beside him.

"Nice meet you both, and what about that young man beside you?" Tiffany asks Mike pointing to the young blonde man.

"Ok yeah, that Adam, he 26 year-old," Mike told Tiffany pointing to Adam, who was sitting at the end of the couch. "Sorry man, you're so quiet," Mike apologizes to Adam.

"That okay, dude," Adam was cool with Mike, sitting on the couch with his friends. Adam look around the room and back at Roselyn, Tiffany, Andrew, and Aaron, "You four are the only ones who live here?" Adam asks them nicely.

"No, we have friends, who shy, living with us. She upstairs on the third floor," Tiffany answer Adam question, pointing to the ceiling to signal the third level.

"I see, can we meet her, if she up for it?" Adam requested to Tiffany kindly with a small on his face.

"Sure she can meet you people," Tiffany got up from her chair and walks out to the living room archway. "I will see if she wants to come down, and meet all of you," Tiffany walks to the stairs and heading upstairs to the second floor to get Sanna.

Tiffany turns to the third staircase and saw Sanna sitting on the steps looking down at her. "Hey Sanna, do you want to come downstairs to meet our new neighbours?" Tiffany asks Sanna looking up at Sanna with a smile on her face.

Sanna look down at Tiffany from the stairs. "I don't feel like it," Sanna say to Tiffany hearing the chatting of people downstairs in the living room.

Tiffany move closer to Sanna up a few steps closer to Sanna. "Hey it will help to meet new people, they are good, not evil," Tiffany putting her right hands on Sanna right shoulder and looking Sanna in the eyes.

Sanna shrug her shoulders at Tiffany, looking down at the stairs in front of her, and back to Tiffany. "I will come downstairs for a bit, but I'm not going to talk much," Sanna told Tiffany in a soft voice.

"That my girl lets go," Tiffany held out her right hand at Sanna. Sanna got up from the stairs, grabbing Tiffany hand, and went downstairs.

Sanna and Tiffany arrive into the living room together. Tiffany let go of Sanna hand and introduction Sanna to the group of people. "Everyone this is our good friend Sanna. Sanna this is our new neighbours," Tiffany pointed to the group of people, and making sure Sanna was okay now.

"Nice to meet you all," Sanna greeted everyone with a wave by her right hand, but nervous about meeting new people and making friends. Her humans friends always die in the battle or use against her in the battle.

"Nice to meet you young lady, I'm Mr. Williston and my wife Mrs. Williston," Mr. Williston introduction his wife and himself to Sanna kindly with a smile on his face.

"I'm Mike: this is Jay, Dave and Adam," Mike introduction his friend and himself to Sanna.

"Nice to meet you all, my name is Sanna, and I'm 24-year-old," Sanna introduction herself to the group walks over in-between the two chairs, that Tiffany and Roselyn was sitting in, and stood there quietly.

Adam look at Sanna stand there between her friends, and seeing the bandage wrap around her upper right arm, "Sanna, what happen to your right arm?" Adam asks Sanna nicely and looking at the bandage around her right upper arm.

Sanna face went pale for a second, and a stun-shock look on her face, and Sanna mind was racing very fast. Sanna look at Adam for a moment, and then say, "I cut it a few days ago on a walk at our old place," Sanna lied a bit to Adam, so no one knows the truth on how she really got it.

"Oh, on what, if I can ask," Adam asks Sanna again nicely, and trying to make Sanna talk more.

"On a tree branch, you see I was walking along a pathway through the tree three. When a black bear came out of the brushes, and started to chase me back home. Lucky when I got out of the tree, the bear stop, and went walking back into the tree. Thankfully Roselyn a nurse, and was able to fix me up," Sanna explain to Adam, trying to hold back her nervous, and her stomach doing flips now.

"Hopefully you get better," Adam tells Sanna with a smile on his face. Sanna try to keep herself happy, but inside she was very nervous. Sanna sat down the floor between the two chairs quietly. She did not want to say anymore to the group.

Jay looks over at Sanna and asking Sanna nicely, "When are your birthday Sanna?"

"June 9," Sanna told Jay nicely from the floor, and trying hard to keep herself together now.

"So in a couple of months, it is April 9, 2064. Are you having a big party?" Jay asks Sanna trying to hit on Sanna.

"I am not sure, I'm just new here, we will see. When June 9 comes around," Sanna say to Jay trying to stay calm around everyone.

"Jay stops hitting on Sanna. You got a girlfriend that can beat you up," Dave says to Jay, hitting Jay in the stomach with the back of his right hand.

"Ouch, I was trying to being friendly okay," say Jay to Dave, rubbing his stomach with his hands.

"Sorry Sanna, he such a ladies man," Dave apologizes to Sanna with a smile on his face.

"That okay, I am not ready for a boyfriend anyways," Sanna explain to Dave, smiling nicely at Dave.

Mr. Williston looks at Sanna, and asks nicely, "Why do a young pretty woman, don't have a boyfriend?"

"Well..." Sanna stumble a bit over her tongue. Sanna could not speak at first, and then slowly spoke, "I don't like talking about my past love life." Sanna lower her head, stood up from the floor, and look at everyone. "Sorry everyone, I must go and finish unpacking," Sanna excess herself from the living room archway, and heading upstairs to her bedroom on the third floor with sad look on her face.

Adam watches Sanna going upstairs, and wondering, *'What wrong with her?'* Adam thought as his friend keep on chatting with everyone. Adam looks at his cell phone for the time, and turn to Dave to say, "I think we better get going you, boys have a date with your girlfriend."

"Yep, I don't like to keep my girl waiting," Dave say to his friends as his friend and he got up from the couch. "We will see you guy and girls later," Dave left the house with Jay, Mike, and Adam behind him.

Mr. and Mrs. Williston look at each other. "Well my dear, we better get going, and let these young people finish unpacking. Goodbye, if you need any help we are just next door," Mr. Williston say as his wife and him left the house behind the boys.

"Nice to meet, and thank-you for coming over to visit," say Andrew closing the front door behind everyone.

Sanna watch from her bedroom window seating, everyone leaving the house, "There something about that Adam guy, but what it is?" Sanna whisper to herself looking down at Adam from the window, Adam walk to his house with his friend joking and laughing. Sanna got off the window seating, walks to the desk, sitting down in the computer chair, turning on her laptop, and started to type on her laptop for a while.

Roselyn and Tiffany enter the bedroom, "Hey Sanna, I see you're almost done unpacking," Tiffany says to Sanna looking around the room at all the stuff, and the empty boxes.

"Yes I am almost down," Sanna say looking at the screen on the laptop, and still thinking too.

"Sanna are you alright?" Tiffany says in a worry voice, and looking at Sanna sitting at her laptop.

Sanna shut her laptop down, turning around in her chair to face Tiffany and Roselyn, got up from the chair, walk to her bed, and stood there looking at Tiffany and Roselyn, "I'm okay, it's just..." Sanna started to speak.

"What wrong sport?" Andrew say coming into the room with Aaron behind him, and up to their wives.

"It just..." Sanna look at her friends together, Aaron and Andrew had their arms around Roselyn and Tiffany waist. "Nothing, I was thinking that all," Sanna shook for her head, and turn around to her bed. "I think I need to go to bed," Sanna say to her friends in an upset voice.

"Okay, sleep tight, and see you in the morning," Tiffany says to Sanna, giving Sanna hug goodnight.

"Goodnight Sanna," Aaron and Andrew say to Sanna at the same time, hugging Sanna together.

"Goodnight Sanna, sleep tight, and any problem we are downstairs," say Roselyn says to Sanna, leaving the bedroom with Tiffany, Aaron, and Andrew behind her, and closing the bedroom door.

Sanna went to the bathroom to run a warm bath in the tub. Sanna turn on the water from the tap, and putting some bubble bath into the running water. Sanna slowly undress herself, taking off her clothes. Sanna look at herself in front of the mirror in her bra and underwear. Sanna put her hand on the countertop, looking at herself in the mirror and sigh with a sad-worry look on her face. Sanna unwrap the bandage from her upper right arm, and throwing the dirty bandage wrap in the garage can that beside the sink. Sanna look at the scar that was slowly healing, and trying to stay calm. Sanna took off her underwear and bra, and throwing them into the dirty clothes pail. Sanna shut off the running water, climbing into the tub, and layback in the tub. Sanna lay there in the tub thinking, her mind was racing and her flashbacks play of in my mind.

An hour later, Sanna climb out of the tub, and wrapping a big towel around her body. Sanna put a glazed pad with some herds on the pad, and rewrap the scar with a bandage wrap. Sanna putting on new underwear on her body, a long flowing white nightgown, and brush her long wet hair with the brush. Sanna exited the bathroom into her bedroom as she walk pass the French doors to the balcony, she can hear someone singing outside, a male voice. Sanna stop and listen for a while, until the music stop. Sanna walk to her bed, sat down on the edge of her bed, thinking for a moment and lay down in her bed. Sanna turn off her lamp beside her bed, and lay there in the dark with the canopy around her bed. Sanna face the ceiling, Sanna was thinking, *'It is too dark in here.'*Sanna clap her hands together, holding her hands close to her chest, whisper something, opening her hands, and letting out a bunch of stars up in the air. Sanna stared at the stars in the air. Sanna slowly closed her eyes, and slowly fell asleep.

All night Sanna had bad dreams, tossing, turning, a few times waking up and trying hard not to scream loudly.

CHAPTER TWO

New Friend & Four Birthdays!

May 9, 2064, Sanna was alone in the house sitting in the living room on the couch under the east window with her sketchbook in her hands, drawing a few pictures. It was late morning, when Sanna was laying down on the couch for a moment. Sanna look up at the ceiling thinking about a few things, when Sanna heard someone coming up the steps of the front deck. Sanna sat up on the couch, looking out the window to see who was there. Sanna saw Adam standing in front in the front door, pushing the doorbell as Sanna hear the bell ringing inside the house. Sanna hunch down on the couch, Adam stood outside waiting for someone to answer the door. Sanna wait for a bit, hoping Adam will leave here soon, and then something inside Sanna made her thinking out aloud to herself, "Why can't I stop thinking about Adam? He is standing outside waiting for someone to answer the door. AARRHH WHY?" Sanna ran her fingers through her long-curly-wavy hair, standing up from the couch, and walks to the front door. Sanna stood there at the door, looking at the doorknob, taking her right hand, putting her hand on the doorknob, and opening the door. "Hello," Sanna ask to Adam, looking through a creak in the door.

"Hey... It is Adam, remember from a month ago, when your friends and you move in," Adam greeted Sanna looking at Sanna through the creak in the door with a smile on his face.

Sanna open the front door all the way and look at Adam standing there in front of her. "Yes, I remember your friends and you," Sanna say to Adam, "Come inside for a visit." Sanna move to the side to let Adam inside the house, and trying hard not to let her nervous getting to her.

Adam enters the house and Sanna closed the front door behind Adam. Adam taking off shoes in the entryway and enters the living room, "Wow, you guys and girls have a put a lot of…" Adam says to Sanna entering the living room with Sanna behind Adam.

Sanna lend against the archway on her left side of her body, "Creative," Sanna say to Adam watching Adam looking around the living room at all the stuff around the living room.

"Yeah, you have a lot of stuff that suits your friends and you," Adam looks around the room at all the pictures and glass fingers on display on the shelves and cabinets. "Did your friends and you buy all of this stuff?" Adam asks Sanna sitting down on the east wall couch, and Sanna was still lending against the archway. Adam saw Sanna sketchbook on the coffee table, picking up the book up in his hands, and started to flip through the pages. Adam look at each of the drawing on the pages, Sanna stood there in the archway with a stun look on her face. Adam look up at Sanna to say, "Sanna are these drawings yours?" Adam asks Sanna looking at each drawing in Sanna sketchbook.

Sanna walk up to Adam and snatching the book out of Adam hands. "Yes," Sanna softly spoke to Adam, closing her sketchbook in her hands, holding the book closer to her body with both arms around the book.

"Your pretty good at drawing, did you take a course or something?" Adam question Sanna looking at Sanna with the book on her arms, and being nice to her.

Sanna sat down on the other end of the couch and say, "I have an art major and writing major from college." Looking at the book in her hands, and thinking that she told the truth to Adam about her having taking course before.

"That cool, are you thinking of getting a job somewhere where there art?" Adam asks Sanna looking at Sanna on the other side of the couch.

"No, I like to keep my art and writing to myself," Sanna spoken softly to Adam holding her sketchbook in her hands, looking over at Adam. "Do you have a job?" Sanna ask Adam nicely trying to stay calm.

"No, there nothing much for someone in music," Adam told Sanna looking at Sanna, and smiling at him.

"You sing or play an instrument?" Sanna ask Adam trying to be friendly, and setting the book in front of her on the couch.

"I play guiltier and sing," Adam told Sanna smiling at her kindly, and looking her over nicely.

Sanna thought for a moment to herself. "You're the one who playing at night every night. I love listening to your music," Sanna say quickly to Adam blushing a bit at the end, "Sorry I have not been myself for along time."

Adam chuckled a bit at Sanna, "That okay... Thanks for the comment," Adam say to Sanna smiled at her nicely, and his cheeks was getting a bit red now.

Sanna put her sketchbook down on the coffee table, and got up from the couch, "Are you hungry?" Sanna ask Adam nicely, and her stomach growling a bit.

"Yeah, I better go home for lunch then," Adam says to Sanna getting up from the couch, and looking at Sanna with a grin on his face.

"You can stay here for lunch, I am having soup and grilled cheese sandwich," Sanna invited Adam to stay for lunch, and trying to finger out why there something about him that she cannot put her finger on.

"Sure, are you a good cook?" Adam was only joking at the end of the sentence at Sanna, about Sanna cooking.

Sanna laugh at Adam and smiled at Adam, "I am a good a cook." Sanna walk out of the living room, down the hallway, and into the kitchen with Adam behind her.

Sanna and Adam enter the kitchen, Adam stood in front of the inland, and Sanna grab the stuff for lunch. Sanna was cooking way over the stove, when Adam asks Sanna a question that makes Sanna upset and mad at the same time, "Why are you not marry like your friends?"

Sanna finish the soup and grilled cheese sandwich, and serve them on the plates and bowels. Sanna put the food in front of Adam, Sanna stood there lending over the countertop of the inland at Adam. "I don't like talking about my past love life," Sanna say through her teeth at Adam, stood back a bit, and started to eat her lunch slowly.

Adam lowers his head and felt very wrong inside, "I'm so sorry Sanna. I never know that you could have a rough love life," Adam apologizes to Sanna with a sad look on his face.

Sanna calm down and look at Adam, "That okay." Sanna lower her head, "It just that what happen to my lover is not that great. I have nightmares of that day here and there," Sanna spoke softly to Adam, and taking a bite of her sandwich.

Adam raise his head to Sanna, look at Sanna standing in front of him with her head lower, and Adam spoke up, "Hey if you want to talk about that anytime, I'm here to listen and help when you're in it."

Sanna look up at Adam, "Thanks, now you better eat before the food get cold." Sanna point to Adam lunch in front him, and trying to smile through the painful thoughts she was having of that one day that happen years ago.

After lunch was done, Sanna start to clean up with Adam help, "Where is everyone?"

Adam asks Sanna washing the dishes in the sink.

"At work," Sanna says to Adam drying and putting away the dishes.

"Where does everyone work?" Adam asks Sanna, finish washing the dishes in the sink.

Sanna finish drying and putting away the last dish away. Sanna look at Adam, and say, "Tiffany works at the bakery shop in town, Roselyn work as a nurse at the client, Aaron work in town office, and Andrew work in the school as a gym teacher."

"I see and you don't," Adam say point to Sanna in the face with his left hand, and wiggle his finger in front of her face.

"Watch it buddy, you might lose that finger," Sanna was joking to Adam, laughing a bit at Adam.

"Oh really," Adam keep on pointing his left pointer finger in Sanna face. Sanna twist the tea towel in her hands and snap the towel at Adam legs, Adam jump a bit. "Watch it," Adam told Sanna jumping a bit with fear.

"Told you, don't mess with me," Sanna was trying to be tough, but smiling at Adam.

Adam grabs another tea towel from the hanger in the wall by the sink; twist it up in his hands, and snapping it at Sanna legs. Sanna jump back to avoid the contact of the end, "You started it," Adam told Sanna getting ready with another snap.

"Okay, but legs, feet, and butt shots. Nothing above the waist line," Sanna set the rules, and getting ready to snap again at Adam legs.

"Agree," Adam nodded with a smile on his face.

"On the count of three, we start," Sanna walk close to Adam with the tea towel at full stretch in her hands. "One...Two...Three...Go!" Sanna snap the towel at Adam feet, and grinning a bit on her face.

"Wooh, that was close," Adam jump back at the snap of the towel on the floor. Adam look at Sanna with a shock look on his face, "Oh it is on." Adam snap back at Sanna legs, and making contact on Sanna upper right leg with the towel end.

"Ouch!" Sanna yelled rub her upper right leg with her right hand, having a pain look on her face, and went back snap the towel at Adam legs and feet.

Around 3 o'clock in the afternoon, Roselyn and Tiffany came into the house from work. Roselyn open the front door and enter the house with Tiffany behind her. Tiffany closed the door behind her, Tiffany and Roselyn can hear snapping of towels with screams and laughing coming from the kitchen. Tiffany and Roselyn walk down the hallway to the kitchen, look in the kitchen, and seeing Sanna and Adam having a towel fight in the kitchen, "What going on in here?" Tiffany yelled at the top of her voice, see the mess, and two people with a shock looks on their face.

Sanna and Adam stop snapping the towels, then staring at Roselyn and Tiffany standing in the kitchen looking at them. "Roselyn, Tiffany, your home already," Sanna say standing up straight and holding the tea towel in her right hand hanging down.

Tiffany looks at Sanna with narrow eyes, then trying to calm down at what she saw going on in the kitchen a moment ago, "What going on here?" Tiffany asks in a calm voice.

Sanna looks at Tiffany, feeling wrong about the whole towel fight, "I'm sorry; we were having a towel fight." Sanna lower her head at the thinking on what she has done now.

Roselyn look at Sanna with a smile on her face, "Are you two okay at lest?" Roselyn ask Sanna and Adam, seeing a few marks on their legs from the towels.

"Yeah, we were aiming for our feet, legs, and butt," Adam told Roselyn nicely, and smiling at Sanna to cheer her up a bit maybe, and standing behind Sanna a bit.

"Okay as long you two are okay, and nothing broken." Roselyn say to Sanna and Adam walking closer to them. Tiffany and Roselyn walk to the fridge to get a glass of water each.

When Tiffany and Roselyn had, their backs turn to Sanna and Adam, Adam snap Sanna with the towel right behind her right behind the kneecap. Sanna try not to scream as she sat down on the bench by the table. "That for the feet shot earlier," Adam whisper to Sanna, giving a nice smile to Sanna.

"I will get you later," Sanna whisper to Adam rubbing behind her right knee with her hands and narrowing her eyes a bit.

"Well I better get going home now. Thank-you Sanna for having me over," Adam says to the girls, putting the tea towel on the table, and walk out of the kitchen to the front door.

Sanna look at Tiffany and Roselyn, "Can I please have one more shot on him?" Sanna beg to Tiffany and Roselyn standing up to the bench.

"One more shot, but you make it a butt shot. We heard that shot on you," Roselyn told Sanna from the inland.

"Yes, thanks Roselyn," Sanna grab her towel and sneaking up to Adam.

Adam was getting ready to open the front door; his back was turn to Sanna, when Sanna snap the towel at Adam, and hitting his butt with the towel end, "OW!" Adam screams in pain, and grabbing his butt with his hands.

Sanna laugh at Adam actions, "Paid back is a bitch," Sanna told Adam smile at Adam with the towel in her hands.

Adam opens the front door; "I'll remember that, thanks for the fun afternoon, bye," Adam exits the house, and walking down the steps from the deck.

"Thanks for coming over, bye." Sanna wave to Adam from the front doorway, closing the door behind Adam with a smile on her face, and feeling happy for once in a long time.

Once Sanna closed the front door tightly behind Adam, Sanna turning around to see Roselyn and Tiffany standing in front of her, they appear from thin air, "Wooh, will you two stop that?" Sanna was staring at Tiffany and Roselyn, Sanna walk pass then to the kitchen with tea towel in her right hand.

"What did you two do all day?" Roselyn ask Sanna crossing her arms and walking behind Sanna with Tiffany beside her.

"Adam came over in the morning; we talk, lave lunch, clean up, and have a towel fight," Sanna explain to Tiffany and Roselyn stopping by the inland, and letting out a sigh at a thought she was having now.

"You two just talk having fun as friends?" Tiffany asks Sanna walking up to Sanna, and thinking the last time Sanna had a human friend.

"Yes, now please let me have Adam over once and a while?" Sanna beg Roselyn and Tiffany putting her hands together in front of her body, and smile came to her face.

Roselyn and Tiffany look at each other, "You know Sanna, it has been years since we seen you smile like that and having fun too," Roselyn was saying to Sanna. Roselyn walk up to Sanna, putting her left arm around Sanna shoulders, "When the last time you had fun like that?" Roselyn ask Sanna.

Sanna lower her head, "399 years ago…was the last time that had fun like that," Sanna say to Roselyn in a lower voice.

Roselyn look at Sanna, "Cheer up, we will let you have your fun with Adam as a friend, but remember with you're here to do," Roselyn told Sanna, tapping Sanna on the head with her finger.

"I'll never forget my duty to be here. Next year Donovan is going down forever," Sanna rub her right upper arm with her left hand, and had a piss-off look on her face.

Tiffany look at Sanna in the face, "He will, and you're not doing it alone again like last time. We almost lose you and many lives. We are here to help, and if we work like a team we can defeat him and his group for good," Tiffany told Sanna putting both of her hands on Sanna shoulders.

"I know, but please I don't want to fight in town," Sanna say moving away from Tiffany and Roselyn and walking out of the kitchen.

"Where are you going?" Tiffany yelled to Sanna from the kitchen, watching Sanna leaving the kitchen and down the hallway.

"I'm going to my room for some quite time to myself!" Sanna yelled walk up the stairs to the second floor, and could not stop thinking about her past now.

"Just leave Sanna alone for a while, Sanna having a hard time now. I think we should let Sanna have her fun time for a while, maybe this can help Sanna be more powerful," Roselyn told Tiffany starting supper over the inland.

"Yeah, plus remember what happen tomorrow is?" Tiffany told Roselyn helping getting supper ready on the inland.

"I know, Aaron, Andrew, yours and my birthday." Roselyn told Tiffany prepping for supper over the stove.

"So do you want to that night?" Tiffany ask Roselyn helping making supper by getting the chicken ready to be bake on the stove.

"How about going out for supper?" Roselyn told Tiffany stirring the rice in the pot on the stove with a wooden spoon.

"That sounds cool my dear," Andrew says entering the kitchen with Aaron behind him.

"Just the four of us for supper tomorrow night," Tiffany turns around from the chicken, and looks at the boys.

"What about Sanna?" Aaron question Tiffany for a worrying voice.

Tiffany thought for a moment, "You know, Sanna always stay home every time. How this time Sanna comes out with us?" Tiffany told her family cooking the chicken on the stove.

“It is up to Sanna is she really wants to come with us,” Roselyn say setting the cook food on the inland, along with dishes and forks, knifes, and spoons.

“True, Sanna like to be alone,” Tiffany told Roselyn, Tiffany put her right hand under her chin, and thinking.

“Please you guys and girls, we don’t want to push Sanna anymore then what she going through alright is. Sanna has a lot on her plate with what going on next year; she doesn’t want to be distracted,” Roselyn told everyone in the room, “But it is up to Sanna if she wants to have fun… Now it is supper time,” Roselyn pointed to the food on the inland with her right hand.

“I’ll call Sanna down for supper,” Andrew says Roselyn, about to go the stairs to fetch Sanna for supper.

“Just text her, I bet Sanna got her bedroom door closed, and music going loud,” Roselyn stop Andrew in the kitchen enters way.

“Okay then Roselyn,” Andrew told Roselyn, starting to text Sanna for supper on his phone for supper.

Ten minutes later, Sanna came downstairs for supper with hair up in a ponytail and her hoodie jacket on. Sanna grab a plate of food, and sitting down at the head of dinning table with everyone else. “Hey sport,” Andrew was saying to Sanna.

“Hey Andrew,” Sanna say to Andrew, playing with her food on her plate with her fork in her right hand, and could not stop thinking on the fight coming here soon.

“We were talking about you maybe coming with us tomorrow night for supper?” Andrew asks Sanna nicely with a smile on his face.

“Tomorrow is you guys birthday… maybe,” Sanna say to Andrew as she took a bite of food, and chewing it slowly.

“Let us know if you want to come,” Andrew told Sanna looking at Sanna from his place at the head of the table.

“We will see Andrew,” Sanna say starting eating her supper. Sanna finish eating her supper, getting up from the table with her dishes in her hands, heading to the kitchen, and started to wash her dishes in the sink.

Everyone finish eating their supper, and stated to clean up. Sanna headed upstairs to bed, Sanna went to have a bath in her bathroom. Sanna was lying down in the tub, thinking to herself,

‘How can I be so stupid…? Why should I have fun, when next year will be very hard to stay force…? I have to stop… but it was fun… maybe I should relax for a bit and has

fun… It has been 399 year still I had real fun with a boy… but when it gets closer to the time, I have to stop having fun, and force on the big picture… getting rid of Donovan and his group.' Sanna tighten her hands into fists. Sanna was getting very angry that her body just glow white, Sanna started to relative what going to happen, Sanna quickly calm down, and everything was good. Silent was the only thing Sanna can hear, her own breathing heavily, Sanna lay in the tub relaxing, Sanna put her head under the water, and in a few minutes came back up for air.

Sanna got out of the tub, putting on her PJS, and look into the bathroom mirror. "You look awful," Sanna told herself looking at her eyes with black bags under her eyes. Sanna ran a brush through her hair and putting her hair into two pig-tail-braids one on each side of her head. Sanna exit the bathroom, stop by the French door, open the doors, and went outside on the balcony. Sanna walk to the railing and put her hands on the railing. Sanna look out at the lake, not far in the distance.

The moonlight was glinting off the lake water and the shadows of the trees were along the ground.

In the distance in the middle of the lake is a large inland with nothing but trees, brushes, and no one living on it, just wildlife "That is where we will finish our battle," Sanna whisper to herself. Sanna heard someone strumming a guitar, Sanna turn her head to the direction of the noise in the north, and saw Adam sitting on his baloney on the third floor of his place, strumming his guitar in his hands. Sanna knelt behind the north railing of the balcony and peaking through the rails at Adam. *'He so cute,'* Sanna thought to herself, as she watches Adam playing his guitar. Sanna was staring at Adam for a long time, her heart was beating fast, and Sanna can feel butterflies in her stomach.

'What the…,' Sanna thought to herself, *'Do I have a crush on Adam?'* Sanna sat on the floor, lending her back against the sliding of the house. *'There something about Adam that I should know…It like my past lover one.'* Sanna look over at Adam place, and watch Adam going inside his house. Sanna got up from the floor, sigh in relief, and went inside to bed.

The next morning Aaron and Andrew left for work, and Roselyn and Tiffany was getting ready to leave for work, when Sanna came downstairs wearing blue jeans, blue t-shirt, and white socks. Sanna hair was still in the two pig-tails-braids. "Morning sleepyhead," Roselyn greeted Sanna getting her shoes on.

"Morning Tiffany and Roselyn," Sanna groan to Tiffany and Roselyn, coming downstairs sleepy eyes, and moving slowly.

"So are you coming tonight for supper?" Tiffany asks Sanna getting her shoes on, and looking at Sanna to see she was tired again.

"No, I want to stay home, and not to bug you guys and girls," Sanna told Tiffany hitting the bottom step, and stood there watching her two friends getting ready for work.

"Okay, but if you change you mind…" Tiffany says to Sanna grabbing her bag of stuff, and waiting for Roselyn to hurry up.

"I will let you know, now have a good day," Sanna say to Tiffany and Roselyn seeing them leaving the house for work.

Sanna hangout all day by herself, Sanna made Aaron, Andrew, Tiffany, and Roselyn birthday gifts. Adam stop by for a bit, "How if going?" Adam says entering the house after Sanna answer the door.

"Good, just finish four birthday gifts for Aaron, Andrew, Tiffany, and Roselyn," Sanna say to Adam watching taking off his shoes.

"Oh, when are their birthdays?" Adam asks Sanna looking at her with a smile on his face, and thinking when the four birthdays is now.

"Today, Roselyn and Tiffany are turning 29 year-old, and Aaron and Andrew are turning 30 year-old," Sanna told Adam walking to the kitchen with Adam behind her.

"Wow that cool, and you're turning?" Adam asks Sanna nicely walking behind Sanna to the kitchen.

Sanna bite her bottom lips for a second, with thoughts of her real life age racing through her mind, and told Adam, "June 9 this year, I will 25 year-old."

"That cool, any plans yet for a party?" Adam asks Sanna friendly like to make Sanna feel better.

"No, not yet… I have no idea it only a month away… Can we please stop talking about that?" Sanna stop Adam for talking on anything that personal with her.

"Okay, what do you want to do today?" Adam asks Sanna nicely standing there in front of the inland, looking at her, and he smiled at her friendly.

"How about playing some pool downstairs?" Sanna say to Adam nicely with a smile on her face.

"That will be cool, let's go," Adam say to Sanna as Sanna and him walk downstairs to play pool.

Sanna was kicking Adam butt in pool, when Tiffany, Roselyn, Andrew, and Aaron came home from work to get ready for their birthday supper. Sanna came running upstairs, after hearing the front door shutting with Adam behind her. "Hey you guy and girls, your home," Sanna say to her friends.

"Yes, we are going to get ready for supper now. Hey Adam," Roselyn told Sanna, and greeting Adam, who behind Sanna by the stairs.

Adam wave to Roselyn with a smile on his face, then looking at Sanna. "Hey I better get going then, so you can get ready Sanna," Adam told Sanna in the hallway behind Sanna.

"You can stay with Sanna for night?" Roselyn told Adam nicely as Tiffany, Andrew, and Aaron walk upstairs to their bedrooms.

Adam look at Sanna, "You're not going with them for supper," Adam asks Sanna with a shock look on his face.

"Nope, they are going to a nice romance restaurant, and I don't feel comfort going to that kind of restaurant," Sanna told Adam looking over her left shoulder, "But they are coming back for birthday cake and gifts later."

"Sure I can stay to keep Sanna happy. In addition, I was winning at pool games," Adam told Roselyn with a smile on his face, Sanna rolled her eyes at what Adam say to Roselyn, knowing the truth at who was really winning at pool games.

"That will be nice; I have pizza coming to the house for supper. Adam, do you like meat lovers?" Roselyn ask Adam friendly.

"Yes I do love meat lovers," Adam answers back to Roselyn, and looking at Roselyn.

"Good, now I better get ready." Roselyn say going upstairs to her bedroom to get ready for supper.

Sanna waited a bit for Roselyn to go upstairs to the bedroom, and then turn around to Adam. "You know I was kicking your butt in pool," Sanna told Adam walking to living room, and flopping down on the couch along the east wall.

"Hey, I had a couple of wins," Adam saying in the entering the living room behind Sanna, and flopping down on the north wall couch. Sanna giggle at what Adam was saying, ya he was right about winning a couple of games of pool too.

Around 6 o'clock, Roselyn, Tiffany, Andrew, and Aaron coming downstairs dress in their formal wear. Tiffany was wearing a light pale green knee-length dress with green high-heel shoes and her hair was pulling back into a bun. Roselyn was wearing a light pink knee-length dress with light pink high-heel shoes and her hair in curls. Aaron and Andrew both were wearing black suits with ties. Andrew had a pink tie and his hair was in a ponytail, and Aaron had a green tie and his hair was grease back. Sanna look up from the couch, "Wow you guy and girls look great," Sanna say standing up from the couch, and walking to the front door with Adam behind her.

"Thanks, now pizza should be here around 6:30pm. Have fun and no towel fights or food fight in the house," Roselyn told Sanna and Adam pointing her index finger on her right hand at them.

"What about outside the house in the yard?" Sanna ask Roselyn nicely with a smile on her face.

"Outside only, now see you two later." Roselyn say to Sanna and Adam leaving the house with Aaron, Andrew, and Tiffany.

"Bye, have fun." Sanna waving to them as the front door shut tight. Sanna walk to the living room windows, watch the car pulling out of the drive, and driving down the street. Sanna turn to Adam, and ask, "What now?"

Adam walk up to Sanna, "How about a movie?" Adam asks Sanna standing in the living room archway.

"Sound cool, but let wait for the pizza. We can go downstairs, and watch a movie," Sanna say to Adam standing by the window, and heading downstairs with Adam chatting between each other on whom really winning the pool games.

Around 6:30 pm roll around and the pizza arrives. Sanna answer the front door, paid for the pizza, and closing the door, "Pizza here Adam comes get it while it hot!" Sanna called out walking into the kitchen with the pizza in her hands.

"Pizza," Adam called out, like a very happy kid, running upstairs from the basement. Adam walk up to the pizza, and smelling the pizza in the air, "Ah meat-lover my favourite."

"Is the movie ready?" Sanna ask Adam walking downstairs to the basement with pizza and plates in her hands.

"Yeah it is ready to go," Adam says to Sanna following Sanna downstairs to the basement.

"That great," Sanna say to Adam setting the pizza down on the coffee table in front of the TV and couches. Sanna walk to the wet bar, and open the bar fridge. "Adam wants a pop?" Sanna ask Adam nicely looking over the pop in the fridge.

"Sure," Adam says to Sanna sitting down on the couch, and grabbing the piece of pizza from the box. Sanna came back with two pops in her hands, and handing one to Adam. "Thanks," Adam thanks Sanna, and opening the pop up.

"You're welcome," Sanna says to Adam grabbing a piece of pizza, and sitting down on the other end of the couch. Adam started the movie and sitting there eating his piece of pizza. Sanna ate her pizza quietly and drinking her pop. Adam and Sanna sat there on the couch one on each end, laughing at a few parts of the movie, and in-shock with a few parts. Adam looks over at Sanna and was going to say something but could not get a word out of his mouth. Instead, Adam sat there quietly watching the movie. Sanna looking over at Adam and shook her head at a thought that came to her mind.

After the movie was over, Sanna and Adam clean up their mess, and head upstairs to the kitchen, "What kind of cake are we having?" Adam asks Sanna, finish washing the dishes in the sink.

"Marble cake with white icing base, and different color of trim icing," Sanna say to Adam putting the leftover pizza away in the fridge, and looking at the cake in the fridge.

"That cool, but there something missing here for a party," Adam told Sanna looking around the house.

"What is it?" Sanna ask Adam wondering what missing now, she plan everything out for the birthday party.

Adam move closer to Sanna, "Decorations," Adam smile at Sanna raising an eyebrow at Sanna.

Sanna smile ear to ear, "That sound great." Sanna ran back downstairs for a few minutes, come back upstairs with a small box of decorations in her head, and say to Adam, "Got them." Sanna show the box to Adam.

"Let's get started," Adam rubbing his hands together as a plan was coming together in his mind.

"Okay, but not to much down here, their bedrooms lets go crazy." Sanna say to Adam putting the box on the dinning room table.

"Okay let's start," Adam open the box; grab a bag of balloons, and using the hand pump to blow up the balloons.

Sanna hang the streamers around the house, once Sanna done hanging the streamers, and Sanna went to help Adam blow up balloons. They where done blowing up the balloons, Adam and Sanna hang up some of the balloons on the wall. Sanna look at Adam after finish hanging up the balloons up. There were a few extra balloons over, Sanna grab an arm full. Sanna ran upstairs with the armload of balloons to Roselyn, Andrew, Tiffany, and Aaron bedrooms. Adam watch Sanna doing her trick, and join in to help. Adam and Sanna fill Aaron, Andrew, Roselyn, and Tiffany bed with the balloons. After they finish with their trick, Roselyn, Tiffany, Andrew, and Aaron was coming home from supper. "Just in time," say Sanna looking out the living room window seeing the car pulling into the driveway, and everyone exit the car.

A few minutes the front door open and Roselyn enter with Andrew behind her. "Hey we are home," Roselyn called out as Tiffany and Aaron enter the house.

"Hey you guys, how was supper?" Sanna ask her friend coming out of the living room.

"It was good," Andrew, say to Sanna rubbing his stomach with his hands.

"Well I hope you got enough room for cake," Sanna say to Andrew walking back into the living room.

"Of course I got enough room for cake, when I don't have room for cake?" Andrew asks Sanna walking into the living room and dinning room.

Everyone enter the living room and dinning room area, and seeing the decorations on the walls and around the room. "Wow... did you two do this?" Roselyn ask looking around the room with a smile on her face.

Sanna and Adam look at each other, and nod their head, "We work hard on it," Sanna say to Roselyn.

"That cool, now how about some cake," Roselyn told Sanna. Sanna left the room to the kitchen, coming back a few minutes later with the cake in her hands, and setting the cake down on the dinning room table. Everyone gather around the table and start to sing 'Happy Birthday' to Roselyn, Andrew, Tiffany, and Aaron. After they where done singing the birthday song, Sanna cut up the cake, and serve a piece of cake to everyone in the room. They sat around the table talking and laughing for along time.

It was starting to get late, and Adam decides to go home. "Well see you later Sanna," Adam was saying to Sanna getting his shoes on at the front door.

"See you around Adam," Sanna say to Adam standing by the stairs, watching Adam putting on his shoes.

Adam gave Sanna a hug, and left the house, "Thanks for the good time, bye," Adam says to everyone in the house, and closes the front door behind him.

Sanna stood there by the stairs in shock, Roselyn walk up to Sanna. "Hey are you okay Sanna?" Roselyn ask Sanna with a concerned voice.

Sanna was still in shock; Sanna was wide-eye in shock. Sanna shook her head, "Yeah, I'm okay... just... that I cannot believe that Adam did that," Sanna told Roselyn.

"As long you're alright," Roselyn told Sanna putting her right arm around Sanna shoulders.

"I will be fine, but I like to know something," Sanna ask Roselyn looking up at Roselyn face.

"What is it?" Roselyn ask Sanna look at Sanna with a confused look on her face.

Sanna sigh, and lower her head, "How can I fight without my sword?"

Chapter Three

Past Love Story & Found Sword!

Roselyn lead Sanna into the living room with her right arms around Sanna shoulders, and sat Sanna down on the couch under the east window. Tiffany, Aaron, and Andrew sat down on the north couch, look at Sanna. "What Sanna question mean how going to fight without your sword?" Roselyn question Sanna with a confused-worry voice.

Sanna sat there on the couch quietly with her head lower to the floor. "Do you remember what happen to my sword?" Sanna ask Roselyn through her teeth, and tighten her hands into a fist.

Roselyn had a confuse look on her face, Tiffany stood up from the other couch, and yelled, "Roselyn! Sanna lost her sword about 100 years ago." Tiffany pointed her right pointer finger at the Sanna.

"I did not lose it... It's was blasted out of my hands!" Sanna say through her teeth, still having her head lower looking at floor, and thinking of the last fight with Donovan 100 years ago.

"You lost it, Anilea!" Tiffany yelled at Sanna standing in front of Sanna across the coffee table, pointing a finger at Sanna.

"I did not, I told you what happen." Sanna was getting piss-off at Tiffany, and did not want to remember from all fighting between Donovan and her.

"You did!" Tiffany called out at the top of her voice, and curling her hands into fist.

Sanna stood up quickly from the couch and look at Tiffany. "I did not lose my sword!" Sanna was breathing heavily, "My sword was blasted out of any hands, when I was fighting Donovan... I almost lost my life, remember after the fight how weak I was," Sanna yelled at Tiffany curling her hands into fists.

Tiffany face went white and Tiffany eyes went wide, "I almost forgot, what you were like after a fight." Tiffany lowers her head, "I'm sorry Sanna. Will you forgive me?" Tiffany apologizes to Sanna.

Sanna calm down effect, Sanna softly spoke to Tiffany, "I forgave you Tiffany, and I just want to go find my sword that it."

Tiffany look at Sanna, "But what happen if Donovan have it?" Tiffany asks Sanna in a worry voice.

Sanna got a little mad at the thought if Donovan got her sword. "He does not have my sword, if he did. He will coming after me and I will be alright died by now," Sanna say through her teeth. Sanna calm down effect and spoke nicely, "My sword is still in this town, where I have no clue?"

Roselyn look at Tiffany and Tiffany nodded back. "Sanna," Roselyn say to Sanna standing up from the couch. "We were thinking maybe we let you outside the house. You know why we want you to stay inside?" Roselyn put her right arm around Sanna shoulders.

"I know why… but you know I'm older then all of you guys." Sanna told Roselyn, and smile at Roselyn.

Roselyn chuckle a bit at Sanna, "We know we do care about you." Roselyn look at Sanna in the face.

"I know, but please let me find my sword on my own?" Sanna ask Roselyn nicely and thinking of leaving the house and the yard after years of staying inside the house.

"Okay," Roselyn agree with Sanna, "But any problems or troubles you come straight to us for help," Roselyn told Sanna, placing a finger on Sanna nose, and taking it off.

"I well… yawn… I think it is time for bed." Sanna yawn, walk to the stairs, and trying to finger where her sword in the town.

"I think we should all go to bed now," Roselyn told everyone else, and talking to each other.

Everyone got off the couches, heading upstairs for bed. Sanna sat on the top step of the third floor staircase and waiting for the fun. It did not take to long for Tiffany, Roselyn, Andrew, and Aaron to know that there balloons in their beds. "ANILEA, YOU BRAT!" Everyone yelled from their rooms as balloons flying out of the rooms.

"Yes," Sanna whisper got up from the step and went to her room to bed.

~~*~*~*~*~*~*~*

May 20, 2064 came rolling around, Adam walk up to Sanna house after her friends left for work. Adam grabs the newspaper off the deck steps and rings the doorbell. Adam waits a few minutes when Sanna answer the front door. "Hey Adam," Sanna greeted Adam in a sad voice, and red-watery eyes.

"Hey Sanna, what wrong? It looks like you were crying." Adam says to Sanna entering the house with the newspaper in his hands.

"It nothing, I just got something in my eyes." Sanna tell Adam rubbing her eyes with her hands, and closing the door behind Adam.

"Are you sure?" Adam question Sanna looking into Sanna eyes and seeing them red from crying.

Sanna took a deep breath, and slowly letting it out. "Today is not a good day for me," Sanna told softly to Adam in an upset voice.

"Why is this day not a good day for you?" Adam walk to the kitchen with Sanna beside him, and thinking what wrong with Sanna now.

They enter the kitchen, Sanna lend her back against the inland, and looking at Adam. "Why you ask me, Adam?" Sanna ask Adam, Adam nodded his head to Sanna. "Okay..." Sanna took a deep breath and let it out. "Today mark the date of my wedding."

"So why so sad? Did something happen on this date?" Adam asks Sanna, still holding the newspaper in his hands, and never knows Sanna was going to be married.

Sanna lower her head, and say to Adam, "Something did happen on this date, something bad." Sanna shed a few tears, rolling down her cheek, and trying to forget what happen on that day.

"What did your fiancé left you at alter or something else?" Adam asks Sanna wanting to know what happen.

"No, my fiancé did not leave me... He was killed right in front of me, along with my family and friends." Sanna started to tell Adam with tears filling her eyes, and wanting to cry or run away from Adam now.

Adam jaw drop to the floor, and his eyes went big, "He was killed right in front of you, along with your family and friends too, "WOW!" Adam was surprise at the thought of Sanna lover, family, and friends killed in front of her on her wedding.

"Yes... here how it went down. I was walking down the aisle; we decided to have an outdoor wedding with my parent's one on each side of me. My parents gave me away to my fiancé, and we were so happy for each other. We were getting ready to say 'I do's', when a guy who hate me and his group came down the aisle, and demanded that I go with him. My fiancé told him 'I am not going anywhere with his group or him.' Next minute the person stabs my fiancé in the stomach and chest with a knife. I watch as my fiancé felling to the ground, and I ran up to my fiancé, and try keeping him alive, but..." Sanna started to tear up in her eyes, and the tears started to roll down her cheeks.

Adam put the paper on the inland, and putting his arms around Sanna. "What happen next?" Adam calmly told Sanna in his arms.

Sanna wipe a tear away from her eyes with her hands, "My fiancé died in my arms. I did not want to go with this mean person or his group. I fought back, but they keep on killing my family and friends. I watch as everyone dieing right in front of me... I ran away as fast as I can, I look back to see a fire burning through the trees. I ran into Roselyn, Tiffany, Andrew, and Aaron. I told them what happen to me, and they got me out of that place. I have been with them for along time," Sanna spoke to Adam trying to not to get so upset.

Adam look down at Sanna in his arms, taking his right hand, placing it under Sanna chin, and raising Sanna head up to his face. "How long has it been?" Adam asks Sanna nicely, smiling a bit to Sanna.

Sanna face went white for a second, her mind was racing fast to find the right words to say. "Adam it was three years ago," Sanna lied to Adam, knowing it was long time ago.

"I see..." Adam nodded to Sanna, "Hey do you want me to stay, just to make sure you're aright?" Adam smile down at Sanna in his arms, and trying to comfort her.

"Sure you can Adam," Sanna smiled at Adam, and moving out of Adam arms a bit. Sanna saw the newspaper on the inland, Sanna look at the cover paper in the right-hand corner was countdown to something. "Hey Adam, what is this?" Sanna ask Adam pointing to the countdown on the paper.

Adam looked at it, "Oh, that countdown to a something that happens every 100 years. Something about two spirits' that fight in this town. I have no clue, but the museum has an exhibit on it. Do you want to go?" Adam says to Sanna, looking down at her, and hoping she will like to get out of the house to cheer her up.

Sanna thought for a moment, then say to Adam, "I am in," Her chance to get out of the house and yard for a while.

"Cool let's get going, I know the caregiver of the exhibit," Adam told Sanna as they walk to the front door.

Adam put on his shoes, and stood by the front door waiting for Sanna. Sanna put on her running shoes, hoodie jacket, and her hat pulling her ponytail through the back. "Let's get going," Sanna told Adam looking at Adam standing by the front door. Adam opens the front door, and walk outside onto the front deck. Sanna stood in the doorway looking outside; Sanna took a deep breath through her nose, and took a step outside onto the deck. Sanna was happy that she was outside the house; Sanna closed the front door, and lock the front door with the key. Sanna turn to Adam, and ask, "How far is the museum?"

"It on the end of Main Street, so about ten blocks from here," Adam told Sanna walking down the step onto the walkway in front of the house; Sanna was not far behind Adam.

They walk along the sideway down to the museum. They was talking and laughing along the way. Sanna was looking at everything along the way, and waving to people as they wave first. Sanna was surprise how everything rebuilt back to normal after her fight with Donavan. "What about Sanna mean?" Adam asks Sanna walking along the street.

Sanna say to Adam, "Sanna mean 'Lilly flower', what about Adam mean?" Sanna keep on walking along the street with Adam beside her.

"Lilly flower that sweet, Adam mean 'Man of the earth," Adam told Sanna keep on walking along.

"Sound powerful," Sanna say to Adam looking over at Adam, and seeing what the name meant now.

Adam and Sanna arrive at the museum, Sanna look up at the two-story brick build, and shaking her head. Adam enters the building with Sanna behind him. Sanna look around the open front way, and the signs to different exhibits. Adam walks up to the front desk, and asks for someone. "Hey Molly is Prof. Jeff in today? Adam asks Molly the front desk person.

"Yes he is in today; I'll call him for you." Molly told Adam picking up the phone, and called Prof. Jeff to come to the front desk.

A few minute later a middle age, dark long brown hair male, wearing a black dress pants, white long shirt, and black dress jacket. Came to the front desk, Jeff greeted Adam, "Adam nice to see you, how everything going for you?"

"Hey Jeff, everything is going. This is my friend Sanna, who interested in that exhibit of yours," Adam introduction Sanna to Prof. Jeff.

"Nice to meet you Prof. Jeff," Sanna say to Jeff shake his right hand with her right hand.

"Nice to meet you too, Sanna." Jeff shook Sanna right hand with his right hand. "Now what do you want to you know about my exhibit? Jeff asks Sanna nicely.

"Everything about the two spirits," Sanna told Jeff, thinking there has to be something from the last fight that she is looking for or a hint to where her sword could be now.

"That very interesting," Jeff was confused at what Sanna was saying to him. "Let's go upstairs, and I will show you two around my exhibit." Jeff show the way for Sanna and Adam to his exhibit upstairs.

"This exhibit was creative about a 100 years ago, but records dating back almost 400 years," Jeff told Sanna walking up the stairs and down the hallway to a large room with display and models.

Sanna eyes grow big, and her mouth drop at the sight of the way exhibit was display. Sanna shook her head, and then ask Jeff, "This is everything about the two spirits fight and some history behind the fighting between them?"

"Yes it does," Jeff told Sanna showing a manikin of a white dress female spirit. "I know everything about these spirits. I study about them for years, well every since I was child."

Sanna stood looking at the white dress female manikin, "What is this spirit name?" Sanna pointed to the white dress manikin, and seeing how close it was looking like her in her spirit form.

Jeff look over the female manikin, then spoke, "Her name is Anilea, she a white spirit, who save people live with her sword. She has a wonderful warrior, white warrior clothes with gold arms and legs covers, and a gold cross necklace." Jeff show Sanna the another white female manikin of Anilea in her warrior clothes. Jeff looks at Sanna, and saw her necklaces. "That looks very close to Anilea necklaces," Jeff pointed to Sanna necklaces with his finger, looking at the manikin and back at Sanna.

Sanna cover the necklaces with her left hand, and putting the necklace in her shirt. "It was gift from my family," Sanna told Jeff with a sad voice, and knowing who really gave it to her the first time, she was set to Earth to save the human kind from the darkness.

Jeff was going to ask something about Sanna family, Adam put a hand on the Jeff left shoulder, and shook his head to Jeff. Jeff care on with his speaking, "Now were I… oh yes," showing Sanna a dark dress male manikin. "This is Donavan the dark spirit, who wants to get rid of everyone or want to control everyone. Donavan never go anywhere, without his groups of evil spirit people. Now any questions you have about anything just ask."

Sanna had a couple questions for Jeff, "Jeff, how old is the spirit? Does the white spirit have a group of good spirits?"

Jeff looks at Sanna, "Well I will answer the second question, and first Anilea has a group of people that fight along side her. We are in making for them we found some old photos of the group and they are very old photos to make out here and there, but they just arrive today and soon will be set up along side Anilea in her warrior form. Now for the other question, I think these spirits are about 2000 years, it is hard to date back how old they are really," Jeff told Sanna nicely.

Sanna whisper to herself in a low voice so no one can hear her, "1314 years-old for Anilea, and 655 years-old for the white spirit four friends. 1614 years-old for Donavan and his group," Sanna walk around the exhibit looking at everything and reading the papers. Sanna shook her head at something is that writing in the newspaper after the fight, and reading the death toll.

Sanna eyes water up a bit, Adam walk up behind Sanna and ask in a worry voice, "Hey what wrong?"

Sanna wipe her eyes with her hands, "I was reading about the day after the fight and how many death of the town people that did not want to die." Sanna did not take her eyes off the papers, and then Sanna ask Adam, "Adam what happen if this flight happens again. Let say something happens to me, what will you do?"

Adam was in-shock at what Sanna was saying, "Wow, that secrecies question..." Adam was thinking for a moment, "Sanna, I will be lost for along time. You such a great true friend that I will hurt in my heart," Adam look at Sanna still looking at the newspapers.

"That all I need to know," Sanna move to the next display, and looking at the display. Adam watch Sanna walking away, Adam was thinking about something. When Jeff came up to Adam and started talking to Adam.

Sanna move around the exhibit at every display and manikins. Then one display catches her eyes, a glass case table display in the middle of the whole exhibit. In the display was a dagger inside in the middle of the large case with informants around the dagger, and wondering came to Sanna mind. *'I hope this is my sword?'* Sanna thought to herself. Sanna look around the room to make sure no one was around; Sanna put her hands on the glass case, and force her powers on the dagger. Sanna look down at the dagger that grows into her sword. "Bingo, I found it finally, my sword," Sanna whisper to herself with a smile on her face.

"Get your dirty hands off the display case now!" yelled a male voice from behind Sanna.

Sanna quickly took her hands off the case, and the sword whet back into the dagger. "Sorry, I wanted a closer look at this dagger," Sanna stood back from the display and ins-shock that someone saw her touch the glass.

A middle age male, mid-built, red short hair, wore sunglass on his face, tight pants and short shelves shirt. A young middle age woman in the right side of him, the woman wore a very tight short dress with her long very curly hair, huge breast and hips to butt, and thin waist. He walks up to Sanna, "Young lady this is very old dagger with some special powers or something like that. You're putting your dirty hands on the glass," The male rub Sanna handprints off the glass with a piece of cloth from his tight pants.

"Sorry, my name is Sanna," Sanna introduction herself to the male watching him wiping off her handprints.

The male turning around, and took off his sunglass, "My name is Robbie, and this is my girl Cookie," Robbie introduction himself and Cookie in a snobby voice.

"Nice to meet you two, I'm new to the town, and wanted to know about..." Sanna started to talk to Robbie and Cookie.

"Yeah, yeah, none of my business, now please move I have very important people coming here soon, and I don't want any dirty fingerprints on anything." Robbie interruptions Sanna, waving Sanna aside with his left hands, Sanna move to the side as Robbie and Cookie walk by her, "Prof. Jeff how everything going? Everything ready to go for our very important guest," Robbie ask Jeff looking around the exhibit.

"Yes, everything is ready to go," Jeff told Robbie, and looking around the exhibit to make sure everything is ready.

"Good, now you and those two people go stand outside the door, and don't say a word about anything, this is my exhibit," Robbie told Jeff pointed to the door, as the Mayor and the newspaper people came walking in. "Show time Cookies." Robbie saw everyone entering as Jeff, Adam, and Sanna stood outside the door, as Robbie and Cookie walk up to the group of people,

"Welcome Mr. Mayor to my awesome exhibit," Robbie greeted the Mayor and everyone else.

"Good to see you Robbie and Cookie, hope you make this visit very were waiting for?" Mr. Mayor told Robbie looking around the room, see everything set up nicely.

"Yes, it wills were waiting for," Robbie told Mr. Mayor, "Now let get rolling." Robbie shows the manikins of the spirit. "Now those are two spirits Anna and Don. Anna is a white spirit, kind of angel that protects people or something like that." Robbie starting to talk to the Mayor and the newspaper people try to know the truth but does not know anything about anything.

Sanna stood by the door with Adam and Jeff, "That Anilea and Donavan, and I prefer spirit not angel," Sanna whisper to herself in a piss-off voice, leading against the doorway with her arms-cross in from of her body.

"Don here an evil-devil, like a spirit, who not so smart. That way he could not win any battles or the war. I bet he can't do anything without his group and Anna too," Robbie and everyone laugh at what Robbie was saying.

Sanna watch Robbie making fun of the spirits, which Sanna look over at Jeff, "How can you stand here and let him do this?" Sanna ask Jeff in an upset voice walking away from the doorway.

Jeff looks at Sanna, "Because he has the money to provide this exhibit," Jeff says to Sanna trying to be nice.

"But you got the knowledge of those spirits, and you know what you talking about," Sanna told Jeff looking at Jeff with wide-eyes.

"Please Sanna, let it be," Adam told Sanna, put an arm over Sanna shoulders.

"I can't let it be, Robbie and Cookie are making fun of Jeff hard work and knowledge of the spirits. I can't let that go," Sanna started to raise her voice in anger at the end, and hate seeing someone making funny of her life.

Sanna look over at Robbie and Cookies standing by the display that has the dagger, "So this dagger has very special power," Robbie told the group of people.

"What kind of powers?" The Mayor asks looking down at the dagger in the display case, then at Robbie to find the answer about the dagger.

"Well..." Robbie started to stumble over his words. "This dagger can turn into a very cool sword that has some very awesome powers," Robbie told the Mayor, sweat beaded on Robbie forehead as nervous set in.

"That does not answer my question, what kind of powers does the sword has?" The Mayor question Robbie again, looking at Robbie in the eyes, and seeing if Robbie know anything.

Robbie nervous set in as the sweat started to run down his face. "Well..." Robbie could not speak for a bit, then made-up something to say to the Mayor. "This sword can heal anyone, just by touching it, even in dagger form, and can also save people from the evil spirit by shooting light beams at them."

The Mayor believes in what Robbie was saying with a smile on his face, but had one more question for Robbie, "How can this dagger turn into the sword?"

Robbie went wide-eyes stun, "Mr. Mayor something are might to be a secret, and how this dagger turning into a sword is one of them. Cookie and I been trying to finger out how the dagger can do that," Robbie was hoping that fool the Mayor and everyone else.

The Mayor nodded his head, "Okay Robbie that can stay your secret, now show us more stuff," The Mayor looking at everyone.

"Sure Mr. Mayor, this way," Robbie told the mayor showing more displays and talking about made-up stuff.

Sanna watch from the entryway of the exhibit with Adam and Jeff listening to Robbie chatting with the mayor. Sanna was trying to stay calm, but one thing that she heard that make her blood boil. "Cookies here are way prettier then Anna here. I bet Cookie will look hotter in Anna white dress then Anna alone," Robbie told the newspaper people and the Mayor laughing at the thought.

Sanna walk up to Robbie, the last thing Sanna heard was Adam calling out to her to stay with Jeff and him. Sanna walk straight up to Robbie and Cookie and looking at Robbie in the eyes, "Listen up Robbie and Cookie," Sanna told Robbie in a piss-off voice. "First off the two spirit names are not Anna and Don, but Anilea and Donavan. They are fighting for live on earth, if Donavan destroy Anilea life as you know it will not exist, Anilea here to save the life on earth from Donavan, and it spirit not angel, they are called." Sanna was nose to nose with Robbie, "The sword that now a dagger cannot shot light beams, it serves as a protector of humans life, in the wrong hands can be the end of the world." Sanna started to walk away, but stop and turn around, "Also Cookie would not be able to fit into Anilea clothes, she too cubby."

Cookies was raging at what Sanna say, Robbie had to hold Cookies back, "Easy Cook, let it go," Robbie told Cookie holding her in his arms.

Sanna walk up to the Mayor, "Mr. Mayor, sir, Robbie here has no information about anything here in this exhibit. Prof. Jeff here has the information about everything," Sanna pointed to Prof. Jeff standing behind her. "Robbie and Cookie provide the money for this exhibit," Sanna told the mayor.

The Mayor looks at Sanna with a confused look on his face. "What are you talking about? The museum makes a lot of money to keep everything going," Mayor told Sanna.

Sanna look at Robbie and Cookie, "Robbie and Cookie nice tan you too," Sanna say to Robbie and Cookie looking over their tan bodies.

"Thanks," Robbie says to Sanna looking over his gold-brown tan body and feeling prove of his fake tan.

"Yeah, it is the middle of May to get that dark of tan," Sanna ask Robbie with a raise eyebrow at them and a crooked smile on her face.

Robbie and Cookie face went white, and they cannot speak. The Mayor look them with a stern look on his face, "Yes, I think this young lady is right. Are you two spending the money on your own needs?" the Mayor asks Robbie and Cookie.

Robbie came out with it, "Yes, we using museum money on ourselves. Okay happy now, let us keep on working here." Robbie felt so stupid about spilling the truth to the Mayor and new people.

The Mayor look at them, "I should fired you two, but how about you to work as the new cleaning people of the museum," The Mayor told Robbie and Cookie.

Robbie and Cookie look at each other, and then say together, "We will take the job."

"Good now, Prof. Jeff," The Mayor say to Jeff look at him.

"Yes, Mr. Mayor," Jeff say to the mayor with a nervous tone to his voice.

"You are the new manger of this exhibit," The Mayor told Prof. Jeff with a happy voice.

Prof. Jeff was so happy, "Thank-you Mr. Mayor, I would not let you down. Thanks Sanna," Jeff told the Mayor shaking hands with the mayor, and look at Sanna.

"Your welcome, now show the mayor what a real tour around here look like," Sanna smiling at Jeff, and feeling good that the real truth will use now.

Prof. Jeff show the Mayor and the newspaper people what the real information about the two spirits. Adam walk up to Sanna, "Nice job, you made someone very happy," Adam told Sanna watching Prof. Jeff giving talk to the Mayor about the truth about the fight and the spirits.

"I know; I just hate to see someone, like Robbie and Cookie, to do something like that to someone, like Jeff, who work hard on a big project," Sanna told Adam watching Prof. Jeff talking to the Mayor. Sanna turn to Adam, "Are you hungry?" Sanna ask Adam walking to the stairs.

"Yes and I know the prefect place for lunch," Adam told Sanna walking down the stairs with Sanna.

"Cool I'm in," say Sanna walking out the front door of the museum. Sanna look over her right shoulder. *'Now I know were my sword is now how to get it back?'* Sanna walking outside the museum with Adam, and heading down the street.

Adam and Sanna walk away from the museum talking and laughing. Five people all dress in black clothes, watching Sanna and Adam walking away from the museum, "Hey Donovan is that Anilea?" ask a young woman to the male leader looking from the shadows of the trees.

"I think so Desdemona, my dear sister, only time can tell," Donovan says to Desdemona looking at Sanna walking down the street, with an evil grin on his face.

"Let go and get her now," say Ryu in a tweak voice and movement, all he wants to do is cause trouble and chaos.

"Easy my dear hubby, Donovan has a planned to get rid of Anilea and her little group," say Eris to Ryu rubbing Rye arms with her hands up and down slowly and smooth, Rye cringe in a good way, and making his eyes rolled in the back of his head.

"Why are we standing here talking, let get out of here before Anilea sights us," Crevan looking at Donovan, lending against the tree, and close to Desdemona, his wife.

"I agree with Crevan, let's go back to our new place," Donovan say to his group walking away down the street in the opposite direction then Sanna and Adam.

Sanna looking over her right shoulder quickly and she saw Donovan and his group walking away. Adam look at Sanna, "What wrong?" Adam asks Sanna nicely.

"Nothing I thought I saw something, but it's not that important," Sanna laird to Adam look at Adam in the face but in the back of her mind was going wild. *'He here and his group too,'* Sanna thought to herself and keep on walk with Adam.

CHAPTER FOUR

Donovan Return & Anilea Fear!

Donovan and his group show up to a large two-story house in the dark part of the woods. Crevan opening the large front door and hold it opens for everyone to enter. Crevan closed the door behind Donovan. "Welcome home my friends," Donovan says to everyone laughing. Donovan is a 6 ft tall, looks 29 year old, well-built male, and a scare on the right side of his face down the cheek from Sanna. Donovan hair is short spike black with dark red highlights. Donovan wear black jean, black or red t-shirts with black leather jacket, and black boots, Donovan and Desdemona are family more he older looking then his sister.

Desdemona is 5 ft 5 in tall, looks 25 year-old. Desdemona long straight black hair with red highlights. Desdemona wear black leather pants or black mini skirt, black thin strap shirts with a black leather jacket, and black knee-high boots. Desdemona is a thin woman, Donovan younger sister, and marry to Crevan.

Eris is 5 ft 5 in tall, look 25 year old, thin woman, black long curly hair with dark purple highlights. Eris wears black or red short length dress, thin straps, and knee height boots. Eris fighter clothes are black leather pants, red leather tank top, and black boots, and Eris is marrying Ryu.

Ryu and Crevan are twin brothers, look 29 year-old. Ryu and Crevan are 6 ft tall each, having black short stick hairs with red highlights for Crevan and purple highlights for Ryu, and both well-built males, wearing red or black t-shirts, black leather pants, and black boots. Everyone has green eyes when calm, but red eyes when mad or fighting. Everyone has been on earth 1614 years.

Donovan sat down on the couch in the living room. Ryu, Crevan, Eris, and Desdemona enter the living room behind me, and Donovan look at them. "My friends," Donovan putting his feet on the coffee table, "Anilea and her friends are here in this town, and I cannot wait for next year it will be so much fun," Donovan told his group.

"Are we going to have some fun before the big battle?" Crevan ask Donovan sitting on the other side of the couch with Donovan. Donovan put his left hand under his chin, and thinking about what Crevan was saying to him. Ryu was tweaking, and waiting Donovan answer.

After a few minutes Ryu bust out with it, "Come on! Please, I have not had any real fun with people for years! Please Donovan, let have some fun for now!" Ryu realize what he did, Ryu felt wrong, and sunk down a bit while standing.

Donovan took his feet off the coffee table, stood up from the couch, walk up to Ryu, and look at Ryu in the eyes. "What do you think?" Donovan question Ryu in a mean voice.

Sweat beaded on Ryu forehead. Ryu eyes shifted side to side. Ryu could not speak as Donovan has his eyes on him. "I... I..." Ryu started to stumble over his words, "I think yes." Ryu say a little calmly to Donovan.

"Of course, but first we need to deal out something that we need to do." Donovan turns to everyone else, and walking around the room to think.

"What that?" Crevan ask Donovan with confused voice, sitting on the couch, and looking at his wife.

Desdemona sat down on the arm of the couch beside Crevan, "My dear husband, my big brother is saying we to plan to get Anilea and her friends by surprise," Desdemona say to Crevan running her left hand up and down his chest, Crevan was enjoying it a lot.

"Your right sister," Donovan told Desdemona sitting down in a chair across the couch. "My idea is you guys spy on Anilea and her friends. We need to find Anilea weakness and use it against her, and then we go to have a wonderful battle that this town well never seen in history." Donovan stood up, and laughing meanly, everyone join in laugh with Donovan, "Enough!" Donovan called out, and everyone stop laughing on the spot. "Now tomorrow you guys and girls are going to work spying and not trouble, not yet. Remember to stay out of Anilea sight, she see you, your toast on the spot, stay out of her sight," Donovan told his group and knowing his group will do his betting.

"We know," Crevan told Donovan, "So what for supper?" Crevan look at Desdemona, looking at his wife sexy body, and think how luckily he is to have a sexy wife.

Desdemona look at Crevan in the eyes, "I tell you what for dessert," Desdemona start to rub Crevan inter-thigh with her hands.

Crevan got the point across quickly, “Oh I see… Like someone said ‘Life is too short, eat dessert first.’” Crevan got off the couch, picking up Desdemona in his arms, and turn to everyone else. “We will be right back soon… In an hour or so,” Crevan went upstairs with Desdemona in his arms.

Ryu look at Eris with sexy eyes, “Do you want too?” Ryu signal upstairs to Eris, and want to have some fun before he go crazy.

“Sure,” Eris says to Ryu walking upstairs together, placing her right hand on Ryu but all the way to their room.

Donovan watch as his group gone upstairs together, “Poor love sick puppies, they are,” Donovan told himself lending back in the chair. “They better keep their heads on the big picture… to get rid of Anilea and her friends for good.” Donovan putting his fingertips together, and moves them evilly. “My dear Anilea this time next year,” Donovan look out the window from his chair, “You will be died, and long gone for good. There no way you’re coming back on this earth and the spirit world.” Donovan started to chuckle evil at the thought, and then Donovan heard loud sex mourning and groaning coming from upstairs bedrooms. “Well you guys keep it down!” Donovan yelled out at the top of his voice.

“Sorry boss!” Four voices called out from the upstairs bedrooms, and then they were quiet now.

“Idiots, but they are good for something,” Donovan told himself. Donovan relaxes in the chair, and thinking plan to get rid of Anilea for good.

~~*~*~*~*~*~*~*

Sanna and Adam walk back to Sanna place, “Thanks for lunch, Adam,” Sanna say to Adam walking up to the steps of the front deck and up to the front door.

“You’re welcome,” Adam says to Sanna, “Hey if you need to talk about anything that bugging you, I am here for you to listen.” Adam blush a bit at the end, and thinking of her hand but pulled back a bit.

“Oh okay, I’ll remember that for next time,” Sanna was surprise at what Adam say to her, Sanna blush a bit in her cheeks. Adam stared at Sanna a bit, wanting to say something, but could not find the right words to say. Sanna look at Adam, “Hey you better get going home. I see my friends are home, and I better get going. Thanks for the great day,” Sanna say to Adam opening the front door,

“See you around Adam,” Sanna say to Adam walking into the house.

"See you later Sanna," Adam told Sanna walking down the step, and walking to his place.

Sanna sigh in relief, and closing the front door. "Hey I'm home!" Sanna called out, taking off her shoes.

"Hey Anilea, I'm upstairs!" Roselyn called from the second floor in her room.

Sanna walk upstairs to the second floor and to Roselyn bedroom. "Hey, how it going?" Sanna say to Roselyn, standing in the bedroom doorway.

"Good, just got home from work a few minutes ago," Roselyn told Sanna taking off her nursing scrubs, and putting jeans and a t-shirt. "And you? How were you today?"

Sanna lend against the doorway, looking at Roselyn, "It was alright," Sanna, say in a mild tone voice.

"May I ask what did you do today?" Roselyn look at Sanna in the doorway, knowing body language, and knowing something was on Sanna mind now.

Sanna lower her head, "Most of the morning I spent crying, then Adam came over, and cheer me up a bit. We talk for a while, and then we went to the museum to an exhibit about something cool," Sanna told Roselyn, looking at Roselyn with mild eyes, and trying hard now to getting upset at what she saw at the museum.

Roselyn look at Sanna, "What was this cool thing that you saw at the museum?" Roselyn question Sanna with a raise eyebrow.

"Well..." Sanna try to drag it out a bit, and thinking of her sword is now.

Roselyn put her hands on her hips, "Come on Sanna, what it was about?" Roselyn told Sanna, looking at Sanna with narrow eyes now.

Sanna came out with it, "Okay, the museum has an exhibit on us and them, and guess what I found there?"

Roselyn look at Sanna, dropping her hands to her side, "What was it that you found?" Roselyn ask Sanna nicely calming down now.

Sanna look at Roselyn in the eyes, "My sword," Sanna told Roselyn in a mild tone.

Roselyn look at Sanna with wide eyes, "You're got to be kidding me. There no way your sword is on display in the museum. They must put a fake one out for the human eyes," Roselyn told Sanna in a panic voice. Roselyn ran her hands through her hair thinking that Sanna found her sword now.

Sanna slowly walk up to Roselyn, Sanna took Roselyn hands in her hands, looking up at Roselyn, and spoke, "It is my sword, right now it is in dagger form. I thought at first that it was a freak one, when I look at it that it was not my sword. When no one was not looking I put my hands on the display, force my power on the dagger and it turn into my sword right in front of me. That when I know that it was my sword."

Roselyn look at Sanna, and say in a mild tone voice, "Did you get your sword back?"

Sanna shook her head, "No, there were too many people around. Listen to me Roselyn, now I know were it is at, when time comes. I will go and get it," Sanna let go of Roselyn hands.

"Did we hear you, Sanna, right that you found your sword in the museum?" Tiffany says behind Sanna in the doorway of the bedroom with Andrew and Aaron behind her.

Sanna turn around looking at her three friends in the doorway of the bedroom, "Yes, but it is impossible to get it back with secretary is so tight and too many people around. I was luckily to put my hands on the glass case with no one seeing me using my powers on the dagger," Sanna told everyone in the bedroom.

"When are you going to get your sword back?" Aaron asks Sanna over Tiffany right shoulder, and knowing when will be the best time for Sanna to her sword back.

Sanna look at Aaron, "Not right now, next year when my sword will be back in my hands," Sanna told Aaron, looking at her hands to an image her sword back in her hands.

"How are you getting the sword?" Andrew asks Sanna, thinking now.

Sanna put her right hand under her chin, and thinking a bit, and then Sanna told Andrew, "I have no idea, but it will come to me soon."

Sanna look at everyone for moment, Sanna face whet white, her eyes whet scare look, and Sanna body just whet stiff as a broad. Roselyn look at Sanna, "Sanna?" Roselyn ask Sanna with a worry voice. "Anilea are you alright?" Roselyn touch Sanna right shoulder with her right hand.

Sanna turn her head to Roselyn, looking at Roselyn in the eyes, in a scared voice say, "They are here."

Roselyn put both hands on Sanna shoulders, looking Sanna in the face. "Anilea, what do you mean they are here? You don't mean?"

Sanna nodded her head to Roselyn, "I thought I saw them outside the museum across the road." Sanna was so scared that her body started to shake badly, "But now I know they are here in this town and Donovan look more powerful then last time." Sanna eyes rolled in the back of her head, her body went limp, and Sanna started to fall down to the floor.

Andrew and Aaron catch Sanna body before she hit the floor. Roselyn look at Andrew and Aaron,

"Let's get Anilea upstairs to her bed now," Roslyn told Andrew and Aaron, a bit scared to see Sanna just collapse so quickly in front of her.

"Let's go sport," Andrew carries Sanna upstairs to her bedroom in his arms. Sanna was silent with her eyes closed.

Aaron open Sanna bedroom door for Andrew, Andrew enter the room with Sanna in his arms, Andrew lay Sanna down on her bed, and cover Sanna with a blanket. Roselyn and Tiffany enter Sanna bedroom, Tiffany look at Sanna lay on the bed, "Roselyn, I never seen Anilea act like that before," Tiffany ask Roselyn keeping her eyes on Sanna.

"I know," Roselyn, told Tiffany looking at Sanna lay on the bed, "Anilea never act this way before when Donovan came to town... Maybe Anilea think she would not be powerful to defeat Donovan. You know she wants to end this battle once and for all." Roselyn walk over to Sanna right side of the bed, and look down at Sanna sleeping, "Anilea look so peaceful right now, and it's been years."

Tiffany look at Roselyn, Aaron, and Andrew, "Have you every thought what will happen to us if Anilea died by Donovan hands?" Tiffany asks everyone in the room.

Everyone looks at Tiffany with a shock look on his or her faces, "I never thought on that question," Andrew says to Tiffany with a stun voice.

"We will be lost without Anilea. You remember how long it took us to find her," Aaron told everyone looking around the room at everyone.

"Almost 250 years-old, before the fighting started again," Tiffany told Aaron looking at Sanna sleeping in the bed, and thinking to herself.

Roselyn look at everyone in the room, "We will be all heartbroken and very upset if anything happen to Anilea. Remember what happen almost 100 years ago. We were so close to losing Anilea from the fight. If Anilea did died I will cry, then I will carry Anilea duty without her, and take care of Donovan and his group." Roselyn spoke to everyone in the room with a strong voice tone.

Tiffany, Andrew, and Aaron look at Roselyn, "Not without us by you side, your not doing that alone," Tiffany told Roselyn pointing a finger at Roselyn.

Roselyn chuckled at Tiffany, "Your right sister. We don't anything without everyone beside our side," Roselyn look down at Sanna, "Anilea be on her own for along time, even in hiding from Donovan. Now being here again in this town bring back memories of her past life, and now I think the pressure is getting to Anilea badly. You seen Anilea passing-out a few moments ago, when she says Donovan was here," Roselyn say to everyone with a worry voice.

Tiffany looks at Roselyn then to Sanna, "I saw Anilea passing-out right in front of you and all of us, it was scary." Tiffany says to Roselyn looking back down at Sanna.

"Yes, now let's leave Anilea to sleep for a bit. I think she need it," Roselyn say to everyone, looking at up at everyone. Andrew, Aaron, and Tiffany left the Sanna bedroom, and went downstairs to the living room. Roselyn took her right hand, and moving a piece of hair away from Sanna face. "You got to be strong to win this fight, Anilea," Roselyn whisper to Sanna, leaving the bedroom, and closing the bedroom door behind her.

A couple hours later, Sanna eyes start to stir, and open quickly. Sanna sat up straight in her bed, "Where am I?" Sanna say quickly, looking around the room. Sanna realize that she was in her bedroom, "I'm in my bedroom," Sanna say to herself calming down. Sanna throw a couple pillows against the north wall behind her, and lend against the pillows with her back against the pillows. Sanna sat there on her bed, thinking about what Tiffany, Roselyn, Aaron, and Andrew was talking about, if she even died. "They will so heartbroken and lost without me," Sanna lower her head, "But I know that they finish my duty for me..." Sanna raise her head up and looking ahead at the end of her bed. "They don't know with will really happen if I died from Donovan hands, they would be his salves and has to do whatever he says." Tears fell from her left eyes, Sanna wipe the tears away, and Sanna mind was on something else. "Why today my memories have to come over my duty?" Sanna started to sob as tears started to flow from her eyes. "Why did you have to die? I miss everyone that had to die!" Sanna called out in the air. Sanna curled into a ball, placing her hands with half-curled fingers, and started to rock back and forward, "What happening to me?" Sanna could not find out what going on with her, "Why are my memories coming more involved?" Sanna started to shake and Sanna eyes started to shift side to side. "I need some air now," Sanna fling the blankets off her, jumping out of her bed, running to the French doors, and opening the doors wide.

Sanna ran outside onto the balcony, Sanna put her outs in front of her, as she hit the front railing of the balcony. Sanna breathing heavily and short too, Sanna eyes were wide and sadly looking. Sanna could not control herself in anyway or form. Sanna mind was racing a million miles an hour, and Sanna had flashbacks of her past life. Sanna scream at the top of her voice, throwing her head back in the air, "PLEASE JUST STOP!" Sanna voice carries through the town, forest, and over the lake. No one could not hear Sanna scream, it was nothing but a breeze blowing through the leaves on the trees. Sanna done screaming, she fell to knees, look through the bars of the railing, as Sanna lend her forehead against the bars. Sanna look down to the grassy ground from the third-story, she started to weep as tears fall to the ground.

Rain started to coming down from the sky, Sanna look up to the sky, and crying more with her eyes red from crying. Sanna fell to hands and knees, weeping more, sitting down on the wooden floor of the balcony, and look out at the lake. Sanna pictures of her love one and her walking around the lake, and having fun in each other arms. Sanna remember when her lover pops the question of marriage to her, and her wedding day. Sanna was in a trace, got up from the floor, walking back into her bedroom, and into the closet.

A few minutes later, Sanna exited the closet wearing the white old dress, and her wet hair down. Sanna walk to the make-up table, open a wooden box on top of the table, grab a crown of flowers with white ribbon down the back, and putting it on her head. Sanna walk back outside onto the balcony with the rain pouring down hard. Sanna walk to the end of the balcony as the rain hit Sanna body and hair. The thunder and lighting was roaring and flashing in the sky, Sanna stood there on the balcony with a blank look on her face. Sanna could only hear the thunder and rain hitting the ground. Sanna was mumbling words to herself, as Sanna mind keep on running a million mile an hour. Sanna body started to glow with a white light around her. Sanna could hear a male voice from the north, yelling her name through the rain and the thunder. Sanna turn her glowing eyes to the voice, through the hard rain and saw Adam yelling through the rain to her. Sanna stared at Adam soaking wet body, and something inside Sanna mind just stop everything. Sanna snap out of the trace, Sanna eyes went back to her hazel eyes, and Sanna stand there in the rain in her white dress. "Why am I wearing my old wedding dress, and flower crown?" Sanna ask herself looking at what she was dress in.

Sanna look at Adam, looking back at her through the rain, Sanna ran back inside the house, and closed the French doors behind her. Sanna stood there in front the door, wide-eye in shock, "I wonder if he saw me going into my spirit form?" Sanna told herself, slowly walking away from the doors, and back into the closet. Sanna got out of her wedding dress, and back into her jeans and shirt. Sanna exit the closet, putting the flower crown back into the wooden box, and closing the box. Sanna did not take her hands off the lid of the box, the only thing Sanna could do was lower her head, and let out a big sigh. Sanna closed her eyes for a bit, trying to forget what she saw outside with Adam. "What an idiot I am," Sanna told herself in a piss-off voice. "Adam saw me glowing in a white light… How could I let myself do that? … What if he asks me, where the white light came from? …" Sanna walk away from the make-up table, and to the window seating. Sanna stood there looking outside the window with a puzzling look on her face, "What will I do?" Sanna told herself in a worry voice, "I'm hoping Donovan group did not found out where I am at?" Sanna watch the rain hitting the glass of the window, and running down the window to the ground.

Sanna could hear the phone ring from the main floor, and someone answering the phone. Sanna open the bedroom door; slowly walk to the staircase, and down to the second floor to listen better. "Hello," Roselyn answer the phone, "Hey Adam… Yes, everything is good with me… Where is Sanna? Upstairs in her bedroom resting now… You want to talk to her… I will go and see if Sanna wanted to talk to you. Be back in a few minutes," Roselyn taking the wireless phone with her, and Roselyn cover the phone end with her right hand. Roselyn turn the corner from the staircase, and seeing Sanna sitting down on the tops steps of the third staircase, looking down at Roselyn. "Oh hey Sanna, you got a phone call. It is Adam, he really wants to talk to you," Roselyn told Sanna, still having the phone cover, and seeing Sanna was up now.

Sanna shook her head to Roselyn, "I don't want to talk to Adam,' Sanna told Roselyn in a worry voice.

"Why?" Roselyn ask Sanna still having the phone cover with her hand, seeing something was not right with Sanna.

Sanna look at Roselyn in the face, "Because I think Adam seen me glowing," Sanna told Roselyn lending back on the stairs, and letting out a sigh.

Roselyn mouth drop down, and Roselyn eyes went wide-eye looking, "Are you sure?" Roselyn ask Sanna, Sanna nodded her head; Roselyn put the phone back to her ear. "Sanna not feeling well effect to talk, Sanna will call you back when she well affect, bye," Roselyn hung up the phone on Adam.

Sanna put her elbows on her legs, and her forehead in her hands. Sanna stared at the stairs, as Roselyn look Sanna with a shock look on her face. "I don't want to see Adam anymore," Sanna told Roselyn in an upset voice, tears falling from Sanna eyes.

Chapter Five

Anilea Birthday and Crush!

June 9, 2064 came around; Sanna woke to the sun rising from the east, Sanna look at her alarm clock on the left bed stand. "4:30 in the morning," Sanna groan when she saw the time on the alarm clock. Sanna rolled onto her back, laying facing the ceiling, "Happy birthday to me," Sanna whisper to herself looking at the white lace hanging over her bed. Sanna sat up in her bed, looking at the French doors, "I need some air," Sanna told herself getting out of bed, putting her light blue robe, and opening the French doors.

Sanna walk outside onto her balcony, Sanna took a deep breath through her nose, and letting it out of her mouth. Sanna looking out to the lake, watching the wind blowing over the water making waves with white caps on top of the water. Sanna could hear the waves crashing against the shore and big rocks in the water. Sanna felt calm down enough to go on with day, but one image Sanna could not off her mind, the night of May 20, when the thunderstorm hit and Adam, seeing Sanna glowing white. "How could I been a fool," Sanna spoke in the whisper, "I wonder if Adam forgot about that night." Sanna turn to Adam house in the north, *'I hope he did... I cannot be hiding from Adam forever... I like him a lot, but there still something about Adam that I should know,'* Sanna thought for a bit, and then yawn with a stretch. *'Why am I up this early? I'm going back to bed,'* Sanna walk back inside the house, and closed the door behind her. Sanna took off her robe throwing back on the chair by the door, and went back to bed. Sanna lay in the middle of the bed in her light blue, thin strap, full-length nightgown, and covering up by a blanket.

Around 9:30 in the morning, Tiffany, Roselyn, Aaron, and Andrew quietly walk upstairs to Sanna bedroom. "Ssshhh," Roselyn say putting a finger against her lips, and quietly open the door to Sanna bedroom. Tiffany, Roselyn, Andrew, and Aaron enter the bedroom with Tiffany holding a breakfast in her hand on a tray, and balloons in Andrew and Aaron hands. Tiffany put the tray on the make-up table, Aaron and Andrew put the balloons on the floor beside the bed, and Roselyn put the little gift by the tray. Roselyn and Tiffany move the white lace curtain back from the bed and tide the curtain back with a light blue ribbon. Roselyn and Tiffany look at Sanna sleeping and slowly laying down beside Sanna on each side, Aaron and Andrew slowly sat down on the end of the bed.

Sanna started to stir and slowly open her eyes. "Morning sunshine," everyone say to Sanna.

Sanna jump up on her feet on the bed with wide-eyes, "Oh it is only you guys," Sanna trying to slowdown her heart from breathing so fast. "What are you guys doing here?" Sanna ask everyone in her bedroom.

"We came to give you your birthday breakfast in bed," say Tiffany getting off Sanna bed and grabbing the tray from the make-up table.

"Oh," Sanna sat down on her bed, "I see." Tiffany places the tray of waffles with whip-cream and raspberries on top in front of Sanna. Sanna look down at the plates of food. "Thanks you guys, this mean a lot to me," Sanna thanks her friends and started to eating the food.

Roselyn look over at Andrew and Aaron. "Don't you two have to get to work here soon?" Roselyn ask the boys.

"Yes," Aaron say to Roselyn, Aaron turn to Andrew, "Let's go bro. See you girls later." Aaron and Andrew left Sanna bedroom, and left the house for work.

Roselyn heard the car starting up and driving away along the street. Roselyn turn to Sanna and realize that small gift on the make-up table. "Oh... Anilea, someone stop by and drop this little gift for you," Roselyn say to Sanna, picking up the gift off the make-up table, and handing it to Sanna.

Sanna took the small gift from Roselyn hands and holding the small gift in her hands. Tiffany took the tray away from Sanna with empty dishes on it. Sanna look down at the gift in her hands, Sanna running her fingers across the wrapping paper, and little bow on top. "Who is this gift from?"

Sanna ask Roselyn and Tiffany still having her eyes on the gift.

Roselyn and Tiffany look at each other, and then back at Sanna. "Anilea, it's from Adam," Roselyn say to Sanna, looking at Sanna face worry looking.

"I see," Sanna looking at the gift in her hands, she at the card on top of the gift, Sanna read through the card, tears fill Sanna eyes, and falling onto the gift. Sanna throw the card onto the bed, "How could he do that?" Sanna was upset at what Adam wrote in the card.

Roselyn pick up the card into her hands, and reading the card. Roselyn look at Sanna, "I think Adam like you a lot," Roselyn told Sanna with the card in her hands.

"Let me read that card?" Tiffany asks Roselyn. Roselyn pass the card to Tiffany. Tiffany read the card, looking at Sanna, "I agree with Roselyn. Adam has a crush on you, and he does care about you a lot," Tiffany told Sanna.

"Still I almost blow my secret to him... Adam saw me glow on the night of May 20... I never forgive myself for doing that." Sanna look at Roselyn and Tiffany, and back to the gift in her hands. "Do you think I should open this gift?" Sanna ask Roselyn and Tiffany.

Roselyn sat down on the edge Sanna bed, "Sanna, you should at lest open it to see what it is," Roselyn told Sanna.

Sanna unwrap the gift to relive a small white box, Sanna open the box, and saw the beautiful thing that she ever saw. Sanna mouth drop at the sight of the thing, Sanna took her hands, and pick up a little angel in her hands, "Wow... it's beautiful." Sanna ran her right fingertip over the details of the angel. "I never seen anything like this... it's... so beautiful," Sanna looking closer at the details of the angel.

Roselyn look at Sanna, "Now how can you be mad at Adam after this beautiful gift that he gave you?"

Sanna shook her head to force herself, "I'm not mad at Adam after this beautiful gift that he gave." Sanna look at Roselyn and putting the little on the left bed stand under the lamp. "There now every morning, when I wake up, I can look at it, and think of Adam," Sanna told Roselyn and Tiffany sitting in her bed with a smile on her face.

Roselyn and Tiffany smile at Sanna, "It is good seeing you smile like that. Now we better leave so you can get dress," Roselyn told Sanna getting up from the bed, and Tiffany too.

Sanna watch Roselyn and Tiffany about to exit the bedroom, when Sanna ask Roselyn, "Rose, can you braid my hair?"

Roselyn stop in the doorway and turn back around to Sanna, "Sure I can, but get dress first so your hair would not be mess up. When you put your shirt on," Roselyn told Sanna with a smile on her face.

Sanna jump out of her bed, when to the walk-in closet to get dress. Few minutes later Sanna exit the walk-in closet wearing light blue jeans, black tank top, and a pink and white button-up shirt over the tank top. Sanna sat down in front of the make-up table as Roselyn started to brush Sanna hair with the brush, then taking the comb and combing Sanna hair, and started to French-braid the back of Sanna head. Sanna watch Roselyn working, trying to smile through whole braiding. Sanna can see the little angel in the mirror, Sanna mind started to race fast. *'He so hot, Adam does care about me, and he does make me happy. In addition, I have not had any fun like that for a long time. Maybe I should try dating again, and if it does not workout I would not date or crush on any more guys,'* Sanna was thinking to herself.

"Hey Anilea, what do you think?" Roselyn as Sanna finish with Sanna hair and looking down at Sanna.

Sanna looked in the mirror, and saw the French braid in the back of her head. "Wow! Thanks Roselyn, it looks awesome," Sanna, told Roselyn getting up from the chair and giving Roselyn a hug.

"Your welcome," Roselyn hug Sanna back, "Now let's goes downstairs and has some fun."

"I'm in sis," Tiffany says to Roselyn exiting the room with Roselyn and Sanna.

After lunch, Sanna decide to go for a walk down by the lake. Sanna put her shoe on exit through the back door, and down the deck steps. Sanna walk down to the lake, and stood by a tall trees. Sanna, could feel the breeze on her face, Sanna closed her eyes. Sanna could hear leafs moving in the tree, the waves crashing along the shoreline, and someone walking up behind her. "Hey Sanna," the male voice spoke behind Sanna.

Sanna open her eyes quickly, turning around fast, with her fist ready for a fight, and seeing Adam standing in front of her. "Oh Adam, it is only you," Sanna say to Adam calming down, and uncurling her hands now.

"Sorry for scaring you, I saw you walking down here, and I thought if you like some company," Adam told Sanna, with his hands in his jean pockets.

Sanna look at Adam, then say, "Sure you can stay with me. I will like a lot," Sanna smile at Adam.

Adam smile back at Sanna, "Hey, do you when to go for some ice-cream? I know a great place by the lake that has the best ice-cream ever," Adam asks Sanna.

Sanna nodded her head to Adam, "Sure I'm in."

"Cool, let's go," Adam say to Sanna start to walk along the pathway to the beach area.

Adam and Sanna arrive at the beach area; there was a stand area by the water, and large grass area with trees and tables. Adam and Sanna walk up to the little ice-cream shack, and order their ice cream. They got a waffle cone with chocolate along the top of the cone. Adam got one scoop of Role, and one scoop of Smartie. Sanna got one scoop of Role, one scoop of Smartie, and one scoop of cookie dough; because Adam told the person that, it was Sanna birthday. Sanna walk up to a table, and sat down on the top of the table part, Adam sat down beside Sanna. They sat there eating their ice cream and looking out of the lake. Adam look at Sanna to ask a question, "So did you get my birthday gift?"

Sanna look over at Adam, "Yes, and it is beautiful thing I ever seen," Sanna answer Adam smiling, "Thank-you for it."

Adam blush a bit in the cheeks, "Your welcome. When I saw it I thought of you, and I know it make you smile... What about the card?" Adam asks Sanna eating his ice cream.

Sanna went quite for a few minute, then looking out at the lake. "It is very..." Sanna look at Adam in the eye, "Kind of you to write those very sweet words to me, and I love the card that you pick out," Sanna blush in the cheeks. Adam look into Sanna eyes. Trying to say something, but could not find the right words to say. Adam look out at the lake with Sanna, eating their ice cream.

Sanna and Adam keep on looking out at the lake. Everything was quite just the sound of the wind through the trees and waves hitting the shored. Adam spoke through the silent, "Your friends told me everything about you," Adam keeps his eyes on the lake, getting ready to tell Sanna, what her friends told Adam about her.

Sanna turn her head quickly to Adam, Sanna was wide-eye in shock, and Sanna mind was racing. *'How could my friends tell the truth about me...? I did not want Adam finding out.... Now what I can I do with him? What if Donovan fines out that Adam knows about the real me. I surprise Adam taking it very well... but I do not want Adam to hurt by my own fault... I like him a lot... more then friends.'* Sanna try to stay calm in front of Adam, and trying hard not to freak out in front of Adam or start glowing white.

"How could I realize, just the way you acting," Adam keep on talking to Sanna, watching the way Sanna body moving.

'Please don't say it,' Sanna keep on thinking, closing her eyes, and hoping for wrong words to come out of Adam mouth.

"You're fighting with..." Adam look at Sanna thinking on the right words to say.

'Don't say dark spirits,' Sanna was still hoping in her mind, and hoping that Adam will not say the words aloud encase someone around that will blow her cover.

"Depression," Adam says to Sanna snapping his finger at Sanna, and pointing a finger at Sanna.

Sanna open her eyes, and a rush of relief race all over her body. Sanna look at Adam, "Your right, I'm fighting with depression, you found out my big secret," Sanna told Adam with a smile, as Sanna mind relaxes.

"Hey the best way to fight it is a good friend by your side, and a lot of hugs," Adam gave Sanna a hug and holding her nicely in his arms now.

Sanna relax in Adam arms, and wrapping her arms around Adam shoulders, "Thank-you Adam for being a true friend," Sanna say in Adam arms.

"Your welcome," Adam let go of Sanna, and look down at Sanna into her eyes.

"Did you ask my friends any more questions?" Sanna question Adam wondering what her friends told Adam.

"Remember on the night of May 20?" Adam asks Sanna, remembering that night, and what he saw on Sanna balcony that night.

"Yes, the thunder storm that night, yes," Sanna was worry about what Adam found out; hoping he never saw her glowing white.

"I went over the next day, ask your friend what I saw, and they told me everything," Adam look at Sanna, "How every year you go into a trance, trying to comminute suicide in your wedding dress, and always waking up in your dress the next morning in your room, because you lost your love ones on that day... Wow I can not an image going through all that hurt for so long, and still having nightmares of that day," Adam look at Sanna in the face, and into her eyes.

Sanna lower her head after finishing her ice cream cone, "Thanks for reminding me Adam." Sanna say in an upset voice, and looking away for a moment.

Adam drop his head feeling wrong on what he told Sanna, "I'm sorry Sanna; I don't want to remind you about that date, and what happen on that date. I am very sorry for that," Adam spoke to Sanna in a mild tone finish his ice cream cone.

Sanna closed her eyes and listen to the sound of the waves hitting shoreline. Sanna try to stay calm, Sanna spoke in a whisper, "I forgive you, and thanks for saving my life," Sanna keep her head down and eyes closed.

Adam turns his head to Sanna, "What do you mean I save your life?" Adam question Sanna in a wondering voice.

Sanna open her eyes and turn her head to Adam, "You snap me out of that trance. I could have jump off the balcony, and kill myself hitting the ground." Sanna putting her left hand on top of Adam right hand, "You called out through the rain and thunder to me, that snap me out of that trance, and I'm the one should be sorry," Sanna told Adam holding his right hands in her left hand.

"Why should you be sorry?" Adam was confused at what Sanna was saying to him.

"Because I was rude to you for a while, it's just I wanted sometime to myself, and I'm sorry for that." Sanna let go of Adam right hand, and sat there on the table looking out on the beach.

Adam lend in closer to Sanna left ear, and whisper into Sanna left ear, "I forgive you, you was not yourself for a long time, and that okay," Adam gave Sanna a hug, Sanna set her head on Adam chest, and started to cry. Adam look down at Sanna, "Hey don't cry," Adam wipe a tear away from Sanna face with his fingertips.

Sanna pull back from Adam, "Sorry, it's just I never had a good friend that care about me this way," Sanna sniff a bit, and wiping the tears away from her face with her hands.

"What about the friends that are you living with?" Adam asks Sanna thinking about her friends living with her.

"They care about me, but outside my four friends is were your at," Sanna told Adam smiling at Adam.

Adam smile at Sanna, "Hey you hair look nice today, did you do it yourself?" Adam asks Sanna looking at Sanna hair.

"No, Roselyn did it. Does its look nice?" Sanna show the back of her head, and smiling a bit now.

"It looks very pretty," Adam look at Sanna French-braid, and thinking Sanna was looking good today.

Sanna turns back at Adam, Sanna look at Adam, "Adam," Sanna spoke in worry tone.

"Yes Sanna," Adam looks at Sanna, and had a worry look on his face.

"What if you have a big secret that you don't want lets say someone you got a crush on, to know about?" Sanna ask Adam still worry, fooling around with her hands together.

Adam putting his right hand under his chins, and ponders on the thought, "Mmm… First, I will think if this secret will hurt the friendship, if I keep it a secret. Then I will tell that person the secret, and see what happen next. If workout or not," Adam told Sanna, thinking to himself on the question Sanna ask him.

Sanna nodded in agreement with Adam, "Your right, but there also the right time to tell, and the wrong time to tell," Sanna told to Adam, and blushing a bit red in her cheeks.

"Your right about that too," Adam nodded to Sanna, "So is there anything you want to tell me?" Adam looks over at Sanna a bit, and blushing a bit more.

"No," Sanna trying to hind her blush fill face from Adam in her hands.

Adam look at Sanna in the face through the finger, "You have something on your mind that you want to tell me," Adam question Sanna looking at Sanna.

Sanna calm down that the red cheeks are gone, and spoke to Adam, "I maybe have a crush on someone."

Adam look at Sanna, "Who?" Adam raises an eyebrow at Sanna, and keeping his eyes in her eyes.

Sanna move closer to Adam right ear, and spoke in a whisper, "On you," Sanna move away quickly from Adam, and blush in the cheeks again.

Adam blush in the cheeks on what Sanna told him, Adam lend closer to Sanna left ear, and whisper back, "I might have a crush on you too," Adam lend back away from Sanna.

Sanna mouth drop at what Adam told her, "Do you really?" Sanna ask Adam in shock.

Adam nodded his head to Sanna, "Yes I do, ever since I land eyes on you in April, when you move in."

Sanna shook her head, "Wow," Sanna look out at the water. Sanna lend forward, putting her elbows on her legs, and putting her head in her hands. Sanna watch two ducks swimming in the lake water, Sanna felt the cold wind against her skin that made her shiver a bit. Adam look at Sanna shiver a bit, Adam took off his jacket, and putting the jacket around Sanna shoulder. Sanna sat up straight and looking at Adam with a stun look on her face. "Thank-you Adam," Sanna thanks Adam, putting her arms through the selves of jacket, and wraps her arms around her body.

"Your welcome, "Adam look at Sanna wearing his jacket, "You look a little cold."

"Thanks, but will you be cold," Sanna ask Adam looking at Adam, seeing him wearing a long shirt and jeans.

"Nay," Adam shook his head, "I'll be fine, beside I'm not cold anyway," Adam told Sanna, feeling warm inside his heart.

"Okay then," Sanna say to Adam, and look back at the lake water.

Sanna took off her shoes and socks, and walk down to the shoreline in her bare-feet. Adam watch from the table at Sanna walking down to the water. Sanna touch the water with her right foot toes, and move them back onto the warm sand. The waves move close to Sanna feet and Sanna watch from a few feet from the water edge. The waves of water hit Sanna feet and Sanna did not move as the wave's crash against Sanna feet. Sanna smile out of the water as her memories play in her mind. Sanna started to cry of her past life playing in her mind. "Why?" Sanna spoke in a whisper to herself, as tears hit the wet sand.

Adam got off the table, walks up to Sanna, putting his hands on Sanna shoulders, "Hey are you alright?" Adam asks Sanna softly in her right ear.

Sanna took a deep breath and letting it out slowly. "Sorry Adam," Sanna told Adam wiping the tears away from her face.

"About what?" Adam asks Sanna in a confused voice.

"About crying in front of you," Sanna told Adam looking at the water hitting her feet.

"That okay, I bet it was you memories of you past life playing in your mind," Adam told Sanna putting his arms around her shoulders and holding Sanna closer to his body.

Sanna look up at the sky, "Your right Adam. What happen in the past should stay in the past," Sanna say to Adam, and trying to feel better now.

Adam look down at Sanna, "Do you think it is time to forget about the whole thing that happens three years ago?" Adam asks Sanna smiling down at Sanna.

Sanna turn around in Adam arms and looking at Adam in the face. "I will try, it is time to move on with my life, and look forward to a new beginning," Sana told Adam in his arms.

"You don't mind my arms around you?" Adam asks Sanna smiling down at her in his arms.

Sanna look at Adam arms around her body, thought to herself for a bit, then spoke in a shy voice, "I don't mind you arms around me, beside I feel comfortable in your arms." Sanna cheeks went bright red, Sanna realize that her cheeks went red that Sanna took her hands and put her face in her hands. Sanna hind her bright red blush fills face from Adam.

Adam looks down at Sanna in his arms and chuckled at Sanna, "Why do you hide your face from me every time you blush?" Adam move Sanna hands away from her face using his hands. Sanna quickly lower her head to the ground, Adam laugh at Sanna a bit, taking his right hand, placing his hand under Sanna chin, and raise Sanna head up to his face, "Your so easy to make blush, and it is cute." Adam looks into Sanna eyes and blush in his cheeks.

Sanna look into Adam eyes, "You have the most gorgeous eyes I ever seen. They remind me of my past lover eyes," Sanna say to Adam, thinking of her past lover in her mind.

"Are you going to be upset?" Adam asks Sanna looking into her eyes, thinking if she going to cheer up now.

Sanna shook her head, "No, I would not be upset. It feels alright and I don't mind your eyes, they the most gorgeous blue eyes I ever seen." Sanna staring in Adam eye, and feeling very relax in Adam arms.

Adam looks down at Sanna and look into Sanna eyes, "Your eyes are so pretty. The pretties hazel eyes ever, they so cool," Adam held Sanna body closer to his body, and his heart was beating fast.

Sanna could smell Adam after-shave; Sanna closed her eyes, and felt at peace, Sanna try to thin to herself about a few things. *'Adam smell, look, and care like my past lover... I have a funny feeling that we are might to be together, maybe Adam a spirit too. Nay,'* Sanna thought to her in Adam arms. Sanna look up at Adam, "Adam," Sanna say in a calm voice.

Adam look down at Sanna, "Yes Sanna," Adam say in a wondering voice.

"Do you want to go for a walk along the beach?" Sanna ask Adam trying not to make she sound stupid.

"Sure and I will take off my shoes and socks too," Adam told Sanna taking off his shoes and socks, and put them with Sanna shoes and socks by the table. Adam walk back to Sanna, "Do you want to hold hands or not?" Adam asks Sanna.

Sanna look at Adam, "Not right now, I feel it not time, but I like hugs from you," Sanna spoke to Adam. Adam gave Sanna a hug, and started to walk along the beach with Sanna beside him.

Sanna and Adam walk along the beach, Sanna suck her hands in Adam jacket pockets as she walk along beside Adam. They talk and laugh along the shoreline, Sanna had a feeling that someone or something was watching Adam and her. Sanna look over her right shoulders to see if this thing or who was following them, Adam look down at Sanna, "Hey is everything okay?" Adam asks Sanna with a worry voice.

Sanna turn her head back to Adam, "Yeah everything okay. I thought I saw something in the tree lines that catch my eyes," Sanna told Adam walking along the beach with Adam.

"Okay, there a lot of animals that comes along this way," Adam says to Sanna smiling down at Sanna.

"Yeah, it must have been animal that I saw in the trees," Sanna told Adam walking along the shoreline, but in the back of Sanna mind, *'Sending your guys to spy on me. It not going to work this time I know your moves and what your going to doing,'* Sanna smile at herself thinking that Donovan trying to up her on this fight coming up.

In the trees, Ryu and Crevan were watching Sanna and Adam walking along the beach. "Do you think Anilea saw us, bro?" Ryu ask Crevan in a nervous voice that his whole body was shacking, behind a large brush.

Crevan took his right hand, and hit his brother across the face. "Anilea will see us if you keep making aloud noise like that. Anilea can sense your fear if you keep on shaking, plus we only here to spying on her, and report back to the Donovan on what we see," Crevan told Ryu in the face, and look back at Sanna through the trees with Adam beside Sanna with slide eyes. "Donovan will like this report," Crevan watching Sanna and Adam walking along the beach.

Ryu look at Crevan with a confusing look on his face, "What do you mean?" Ryu say scratching the top of his head with his left hand.

Crevan turn to Ryu and explain to Ryu, "Anilea has a crush on that young man. Ryu was still confused, Crevan shook his head at Ryu putting his left arm around Ryu shoulders, and Crevan turn Ryu to the distance of Sanna and Adam, "My brother remember almost 400 years ago?"

Ryu nodded, "Yeah, yeah. We killed Anilea family, friends, and love one on her wedding day," Ryu told Crevan happy at the memory.

"Yes and do you remember her weakness?" Crevan ask Ryu squeezing his brother body with his left arm.

"No, I cannot remember that," Ryu told Crevan looking out through the trees at Sanna.

Crevan smack Ryu in the back of the head with his left hand. "It was her love ones that her weakness and I think here a new one in the picture," Crevan looking at Adam. Adam had his right arm around Sanna, Crevan narrow his eyes at the sight.

Ryu got what Crevan was saying, "Oh I see. Donovan will love it," Ryu laugh with a chuckled.

"Yes, now let's go before Anilea finds out that we are here, and come after us." Crevan told Ryu walking away through the trees back home with Ryu behind him.

Sanna was sitting on the sand with Adam sitting beside her. Sanna could hear footsteps through the trees, *'They are trying hard to keep up with me. This time it would not work, I will out do them this time, and finish this fighting for good,'* Sanna was thinking to herself that two of Donovan people were spying on Adam and her.

"Hey what are you thinking?" Adam asks Sanna with a concerned voice looking at Sanna.

Sanna snapping out of thought. "What? None thing much on my mind I was thinking. Just something that I reminded to do today," Sanna say to Adam in a kindly voice. Sanna turn her head to Adam.

"What that?" Adam asks Sanna, looking at Sanna with a wondering what Sanna was thinking about all the time.

Sanna look at Adam in the eyes, and whisper to him, "It's a secret," Sanna look back at the lake.

"I see," Adam nodded his head, and look at the lake with Sanna.

The wind blow across the lake water and the trees, Sanna watch the wind moving the water closer to the shoreline. The wind whistle around the trees and brushes, Sanna closing her eyes and listen to the sounds area. Sanna try hard not getting upset around Adam, *'What will happen this time next year? What will happen to this beautiful place? I want to stay after the fight; I do not care what anyone says... I'm staying,"* Sanna thought to herself, lowering her head. *'Is that maybe that I'm in love... that I want to stay... or maybe that I was born here 425 years ago... I cannot believe that I am 1315 years-old now... Wow I'm old.'* Sanna was think to herself, Sanna raise her land to the white-cloudy-blue sky and open her eyes looks up at the sky.

Adam look over at Sanna, "Thinking again," Adam spoke to Sanna.

Sanna lower her head to Adam, "Yes, I was," Sanna told Adam nicely.

Adam look at Sanna in the face, spoke in a whisper to Sanna, "You do that a lot... What on you mind most of the time...? That making you thinking a lot, is there something that you're hiding from me, that you don't want me to know?" Adam look into Sanna eyes, and trying to finger out what really on Sanna mind now.

Sanna started to panic, Sanna heart started to beat fast, her breathing was fast, and her eyes widen in fear that Adam could find out the truth about her spirit side. Sanna got off the sandy ground, took off Adam jacket, handing the jacket back to Adam. "I have to go home now," Sanna ran back to the table, putting on her socks and shoes, and ran all the way home without stopping.

The last thing Sanna could hear was Adam calling out to her, "Wait!" Adam yelled holding his jacket in his hands. Adam look down at his jacket in his hands, and wondering what going through Sanna head. Adam stood in the sand looking at the lake water.

CHAPTER SIX

Donovan Plan and Anilea Spell!

Crevan and Ryu enter the house, closing the door behind them, "What do you think Donovan do when hear the news?" Ryu ask Crevan nervous in his voice, walking into the living room.

"Calm down bro, Donovan will like, no wait love this news," Crevan told Ryu walking into the living room.

Crevan and Ryu enter the living room, "Well Eris our sexy play toys are back." Desdemona look over at Eris, lying on the couch on her side and Eris lying on the other couch on her side, both wearing short dresses that show their naked butts more.

"I agree, I need any daily douse of hardcore sex at least three times a day," Eris told Desdemona looking at Ryu with sexy eyes and licking her lips with her tongue.

"Oh, did I miss your sexy body and moist-wet pussy," Ryu running up to Eris, and starting to kiss Eris on the lips and down her body crazy-like.

"My dear wife how I miss you," Crevan say to Desdemona, walking up to her, sit down on the couch besides Desdemona making-out on the lips with passion.

Donovan came downstairs, walking into the living room, seeing Ryu, Eris, Crevan, and Desdemona making-out on the couches, "Enough!" Donovan yelled at the top of his voice in the doorway. "I wanted you guys to report back to me, and then go have fun with your wives upstairs in your bedrooms!"

Everyone stopping kissing each other, and stand up from the couches, and looks at Donovan. "Sorry my dear brother, it was Eris and I fault, we made them do this," Desdemona apologizes to Donovan.

Donovan walks up to Desdemona, looking at Desdemona face, "If we won't family, I would kill you on the spot, but you're the only one I know who can play mind games with Anilea. Making Anilea weak enough for me to kill her," Donovan told Desdemona rudely, Desdemona lower her head to Donovan. Donovan turns to his attention to Crevan and Ryu, "What did you two find out about Anilea?" Donovan questions Crevan and Ryu sitting on the chair across from the couches.

Crevan spoke up first, "Ryu and I found out that Anilea might have a new lover in her life."

Donovan smile evilly at Crevan and Ryu, "Good job you two. Now I need more information about this new lover, so I let my dear sister have her fun with Anilea mind," Donovan say to Crevan and Ryu.

Crevan and Ryu sat down on the couch across from Donovan with their wives beside them. "The new lover name is Adam, he live next door to Anilea on the north side. He plays the guitar and sing," Crevan told Donovan.

"Okay I need more information on this Adam guy," Donovan asks Crevan and Ryu with a huge smile on his face.

Crevan and Ryu told Donovan everything they found out about Adam, "Now you know boss... So did we do well?" Crevan ask Donovan a little scare tone in his voice.

Donovan stood up from the chair, looks at Crevan and Ryu, and spoke to them, "You boys did great, keep up the work on spying on Anilea, but now include this Adam guy to your list. Now you guys and girls go have some sex fun upstairs in your bedrooms," Donovan was please at the work that Crevan and Ryu did.

"Thank-you sir," everyone say getting up from the couch, leaving the living room to his or her bedrooms upstairs to have some sex fun.

Donovan watches Crevan, Ryu, Eris, and Desdemona leaving the living room. Donovan walks over to the fireplace along the wall, looking at the wood inside, and snapping his right fingers. The fire roar as the wood lit quickly in seconds. Donovan looks down at the fire, watching the flames flicking, and hot heat touching his body as Donovan smile evilly. Without using his hands, Donovan pulls a big chair up closer to the fireplace, sitting down in the chair. Donovan looks into the fire, focusing his powers on the fire. Suddenly the fire swam around Donovan, flames touching everything, but nothing burning or a signal burn mark on anything. Donovan lend back in the chair, thinking to himself as a glass of cold red wine appear in his right hand. Donovan took a slip of the wine, looking into the wineglass, Donovan say, "Donovan, you're the most evilly dark spirit ever, and the handsome on too." Donovan looks at the scar on the right side of his face.

"You will pay Anilea for this scar on my face... but I did leave you with a nice scare on your right upper arm," Donovan took another slip of wine from the glass. "I should finish you off, when I had the chance, but I should have known not kill your love ones in front of you... Oh well, I wanted the fun back... now we got a new player to this game. Adam person that you got a crush on, well he will not last very long. When our fight with each other starts, I'm going to use Adam to do my dealing or kill him in front you," Donovan laugh evilly, throwing his head back laughing, and keep on drinking his wine in the flames of the fire.

~~*~*~*~*~*~*~*~*~*

Sanna come flying through the backdoor into the sunroom with a scared look on her face. Sanna took off her shoes, walks to the couch under the east wall widow, flopping down into the couch, and trying to calm down as she lay down on the couch. Sanna took her left arm, and laying the arms across her eyes, Sanna could only see darkness. Sanna lay there in the silent as an image came to her.

~~*~*~*~*~*~*~*~*~*

Flames of fire around her as she stood there in the middle of the fire in her white spirit dress. Sanna looking around her, the only thing she can see large walls of flames. Sanna could hear her name called through the flames. 'Sanna... Sanna...' it called out echoing around her.

'Adam is that you?' Sanna called out to see if she could find Adam any where in the flames now.

Sanna spin around in a circle for a bit, as the voice came louder to her. 'Sanna... Sanna,' it keeps on calling out to her coming closer.

Sanna keep on turning around in circles, suddenly Sanna turn right into Adam chest, 'Oh Adam, it's you,' Sanna calm down as she put her hands on Adam chest, and her forehead down on his chest. 'I thought you were a goner,' Sanna spoke to Adam, not looking up at Adam, and feeling good that Adam was safe now.

'That okay Sanna,' Adam told Sanna wrapping his arms around Sanna shoulders. 'I will never leave you Sanna nor should I say... Anilea,' Adam voice changes at the end to deeper voice.

Sanna came face to face with Donovan quickly looking, 'Donovan!' Sanna yelled with fear in her voice and wide-eyes. Sanna push Donovan away from her body with her hands,

'Where Adam you fucking asshole?' Sanna scream at Donovan, pointing her right inbox finger at Donovan.

Donovan looks at Sanna in her eyes, 'My dear Anilea or Sanna, your dear lover Adam is at my mercy,' Donovan spoke evilly to Sanna, pointing through the flames. Sanna saw Donovan group holding Adam up by his arms with chains around his body.

Blooding dripping from Adam mouths cuts on his body from the chains, Adam face looking down at the ground, 'Sanna,' Adam spoke in the whisper.

Sanna heard Adam saying her name in the whisper, 'Adam stay with me please.' Sanna called out to Adam, Sanna looks at Donovan, 'Let Adam go now, he not involve with this fight at all. Your fight is with me always,' Sanna yelled at Donovan.

'Oh yes he is,' Donovan told Sanna, 'He my way to getting rid of you for good,' Donovan touch Sanna face with the back of his right hand.

Sanna smack Donovan hand away from her face; 'Get your evil hands off of me,' Sanna yelling in angry with Donovan.

Donovan looks at Sanna, 'I know your weakness…' Donovan walks up to Adam, taking a large knife, and stabbing Adam in the stomach. Adam quickly coughs up blood from his mouth, hunching over in pain, and feeling his life spilling away.

'NO!' Sanna scream watching Donovan stabbing Adam in the stomach, and Adam falling to the ground, half-died, with blood pouring from the wound. Sanna ran up to Adam on the ground, holding Adam in her arms, 'Stay with me Adam,' Sanna cry over Adam body. Tears fell from Sanna eyes onto Adam face, Adam breathing was getting shorter, and then nothing left in Adam life. Sanna cry over Adam body, Donovan stood behind her. Sanna lay Adam down on the ground, got off the ground, Sanna turn around, and looking at Donovan in the face, 'You bastard! You son of a bastard, you did it again! You kill another love one! I will kill you!' Sanna yelled at Donovan, hitting Donovan in the face with her right fist.

Sanna started to glow white, Donovan quickly grab through Sanna chest to her heart with his right hand, and looking into Sanna eyes. 'Good-bye Anilea forever,' Donovan holding her beating heart in his right hand.

Sanna stop glowing and looking into Donovan eyes with fear, 'Please don't,' Sanna beg Donovan.

'Sorry my dear Anilea, it has been fun, but you time is up,' Donovan told Sanna, squeeze Sanna heart quickly as Sanna heart explored in his hand. Sanna eyes roll back in her head, Donovan pull out of Sanna chest, and his right hand cover with Sanna blood. Sanna fell to the ground and Donovan laugh evilly over Sanna lifeless body. Flames of the fire grower bigger around Donovan as the heat burn every living thing.

~~*~*~*~*~*~*~*~*~*

Sanna scream loudly at the top of her voice, sitting up in the couch quickly, breathing heavily. Sanna looking around the room, "Oh, it was only another bad dream," Sanna told herself putting her right hand on her chest.

Tiffany, Roselyn, Andrew, and Aaron came running into the sunroom, "Anilea are you alright?" Tiffany say quickly panic a bit if Sanna was hurt or something wrong.

Sanna did not looks at her friends, and say, "I'm alright, it was a bad dream I had," Sanna sat up straight on the couch, putting her feet on the floor, and looking down at the floor.

Roselyn and Tiffany sat down beside Sanna, one on each side of Sanna. Roselyn put her right arm on Sanna back, "Tell us what the bad dream about?"

Sanna looks up at Roselyn, and then spoke with a shaky voice, "The dream was about Donovan killing Adam. "Donovan told me that he found my weakness, and it was Adam. In addition Donovan killed me by grabbing through my chest, and crushing my heart in his hand," Sanna started to shake all over her body.

Roselyn put her right arm around Sanna shoulders, "Sweetly, it will be alright you know it was a bad dream, and you know Donovan won't find out your weakness," Roselyn told Sanna comforting Sanna in her arms.

Sanna shook her head at Roselyn, "They been spying on me,' Sanna told Roselyn, and thinking of all the time she sense them spying on her.

"They have been spying on you!" Tiffany jump up from the couch with a stun look on her face. "Roselyn, we need to put a spell around here to protect this neighbourhood. They might come into this house and kill us at night or start the fight early," Tiffany told everyone else.

"I know for Sanna protection, we need do it now," Roselyn spoke to Tiffany, getting off the couch, walking up to Tiffany.

Roselyn, Tiffany, Andrew, and Aaron walking out of the sunroom to the living room, closing the curtains along the way to darken the house. Sanna got off the couch and following them quietly. "Everyone ready," Roselyn ask everyone forming a circle around a little lit white candle in the middle of the living room. Sanna was about to join hands with Andrew and Roselyn, but Roselyn stop Sanna, "Anilea, you need to save your powers for the battle," Roselyn told Sanna.

Sanna looking at Roselyn in the face, "Please let me help, I'm the only one who can control the spell," Sanna beg Roselyn to let her join with her friends.

"No, you're still weak from the last battle 100 years ago. You do the spell you could died right here on the spot," Roselyn told Sanna trying hard to keep Sanna away from the Candle. "Now go upstairs to your bedroom, lay down on your bed, and try to relax," Roselyn look at Sanna in the face, and pointing upstairs. Sanna nodded to Roselyn, and left the living room to her bedroom upstairs. Roselyn turn back to everyone else, joining hands between Andrew and Aaron, and started the spell.

A white light came from the candle, and started to spread through out the house and outside. The white light covers the whole neighbourhood without anyone knowing what going on. The light covers every house, yard, people and animals with a protection light from the darkness. Sanna could see the light spread through out everything, "They would not be able to control the light with out me," Sanna told herself, sitting up in her bed, getting off her bed, and stood in the middle of her room. Sanna lift up her arms in the air, closing her eyes, and force her powers on the light. ***"Light of the world... Take the darkness with in this neighbourhood... Let the light protract everyone and everything from the darkness... Do not let the darkness win... Light glow brighter and protract everyone were ever they go,"*** Sanna spoke loudly in the air, as the light grow brighter.

Downstairs in the living room, Tiffany, Roselyn, Andrew, and Aaron realize something was not right with the spell. Roselyn and Tiffany look at each other; they realize that Sanna had a control over the spell, "Sanna! Anilea!" Tiffany and Roselyn called out taking off running out of the living room and upstairs to Sanna bedroom with Andrew and Aaron behind them.

They arrive outside Sanna bedroom on the third floor, the light glow around the bedroom door. Roselyn open Sanna bedroom door, and saw Sanna finish casting the spell. The light slowly disappears around Sanna body, Sanna stood there in the middle of the room looking at Roselyn. Sanna eyes looks at Roselyn in the eyes, Roselyn stood in the bedroom doorways with a stun look on her face. Sanna spoke in a whisper as her friends enter the bedroom staring at Sanna, "The spell is done," Sanna started to collapsing to the floor.

Sanna lay on the hardwood floor; face down, eyes closed, and trying to breathe. Her friends ran up to Sanna, everyone sliding across the floor to Sanna on their feet. Andrew turns Sanna over, Aaron check Sanna pulse at the neck, "Anilea pulse is very low," Aaron told Roselyn panic in his voice.

"First off don't panic, second off Andrew get Anilea onto her bed, so I can exam her," Roselyn told Andrew and Aaron.

Andrew pick up Sanna into his arms, "Come on sport," Andrew lay Sanna down on Sanna bed.

"Tiffany can get a cold wet cloth, so I cold Anilea down," Roselyn told Tiffany after feeling Sanna forehead that very hot with a fever now.

Tiffany ran into the bathroom, grabs a facecloth by the sink, running the cloth under cold water, shutting off the water, ran back to Roselyn, and handing the cold wet cloth to Roselyn. "Here sis," Tiffany says to Roselyn holding the cloth to Roselyn.

Roselyn took the cloth from Tiffany hands, "Thanks sis," Roselyn thanks Tiffany, putting the cold cloth on Sanna forehead. "Tiffany grabs another wet cloth for me," Roselyn ask Tiffany trying to keep Sanna cool, and knowing this cloth will not work for Sanna fever now.

"Sure," Tiffany says to Roselyn running back into the bathroom. Few minute later coming out with another wet cloth, and a large bowel of cold water. Tiffany set the bowel on the floor, and looking at Roselyn. "I know you might need this later," Tiffany pointing to the bowel on the floor.

"Thanks sis," Roselyn looks down at the bowel of water, and taking the cloth from the bowel. "Tiffany can you put this bowel on a chair for me?" Roselyn ask Tiffany wiping Sanna body with the wet cloth. Aaron grabs the chair from the make-up table, putting it close to Roselyn, and Tiffany placing the bowel on the chair bottom." Thanks you two," Roselyn thanks Aaron and Tiffany.

Tiffany move to the end of the bed with Aaron, Tiffany was scared for Sanna life; Aaron put his arms around Tiffany shoulders. Andrew walks up to Roselyn and asks Roselyn in a strong voice, "How Anilea is doing?"

Roselyn put the cloth in the bowel, looks at Andrew, then say, "It hard to tell, Anilea different then us. She very powerful and older then us, Sanna has more exertions, fighting, and life then all of us. We do not know what happen in the Dark Ages between Donovan and her. Anilea like to keep everything to herself." Roselyn looks down at Sanna sleeping, "We should keep an eye on her, when we did that spell, then she won't be like this," Roselyn touching Sanna face with her right hand, feeling the heat coming from Sanna skin.

"Honey, Anilea did tell you that she the only one who can control that spell. We should let her do it with us, then she would not be so weak," Andrew told Roselyn putting his left arm around Roselyn shoulder.

"I know, we should did that," Roselyn blame herself, lowering her head in shame, and thinking she should let Sanna help them with the spell.

"It is okay Roselyn, Anilea will be alright. She will jump back to normal soon, Anilea will away has jump back to normal in no time," Aaron told Roselyn standing at the end of the bed, looking at Roselyn and Sanna a bit.

"I know, but we need Anilea at full strength when the times come next year on May 20," Roslyn told Aaron, looking at him at the end of the bed with Tiffany.

"We all know, now lets Anilea rest," Aaron told everyone, and looking at Sanna sleeping now.

"I agree, Anilea will be alright for a bit," Andrew told Roselyn, looking at Roselyn with a smile on his face.

"I'm not leaving Anilea, until her alright," Roselyn told everyone, moving away from Andrew arms, re-wetting the cloth on Sanna forehead, and setting it back on Sanna forehead.

Then the doorbell rang from downstairs, everyone frozen in fear, and Sanna started to stir a bit more in her bed.

CHAPTER SEVEN

Party Time & Worries!

Tiffany look up at Aaron from his arms, "Who here?" Tiffany says with fear in her voice.

"I have no idea," Aaron says to Tiffany looking down at Tiffany in his arms with a worry look on his face.

The doorbell rang again, Andrew looks at Roselyn with courage going through his blood, "I'm going to find out who it is," Andrew told Roselyn walking away from Roselyn side and out of the bedroom to the front door.

Aaron watch Andrew walking out of Sanna bedroom, Aaron let go of Tiffany quickly. "Hey bro, I right behind you," Aaron yelled quickly leaving the room behind Andrew, running down the stairs behind Andrew.

Tiffany watch Aaron leaving the room and quickly follow Aaron, "Hey what about me?" Tiffany called out leaving the room, running down the stairs to the main floor.

Roselyn looks down at Sanna, "I'll be right back in a few minutes," Roselyn told Sanna as the doorbell rang again, and Roselyn left the room behind Tiffany quickly.

Andrew walks downstairs to the front door with Aaron, Tiffany, and Roselyn not far behind him. Andrew saw a shadow finger in one of the side windows, Andrew carefully open the front door and sigh of relief came over Andrew and everyone else faces. Adam stood in front of the door, "Hey you guys and girls, I was wondering if Sanna is around?" Adam asks everyone in the room standing on the front deck.

Everyone looks at each other, and then Roselyn spoke up, "Adam," Roselyn moving closer to Adam passing everyone, "Sanna is..." looking at Adam in the face to tell him that Sanna was not feeling well now.

"Sanna is what Roselyn?" a female voice came from the stairs, about halfway up the stairs, and she was looking down at them all.

Roselyn and everyone turn around, and saw Sanna standing on the stairs looking down at them. "Sanna is here right now," Roselyn told Adam a little confuse at what she seeing Sanna standing there on the stairs.

Sanna walks downstairs, and up to Adam, "Hey Adam, what are bringing you here?" Sanna ask Adam try hard not to collapse in front of Adam or show her friends how weak she is right now.

"I came for your birthday supper, you invited me, a few days ago," Adam told Sanna smiling at her with a sweet smile on his face.

"Oh yeah, sorry I almost forgot that. I was sleeping for a bit," Sanna told Adam smiling back at him, and feeling her head spinning a bit now.

"I can see, you look a little bit sleepy," Adam chuckled at Sanna, seeing her long hair mess up a bit, and sleepily eyes a bit.

Sanna ran her fingers through her hair, "Come on in, and lets this party started," Sanna move to the right side of the doorway to let Adam into the house.

Adam walks into the house, taking off his shoes, and walks into the living room with Aaron, Tiffany, and Andrew behind him. Roselyn walks up to Sanna, "What are you doing down here? You should be upstairs in your room resting," Roselyn whisper to Sanna in a worry voice looking her in the face with a shock looks on her face.

"I spring back quickly remember, plus I don't want Adam to know who I am really," Sanna whisper back to Roselyn with strong voice, walking by Roselyn to the living room.

Roselyn put her left hand on Sanna right shoulder, "Just be careful Anilea, your not strong enough," Roselyn whisper to Sanna, and had a worry look on her face for Sanna health.

Sanna put her left hand on Roselyn hand, "I will," Sanna whisper to Roselyn. Roselyn let go of Sanna shoulder, Sanna walks into the living room. Roselyn shaking her head slowly and follow Sanna into the living room. Sanna enter the living room with Roselyn behind here, "Andrew, Aaron can you two start the BBQ up, and get the meat started," Sanna say Andrew and Aaron.

"Okay Sanna, let's go bro," Andrew say to Sanna, then to Aaron leaving the living room with Aaron being him.

Roselyn turn to Tiffany, "Tiffany lets get the rest of the food ready," Roselyn told Tiffany, then turn to Sanna and say, "Sanna, you relax until supper is ready," making sure to use Sanna fake name in front of Adam.

Sanna sigh, and then say to Roselyn, "Okay Roselyn." Sanna sat down on the couch under the north window, Roselyn and Tiffany left to the kitchen.

Adam looks at Sanna, Adam saw that Sanna was pale in her face. Adam lend over to Sanna from the east couch, "Sanna are you feeling alright?" Adam asks Sanna with a worry voice, keeping his eyes on her now.

Sanna looks at Adam, and say, "Adam, I have not feeling good for a bit. Something, or I proudly sick I have not been sleeping very well for years, and sometimes it take a troll on me. Sorry for the way I look now, I'm not like this all the time," Sanna rubbing her eyes with her left hand, and trying to stop her head spinning now.

Adam got off the east couch, moving closer to the north couch and sitting down beside Sanna. Adam putting his right arms around Sanna shoulders, and pulling Sanna closer to him, "Hey it's alright. I have not been sleeping very well too, so we are both in the same boat," Adam chuckle to Sanna, running his fingers through her hair a bit.

Sanna laugh a little bit at Adam, moving away from Adam, pulling her legs up onto the couch, and curling her legs, Sanna look at Adam. "You don't look like you have not sleep very well," Sanna joke with Adam and feeling her stomach flipping now.

Adam looks at Sanna, putting his right hand on Sanna lower legs, and say to Sanna, "I'm trying hard not to show that I am tired." He look at her, not showing how worry he was now about her health.

"Thanks Adam," Sanna lend back against the armrest on the couch, and smile at Adam.

"You're welcome Sanna," Adam told Sanna removing his hand off Sanna lower legs, and smile at Sanna.

Sanna closed her eyes a bit, and then spoke to Adam, "I'm hoping that I get some sleep tonight," opening her eyes a bit to look up at the ceiling for a while.

"I hope so too, because you're not yourself right now," Adam spoke to Sanna, looking at Sanna pale face more, and feeling his heart breaking slowly on seeing Sanna this way.

Roselyn walks up to Sanna and Adam, say to them nicely, "Supper ready," Roselyn walks to the back door and outside on the deck. Sanna and Adam got off the couch, and follow Roselyn outside onto the deck.

"Hey it's the birthday girl," Aaron announce to everyone as Sanna walk outside with Adam behind her.

"Thanks Aaron," Sanna say to Aaron smiling. Sanna looks at the table set up with food, drinks, and party decoctions', "Wow this looks awesome," Sanna sitting down at the head of the table, and smiling at all the stuff her friends did for her.

"You're welcome," everyone say to Sanna sitting down around the table, and Adam sitting across from Adam on the other end of the table.

Everyone dig into the food and drinks, started to eating their supper. Sanna did not have very much; because she had a funny feeling that someone from the dark-spirit was watching them. Roselyn lend close to Sanna left ear and whisper, "What wrong?"

"I have a feeling we are being watch," Sanna whisper to Roselyn, pointing under the table to the diction of the feeling coming behind Roselyn.

Roselyn looks over her right shoulder, seeing two dark fingers in the trees looking at them, and turning back to Sanna, "Your right, just stay calm, and don't worry about them. The spell is working to keep them away from here," Roselyn whisper to Sanna. Sanna breath a sigh of relaxes and continues to have fun. Once and awhile, Sanna keep on checking if the two dark fingers were still watching them.

Once supper was done Roselyn, Tiffany, Andrew, and Aaron clean up the table, and Roselyn brought out the cake for Sanna. Everyone sang 'Happy Birthday' to Sanna. "Make a wish and blow out the candles," Adam says to Sanna. Sanna closed her eyes, making her wish, and then blowing out her candles on her cake, expert for one. Sanna was in shock that one candle did not blow out.

Sanna blow it out, and then sat back in her chair. Aaron looks at Sanna, "Who the boyfriend?" Aaron says to Sanna with kidding in her voice, with a smile on his face.

Sanna blush in the cheeks, sinking down in her chair, and covering her face with her hands, "I don't have a boyfriend, Aaron," Sanna say through her hands feeling her face getting hot from the blushing.

"You know I was joking with you," Aaron says to Sanna with a smile on his face.

Sanna sat up straight in her chair, uncovering her face, and looks at Aaron with a smile on her face. "I know you are only joking, Aaron," Sanna laugh with everyone else along with Sanna.

Adam look at Sanna and say, "So Sanna what did you wish for?"

Sanna looks at Adam and say child-like, "It's a secret. I'm the only one who knows, so there," Sanna chuckled at Adam then sticking her tongue out a bit at him.

Adam laugh with Sanna and shook his head, "Your right," Adam say to Sanna with a smile on his face.

The evening carries on with music, games, and fun. Adam look at his cell phone, "I better get going home. It's like 10 o'clock, so see you guys around, bye," Adam say to everyone waving as he walking down the down the steps from the back deck and walks home from Sanna place.

Sanna stood there watch Adam walking away from her place, Sanna turn around, and saw Roselyn, Tiffany, Aaron, and Andrew staring at her, "What?" Sanna throw her arms out to the side of her body.

Roselyn cross her arms in front of her body, "I cannot believe you are still standing, after that spell you took over from us," Roselyn told Sanna in a tick-off voice.

Sanna walks pass everyone, "If I did not take over that spell, it would kill all four of you," Sanna told everyone walking into the house with a weak voice.

Roselyn, Tiffany, Aaron, and Andrew follow Sanna into the house, Roselyn spoke up walking through the house to the living room, "What do you mean the spell would killed us?"

Sanna stop in front of the fireplace, turning around to Roselyn, and spoke through her teeth, "The spell takes a spirit blood to seal it up, and you four are not as strong as me all together. I need my friends to help me in this war coming up against Donovan."

Sanna friends mouths drop at the thought, "What?" Roselyn spoke up what shocking in the voice, and then saw blood dripping down Sanna face from the corner of her mouth, hitting the floor. "Anilea are you alright?" Roselyn walks closer to Sanna with a worry look on her face.

Sanna wipe the blood from her mouth with her right hand, looks at the blood on her fingertips. Sanna spoke slowly having her eyes on the blood, "I'll be fined," Sanna walking away from her friends, Sanna stop at the archway of the living room doorway, looking over her right shoulder at her friends, and say,

"Don't follow me," Sanna went upstairs to her bedroom. Roselyn knelt down on her knees, taking her right hand, wiping the few blood drops off the hardwood floor, and looking at the blood on her fingertips. Roselyn stood up from the floor, curling her right hand into fit, and placing her right fit on her chest. Roselyn, Tiffany, Aaron, and Andrew were worry about Sanna health.

Sanna was having a bubble bath, blood slowly dripping from the corner of her mouth, "Anilea, how stupid are you for doing that... You almost killed yourself... You need you to at full power for next year battle," Sanna say angry with herself, the blood stop dripping from her mouth. Sanna lend back in the tub relaxing. After a while, Sanna got out of the tub, got dress for bed, and left the bathroom. Sanna walk to the French doors, opens the doors, and walks outside onto the balcony. Sanna climb onto the right railing, sitting down on the railing lending her back against the sliding of the house, and looks out on the night life. Sanna looks out at the lake through the trees, the moonlight glistening off the lake water as the waves move over the water. Sanna think for a while with memories play in her mind, "I cannot believe it's been 399 since I lost everyone, but 1314 years I been on earth, and fighting with Donovan and his group. Even if a good chunk of it was we were hiding, after our last fight during the Dark Ages," Sanna told herself looking down at her feet.

Roselyn walks outside onto Sanna balcony with a cup of tea in her hands, "Hey Anilea," Roselyn say to Sanna walking outside through the French doors.

Sanna look at Roselyn turning her head to the side, "Hey Roselyn," Sanna greeted Roselyn.

"Do you want some tea? I brought you a cup," Roselyn ask Sanna holding out the cup in her hands.

"Sure," Sanna held out her left hand for the cup of tea.

Roselyn handed the cup to Sanna; Sanna took a slip of tea, "How are you feeling?" Roselyn ask Sanna a little bit worry.

Sanna looks at Roselyn, "I'm fined, I don't bleeding anymore," Sana told Roselyn and keep on drinking her tea.

Roselyn walks up to Sanna left side, looks at Sanna in the face, "Don't try to anything stupid again, promise," Roselyn spoke to Sanna.

Sanna sigh, handed Roselyn an empty cup, and got down from the railing. Sanna looks at Roselyn in the face, "I promise for now, but when the fighting starts. I would not keep on any big promise to anyone, just one does not die," Sanna told Roselyn curling her hands into a fist that Donovan trying to one up her in this fight.

Roselyn put the cup down on the floor, and throwing her arms around Sanna body, "Don't died on us, we are your family," Roselyn sob to Sanna with tears running down her face.

Sanna stood in Roselyn arms surprise, Sanna wrap her arms slowly around Roselyn body, "I know," Sanna softly spoke to Roselyn.

A few minutes later, Roselyn let go of Sanna, "I know, we are not relative through blood, but you like a little sister to all of us. We worry about you everyday, and its scary us when you do stuff that can hurt you a lot," Roselyn told Sanna looking at Sanna in the face.

"You mean a big sister then little sister," Sanna say to Roselyn, thinking the age different between both of them.

"Hey you maybe older spirit to us, but human your little sister… You are awesome big sister spirit to us," Roselyn told Sanna chuckling a bit.

Sanna chuckled along with Roselyn; Sanna looks at Roselyn, then spoke to Roselyn with smile on her face, "Rose… I'm happy to have wonderful big sister like you, and everyone else as a wonderful," Sanna yawned a few times.

Roselyn looks at Sanna, putting her right arms over Sanna shoulders, "I think it is bed time for you," Roselyn told Sanna leading Sanna back into house, and to Sanna bed.

Sanna lay down on her bed, and Roselyn cover Sanna with the blanket, "Goodnight," Sanna softly spoke fall a sleep.

"Goodnight Anilea," Roselyn say to Sanna, kissing Sanna on top of Sanna head, and leaving the room.

Sanna slept through the night peacefully with peacefully dreams for once in a long time.

Chapter Eight

The Waterfall!

Through out the summer months, Sanna and Adam hangout a lot more, and their friendship was slowly growing into something more. They hangout at the beach, hike through the woods, and having fun together. One day close to the end of the summer in August, Sanna and Adam were walking through the forest to a waterfall deep in the woods. "Adam, where are you taking me?" Sanna ask Adam, walking along the pathway with her backpack on her back.

"You will see, we are almost there anyways," Adam told Sanna, walking along the pathway, and looking at Sanna behind him walking along the trail.

Sanna stay quiet just listening to the birds singing in the trees, and the wildlife moving around the woods. Sanna looks around at all the nature, stopping a few times to take a closer look at some plants. Sanna keep on following Adam along the pathway, thinking about where Adam was taking her, *'I remember this pathway, it leads to the waterfalls deep in the woods,'* Sanna thought to herself, listening the roar of the falls in the directions, and a small flashback to her old life came to her mind with her family.

Few minutes later, Adam stop at the end of the pathway, turning around to Sanna, and spoke to her, "Be ready to be amazons at the beautiful thing that nature made."

Adam move to the right side and Sanna walks forward to the opening area in the woods. Sanna mouth drop at the sight of the waterfall in front of her, *'Wow, it is like I remember,'* Sanna thought to herself, looking around the area. Sanna turn to around to Adam, and say, "Adam, this is so beautiful. How tall are the waterfalls?"

Adam walks up to Sanna, and explain to Sanna, "About 50 feet height with this one, there another 50 feet tall up top and 20 feet away from the ledge of this one," Adam took off his backpack, and setting the backpack on the ground.

Sanna took off her backpack, putting the backpack on the ground, and looking at Adam, "Why did you bring me here to this wonderful place?" Sanna ask Adam moving closer to Adam, and feeling a weird feeling coming over her body.

Adam looks at Sanna in the face, "I brought you here, because I want you feel more comfort around here, and there something I want to tell you," Adam told Sanna, smiling at Sanna, trying hard not blushing in front of her.

"What that you want to tell me?" Sanna ask Adam with a confused look on her face.

Adam blush in the cheeks, a bright red, Adam shift his eyes side to side with nervous, "Well... you see..." Adam could not speak with nothing about nervous. "I was wondering if you want to go behind the waterfall, and cold down that why," Adam says to Sanna, trying to calm down.

Sanna thought for a moment, then say, "Sure that sound nice, I'm very hot from all that walking."

"Cool," Adam agrees with Sanna, "Follow me then, I think you should hold my hand, because the rocks are slippery. I don't want you to fall and hurt yourself," Adam held out his left hand to Sanna.

Sanna took her right hand, and grabbing Adam left hand, "Make sure I don't fell into the water or you will be in big trouble," Sanna told Adam laughing a bit at the end of the sentence.

Adam laughs at Sanna, and started to walk along the pathway to behind the waterfall, "I want let you fall, beside I don't want anything bad happening to you, I do like you a lot," Adam say to Sanna walking along the pathway.

Sanna looks down at her feet as she walks along the narrow pathway with Adam hand and hand. Sanna whisper quietly, "I like you a lot too, Adam." Adam could not hear what Sanna whisper, walking closer to the small entryway to behind the falls.

Adam enters behind the falls with Sanna behind him with her hands in his hands. Sanna looks around at the howl cave at all the wet rocks, and water dripping from the roof. "Adam this is huge and awesome," Sanna say to Adam letting go of Adam left hand and walk a few steps from Adam.

"I know, and it is the only place where I can calm down from a rough week," Adam told Sanna walking up to her, and looking at the way her body was acting now.

Sanna turn around to Adam, "Then why did you bring me here?" Sanna ask Adam with a confusing voice and raising an eyebrow at him.

Adam put his hands on Sanna shoulders, and looks into Sanna eyes, "Because I wanted you to know you're my true friend, and I wanted to show this wonderful place so you can calm down. You been very upset and stress out for the last few months, and I do not like seeing you like that. I want you to be happy and relax," Adam spoke to Sanna with a worry voice.

Sanna lower her head, "I'll try to stay happy and relax for you," Sanna lifted her head up to look around that cave, and back to Adam, "If I'm not home I will here then to calm down and relax," Sanna smile at Adam, thinking the last time she was around the falls.

Adam smile at Sanna, and letting Sanna go. Sanna move over to big rock and sitting down on the wet rock. Adam sat down beside Sanna, and look at Sanna, "How are you feeling today?" Adam asks Sanna, looking at her.

"What? Oh I'm fine, just the summer flu," Sanna snap out of thought, and spoke to Adam lairing to him about the truth why she not feeling well.

"That good that your feeling well," Adam say to Sanna, thought for a moment, and ask Sanna a question, "Why are you always sick?"

Sanna look quickly at Adam with wide-eye, and then say to Adam. "Because of all the stress that I been having that making me sick, maybe if I calm down then I would not be sick all the time."

"What are you stressing out so much at it is making you sick to your stomach?" Adam asks Sanna wanting to know why she always sick now.

Sanna shook her head at Adam, "There a few things that I don't want you to know about me, and those things are the ones that stressing me out," Sanna told Adam calmly, and fooling around her hands together.

"I see... Are you ever going tell me any of those things when you're ready?" Adam asks Sanna looking at Sanna.

Sanna spoke calmly, "Maybe or never, because those things can hurt our friendship big time," Sanna look at Adam with a small smile on her face.

Adam smile at Sanna, and chuckle at Sanna, "You look so wet now," Adam told Sanna, looking at Sanna wet body and her clothes was soak now.

Sanna looks at herself and laughing at her, "You looks so wet too, Adam," Sanna told Adam looking at Adam wet body and his clothes were soaking now.

Adam laugh with Sanna, "Do you want to go swimming?" Adam asks Sanna with a smile on his face.

Sanna looks at Adam, "Adam, I did not bring my swimsuit," Sanna told Adam, and getting up from the rock now.

Adam looks at Sanna to say, "Who say you need a swimsuit."

Sanna eyes got bigger, then Sanna quickly say to Adam, "We are not going swim naked?" Sanna stood back from Adam.

Adam laugh at Sanna, Adam shook his head, "No, we swim with our clothes on," Adam chuckled at Sanna, getting up from the rock.

"Oh I see, that sound nice, beside we are already wet anyways," Sanna say to Adam laughing at Adam.

"Let's go then," Adam says Sanna walking out from behind the waterfall with Sanna behind him.

Adam stop a few feet away from the opening, turning around to Sanna and saying, "You know the best way to get into the water?"

"What is the best way down to the water?" Sanna ask Adam crossing her arms in front of her.

Adam shift her eyes to the left, and Sanna look in the diction that looking too, and looking ten feet down from the ledge. Sanna jump back to the rock wall behind her, Adam chuckle at Sanna, "Come on Sanna, it's not that scary. Maybe at first, but after a few times it's really fun," Adam told Sanna. Adam held out his right hand to Sanna, "Come on I'll hold your hands."

Sanna grab Adam right hand with his left hand, and walking slowly to the end of the ledge. Sanna looks down, and thought to herself, *'Come on Anilea, you fought Donovan many times, and not show that your afraid. Why are you afraid now? Is it that Adam here with me? Come Anilea snap out of it and have fun'*

"Okay Sanna on the count of three we jump... Ready?" Adam told Sanna holding her left hand. Sanna took a deep breath, and letting it out slowly, "One... Two ... Three ... Go." Adam and Sanna jump off the ledge, and hitting the water feet first.

Adam and Sanna swim back up to the top of the water, and laughing at each other, "Adam, I think we should took off our shoes first then jump," Sanna spoke up at Adam, knowing they were still wearing their shoes now.

"Oops," Adam says to Sanna. Adam swam to the edge of the water area to where the backpacks were with Sanna not far behind him.

They exit the water, walks up to the backpacks, took their shoes and socks off, and leaving them to dry. Sanna walk back to the ledge alone with Adam watching from the bottom. Sanna arrive at the ledge, looks down at the water, and her heart was beating fast. *'Okay Anilea calm down, and just have fun you have done this before many times. Many years ago growing up in the 1600's,'* Sanna thought to herself looking out at the water running down the stream through the trees. Sanna got ready to jump with one good jump off the ledge, Sanna was in the air, and coming down into the water. Sanna hit the water feet first, waited a few minutes under the water. Sanna looks at the clear water, the bubbles from the falls hitting the water, the plant life under the water, and some fish swimming around. Sanna swam to the top, hitting the water top, and took a deep breath in. Sanna look at Adam, standing along the water edge, Sanna smiled at Adam.

Adam jump into the water from the ledge, and swim up to Sanna," You scared the shit out of me," Adam told Sanna with a bit of worry in his voice.

"Why?" Sanna was confused at Adam, and tilting her head to the right side.

"Because you never came up right away, and I thought you got hurt," Adam told Sanna still worry a bit.

Sanna felt sorry at the thought, "Sorry Adam, I can hold my breath for along time, and I was enjoying the beautiful that under the water. I did not mean to scare you badly," Sanna lower her head at Adam.

Adam took his right hand, putting his hand under Sanna chin, and raising Sanna head up to his eyes, "Its okay, beside you had a great jump I ever seen. Did you do that at your old place?" Adam says to Sanna nicely.

Sanna look at Adam, then say, "No, we did not have a waterfall to go to, but we did have a wonderful swimming pool with a high dive place at different levels," Sanna told Adam and it was the truth where she was living last time in a city.

"I see, I never seen anyone have that awesome jump, and can hold their breath that long," Adam told Sanna, removing a piece of hair from her face. Sanna took her right hand, scooping up some water, and slashing Adam in the face. Sanna just laugh at Adam, swimming away from Adam. Adam shook his head, and looks at Sanna a few feet away, "You want to start a water fight!" Adam yelled at Sanna laughing at Sanna, quickly swimming up to Sanna.

Adam was about to slash Sanna, but Sanna got him first, "You need to be faster then that," Sanna say to Adam laughing at Adam.

Adam quickly got Sanna back with water, "Like that," Adam laughing at Sanna as the water hit her face.

Sanna wipe her face with her hands, "That good shot, but I bet you cannot get me again," Sanna quickly swim away from Adam.

Adam chases Sanna around the watering hole and Sanna dive under the water a few feet to get away from Adam. Adam look down and seeing Sanna swimming under his feet, *'She crazy, but it is nice to see her like this,'* Adam thought to himself. Sanna pop up a few feet away from Adam, turning around, and looking at Adam. Sanna smiled a sweet smile at Adam with her long wet hair hanging along the side of her head. Sanna swim to a large rock in front of the falls, climbing up onto the rock, and sat down on the rock looking out at the waterfall. Sanna crossing her legs in front of her, putting her elbows on her legs, and her head in her head. Adam swim up to the rock, climbing on the rock, and sit down beside Sanna, "Tired out are we?" Adam asks Sanna looking at her.

Sanna look s at Adam, "Yeah a little bit," Sanna softly say to Adam. Sanna looks back at the waterfall, sighing a bit, and stood up onto the rock, "I think I'm ready to go home, it's getting dark out." Sanna stretch up in the air, and getting ready jump back into the air.

Adam stops Sanna, "What are you always running from every time?" Adam spoke to Sanna looking at the waterfall.

Sanna stop in her tracks, turn around, and staring at Adam with wide-eyes. Sanna thought for a few minutes, then say, "Adam, I'm running from my past, and I'm not going to tell you anything that happen in my past." Sanna jump off the rock, hitting the water feet first, and swam to the water edge where the backpacks were.

Adam stood up on the rock, jumping into the water, swimming to the water edge, and stepping out of the water. Adam watch Sanna putting on her shoes, her backpack on her back, and about to leave, when Adam spoke, "What was you past like?"

Sanna stop in her tracks, turn her head over the right shoulder, looks at Adam, "My past was not that good, I live in the darkness, and that all you are going to know," Sanna turn her head straight, and keep on walking down to the trail.

Adam grabs his backpack from the ground, putting on his shoes, and running after Sanna. "Sanna, wait up!" Adam yelled at Sanna running up behind Sanna. Sanna stop in the tracks, and try not looking back at Adam. Sanna closed her eyes, and breathing calmly. Sanna heart started to beat faster. Adam catch up to Sanna, "Sanna..." Adam say trying to catch his breath, "Why do you live in darkness, because what happen on your wedding day three years ago?" Adam asks Sanna with a worry voice, and staring at Sanna back.

Sanna took a deep breath as Sanna mind ran million miles an hour, *'How can I lie to Adam? I'm falling in love with him.'* Sanna let out her breath, turning around to Adam. "Adam," Sanna slowly say to Adam, "My past is none of your business," Sanna was getting a little piss off at Adam, trying to stay calm without showing her powers in front of him.

"But at the falls? You say..." Adam was confused at what Sanna told him.

"I say nothing to you there?" Sanna interrupted Adam by yelling at Adam. Adam stops talking, and stared wide-eye at Sanna.

Few minutes there was nothing, but the breeze going through the trees, the birds sing in the trees, and the movement of animals in the brushes. Adam lowers his head, and softly spoke to Sanna, "I'm sorry Sanna, and I did not mean to get you mad... Maybe I should keep my mouth shut."

Sanna drop her backpack to the ground, running up to Adam, throwing her arms around Adam body, and start to cry. "No, I'm the one who should be sorry," Sanna apologizes to Adam tears fell onto Adam chest.

Adam put his arms around Sanna body, "I forgive you," Adam whisper to Sanna holding Sanna closer to his body.

Sanna looks up at Adam, "You been such a good friend, and I like more from you," Sanna told Adam blushing in her cheeks, and heart beating quickly in her chest.

Adam looks into Sanna eyes, "You mean a like a boyfriend?" Adam spoke to Sanna, blushing a bit in his cheeks.

Sanna nodded her head a bit to Adam, and whisper, "I think I'm ready for the dating world," Sanna smile at Adam, and keeping her arms around his body.

Adam looks at Sanna, and asks Sanna a question, "So do you wanted to go out on a date?" Adam smile at Sanna.

Sanna blush bright red in her cheeks, and slowly answer to Adam, "I will love to go out with you on a date," Sanna smile at Adam feeling better now.

"What about tomorrow night, Sanna?" Adam asks Sanna nicely, looking into her eyes, and his heart beating quickly in his chest.

Sanna thought for a second, then say, "Sure, around six, you can pick me up."

Adam let go of Sanna, and say, "It's a date, now let's get home. It's getting dark, and I don't want my girlfriend walking home in the dark without me."

"Sure," Sanna walk up to her backpack, picking up the backpack, and putting it on her back. Sanna walks along the trail with Adam beside her. They walk all way home, beside each other.

Four glowing red eyes watch from a blush, and disappear into the blush.

Chapter Nine

First Date & Trouble!

The first sign of autumn start to show, leafs was changing color from green to red, orange, brown, and yellow. The children run along to the first day of school, along the sidewalk. Sanna watch from the window seating as the younger children walks along the sidewalk with their parents with them. Sanna watching Aaron, Andrew, Tiffany, and Roselyn leave for work. Sanna watching the car backing out of the driveway, and driving away down the street. Sanna got off the window seat, walking out of her bedroom and downstairs to make some breakfast.

When Sanna got to the kitchen, Sanna looks through the cupboards and fridge for any ideas for breakfast. "Why can't I finger out what I want to eat?" Sanna told herself looking in the fridge. Sanna grab one egg, the cheese, and closing the fridge door behind her. Sanna walks to the stove, grabbing a flying pan from the drawer under the stove, and turn on the stovetop placing the pan on the burner. Sanna walk over to the baking cupboard grabbing the cooking spay, and spaying the flying pan. Sanna creak the egg into the pan, and scrambling the egg with a fork. Sanna added some cheese on top the egg, and watch the cheese slowly melt on top. When the egg was cook, Sanna remove the egg with the flipper, and putting the egg on a plate. Sanna shut off everything, and sitting down at the table. Sanna looks down at the scramble egg, *'Am I really hungry or just nervous that I have a date tonight with Adam?'* Sanna thought to herself that, 'I need to eat, and then I have to finger out what to wear tonight,' Sanna started to eat her breakfast. Once Sanna done eating, Sanna clean up her dishes and head upstairs to her bedroom.

Sanna had a shower in the early afternoon, got dress in her white bra and underwear. Sanna walk out of her bathroom to her make-up table, and sat down in the chair in front of the table. Sanna took the brush in her right hand, and started to brush her hair. Sanna finish brushing out her hair, pulling her hair back from her face with a few bobby pins on the each side of her head. Sanna look at herself in the mirror, and smile at herself, *'Man, it's has been forever since you were so happy at yourself. You look nice, now for some make-up, and find something to wear,'* Sanna thought to herself, putting some make-up on her face, got up from the chair, and walk to the walk-in closet.

Sanna look through her clothes, "Nothing here!" Sanna yelled anger at herself, looking over all her clothes, and finding nothing to wear for her date with Adam.

"What are you looking to wear?" Roselyn spoke from the doorway of the closet with Tiffany beside her; they came home from work now, and hearing Sanna from downstairs in their bedrooms.

Sanna scream with fear, and turn around to Roselyn and Tiffany standing in the closet doorway. "Don't scary me like that; do you want me to pass-out?" Sanna putting her left hand on her chest, and try to calm down enough.

"Sorry sweetly, we came home, and we can hear you from our rooms. What are you looking for?" Roselyn ask Sanna looking at some T-shirt on the shelves, and looking at Sanna a bit.

"Nothing and I'm not telling you anything," Sanna say to Roselyn and Tiffany trying to looks over some clothes.

Tiffany looks at Sanna, seeing Sanna hair has done up, and the make-up on Sanna face, "Anilea, do you got a date tonight?" Tiffany asks Sanna, raising an eyebrow at Savanna.

"No," Sanna shook her head, trying hard not to tell, but her eyes gave it away.

Roselyn looks at Sanna, "You do, and I bet it is with someone we know pretty well," Roselyn told Sanna, walking up to Sanna, and looking into her eyes.

Sanna came out with it, "I have a date with Adam tonight at six," Sanna told Roselyn and Tiffany, letting a huge breath of relief to get that offs her chest now.

Roselyn and Tiffany look at each other, and back at Sanna, "We will help you finding something nice to wear," Roselyn told Sanna, starting looking through some drawers. "No jeans and t-shirts, you need something nice," Roselyn spoke to Sanna going through Sanna clothes.

"So sis, nothing like this," Tiffany told Roselyn holding up a pair of bell-bottom pants from the 60's.

"I remember that era... and those look like my pants... They are my pants that I thought I lost the end of that era," Roselyn pointing at the pants that Tiffany held up.

"I borrow them, and I forgot to give them back," Sanna told Roselyn, "You can have them back."

"Thanks Anilea... Tiffany do you remember the boys hairs through the years?" Roselyn ask Tiffany as they keep on looking through Sanna clothes.

"Yeah Aaron with his big hair, and Andrew twisted hair," Tiffany told Roselyn laughing at the thought. "When they have to cut their hairs. Aaron never grows his hair after that," Tiffany says to Roselyn looking through Sanna skirts.

"Andrew like his long hair," Roselyn say to Tiffany looking through Sanna dresses. Sanna stood in the middle of the closet watching Roselyn and Tiffany going through her clothes to find something nice to wear for her date.

Roselyn search through Sanna dress, and came across the prefect dress for Sanna, "I think I found the one for you to wear, Anilea." Roselyn told Sanna taking the dress off the hanger, and turning around with the dress in her hands to Sanna.

Sanna look at the light blue knee-length with thin straps, light blue lace around the waist and hang down to the bottom of the dress, and some beadwork was along the top of the dress. Sanna took the dress in her hands, looking at the dress for a minute, and putting the dress on. Sanna look at herself in the long mirror on the wall, seeing the dress flowing from the waist down to her knees. "Its prefect," Sanna says to Roselyn and Tiffany, just staring at herself in the mirror for a while.

"Its looks beautiful on you, and do you remember made this dress. It was 30 years ago right," Roselyn say to Sanna standing behind Sanna.

Sanna look over the dress on her, "I remember making this dress and many other clothes too. I never wore this one dress, because I was saving it for a special time," Sanna told Roselyn looking in the mirror at the dress, and twisting a bit to make the dress flow a bit.

"This is a special time to wear it," Roselyn told Sanna, putting her hands on Sanna shoulders, and looking at Sanna in the mirror from behind Sanna back.

"It is; I'm nervous about this. Please don't follow me, I want to do this on my own, any trouble I will call you guys," Sanna told Roselyn and Tiffany looking at them, and making her nervous are calm enough to go on her date with Adam.

"We would not, but you call we will be there quickly," Roselyn told Sanna, then Roselyn look at Sanna hair. "I think your hair need a little touch up," Roselyn taking her hands off Sanna shoulders, and playing with Sanna hair.

"I agree Roselyn," Sanna smile at Roselyn, and chuckle at the thought she got.

"Let's go, and get you ready for tonight Sanna," Tiffany told Sanna walking out of the closet, with Roselyn and Sanna behind her. Sanna walk up to the make-up table, sitting down in the chair, and Roselyn stood behind Sanna taking out the bobby pins out of Sanna hair. Tiffany ran back into the closet, and coming out with light blue small high heel shoes. Sanna slip on the shoes on her feet as Roselyn did her hair.

After 20 minutes, Roselyn finish up with Sanna hair, and putting a couple of little blue rose on the left side of Sanna head. "There what do you think Anilea?" Roselyn ask Sanna, Roselyn standing back from Sanna.

Sanna look closer at her hair in the mirror, "Its looks awesome Roselyn, you're a miracle worker on hair. Are you sure doing want to switch jobs for this?" Sanna joke with Roselyn.

"No, because I need to keep up with you anyway, plus thank-you for the nice comment," Roselyn told Sanna looking at Sanna, "Anilea?"

"Yes Roselyn," Sanna ask Roselyn turning around in the chairs, and looks at Roselyn.

"It's so nice to see you happy, and finding someone to love you," Roselyn smile at Sanna, and thinking it was a long time since she saw Sanna happy about something.

Sanna stood up from the chair, and hug Roselyn, "It's all because Tiffany, Aaron, Andrew, and you being with me along the way. If you people was not being around I will proudly not be here, and you people help me be more myself. I own you guy my life... Thank-you," Sanna told Roselyn.

"Hug time," Tiffany joins the hug with Sanna and Roselyn.

The girls were laughing for joy, when Aaron and Andrew came upstairs to Sanna bedroom, "What going on here?" Andrew asks the girl, looking at the group hug girls.

"Hey you two, you're back from work early," Roselyn say to Andrew and Aaron letting go of Sanna along with Tiffany. "We were giving Anilea a big hug, and helping her get ready for her date tonight."

Andrew looks at Sanna and saw Sanna dress-up all pretty, "Sport, who the lucky guy that taking you out?" Andrew asks Sanna nicely, and thinking whom Sanna could be in love with now.

Sanna lower her head, and nervous say "Adam," Sanna blush at the thought having a crush on Adam now.

Andrew look at Sanna with a shock look on his face, "Did you say Adam?" Sanna nodded her head, "That so cool and it's been forever since you dated," Andrew was so happy at Sanna.

The doorbell rang from downstairs, Sanna look at her alarm clock it was six o'clock. "Adam is here," Sanna say to her friends as the nervous setting in.

Andrew and Aaron went downstairs to greet Adam. Roselyn and Tiffany stay with Sanna a little longer, "Nervous Anilea?" Tiffany asks Sanna, looking at Sanna to see Sanna a bit nervous now.

"A little bit Tiffany," Sanna say to Tiffany trying to calm down.

"Just calm down, and enjoy yourself tonight. Don't worries about anything just have some fun," Tiffany told Sanna, Roselyn and Tiffany left the room to go downstairs to greet Adam.

Sanna took a deep breath and letting it out slowly, "Showtime," Sanna told herself leaving the room.

Andrew answers the door with Aaron beside him, Andrew opens the door and saw Adam standing there with a red rose in his right hand, "Hey Andrew, hey Aaron, is Sanna ready?" Adam greeted Andrew and Aaron.

"Yep Sanna will down in a few minutes, come in and wait for her," Andrew say Adam, letting Adam in the house. Adam stood by the doorway in his black pants, black suit jacket, black shoes, and white long shelve shirt with the two top buttons unbutton. Adam held the red rose nervously in his hands, and thinking he loves Sanna very much.

Roselyn and Tiffany came downstairs, "Hey Adam, Sanna will down here soon," Roselyn say Adam coming down the stairs, stepping off to the side.

"Thank-you," Adam thanks Roselyn, holding the rose close to his body. Adam waited nervously for Sanna came downstairs.

A minute later Sanna same slowly downstairs, Sanna stood a few steps from the bottom, looking at Adam with a smile on her face, and say sweetly, "Hello Adam."

Adam walks up to the stairs, looks up Sanna, and held out the rose to Sanna, "This is for you," Adam spoke in a nervous voice.

Sanna step down to the bottom step, take the rose from Adam hand genially, and sniffing the rose sweetly. "Thanks Adam for the rose," Sanna say to Adam holding the rose in her hands, looking up into Adam eyes, and blushing in her cheeks.

Roselyn walk close to Sanna, "Sanna, I will take the rose from you, and putting the rose in the vase of water," Roselyn told Sanna.

Sanna turn to Roselyn, and handed the rose to Roselyn, "Thanks Roselyn," Sanna say to Roselyn then turn to Adam. "We better get going for dinner," Sanna say to Adam.

"Your right," Adam told Sanna walking to the door with Sanna beside him.

Adam exits the house with Sanna not far behind him, "Remember Sanna, your home at nine o'clock," Andrew told Sanna as Sanna exit the house.

"Andrew, I'm not a little girl anymore," Sanna told Andrew looking at Andrew, with you-got-to-be-kidding look on her face.

"I'm joking, but don't too late," Andrew told Sanna with a chuckle in his voice.

"I won't, see you later," Sanna wave to everyone walking down the steps to Adam car.

"Good-bye! Have fun you two on your date," Everyone yelled to Sanna and Adam closing the front door.

Adam open the car passenger door for Sanna, Sanna enter the car, and closed the door for Sanna. Adam ran around to the other side, and got into the car. Adam started the car up, and looks over at Sanna. "You look beautiful this evening," Adam say to Sanna looking over at what Sanna was wearing.

"Thank-you Adam, and you looks handsome this evening too," Sanna say to Adam looking at Adam.

"Thank-you, I hope tonight will the best night for you. I got reservation at a nice restaurant, and maybe we can walk along the beach later," Adam drove along the streets to the restaurant.

"Sound wonderful," Sanna told Adam listening to the music over the stereo, and look out the side window at the scene going by.

They arrive at the restaurant on the edge of the town close to the lake. Adam parks the car, shutting off the car, exit the car, running around to Sanna side, and open the door for Sanna. Sanna exited the car, fix her dress, and say to Adam, "Thanks-you Adam."

Adam closed the car door, held his left hand out to Sanna, Sanna grab Adam hand with her right hand, and walk along the sidewalk to the restaurant front doors. Adam open the door for Sanna, Sanna smile at Adam walking by him into the entryway, "We need to go upstairs to the second floor to dinning," Adam told Sanna leading the way to the stairs.

"Let me guess the bar in downstairs?" Sanna ask Adam walking upstairs, looking at the place they were at now.

"Yeah it is," Adam says to Sanna reaching the top steps with Sanna beside him.

Adam enter the doorway to the dinning room, a French male waiter came up to Adam and Sanna. "How can I help you two this lovely evening?" the waiter greeted Adam and Sanna with a smile on his face.

"I made reservation for two this evening, under Adam," Adam told the waiter in a nice voice.

The waiter walk to the front deck, looking through the book, and found Adam name, "Yes you did, table for two, outside on the balcony." the waiter grab a couple menus, and looks at Adam and Sanna, "This way you two," The waiter start walking. Adam and Sanna follow the waiter outside to the deck, the waiter putting the menus down on the table, and pulling out the chair for Sanna.

Sanna sat down in the chair, "Thank-you sir," Sanna thanks the waiter as the waiter pushing the chair in for Sanna chair nicely.

"Well you want any drinks this fine evening?" the waiter asks Sanna and Adam.

"I will have a Pepsi," Adam told the waiter nicely.

"And for the lovely lady?" the waiter ask Sanna looking at Sanna.

"I will have a Pepsi too, thank-you," Sanna told the waiter nicely.

"I will be back with your drink," the waiter left the table.

Sanna looks around at the view from the deck over looking the lake, "Wow, this is awesome view," Sanna told Adam looking out at the lake with the moon glassing off the water and the stars shining off the water now.

Adam looks at the lake, and say to Sanna, "Not as awesome as you looking this evening," Adam looking at Sanna, and blushing a bit in his cheek.

Sanna turn her head back to Adam, "Really?" Sanna was stunned at what Adam say to her, and blinking a few times at Adam.

"Yes I do mean that," Adam held Sanna left head with his right hand on the table. "You're like angle that came to me from heaven, and there nothing going to ruined this lovely evening with you," Adam told Sanna.

The waiter came back with Adam and Sanna drinks, "Here you two go, two Pepsi," the waiter pass the drinks to Sanna and Adam.

"Thank-you," they both thank the waiter taking the Pepsis to drink.

"Have we decide want to eat this evening?" the waiter ask Sanna and Adam, getting his book ready to write down the order.

"I will have the BBQ chicken with bake potato," Adam told the waiter, looking over the menus at one thing that catch his eyes to eat.

"And for a starters: soup or salad?" the waiter ask Adam, writing down Adam order.

"Caesar salad for starter," Adam told the waiter.

"And for the lovely lady?" the waiter ask Sanna nicely looking over at Sanna.

"I will also have the BBQ chicken with bake potato too, and a Caesar salad with no dressing for starter," Sanna told the waiter nicely closing the menus.

"Thank-you, I will be back with your meals," The waiter told Sanna do Adam leaving the table with the order.

Adam looks at Sanna, "What are you thinking about?" Adam asks Sanna, seeing Sanna looking over the lake with her thinking face on.

"Just how lovely everything is, and how wonderful you been to me," Sanna told Adam looking at Adam in the eyes, and smile at Adam. Something catch the corner of Sanna eyes, Sanna was not trying think who show up with few people with him, *'Please don't let it be Donovan?'* Sanna thought to herself.

Sanna could hear the waiter talking to the group, and a male voice strike fear in Sanna heart. "Thank-you sir, my group and I have the best fine red wine to drink. Bring a couple of bottles," The voice spoke to the waiter.

Sanna look over her left shoulder, and came eye to eye with Donovan. Sanna turning back around, and thinking to her, *'What is he doing here? I thought he would not come out until the fight.'*

Adam looks at Sanna, "Sanna, are you okay?" Adam asks Sanna, a little worry voice.

"Yeah, just something catch my eyes that I was wondering what it was," Sanna told Adam turning her head back to Adam.

"I see, don't worry about that, just enjoy yourself and this wonderful evening," Adam told Sanna, letting go of Sanna hand.

The waiter came back to Adam and Sanna table with two Caesar salads on a tray, "Here you go, two Caesar salads one with dressing and one without dressing," The waiter pass-out the bowels of salad to Sanna and Adam. "Enjoy your starters, your meal will be here soon," The waiter told Sanna and Adam leaving the table.

Sanna look down at the salad, taking the salad fork, and started to eat her salad. Sanna took a bite of salad, and amazons for the favours, "Adam this salad is good. There so many favours in this salad that I can't image," Sanna told Adam with smile on her face.

"It is a great salad, I ever ate," Adam agrees with Sanna eating the whole salad.

The waiter came back to take the empty bowels from the table, "How was the salads?" the waiter ask Sanna and Adam, holding the bowels in his hands.

"The salad was awesome, we both agree with each other," Adam told waiter, with a huge smile on his face.

"Thank-you I will let the chief know, I will be back with your meals," the waiter left the table with the bowels in his hands, entering the dinning area to the kitchen.

Adam looks at Sanna, "You look lovely tonight," Adam sweetly say to Sanna.

"You already told me that, but I like it a lot," Sanna say to Adam. Sanna notice that Adam had some salad dressing in the corner of his mouth. "Adam, you got some salad dressing on the corner of your mouth," Sanna pointed to the corner on her mouth.

"Oh," Adam wipes the dressing off his mouth with his cloth napkin. "That must been stupid," Adam whet red cheek quickly.

Sanna giggle at Adam, "I don't mind, it was cute," Sanna told Adam, blushing in the cheeks.

Adam looks at Sanna, "I hope you did not mind my screw-up," Adam say Sanna.

"I don't mind your screw-up, if you don't my screw-up too," Sanna say to Adam, thinking about the truth that she hiding from Adam now.

Sanna could feel an ice-cold stare in the back of her head, Sanna try not to let Donovan or his group getting her, mostly around Adam. Sanna feel Donovan eyes staring at her like knifes going through her body. Sanna trying to use the strength she had to not freak-out, and goes after Donovan right now. Sanna try stay calm in front of Adam, *'Don't lets him get to you Anilea... You need to stay strong... Do not become extremely angry on Donovan... You need to enjoy this date with a wonderful man... that you love with all my heart,'* Sanna thought to herself, trying to stay calm.

The waiter came back with Sanna and Adam meals, "Here you to go two BBQ chicken with bake-potato, enjoy," the waiter pass the food to Sanna and Adam.

"Thank-you," both Adam and Sanna thank the waiter nicely as the waiter left the table.

Adam look at Sanna, "Enjoy, you need it," Adam told Sanna, starting eating his meal.

Sanna started to eat her meal, and enjoying the taste of the food, "Yummy," Sanna say after the first bite.

Over at Donovan table, Donovan watches Sanna enjoying her food. Donovan lend back in his chair with a glass of red wine in his right hand, "I think we got poor Anilea scared to attack in front of that young man," Donovan spoke to his group drinking his wine slowly.

Desdemona look over her right shoulder at Adam, "Oh I can have some fun with fresh meat," Desdemona was licking her lips with her tongue.

Crevan looks at his wife, "My dear wife, what about me?" Crevan felt left out, that Adam could be Desdemona new sex toys.

Desdemona looks at Crevan, putting her right hand on his penis and say while patting Crevan penis, "My dear hubby, you're my first sex toy, and will be always. I was talking about maybe using Adam or I can poison him by my death kiss," Desdemona started to rub Crevan penis.

Crevan cringe in his seat at Desdemona doing, "Oh boy," Crevan squirms in his chair, Desdemona keeps on rubbing Crevan penis. Crevan lend forward in his chair, trying to stay calm.

"Desdemona enough of that," Donovan called meanly to Desdemona, glaring at Desdemona with narrow eyes.

Desdemona took her hand off Crevan penis, and Crevan felt relax, "Sorry brother, I could not control myself," Desdemona say sorry to Donovan, lowering her head.

Donovan lends closer to Desdemona, and whisper meanly to Desdemona, "Remember if we were not family, and you will died. Remember that from now on, and keep your head in the main game plan of this battle to end Anilea life for good."

"I will," Desdemona whisper to Donovan. Donovan sat back in his chair, enjoys the rest of the evening of good food, and putting the fear in Anilea from a far.

Adam and Sanna finish their meals, and ready to order dessert. The waiter took their plates away, handed the dessert menus to them, and left for the few minutes. "Everything looks so on here, I can't decide what I want for dessert," Sanna told Adam looking at the menus.

"Order what you really want," Adam told Sanna looking at the menus.

Sanna looking at the menus, when the waiter came back to the table, "What do you two want for dessert?" the waiter ask Sanna and Adam.

"I will have a banana foster," Adam told the waiter.

"Mmm... I will have a mud pie," Sanna told the waiter.

"Okay," the waiter took the menus from Sanna and Adam, "I will be back with you dessert," the waiter left the area to the kitchen.

Adam look at Sanna, "Are you enjoying the evening?" Adam asks Sanna with a smile on his face.

Sanna looks at Adam, and say, "I'm very enjoying myself very much. Everything is prefect, thank-you," Adam saying looking out at the lake.

Sanna and Adam looks out at the lake from their table, "This evening is so nice," Adam saying looking out at the lake.

"Yeah it is," Sanna replied to Adam looking out the lake.

The waiter came back with their dessert in hands, "Here you two go, one banana foster, and one mud pie," the waiter put the dished in front of Sanna and Adam.

"Thank-you," both Adam and Sanna say to the waiter looking down at their desserts. Sanna and Adam started to eat their dessert.

Adam look at Sanna dessert, "Sanna can I have a bite of that mud pie, and I will let you have a bite of my banana foster?" Adam asks Sanna looking at Sanna in the face.

Sanna looks at Adam, and say, "Sure you can Adam," Sanna move the plate of mud pie closer to Adam.

Adam moves the bowel of banana foster closer to Sanna, takes a spoon, and taking a piece of Sanna mud pie. Adam taking a bite mud pie, and loves the taste of the mud pie. "That good mud pie," Adam told Sanna, smiling at Sanna.

Sanna take her spoon, and took a bite of Adam banana foster. Sanna love the banana foster, "That good banana foster," Sanna told Adam smiling at Adam.

They take their dessert back, and finish eating your dessert. The waiter came back, handed Adam the check, took the dishes the away, and say. "How was everything?"

"It was awesome." Sanna say to the waiter smiling.

"Thank-you, just pay inside," waiter say Adam and Sanna, leaving the table back inside.

Adam looks Sanna, "Ready to go to the beach?" Adam asks Sanna nicely.

Sanna look at Adam, but Sanna could still feel Donovan ice-cold staring in the back of her head. Sanna try not letting Donovan get to her, Sanna say to Adam, "Yeah I'm ready to go." Adam got up from his chair, walks to Sanna chair, pulling out Sanna chair for her, and Sanna stood up from the chair. Adam took Sanna right hand, and led her inside the restaurant. Sanna with Adam pass by Donovan table, slowly motion feeling set in for them, Sanna eyes and Donovan eyes meet. Donovan glared at Sanna evilly with an evil grin on his face. Sanna felt Donovan ice-cold evil glazed, Donovan slip on his red wine. Sanna saw the scar on Donovan face, chills went down Sanna spine, and Sanna cover the scar on her upper right arm with her left hand. Sanna turn her head straight, and care on walking with Adam.

Adam lend closer to Sanna left ear, and spoke in a whisper, "Are you alright?" walking to the cash area.

Sanna spoke in a whisper to Adam, "Yeah, why do you ask?" Sanna watch Adam pay the check, and walking down the stairs to the entryway.

Sanna and Adam exit the build, walking to the car, Adam open the passenger door for Sanna, and closed the door after Sanna got into the car. Adam walks to the driver side, open the door, got into the car, and started the car up. Adam looks over at Sanna and asks Sanna a question again, "Are you feeling alright?"

Sanna look out the windshield, watching Donovan and his group leaving the restaurant, and walking pass Adam car. Sanna eyes contracted with Donovan eyes and fear fill Sanna body quickly. Sanna quickly look away from Donovan stared, and ask Adam with a little fear in her voice, "Why do you ask?"

Adam took Sanna left hand in hands, held Sanna hand up to see, and look at Sanna, "Because I'm worry about you. You say things to hide your past, and it scare me seeing you so pale," Adam look into Sanna eyes. "I love you very much, and hurt my feels when you runaway from me without talking the problem out." Adam put Sanna hand down, let go of Sanna hand, and drove the car away.

All the way to the beach, Sanna sat there in the passenger sit quietly. Sanna put her hands on her lap, the right over the left hand. Sanna mind was racing quickly with thoughts that Sanna was trying hard to stay calm around Adam. *'I love Adam too, from the bottom of my heart, and it hurt my feels too. Why do I have to lie to Adam…? I wish I could tell Adam the truth about me… That I am not human, that I am a white spirit sent to each 1314 years ago to put an end to Donovan evil plans… I wish I can tell, but I'm afraid that it will hurt our relationship between each… sigh.'*

Adam pull into the beach parking lot, exited the car, and open Sanna door. Sanna exited the car, and watch Adam closed the car door. Adam walk up to Sanna right side, held out his left hand to Sanna, holding a blanket in his right arm, Sanna took her right hand, and held Adam left hand in her. Adam and Sanna walk down to the sandy beach, found the prefect spot along the beach. Adam set up the blanket on the ground, and sat down on the blanket. Sanna sat down beside Adam on the right side of Adam. Adam looks over at Sanna, smile at Sanna, and looks out at the lake as the full moon shine off the lake water, the stars shimmer like diamonds up the night sky. Adam lay back on the blanket, putting his left arm behind his head, looking at up at the star fill sky, and spoke softly to Sanna, "Wow! You look so pretty right now," Adam look at Sanna with a moonlight hitting Sanna body.

Sanna look down at Adam, and spoke nicely, "Thank-you Adam," Sanna smile at Adam.

"The way the moonlight hit your hair, and pretty face, it make you look so awesome. Come lay down beside me, and look up at this beautiful night sky," Adam told Sanna putting his right hand on her back of her dress.

Sanna eyes went wide quickly as a picture of one her nightmares play out in her head. Sanna saw the wall of flames, the hand reaching through the flames, grabbing the back of her dress, and bring drag back into the flames. Sanna sat there on the blanket with a scared look on her face. Sanna trying to calm down around Adam, Sanna was not showing her face to Adam. Sanna felt hot and sweaty all over her face. Sanna quickly stood up onto her feet, "I need to use the washroom," Sanna told Adam walking away to the washroom. Sanna walking to the washroom, Sanna felt someone watching from the brushes, someone evil and dark. Sanna was walk about to walk into the female washroom, Sanna open the door and Sanna look over her right shoulder. Sanna quickly ran into the brushes, grab the female dark character by the neck, and slam the female in a tree. Sanna look into the face of the female, "Eris, nice to meet you?" Sanna say through her teeth, Sanna had Eris neck in her right hand, and squeeze a bit harder up against a large tall tree.

Eris looks down at Sanna, "Anilea, nice to meet you? How everything going with you, Anilea, are you still living in fear?" Eris nicely spoke to Sanna with Sanna holding her neck tightly.

Sanna squeeze a little harder on Eris neck, "Tell me why you're here?" Sanna ask Eris through her teeth.

Eris try to breath a little more, and try to tell Sanna, "Donovan want to know your weakness, and he sent Desdemona and I to spy on Adam and you," Eris put her hand on Sanna right hand, trying to get Sanna right hand off her neck.

Sanna pointed her left index finger in Eris face, "Stay away from Adam and I!" Sanna yelled at Eris.

"Let Eris go now, Anilea," A stern female voice called behind Sanna back.

Sanna let go of Eris neck, turn around to come face to face with Desdemona, "Desdemona, what are you doing here?" Sanna spoke to Desdemona with a courage voice. Eris slid down the tree, and stood up from the ground to walk to Desdemona

"I'm spy on Adam and you, and report to Donovan the following report," Desdemona told to Sanna, looking into Sanna eyes, "And you should be afraid of Donovan. My dear big brother is enjoy with ewe are bring back to him about you," Desdemona smile evil to Sanna.

Sanna tight her heads into a fist, and spoke though her teeth, "Stay away from Adam and I for good or you will be sorry you mess with me right now," Sanna looks at Desdemona and Eris with narrow eyes. "Now leave Adam and me before the rest of the night or you will loose your hair," Sanna held up her left fist to Desdemona face that was glowing white.

Desdemona and Eris step back from Sanna, about to leave Desdemona was walking away, stopping in her tracks, looks over her right shoulder, and spoke to Sanna in a slid voice, "You better watch your back Anilea. Donovan is more powerful from last time you fought each other," Desdemona and Eris walking away from Sanna.

Sanna stood there in the brushes, watching Desdemona and Eris walk away from her, once Desdemona and Eris were gone out of sight, and there was no one around to spy on Adam or her. Sanna let out a big sigh of relief that a lot of pressure was lifting off Sanna shoulders. Sanna look up at the starlight sky through the trees, Sanna remember of the first time she fought Donovan and his group during the dark ages, one picture came to Sanna mind. A tear ran down Sanna left cheeks, Sanna spoke in whisper, "I will revenge you two." Sanna was upset that one lost memory that happen 1000 year ago during the end of the Dark Ages. During the last battle, that Sanna had with Donovan, before them, both went into hiding. Sanna looks down to the ground, and tears fell to the ground. Sanna calm down enough to walking out the brushes, heading to the washroom.

CHAPTER TEN

Facing The Truth & More Planning!

Sanna finish going to the bathroom, she was washing her hands in the sink, Sanna looking up into the mirror for a moment, coming face to face with her spirit side. Sanna look at herself in the mirror, her long wavy-curly hair down, a golden headpiece with a small heart sharp light blue jewel hanging down in the middle of her forehead. Sanna saw her white, thin straps, flowing dress on her body. Sanna staring at herself in the washroom mirror, hoping she will not tell or show Adam that she spirit for over 1,000 years. *"Come on Anilea, your stronger then that,"* a female voice coming out of nowhere and echoes the washroom.

Sanna looks around the washroom to see if anyone was around. Sanna was getting scare, Sanna looking like seeing a ghost, Sanna was wide-eye, white face scare still hearing the voice. "Who are you? Where are you?" Sanna called out in the air with her back to the mirror.

"Right behind you, Anilea," the voice called out behind Sanna, around the mirror area.

Sanna turn around to the mirror, and saw her reflection in the mirror looking back at her. Sanna face just drop with shock, "It can't be true... Am I going crazy?" Sanna say rubbing her eyes with her hands.

"You're not going crazy... Are you starting to lose who you are? Your Anilea a white spirit that fighting with dark spirits," the reflection spoke to Sanna in a strong voice, pointing her finger at Sanna.

Sanna lower her head, "I almost forgot who I am, but I'm in love with Adam. There something about Adam that driving me crazy," Sanna told her reflection, raising her head to the mirror.

The reflection looks at Sanna spoke to Sanna kindly, "There is something about Adam that you should know, and time will tell if that thing that bugging you about Adam will come true. *So just stay forces on what your here to do... to defeat Donovan and his group."*

Sanna look at the reflection, and say with worry voice, "How can I fight with out... You know whose," a tear ran down Sanna cheeks thinking about her past lives now.

The reflection spoke in an uproar voice, *"You have your group right now: Tiffany, Roselyn, Aaron, and Andrew, your friends and helpers with the fight. You forgot that... or is it that you're afraid to lost them like you're...,"* the reflection was thinking about a memory.

"Enough don't say it!" Sanna yelled at the top of her voice, breathing heavily at the end. Sanna spoke quietly to the reflection, "Please don't bring them up again. I lost them for good, and I'm trying to forget them for good." Sanna put her hands on the edge of sink, lowering her head down letting her tears hitting the sink edge now.

"You try to forget them, but remember what they did for you. If they did not sacrifice themselves, you will be the one gone forever," the reflection told Sanna remembering the one fight that Sanna will never forget.

"I know, but..." Sanna started to talk, when a knock at the washroom door happen.

"Sanna, are you okay?" the male voice spoke through the door.

Sanna raise her head up, and look at the door, "Yeah Adam, I am okay. I am just fixing my hair," Sanna told Adam staring at the door with wide eyes.

"Good luck," the reflection whisper to Sanna as it disappears from the mirror. Sanna fix her hair up in mirror, walks to the washroom door, and walking outside the washroom.

Sanna exited the washroom, seeing Adam standing in front of her, "Hey Adam," Sanna told Adam smiling at Adam.

"Hey Sanna, I was worry that something happen to you. You took so long time in the washroom, and I was afraid for you're safely," Adam told Sanna looking at Sanna in her face.

Sanna walks along the pathway with Adam beside her, "I'm sorry for scaring you. I was having a little problem that all," Sanna was telling Adam walking to the blanket, and sitting down on the blanket.

Adam sat down beside Sanna, "What kind of problem?" Adam asks Sanna looking at Sanna in the eyes.

Sanna blush in her creeks, "I don't want to say it's too personal," Sanna told Adam, looking into his eyes.

Adam got the point, "Oh I see female things, gotcha," Adam did not want to find out about Sanna female problems.

Sanna lay down on the blanket, looking up at the star night sky, and felt so relax, "The star are so bright," Sanna say to Adam looking up at the night sky.

Adam lay down beside Sanna, looking up at the night star sky, 'You're the most beautiful star here," Adam told Sanna looking up at the sky.

Sanna look at Adam, "Thanks Adam," Sanna spoke to Adam, then back at the sky.

Adam put his right arm around Sanna shoulders, and pulling Sanna closer to his body, "Sanna, you feel cold. Are you cold?" Adam asks Sanna looking at Sanna laying on the blanket.

Sanna put her arms around her body, and rubbing her upper arms with her hands, "Maybe a little bit cold," Sanna told Adam, she was feeling cold now.

Adam let go of Sanna, sitting up on the blanket, took off his jacket, and lay the jacket on Sanna upper body. Adam lay back down on the blanket, putting his right arms under Sanna shoulders, and look up at the sky, "There nice and warm," Adam told Sanna, holding Sanna in his arms around her.

Sanna snuggle against Adam body with his jacket on her upper body, "Thanks Adam," Sanna say to Adam feeling the warmth from Adam body to her own body.

Sanna was laying there on the blanket in Adam arms, looking up at the night sky. Sanna could hear the waves on the lake hitting the rocks and shoreline, making her thinking on something that happens back in the past that Sanna started to tear up, but hid the tears from Adam good. *'Why are past memories keep coming back to me? It happens at the end of the Dark Age… I hate those memories from the Dark Ages, their too bloodily… All those people dieing in the hands of Donovan,'* Sanna thought to herself. Sanna couple of deep breath, letting the breath out slowly, calming down herself without knowing that she was so upset, and Sanna look back up at the stars with Adam.

Adam looks at Sanna, and asks, "Sanna are you ready to go home?"

Sanna looks at Adam, and say, "Do we have to? I want to stay here in your arms for along time," Sanna snuggle against Adam body more.

Adam chuckle a bit, then say, "Come on Sanna it's almost midnight and your friends will be worry about you." Adam smile at Sanna letting go of Sanna, sitting up on the blanket, and looking down at Sanna, who was still laying down on the blanket.

Sanna looks up at Adam, "We got to go now, but I will do this again," Sanna told Adam sitting up on the blanket. Adam stood up from the blanket, and help Sanna off the blanket hand to hand. Sanna stood up, straight her dress, and looks at Adam with a smile. Adam took Sanna right hand, and held her right hand in his left hand. Adam pick-up the blanket in his right hand walks along the beach to the parking lot. When Adam got back to the car with Sanna, Adam open the passenger door for Sanna, Sanna enter the passenger side of the car, and Adam closed the door for Sanna. Adam walks around to the driving side, opening the back door, throws the blanket into the back seat, closed the door, open the front driver door, and enter the car. Adam started up the car up, and drove home with Sanna.

When they arrive back at Sanna place, Adam got out of the car, opens the passenger door for Sanna. Sanna exit the car, took a few steps away from the car. Adam closed the car, and walk across the street with Sanna beside him. Sanna walks along the sidewalk up to the house with Adam beside her, "So did you a good time tonight?" Adam asks Sanna, walking up the steps to the deck.

Sanna walks up the steps to the deck, and say to Adam, "I had a wonderful time with you, Adam," Sanna smiling at Adam. "What about you? Did you have a good time with me?"

Adam took Sanna hands in his hands, and held Sanna hands nicely, "I had a wonderful time with you, Sanna, and I will do this again in a heart beat," Adam told Sanna with a smile on his face, Adam look into Sanna eyes, and ask Sanna, "How a goodnight kiss?"

Sanna look into Adam eyes, and say to Adam nervously, "I don't kiss on the first date... at less not on the lips."

"Will the cheeks be fine?" Adam asks Sanna if it was okay to kiss on the cheeks.

"I would not mind that idea," Sanna say to Adam, and had a feeling that eight eyes were watching her from the living room window. Adam lend down to kiss Sanna on the right cheek, and looking into Sanna eyes with a smile on her face. Sanna stretch up to Adam left cheek, kiss Adam cheek, lower herself, and looking into Adam eyes with a smile on her face. "Thank-you Adam for the great night," Sanna say to Adam, letting go of Adam hands, and walking to the front door.

"Your welcome, and have good night sleep," Adam says to Sanna getting ready to leave.

"Goodnight Adam," say Sanna opening the front door, and about to walk into the house.

"Goodnight Sanna," Adam says to Sanna running to his car.

Sanna watch Adam pulling away in his car, closing the front door, putting her back against the front door in the dark house, Sanna heart was fluttering with love. Sanna took a deep breath, and letting it out, "I know you guys there," Sanna say turning her head to the living room that was dark.

"How did you know?" Tiffany enters the entryway with Aaron, Andrew, and Roselyn, all wearing their nightclothes, and turning some lights on in the living room and entryway.

"I can sense you guys watching from the living room window," Sanna say to Tiffany stepping away from the front door.

"How was your first date with Adam?" Tiffany asks Sanna wanting to know what Sanna and Adam did on their date.

"Well… we," Sanna walks into the living room, and sat down on the couch under the east window, "We went to a wonderful restaurant by the lake, had a great meal and dessert. Then we went to the beach after supper, and lay out under the stars on a blanket," Sanna explain to everyone with a smile on her face.

"So it sound like you had a fun time without any problems you-know-who," Roselyn spoke to Sanna sitting down beside Sanna on the right side of the couch.

"Well…" Sanna started to speak, fidgeting with her hands together on her lap. "Donovan and his group show up at the restaurant, and Eris and Desdemona show up at the beach," Sanna told everyone nervously, fooling around with her hands, thinking what happen that night.

Andrew face drop with shock, "Donovan show up in a public place with his group. I thought he would not show up on the day of the battle?" Andrew says with a shocking voice.

"I know that what I thought so too, but the only thing Donovan did was stare his ice-cold eyes at me that it," Sanna told everyone, shivering to be reminding of Donovan icy cold eyes staring at her.

"What about Eris and Desdemona?" Tiffany asks Sanna sitting on the left side of Sanna on the couch.

Sanna looks at Tiffany, "They were spying on Adam and I down at the beach," Sanna told Tiffany through her teeth.

"How did you know it was them spying on Adam and you?" Tiffany question Sanna, trying to calm Sanna down.

"I heard them in the brushes by the washrooms, went I was walking to the washrooms. I ran into the brushes, and grab Eris by the neck with my right hand," Sanna started to explain to everyone, looking a bit at everyone.

Tiffany looks at wide-eyes at Sanna, "You grab Eris by the neck by one hand. Man, you got the gust to do that. What about Desdemona?" Tiffany say to Sanna, clearing her head after the thought Tiffany got of Sanna grabbing Eris by the neck.

"Oh Desdemona show up behind me, before I let go of Eris neck, and we had argument, after I let go of Eris neck," Sanna told Tiffany starting to get a little mad at the thought of Desdemona showing up.

Roselyn looks at Sanna, moving a piece of Sanna hair away from Sanna face with her left hand, and spoke to Sanna, "What did you two argue about?"

Sanna tight her hands into a fit, and sat there with a piss-off look on her face. Sanna spoke through her teeth, "We argue about them spying on Adam and me. I told them to leave Adam and me alone for the rest of the night or they will lose their hair on the spot."

"What did they do?" Roselyn ask Sanna thinking of the worse thing that Desdemona and Eris can do to Sanna.

"They left me alone, but it was Desdemona say to me that got me scare about Donovan," Sanna trying hard not to shake in front of her friends, and trying to calm down.

Roselyn put her left hand under Sanna chin, turning Sanna face to her own face, and looking into Sanna eyes to say, "What did Desdemona say about Donovan that got you so scare?" Roselyn had a worry look on her face, letting go of Sanna chin Sanna started to speak to everyone, "Desdemona say that I should be afraid of Donovan, because he more powerful from the last fight." Sanna lower her head to the floor, and trying to stay calm. "I will never win this time," Sanna spoke in a whisper with her head lower.

Roselyn put her left hand on Sanna back, and starting to rub Sanna back in circles, and up and down. Roselyn look at Sanna, and spoke to Sanna, "You will win this time. You got us, your friends, with you always, along the way. In addition, you should know by now about that. We will never let you fall, and we will never let you died in the hands of Donovan."

Sanna thought for as moment on the words Roselyn told her, Sanna raising her head up, and looks at Roselyn, "The only thing I'm afraid of is loosing you guys that all," Sanna told Roslyn with an upset look on her face.

Roselyn put both of her hands on the sides of Sanna face, looking into Sanna eyes, and saying, "You will never lose us. We are family, and a damn good family, even if you are not through blood with us. Your always be a sister to all of us, and we love you very much, remember," Roselyn letting go of Sanna face.

Sanna started to tear up a bit, wiping the tears away from her face with her fingers, and looks at her friends, "I remember," Sanna say to her friends nodding a bit now.

"Hey Anilea, you will always be a sister to me, sport," Andrew say to Sanna sitting on the coffee table in front of Sanna.

"What am I? Crop liver? I am think you're a sister me too, Anilea," Aaron say to Sanna sitting down beside Andrew on the coffee table.

"You're not crop liver Aaron, more tuff meat, and Anilea you're a sister to me too," Tiffany say to Sanna looking at Sanna in the face with a smile on her face.

Sanna looks at Roselyn, and Roselyn say to Sanna with a smile on her face, "Me too, forever in my heart."

Sanna looks at everyone around her, and smile at him or her, "I'm happy to have such a great family with me," Sanna say to everyone happy.

"Aw, group hug," Aaron say to everyone. Everyone hug in a big group, and laugh at each other. When they were hugging each other, they smile at each other.

"Thanks you guys, I need that," Sanna say to everyone, then looking up at the clock on the wall, and realize that it was after midnight. "Wow, it is time for bed big time," Sanna told everyone getting off the couch, and watching her friends standing up from their spots. "Let's got to bed," Sanna walks to the stairs with everyone behind her. Sanna head straight upstairs to the third floor,

"Goodnight everyone," Sanna called out to everyone.

"Goodnight Anilea," Everyone called out to Sanna from his or her bedrooms. Sanna headed upstairs to the third floor to her bedroom.

Sanna arrive in her bedroom, Sanna headed to the bathroom to have a shower. Sanna turn the bathroom light on, closing the door behind her. Sanna got undress to her naked skin, took out the bobby pins on her hair, and stepping into the shower. Sanna turn on the water, letting the water run on her body, and Sanna washing her hair and body. Sanna lower her head in the shower letting the water from the showerhead running down over her face. Sanna hair fell in front of her face, and water ran down from the top of her head to the shower floor. Sanna could hear screams and cries from her past fights with Donovan from women, men, and children. It felt like something hitting her stomach, making her hunch over in the shower, wrapping her arms around her stomach, and trying hard to breathe. Sanna cough hard, some blood came out of her mouth, and hitting the shower wall and floor. "What wrong with me? Am I that weak from the fighting with Donovan or from that spell that was cast a couple of months ago or both," Sanna spoke to herself with a worry voice in the shower. Sanna wait a few moments for the pain to go away, standing up straight in the shower, took a few deep breaths, and shutting off the water.

Sanna exit the shower, wrapping a big towel around her body, and walks over to the sink to brush her hair. Sanna was brushing her hair in the mirror, when Sanna saw her spirit side showing up in the mirror again. "Can you leave me alone for the rest of the night?" Sanna told the reflection finishing brushing her hair.

"No, I'm not done with you," the reflection spoke to Sanna, looking the way Sanna was looking now, and raise an eye brow at Sanna.

"What do you want from me?" Sanna ask the reflection with a tick-off voice, slamming the brush down on the countertop, and looking at the reflection in the eyes.

The reflection looks at Sanna body, *"Man, just look at yourself, your so weak now. How will you fight Donovan in the state your in? I never have seen you this thin and pale,"* The reflection told Sanna with a worry voice.

Sanna look down at herself, seeing her thin arms and legs, Sanna remove the big towel from her body, and almost seeing her ribs clearly. Sanna raise her face to the mirror, the reflection move to the left side of the mirror, showing Sanna pale face in the mirror. Sanna just stared at herself, "What have I done to myself?" Sanna say to herself looking at herself in the mirror with a stun look on her face.

"You have been so worry about everything around you that you're not taking care of yourself. You need to force on yourself, and do not worry about everyone else. Their old enough to take care of themselves, and they call you if they need help," the reflection told Sanna moving back into the mirror, and looking at Sanna in the face.

"Your right, but I'm still having fun with Adam," Sanna told her reflection feeling more proud in herself for going to have some fun before the fight in a year.

"You can be in love with Adam, but do not let love get to her head. You need to stay force on your task to defect Donovan and his group," the reflection told Sanna pointing her left index finger at Sanna.

"I would not let love get to my head. I will be force on my task," Sanna told her reflection smiling. "Now it's time for bed, I need my strength to fight Donovan."

Sanna was getting ready to leave the bathroom, *"Have a goodnight, and I will be watching you to see if your getting healthy or not. If not, I will show up, and bugging you again,"* the reflection told Sanna slowly disappearing back into the mirror. Sanna look at the mirror, and saw her pale thin face looking back at her. Sanna shook her head, and left the bathroom. Sanna arrive in her bedroom, getting her nightgown on, went to bed, and trying to get some sleep without a bad dream of her past bug her.

Desdemona and Eris arrive back to their house, "The boys must not be home right now," Eris told Desdemona walking to the front door.

"Proudly still at the bar trying to get my brother a girl to have some sex fun," Desdemona say to Eris, turning the key in the door, and opening the door.

"You're proudly right about that," Eris says to Desdemona entering the house, and closing door behind her. Desdemona and Eris laugh at the thought, walking into the living room, and waited for the boys to come home from the bar.

A few hours later Donovan, Crevan, and Ryu coming back home. Crevan and Ryu were piss-ass-drunk, stumbling up to the house laughing all the way. Donovan opens the front door, "Get in there now you two idiots!" Donovan yelled at Crevan and Ryu to get into the house.

Ryu and Crevan stumble into the house drunk, tripping over everything, and stand in the living room doorway swaying side-to-side, "Hey bro, there two hot chicks on the couch. I wonder if they are single," Ryu say to Crevan hiccupping at the end, and so drunk now.

"Hiccup, I have no idea, but I want the one with the red streaks in her hairs, and the hot ass body," Crevan say to Ryu in a drunken voice looking at Desdemona with sexy eyes looking at her.

Donovan stood behind Crevan and Ryu, "Get in there now you two!" Donovan yelled at Crevan and Ryu pushing them into the living room. Crevan and Ryu fell to the floor laughing at them. Donovan just looks at them as he walking passes them, "Drunken idiots," Donovan say to Crevan and Ryu walking by them. Donovan sat down in his chair across from the couches, and looks at

Desdemona and Eris, "Please tell me you two found something about Anilea and that Adam guy?" Donovan begs Desdemona and Eris for anything better then what Crevan and Ryu is doing now.

Desdemona looks at Donovan from the couch, "We found out that they are dating each other, and that Anilea is still strong," Desdemona say to Donovan, sitting back on the couch, and looking over at the boys once and a while.

"Yeah Anilea is strong, she grab my neck with her right hand," Eris told Donovan showing a red mark on her neck from Anilea hand.

"I see, and what did you do to have Anilea grab you by the neck?" Donovan question Eris about the red marks on Eris neck by Anilea hand.

"Nothing, just on Anilea spying in the brushes by the washrooms, she came running into the brushes. Grabbing me by the neck, and slamming me into a tree, I did nothing to have Anilea grab me, "Eris told Donovan and it was the truth.

"I see, and Desdemona, you were there to see Anilea grabbing Eris neck?" Donovan turns his head to Desdemona, and asks his question to her.

"Yes my dear brother, I saw everything that Anilea did to Eris. Plus..." Desdemona told Donovan, then stood up the couch, walking over to Donovan, and lend on the right arm of the chair that Donovan was sitting in. "Plus Anilea maybe strong now, but she could not show that she afraid of you. Eris and I almost lost our hair if we did not go right away from her, and told to leave Adam and her alone for the rest of the night," Desdemona told Donovan everything.

"How does poor-weak Anilea look like, and how did her reaction when you told her how powerful I am?" Donovan asks Desdemona with an evil grin on his face.

Desdemona was talking to Donovan about Anilea, and how afraid Anilea of Donovan. Crevan crawl on his back between Desdemona legs, and looks at Ryu drunken, Crevan whisper to Ryu, "Ryu, I see a wet moist pussy up there." Pointing up to Desdemona underwear with his finger, and having a drunken smirk on his face.

"I dare you to touch the pussy with your hand," Ryu dare Crevan to touch Desdemona pussy with his hand.

"Okay then," Crevan whisper to Ryu, taking his right hand, raising his right hand up Desdemona skit without Desdemona knowing, and touching Desdemona pussy with right hands.

Crevan rubbing Desdemona pussy, when Desdemona went silent quickly, closed her eyes with a piss-off look on her face, and looks at Donovan in the face. "One seconds my brother, I have to do something now," Desdemona told Donovan through her teeth about Crevan actions.

"Just stomp on him, and you can do your thing later downstairs, carry on telling me more about Anilea fear of me," Donovan told Desdemona, knowing Crevan was being an idiot now being so drunk, and what he was doing to Desdemona now.

Desdemona took her left foot in her high-heel shoe on, and stomp in the middle of the chest of Crevan. Crevan roll away from under Desdemona in pain, grabbing his chest with his hands, and curling into a ball on his right side. Desdemona finish talking to Donovan, "Now you know my dear brother about Anilea health," Desdemona told Donovan at the end of the talking.

"Very good my sister, now I know that it should be easy to get rid of Anilea for good this coming year. Now you can deal with that drunken fool on the floor in pain, and you too Eris deal with Ryu too downstairs," Donovan spoke to Desdemona and Eris about Crevan and Ryu drunken. Donovan stood up from his chair, and walking to the living room archway. Donovan looks over his right shoulder, and says to his group, "I'm going to bed. Don't disturb me or you would not see the next day," Donovan walks away upstairs to his bedroom.

Desdemona looks down at Crevan, Crevan looks up at Desdemona, "Hey cutely, do you have a boyfriend?" Crevan drunken say to Desdemona sitting up from the floor.

Desdemona rolled her eyes at Crevan, Desdemona lend down to Crevan face, and told Crevan, "I have a hubby, now you been a bad boy, and you need your punishment from me downstairs."

Crevan face lit up quickly, "Oh punishment," Crevan says to Desdemona with a drunken smile on his face, getting up from the floor.

Eris got up from the couch and walks over to Ryu, who was sitting up from the floor, "Come dear hubby, I have a gift for you downstairs," Eris told Ryu, looking down at Ryu.

"Oh a gift for me, you should not have," Ryu drunken say to Eris, getting off the floor with a smile on his face.

Desdemona and Eris held on to Crevan and Ryu arms, leading them downstairs to the basement, and close the basement door behind them. A few minutes later, the sounds of whips creaking, and screaming of men, tie up in chains. "More my mistresses... move please!" Crevan yelled to Desdemona through the pain. The sound of the mourning and groaning came from downstairs.

CHAPTER ELEVEN

Halloween Time!

Halloween came around; Sanna woke to the sound of her alarm clock going off, around nine o'clock in the morning. Sanna roll over in her bed, turning off her alarm clock, and getting up from her bed. Sanna wonder to her bathroom to do her business, sleepy eye all the way there. Sanna was washing her hands in the sink, Sanna washing her face, Sanna slashing some water on her face, Sanna look up at the mirror, and sigh at herself. "Anilea, you do look so bad now, but still looking weak. I'm hoping will be stronger for the fight next year," Sanna told herself looking into the mirror. Sanna saw something starting to appear in the mirror, "Don't start!" Sanna yelled at the reflection that slowly appearing in the mirror, and disappearing back into the mirror. "I know myself, and I'm resting and enjoying my life," Sanna told the reflection once gone from the mirror. Sanna exit the bathroom walking into the walk-in closet, got dress into her blue jeans, white t-shirt with blue butterfly on the front, and blue socks. Sanna exit the closet, walking over to the make-up table, taking her hairbrush in her right hand, starting to brush her long hair with the brush, and pulling her hair back into a ponytail. Sanna could hear the leaves rusting in the trees with the breezes blowing. Sanna looks over at the French doors, and thought to herself, *'I hope that tonight; nothing go wrong.'* Sanna walks over to the French doors, opening the doors, and stepping outside onto the balcony.

Sanna walks over to the railing in front of her, and lending against the railing staring out at the different colors of leafs in the trees, slowing falling to the ground. Sanna was staring out in the distance, when her cell phone in her jean right side front pocket started to ring. Sanna reach into her jean pocket, grabbing the cell phone with right hand, pulling out her cell phone, and looking at phone number on the front screen. "Hey it's Adam," Sanna say to herself, flipping open her cell phone, and putting the cell phone up to her right ear. "Hello," Sanna sated to talk into her cell phone.

"Hey sweetheart, that look so beautiful today," Sanna can hear Adam voice on the other end talking to her.

Sanna just smile at what Adam say to her, "Where are you?" Sanna ask Adam into her cell phone.

"Look to your right," Adam told Sanna where to look fro him.

Sanna turn her head to the right, and saw Adam standing on his balcony looking back at her. "Adam, your one strange person, and I like it a lot," Sanna just shook her head, and laugh at Adam actions.

"I cannot wait for tonight... What are dressing up as for Halloween?" Adam asks Sanna over the cell phone, looking at Sanna across the yards.

Sanna thought for a moment, and then told Adam what she going to dress up Halloween, "I was thinking as someone who live in the medieval days."

"Like a princess or a present or someone else?" Adam asks Sanna over the cell phone with a surprise voice.

"You have to wait to see what I'll be tonight for Halloween. In addition, I will be passing out candy to the kids. Remember I told you a few days ago, when we were out for that walk around the park," Sanna remind Adam, what her plans was for that night.

"I remember you telling me that, and do you remember me saying I will come over to help you and to keep you company tonight," Adam remind Sanna on what he doing that night.

"I know... I have to go... Roselyn and them are home today, and I promise them that I will help with the outside stuff," Sanna say her goodbye to Adam, before shutting off her cell phone.

"Okay, see you later on tonight at your place... Take care until then," Adam says his goodbye to Sanna before shutting off his cell phone. Sanna look down at her cell phone in her right hand, and sigh at the cell phone. Sanna walks back inside the house, and headed downstairs to help her friends.

Roselyn, Tiffany, Andrew, and Aaron were downstairs in the living room pulling out Halloween stuff from boxes on the floor. Aaron pulls out a scary mask from a box, and getting an idea in his head. Aaron heard Sanna coming downstairs, he looks at Tiffany with a sneaky-smile on his face, and "I bet I can scared Anilea good with this mask?" Aaron says to Tiffany putting on the mask on his face.

Tiffany looks at Aaron, wearing the mask on his face, and telling Aaron with a worry voice, "I don't think you should do that to Anilea? You could get hurt by Anilea if you're not careful around Anilea."

Roselyn looks at Aaron, and told Aaron, "I agree with my sister, you could get hurt by Anilea if you're not careful. Anilea has been on edge for a while about Donovan and his group are in town, and Donovan looking more powerful then last time they met. If you want to scare Anilea go right a head, but don't say we warning you if Anilea hurts you."

"I will be careful, now it is almost show time," Aaron says through the mask to Tiffany and Roselyn, hearing Sanna footsteps on the second floor. Aaron ran to the staircase and crouch down by the staircase waiting for Sanna to come downstairs. Aaron could hear Sanna slowly coming down the stairs to the main floor. Aaron chuckled at the thought of scaring Sanna, and getting ready to attack on Sanna.

Sanna was almost was a few steps from the bottom, when Aaron jump out from his hiding spot, and roar loudly with the mask on his face. Sanna just scream loudly at the top of her voice for a second, quickly jumping from the stairs, and tackling Aaron to the ground in rage. Sanna knelt over top of Aaron, her left hand on his chest, and her right hand glowing white, "Any last words?" Sanna ask in rage at Aaron, and pulling her right hand back getting ready to punch in the face.

"Hold up Anilea, it is me, Aaron," Aaron quickly took off the mask his face to show Sanna it was only him, and staring at her with wide eyes.

Sanna calm down, dropping her right hand, that stop glowing, and getting off Aaron. Sanna stood up from the floor, and looking down at Aaron, "Your lucky that I let you talk, before killing you," Sanna say to Aaron, watching Aaron getting off the ground with the mask in his right hand.

"Wow, you still got it Anilea," Aaron say to Sanna, rolling his right shoulder in a circle, and putting his left hand his right shoulder. "I think you almost pop my right shoulder out with your tackling. Next time I will listen to everyone else before doing any pranks on you," Aaron says to Sanna walking up to Sanna, and giving Sanna a hug.

Sanna hug Aaron, then looks at Roselyn, who was shaking her head at Sanna, "What?" Sanna throwing her arms out to the side, and stared at Roselyn with wide-eyes.

Roselyn walk up to Sanna with cross arms, and looking into Sanna eyes. "You look like your getting stronger, plus I think you are starting to get some color in your face. I'm not mad, I am happy that you're starting getting healthy,"

Roselyn spoke to Sanna, wrapping her arms around Sanna shoulders, and hugging Sanna in her arms.

"I know, I am getting healthier, I stop being afraid of Donovan and how powerful he is..." Sanna looking at everyone else, "Donovan maybe powerful now, but I will still kick his ass every time we fight. I am the winner every time." Sanna raising her arms in the air, and keep on talking to her friends, "Because I am stronger then Donovan and his group," Sanna lower her arms, and smile at her friends. "I am stronger, because of my friends. Who never gave up on me, when I was ready to call it is quite. When I hit rock bottom, they help me out every time. I put my trust in them and my life too. I'm happy to call them my true friends, and nothing with break our bond that we have for each other," Sanna told Roselyn, Tiffany, Aaron, and Andrew with one big smile on her face.

Roselyn, Tiffany, Aaron, and Andrew smile at Sanna with big smiles on their faces. Andrew looks at Sanna, and spoke happily to Sanna, "I think we all agree that you're a true friend to us, and we well put our lives in the line for you. We are all family, and family stick together like glue."

"I know that Andrew, moreover I don't think all this talk will get the house ready for tonight," Sanna told her friends walking to the front door. "I'm going to rack the leaves in the front yard, and if you need me," Sanna exit the house, and start to rack the front yard.

Once Sanna closed the front door behind her, Andrew walk to Aaron, and putting his right arm around Aaron shoulders, "You did good bro, but next time be more careful Anilea could have kill you," Andrew told Aaron, looking at Aaron.

"I know, but it was fun," Aaron told Andrew walking to the living room with Andrew beside him and the girls behind Andrew and Aaron. They were talking about what Aaron did to Sanna, and what she did to him.

Outside Sanna was racking away in the front yard, when Adam came walking up to Sanna, "Hey Adam," Sanna say to Adam looking up at him.

"Hey Sanna, have fun racking the leaves up?" Adam asks Sanna watching her racking the leaves into a big pile.

"Yeah, it is fun racking the leaves up, and I am almost done racking the front yard so my friends can set up the Halloween stuff in the yard," Sanna saying to Adam racking the last bit of leaves into the pile.

Adam looks down at the pile of leafs, and an idea come to him. Adam grabs a hand full of leaves and looking at Sanna with a smile on his face. "Hey Sanna, you know what the best thing about fall leafs?" Adam asks Sanna holding the hand full of leafs behind his back.

Sanna raise an eyebrow at Adam, "What is the best thing about fall leafs?" Sanna question back to Adam, after putting the rack by the tree, and looking back at Adam with a confuse look on her face.

"This," Adam throws the hand full of leafs at Sanna face, and laughing at Sanna.

The leaves hit Sanna in the face, and Sanna stood there stunned at what Adam did her with the leaves. Sanna grabs a hand full of leaves, and looking at Adam, "It is so on now." Sanna throwing the leaves at Adam face, and hitting Adam in the face, Sanna just giggle at Adam.

Adam looks at Sanna with a stun look on his face, "Now you ask for it," Adam tackled Sanna in the leaf pile, and started to trickle Sanna.

Sanna laugh loudly with happy in her voice, "Stop... Please... Uncle," Sanna say laughing at Adam rolling in the leaves.

Adam stops trickling Sanna, lending over Sanna body, looking down at Sanna into her eyes, and saying, "How much do you love me?"

Sanna grabs Adam by the shoulders with her hands, rolling Adam onto his back, sitting on Adam chest, and looking into Adam eyes, "I really love you from the bottom of my heart, and nothing will change that." Sanna kissing Adam on the forehead, and getting off Adam, and lay down beside Adam left side in the leaf pail.

Adam put his left arms, under Sanna shoulders, and held Sanna close to his body. Sanna put her head on Adam chest, and looking up to the sky. Adam kisses Sanna on top of her head, and whisper to Sanna, "I love you from the bottom of my heart too, and nothing will ever change that."

"I know," Sanna whisper, but inside Sanna felt wrong about keeping her big secret of her life from Adam. Sanna sat up from the leaf pile with some leaves sticking on her back and hair. Sanna looks at Adam for a moment, and asks Adam kindly, "Do you want to help me move the pile around to the back, and help me rack the leaves in the back yard?"

Adam sat up in the leaf pile with leaves sticking on his back and hair, and say sweetly to Sanna, "Sure then we can make a bigger leaf pile in the back to jump into." Adam stood up from the leaf pile, and help Sanna up from the ground.

Sanna and Adam move the pile of leaves from the front yard to the back yard, and start to rack up all the leaves in the back yard into a big pile. Sanna and Adam finish racking up the leaves; they put the racks away in the garage, and went to jump into the leaf pile. Sanna and Adam ran as fast as they can, and driving into the pile of leaves. They laugh and giggle all afternoon having fun in the leaves, and having one big leaf fight. Sanna lay down in the leaves looking up to the sky, and thinking on how wonderful Adam to her. Adam lay down beside Sanna on the right side of Sanna, and putting his left arm under Sanna shoulders. Adam held Sanna closer to his body, and kiss Sanna on top of her head. "Your one amazons' woman and I are proud to be your boyfriend... I love you very much," Adam, whisper to Sanna, looking up at the sky.

Sanna move her head onto Adam chest, and looking up at the sky to say to Adam with a wonder tone to her voice, "Hey Adam, do you think there will a future between us?"

Adam look down at Sanna for a second, then back up to the sky, and say to Sanna in a wonder voice tone, "Maybe, but only if faith will let us. Only time will tell... but now the only thing I want to be is your boyfriend, and tell you how much I love you from the bottom of my heart," Adam held Sanna closer to himself.

Sanna just sigh, and thinking to herself, *'If faith lets us? Time will tell that we are may to be together... I still in love with Adam... Why can I tell the truth to Adam? AARRGGHH!'* Sanna closed her eyes for a while, and calm down.

Around 3 o'clock in the afternoon, Roselyn step out onto the back deck, and calling for Sanna inside. "Sanna time to come inside to crave a pumpkin," Roselyn looks down from the deck railing at Sanna and Adam lying in the leaf pile.

Sanna looks at Adam, and say to Adam, "I guess it is time to say good-bye." Sanna getting out of the leaf pile, and brushing leaves off her body.

Adam got out of the leaf pile, brushes off leaves off him, and says with a bow, "Good-bye for now my lady. Until later on tonight I will see you," Adam walks to his house.

Sanna headed up the stairs to the deck, when Sanna hit the top step, Sanna looks at Roselyn with a smile on her face, and saying to Roselyn happy, "Lets go crave us some pumpkin for tonight." Sanna enter the house with Roselyn behind Sanna.

Sanna and Roselyn enter the kitchen, where Tiffany, Aaron, and Andrew starting to craving their pumpkins. "We clean out a pumpkin for you, now you can design your pumpkin," Tiffany says to Sanna. Roselyn sitting on the breach behind the table, starting to crave her pumpkin with a small knife. Sanna sat down at the head table, grabbing her pumpkin from the pile on the table, putting the pumpkin in front of her, taking a small knife in her right hand, and start to crave her pumpkin. Aaron did a werewolf face, Andrew a vampire face, Tiffany did a witch face, Roselyn did a pumpkin face, and Sanna did 'Happy Halloween' in creative writing. Aaron and Andrew put the pumpkins outside on the front deck, and went back inside the house to get ready for tonight.

Around 6 o'clock that evening, Aaron and Tiffany coming downstairs dress as 60's hippies, Roselyn and Andrew came downstairs dress as pirates, and Sanna came downstairs in her medieval dress for her year. Aaron and Andrew mouths hit the floor at the sight of Sanna in her dress and hair down with flower headpiece on her head. "What?" Sanna spoke looking at Aaron and Andrew mouth wide open.

Roselyn and Tiffany took their hands, and closing Aaron and Andrew mouths. Roslyn looks at Sanna standing on the stairs, and spoke kindly, "Anilea, you look great this evening. Now remember what we like you to do for the children this evening for candy?"

Sanna nodded her head to Roselyn, and say, "Yes I know how to do it, little children give the candy too, and older ones make them sing or dance for the candy," Sanna walks down the rest of the stairs to the bottom.

There was knock on the front door, Sanna walks to the front door, and answering the front door. Sanna saw Adam dress up in medieval clothes, "Hey Adam," Sanna greeted Adam standing in the door.

"Good evening my lady, how are we doing this fine evening?" Adam greeted Sanna entering the house, and Sanna closed the door behind Adam.

"I am doing fine," Sanna answer Adam question walking up to him.

"Okay you two have fun this evening, and any problems call my cell phone," Roselyn told Sanna and Adam getting ready to leave the house with Andrew, Aaron, and Tiffany.

Sanna walk up to Roselyn, and whisper to Roselyn, "You four are careful, this night Donovan group will be out to causing trouble. Just be careful please for me." Sanna try to Roselyn and the rest of them safe.

Roselyn whisper to Sanna, "We will be careful, don't worry about us. If you start, you will start getting sick again and you are starting to get healthy again. So you don't worry about anything we are older enough to take care of ourselves," Roselyn hug Sanna and turn to the rest of them. "Okay lets go and have some fun tonight," Roselyn say to the rest of them, and open the front door.

Andrew, Aaron, and Tiffany exit the house walking to the car. Roselyn exit the house, and say, "Good-bye you two. We will see you two later on tonight, have fun, and don't scare the little children too much."

"We won't, have fun. Good-bye, see you later," Sanna and Adam say at the same time, watching Roselyn closed the front door behind her.

Sanna and Adam stood in the front entryway for a bit looking over each other costumes. "Wow, you look so awesome in your dress," Adam told Sanna with smile on his face, and looking over Sanna light blue flowing with white and yellow designed in the middle of the dress, and on the sleeves.

Sanna look down at her dress, looking up at Adam, and saying, "You look great too." Sanna looking at Adam white puffy shirt, dark brown tight pants, and brown shoes.

"Yeah, I look all over town to find this costume for you," Adam say to Sanna about finding his costume for Halloween. "What about you? Where did you find that pretty dress?" Adam asks Sanna looking over the dress again.

Sanna grab the bowel of candy off the table by the door, and open the front door. "I made this dress years ago for a play that I was in at school," Sanna told Adam with a little bit of a lied to Adam with the bowel of candy in her hands.

Adam head out the door with Sanna to the front deck to head out candy to the Trick-or-Treat. "I see that the dress look lovely on you. I wish we could wear clothing like this all the time. They are so comfort to wear," Adam told Sanna sitting down in one of the chairs on the deck.

Sanna sat down on the other chair, and put the bowel of candy on the small table between the chairs. "I know, but living in the Medieval days is not that good," Sanna told Adam staring out to the street.

"I know living back then will not that pretty with illness, mean people, and so much more bad things. The only thing I want is to wear these clothes always," Adam told Sanna looking at her with a smile on his face.

Sanna chuckled at the thought and watching the children walking house to house to get some candy in their bags. Sanna saw a couple of children walking up to them wearing a princess and prince costumes. Sanna smile at them as they walk up to Sanna and Adam on the deck. "Trick-or-Treat," the children say sweetly to Sanna and Adam.

Sanna look over at Adam, "Aw, Adam look a little princess and prince. They are so cute, here some candy for you two," Sanna handing the children some candy in their bags.

"Thank-you lady," say the little girl in the princess costume. "You look nice too, I love your dress," the little girl looking at Sanna dress.

"Thank-you, have safe Halloween," Sanna say to the little girl as the two children leaving the deck. Sanna could hear the little girl talking to her mother about how much she loves Sanna dress. Sanna smile as more children came up to the house to get some candy.

The rest of the evening went great with no problems, Sanna and Adam enjoy giving out the candy to the young children, and making the older children sing for their candy. Sanna and Adam had a few good laughs with some of the older children where sing their songs. Adam and Sanna watch so many children running up and down the street, door to door of the houses. Sanna was thinking to herself, '*These children have no idea what is coming in the following year to come. What will life be after the battle ends? Will the children still come outside to play or stay inside the house scares to leave? I wish I have the answer to those questions.*'

Chapter Twelve

Nightmare Past!

Sanna look over at Adam friend's place, and could hear the screams of children. "Your friends are having too much fun," Sanna told Adam watching some children running away from the house in fear, but laughing a bit too.

Adam looks at Sanna, and says to her, "Yeah every Halloween they love to scare the older children, but not the little ones. They always play it nice for them. "Adam looks at Sanna, "I told them that I wanted to hangout with you this year for Halloween." Adam smile at Sanna, taking Sanna left hand in his right hand, and kissing Sanna left hand. "I love you, Sanna," Adam whispering to Sanna, looking into her eyes, and blushing a bit in his cheeks.

Sanna sat there in her chair, looking at Adam with thinking face, taking her hand out of Adam hand, and putting her hands on her lap. Sanna lower her head to looks down at the floor, and whisper to Adam, "I love you too." Sanna could not look at Adam eyes right away; her mind was going very fast. Sanna just had a feeling that something was not right now, that Donovan group was up to something evil. Sanna try to put the feeling a side in front of Adam, she knows that her friends will be all right, and everything will be all right for the rest of the night.

"Sanna are you alright?" Adam asks Sanna a little worry, looking over at her, and seeing Sanna was not herself right now.

Sanna raise her head to Adam, "Yeah I am okay, I just had an attack of some source. I will be all right it was a small one. Don't worry about me, I'll be fine," Sanna lied to Adam, a bit about what going on around her for real, and wanted to go after Donovan right now.

Adam sigh of relief, putting his left hand on his chest, and calm down at what Sanna say to him, "That great that you're okay, I was worry about you." Adam look at Sanna face, "You are looking so healthy; you got some color in your cheeks, and putting a little bit of healthy weight. I am so proud of you getting healthy," Adam told Sanna with a smile on his face.

"I know, and I am getting stronger too," Sanna told Adam looking down at herself, seeing that her thin arms and leg getting some muscle on the bone, and she cannot see her ribs cage anymore. "Once I stop worrying about things, I started to get healthy... Plus I did have help getting healthy too," Sanna looking at Adam in his eyes.

Adam looking at Sanna into her eyes, and asking Sanna a question kindly, "Who help you get healthy again?" Adam lend on the right arm of the chair looking at Sanna, crossing his arms on the chair arm.

Sanna lend closer to Adam, and answer Adam question kindly, "Well there Andrew, Aaron, Tiffany, Roselyn, and..." Sanna drag out the last person for Adam, and slowly say to Adam, "There you who were really helpful, getting me better. I like to thank-you for being there for me through everything I been through in the last seven months in this town. Thanks and I love you very much."

Adam sat back in the chair smiling at Sanna, and say to Sanna, "Your welcome, and I love you too. If you need to tell me anything that bugging you, you can tell me, and I can help you the best I can."

Sanna mind was running quickly, *'There will be one thing that you will never know about me. I am scare to tell you the truth about the real me. That the truth will hurt our relationship we have now... I wish, I could tell you now, but something tell me later to tell you... AARRGG! Why?'* Sanna mind was thinking on the truth about her life for real.

For the rest of the evening, the last of trick-or-treats went home to look through their bags full of candy, and getting ready for bed. Adam says his good-bye and goodnight to Sanna, kissing Sanna on her left cheek, and walking to his house. Sanna watch from the front deck Adam walking home, Sanna heart was racing with love for Adam. Sanna try to stay force as the car pull into the driveway, and everyone exit the car. "Hey you guys, how was everything?" Sanna ask her friends, lending against railing of the deck, watching her friends walking up to the house.

"It went great, no problems from you-know-who or his group all night," Aaron says to Sanna walking up the steps of the deck, and looking at Sanna standing there looking at them.

Sanna look over at Roselyn, and ask with a worry voice, "Is this truth Roselyn. You guys never had a problem with you-know-who group?" Sanna took a step away from the railing, and standing there in her dress.

Roselyn walk up to Sanna, putting her hands on Sanna shoulders, looking into Sanna eyes, and saying, "Aaron told the truth, we never had a single problem all night. We never saw them or felt them all night." Roselyn hug Sanna, and letting go of Sanna. Roselyn turn to everyone, and say. "Come everyone it is time for bed, we all need our rest." Roselyn walks to the front door, opening the door, and walking inside the house with Sanna beside her. Andrew, Aaron, and Tiffany follow behind Roselyn and Sanna into the house, closing the door behind them.

Sanna was getting ready for bed, went Roselyn knock on Sanna opened bedroom door. "Hey Anilea," Roselyn say to Sanna, watching Sanna brush her wet hair in front of mirror on the make-up table.

"Hey Rose," Sanna say to Roselyn finishing brushing her hair in the mirror, then turning around to stand there looking over at Roselyn in the doorway.

"I was wondering how your feeling?" Roselyn ask Sanna lending against the doorframe, looking at Sanna.

Sanna walk up to the window seating area, and looking outside at the wind blowing through the trees, removing the last bit of leafs from the branches. Sanna watch the wind blowing, and say to Roselyn with her back to Roselyn, "I am doing well, but all night I had a feeling that Donovan group was up to something without you or anyone else knowing that they are causing trouble." Sanna putting her heads down on the seat part, and lower her head. Sanna say through her teeth, "I wish, I was out there with you guys, instead of handing out candy to children. I feel so un-useful to this group." Sanna tighten her hands into fists, and slamming them down on the seat with rage.

Roselyn walks up to Sanna, putting her right hand on Sanna right shoulder, and speaking kindly to Sanna, "You're not un-useful to this group... You are our leader and a damn good one too... You are more powerful then all four of us put together... You have been through a lot of stuff before we came along, all by yourself... Plus we worry about you all the time, and we want you to be stronger for the fight..." Roselyn turn Sanna around and looking into Sanna eyes, "I don't ever want to see you like the way you look after the last fight. We almost lost you after that fight," Roselyn placing both hands on Sanna shoulders, as a small tear form in Roselyn right eye, and Roselyn try hard not to cry in front of Sanna.

Sanna turn her head to the right looking at the window. "Roselyn tell me how weak I was after the last battle," Sanna say in a worry voice.

Roselyn took her right hand, putting it on the left side of Sanna face, and turning Sanna face back to her face. Roselyn took a deep breathe, letting it out, and reminding Sanna after the fight. "You were so weak that Andrew carries you in his arms. You were losing a lot of blood from the wounds on your body, you cannot force your eyes, and your breathing was shallow and short. Even you were so weak, you still want to fight Donovan. You were telling at Andrew to put you down, so can finish Donovan for good. We got you out of there quickly before Donovan come notice that we were missing from the battle. We ran to the waterfalls outside of town to clean you up from all the blood, and wrapping your wounds with bandages. You were trying to move your arms and legs, but Andrew and Aaron had to hold your arms and legs downs, so Tiffany and I can clean and wrap your wounds. Do you remember sitting up quickly with piss-off eyes and breathing heavily?"

"I remember sitting up straight and yelling Donovan name in the air with rage. I did hit both Aaron and Andrew by accident with my hands and feet. I was so piss-off at Donavon and you people for a bit, because you would not let me finish Donovan off for good. Once you show me how damage I was, I realize that I could have died there. Man, I felt so stupid about that," Sanna was telling Roselyn. Sanna lower her head for a second, and then slowly spoke to Roselyn, "Rose?"

Roselyn looks down at Sanna for a moment, "Yes Anilea," Roselyn ask Sanna with a wonder voice.

Sanna slowly told Roselyn something that Roselyn was surprise at Sanna. "Rose, the truth is about me being so sick looking, weak, and afraid of Donovan. Is that every time I fought Donovan and a get wound from Donovan, I always shook the pain off, and carry on fighting with Donovan. Once you show me how wounded I was after the battle with Donovan, I been worry for the last 100 years that I could not take care of myself. Moreover, coming back to this town my memories is playing more, and we are not talking more then 399 years ago. Nevertheless, when I came to earth, halfway through the Dark Ages, those memories are coming back to me more. There something in this town that making my memories plays more in my mind. I wish I could find out what it is?" Sanna walks away from Roselyn to her bed, and say Roselyn, "Roselyn, I would like to go to bed now. I will see you in the morning." Sanna pull back the covers on the bed, climbing into her bed, and pulling the covers up on her body.

Roselyn walks to the bedroom door, turning back to Sanna, and saying to Sanna in a worry voice, "Please try to get some sleep tonight, and don't worry about anything for now on, you are okay with us. Goodnight," Roselyn turn off Sanna bedroom light, and leaving the room closing the door behind her. Sanna lie down in her bed, trying to relax effect to go to sleep, slowly closeting her eyes, and slowly fell a sleep on her back.

Sanna could see nothing but flames of fire everywhere and blood all over the place. Sanna could hear screaming of people being slaughter by a sword. Sanna could see a dark finger in the distance of her, killing people every second the sword swing side to side. Sanna could see the blood flying through the air and the bodies falling to the ground. She watch men, women, and children being slaughtering, that something snap inside of her big time. Sanna yelled at the top of her voice, "STOP!" Sanna watch the dark finger stop slaughtering the people. Sanna could see the eyes of a small girl looking back at her, the little girl were afraid of the dark finger with a long sword in the right hand.

The dark finger turns around to Sanna, slowly walking up to Sanna. Once the finger was face to face with Sanna, it spoke to Sanna in a deep male voice, "Anilea, we finally met. I will love to kill you with my sword here, my sword thirst for your spirit blood and want to hear your shriek of pain in your voice." The dark finger held up his sword straight in-between Sanna and his face with human blood drizzling down the blade of the sword to the handle, and over the male fingers dripping to the ground.

Sanna look at the dark finger with fear in her eyes. "Who are you? How do you know my real name?" Sanna ask the dark finger with a tremble in her voice.

The dark finger moves his sword away from his face, and saying to Sanna, "You should know me." The dark finger shows the face of Donovan, and smile evilly at Sanna.

"Donovan!" Sanna jump back from Donovan with fear racing through her body. Sanna look down at herself to seeing her spirit armour on her body. The gold wrist and legs covers, her dagger on her left side, white leggings and white tank top shirt, and her gold cross necklaces around her neck. Sanna hair was pulling back into a ponytail and Sanna stood there in shock at what was going on now.

Donovan laugh evilly at Sanna, walking around Sanna in circles, looking at her fighting clothes, and saying with a laugh in-between, "You think you will beat me with that very little armour, and that dagger, HA! You will never win this fight." Donovan throws his head back laughing evilly into the air in front of her.

Sanna lowering her head to the ground, seeing the puddles of human blood everywhere along the ground. Sanna tighten her hands into fists and getting angry with Donovan. That Sanna scream at Donovan, grabbing her dagger from the sheath revealing a long sword. Sanna pointed the end of the sword in Donovan face, and saying through her teeth,

"I am be smaller then you, but I am more powerful then you." Sanna keep the sword tip in Donovan face, cring her teeth together and ready for a fight Donovan.

Donovan step back from Sanna with a surprise look on his face, "Well someone has the guts to stand up to me. You maybe strong enough to defect me alone, but what about four more dark spirits." Donovan moves to the left side showing Desdemona, Eris, Crevan, and Ryu walking up to Donavon side. Donovan steps into the middle of his group, and spoke to Sanna, "Well Anilea, you seem to be out number five to one, too bad there no one else to help you." Donovan laughs at Anilea with his group joining in with their laughing.

Sanna felt wrong and worry that she will never defect Donovan and his group. Sanna drop her sword to the ground and into her hands and knees hitting the ground. Sanna shook her head at what she was seeing, and she called out in fear, "No! How can I defeat a large powerful group that dark spirits, how?" Sanna keep her head lower and fear came all over her body.

Two voices came from behind her, one female and one male. "Come on Anilea, you can defeat Donovan and his group," say the young female behind Sanna.

"I agree your stronger then them as long as you got us behind you," say the young male behind Sanna.

Sanna turn her head around to see two white spirits walking up behind her, a young 20-year-old male and a young 18-year-old female in white clothing with silver armour around their legs and wrist. Both had sword on the left side of their bodies. Sanna look at then with a shock look on her face. "It can't be," Sanna say with a shock in her voice.

The young male held out his right hand to Sanna, Sanna grab his right hand with her left hand, and he pulled Sanna off the ground. "Good to see you again, Anilea," say the young male to Sanna with a smile on his face with his short brown hair, 5 ft 8 in tall and med-built body.

"It can't be, I thought I lost you two for good," Sanna told the two young spirits with a surprise look on her face, at what she was seeing in front of her right now.

"We never left you, we been with you all the time. It is the end of the Dark Ages," say the young female spirit with her med-length light brown hair, 4 ft 8 in tall, and fit body.

'End of the Dark Ages?' Sanna thought to herself, as Sanna look around at all the old builds, and the clothes that the people were wearing. Sanna try to force herself back to the fight and then turn to Donovan. "Let's end this for good," Sanna say to Donovan turning around to back to Donovan. Sanna picking up her sword from the ground back in her right hand, and holding the sword tightly in her right hand.

Donovan laughs at Sanna, "You will still not win against us. We are still powerful then you three," Donovan told Sanna evilly, and signal his group to attack.

Donovan group moving pass Donovan closer to Sanna group. "How can we defeat them there five against the three of us, we will never win," Sanna told her group getting ready to fight Donovan group, keeping a tighten hold on the handle of her sword.

"Don't worry about those four, we will deal with them. Anilea, you deal with Donovan, don't worry about us, we will be okay," the male spirit say to Sanna, pulling out his sword from the left side of his body, along with the female spirit pulling out her sword too. They start to fight with Donovan group with their swords, and clashing with every blow against the steel swords.

Sanna watch her two friends fight Donovan group, Sanna turn her attention back to Donovan, and held her sword in her right hand. Sanna walk up to Donovan, face to face, and slap Donovan across his face with her left hand. Donovan face turn to the right, Donovan put his left hand on the left side of his face, and turn back to Sanna. "Smart move Anilea... very smart move Anilea... You got guts to face me now," Donovan saying to Sanna, punching Sanna in her stomach with his left fist.

Sanna cough up some blood from her mouth with the blood dripping from her mouth, taking a few steps back fro Donovan. "That was smart," Sanna told Donovan wiping the blood away from her mouth with her left hand, and chuckling at the sight of the blood on her hands. "You think that this will scare me... No way this will scare me," Sanna look up quickly at Donovan with a crock smile on her face.

Donovan smile evilly at Sanna, "You will never win against me," Donovan says to Sanna evilly. Donovan run up to Sanna sword ready to fight, Sanna put her sword across her body as Donovan hit Sanna sword with his sword. Donovan closer to Sanna face, and looking into Sanna eyes, "Anilea, you got one pretty face, and I hate to see this pretty face go to waste."

Sanna try to keep her strength against Donovan strength with her sword across her body and Donovan sword against her sword. "I will win," Sanna say to Donovan putting her strength on her sword, and pushing Donovan away from her body to send him flying a bit across the ground.

Donovan was surprise of Sanna strength, Donovan looking at Sanna, getting ready to fight, and say, "You will never win."

Donovan ran toward Sanna, sword ready off to his right side, Sanna stop Donovan sword move with her sword. Every sword movement Donovan made, Sanna stop Donovan sword moves, and Sanna fought back against Donovan. Until Donovan got the upper hand on Sanna, Donovan drains Sanna strength, knocking the sword out of Sanna right hand with his sword, and knocking Sanna to the ground with his left fist. Sanna lay there on her back with Donovan standing over top of her. "Well Anilea, your time is up. I did enjoy this fight, but it is time to disappear for good," Donovan pointed his sword tip in front of Sanna face.

Donovan raises his sword, tip down over his head, and coming down quickly to kill Sanna. The male spirit saw what Donovan was about to do to Sanna, he punch Crevan in the face, running up to Sanna, and driving in-between Donovan and Sanna. Donovan drives his sword downwards through the male spirit back to his heart. The male spirit wide-eyes, his mouth dropping with blood dripping from his mouth, and he was coughing up some blood. "Are you okay?" he asks Sanna looking down at Sanna. Sanna nodded her head to him, "Good, now it is my time to go," Donovan pulls the sword out of the male back. The male spirit fell to the right side of Sanna with no life left in him.

Sanna sat up from the ground, and look at the male spirit lifeless body lying off to the side. Sanna got to her feet with her sword in her right hand, and looking at Donovan, "You bastard!" Sanna yelled running closer to Donovan, sword ready to fight.

Donovan block Sanna move with his sword across his body, pushing Sanna a few feet away with his sword, and got ready to fight back to Sanna. Donovan stood up straight, looking at Sanna with narrow eyes, and a crock smile on his face. Donovan chuckled at Sanna, "You maybe strong now, but your still weak to defeat me," Donovan laughs at Sanna, and tries to scare Sanna. Sanna stood in terror at Donovan; Donovan started to run toward Sanna sword pointed in front of his body.

The female spirit punch Desdemona in the face, running in-between Sanna and Donovan, and Donovan stab the female spirit right in the heart. The female spirit coughs up blood, and slowly dieing on Donovan sword. Donovan remove his sword from the female spirit body, and letting the female spirit body fall to the ground, her blood flowing out of the wound. Donovan looks down at the female spirit died body and kicking the female spirit in the head with his right foot.

Sanna fell to her knees, wide-eye scare, and could not believe that Donovan kill two spirits friends in front of her. "No!... I will never win," Sanna told herself in a worry voice, lowering her head to the ground.

Donovan stood over top of Sanna, "Come on Anilea... You can try again... Oh, wait... you cannot... I have so much fun, but it is your turn to die." Donavan raise his sword over his head and coming down quickly to Sanna body.

Chapter Thirteen

Trouble Starting & Two Falling Rest in Peace!

Sanna sat straight up in her bed, breathing heavily, putting her left hand on her chest, eyes was widen as dinner plates, and try to calm down with sweat forming on her forehead.. The sunlight shine through the window, Sanna turn her head to the window, and looking at the light coming through the curtains. Sanna looking at the window for a minute, then turning her head to her alarm clock, and seeing it was 8 o'clock in the morning. Sanna throw the covers off her body, placing her feet on the floor, and stand up from her bed. "It was all a bad dream, but it was all real to me... That did happen years ago, but I know Donovan was on earth before me, causing troubles... The fight was so real, I did lose you two forever... I was not strong effect to protract both of you two from Donovan deathly kills... Why was I not strong effect to finish Donovan off?" Sanna spoke to herself walking to the bedroom door. "Now I need to be strong now to fight Donovan next year... I will not let that happen to my new friends at all," Sanna turn the doorknob, and opening the bedroom door.

Sanna walks downstairs to the basement, where Tiffany, Roselyn, Andrew, and Aaron was watching the News on the big T.V. Sanna heard the newsperson on the T.V. with one report that struck fear in her heart. "Today in alert report; two young children whet missing last night. A young boy dress as a prince and his young sister dress as a princess went missing last night around 9 o'clock." Sanna saw the picture of the two children on screen, "If you seen or heard anything about these children anywhere after 9 o'clock last night. Call the cops or missing person phone line, the parents will like to know where they are now. Please help find these children, before anything bad happen to them," the newsperson carries on talking about other things in the News.

Sanna lend against the back of the couch, and spoke through her teeth, "Donovan that bastard! Kidnapping children now, how lower can he go now? That son of a bastard, Donovan," Sanna hit the back of the couch with her right fist.

"Easy Anilea, we don't want you to get hurt or more weaker then you are now, calm down," Roselyn told Sanna looking up at Sanna from the couch.

"That bastard Donovan, he taking children now, can you imaged what him or his group doing to those children now," Sanna walks around to the front of the couch, and sitting down beside Roselyn on the left side. "I saw those children last night. They came to the house for some candy, and the little girl and I was talking about our dresses... Now her brother and she are now missing... How can Donovan group do that without any of us knowing? I know something was wrong... I know it." Sanna fell against the back of the couch, putting her hands on top of her head, and trying to stay calm.

Roselyn looks over at Sanna, and saying to her, "Donovan group is getting craftier now. They knew we would watch for them last night. They must grab the children, when we were not looking..."

Sanna interruption Roselyn rudely, "That does not matter were you guys were watching... I let those people down... If I was out there helping you people watching for Donovan group, those children will still be here... I am the one at fault for their kidnapping... I'm the one, not you guys."

Sanna stood up from the couch, and walks to the staircase. Sanna stop at the staircase, looking over her right shoulder at her friends, and saying to them, "I'm going for my jog now; I don't want to be disturbed for a few hours." Sanna walks up the stairs to the main floor, and heading to her bedroom.

Roselyn looks over at Andrew sitting beside her on the right side, and spoke to Andrew, "Anilea seem a little mad at herself... Anilea need to calm down, and try to keep that bottle up rage and angry under control or Anilea will not be strong enough and powerful enough to defeat Donovan for good."

Andrew putting his left arm around Roselyn shoulders, holding Roselyn closer to his body, and spoke to Roselyn, "I know sweetly, Anilea been fighting against Donavan for along time, and Anilea is getting tired of fighting against Donovan, that Anilea wants to end this once and for all next year." Andrew thought for a second, and then spoke in a worry voice, "Maybe this will be Anilea..."

"Don't say it Andrew or you be sleeping on the couch tonight!" Roselyn yelled at Andrew, trying not to think about the worst thing that could happen to Sanna in battle.

Andrew taking his left arms off Roselyn shoulders, and lowers his head to the floor. "I'm sorry my dear wife, I was thinking out loud that all. I did not mean to upset you, I do care about Anilea health, but Anilea is older then us, and maybe Anilea does not want to fight anymore. That the fighting is taking a toll on her body and her mind," Andrew spoke quietly to Roselyn.

Roselyn looking at Andrew, "Andrew," Roselyn watch Andrew raising his head to Roselyn. "I forgive you, Andrew, on what you say about Anilea health and you are right about Anilea wanting to end this fighting for good... We need to keep on Anilea... In addition, it does not matter how old she is, Anilea can still kick Donovan ass. It just Anilea been doing this forever, even the few 100 years in-between that they were both resting. Anilea wants to end the fight, but it is up to Anilea if she wants to live or not. We need ready for the worse after the next year," Roselyn told Andrew, Aaron, and Tiffany, with worry-upset voice as tears started to fall from Roselyn eyes down her face.

Tiffany looks at Roselyn from the other couch, and say, "Rose, don't worry about Anilea, but we know to be prepared for the worse next year after the fight in May. First we need to be strong for Anilea, so she can stop worrying about stuff, and force on the fighting with Donovan next year."

Roselyn wipe away the tears with her hands, looking over at Tiffany, and saying, "Your right Tiffany, we all need to be strong for Anilea... We are all worry about Anilea, and we cannot show it in front of her. Anilea will not get stronger for the fight, if she knows that we are worry about her all the time," Roselyn could hear Sanna coming down the second floor stairs to the front door. "Give me a few minutes," Roselyn got off the couch, heading to the stairs, and walking upstairs to the main floor.

Roselyn turn the corner to the hallway, and walks to the front door, where Sanna was getting her running shoes on. Roselyn stood by staircase, looking at Sanna jogging clothes, the black jogging pants, light blue tank top, blues running shoes, and grey hoodie, Roselyn just sigh at Sanna. Sanna finish tying her shoes, Sanna spoke to Roselyn in a piss-off voice, "What do you want Roselyn?" Sanna turn on her blue I-pod, looking through her play list for her workout songs, and putting in her left earphone in her left ear.

Roselyn step forward toward Sanna, and spoke to Sanna, "Anilea just be careful on your jog for us," Roselyn trying to stay calm.

Sanna put her black hat on her head, pulling her ponytail through the back of the hat, and putting her other earphone in her right ear. "I will be careful Roselyn," Sanna open the front door, turning on her music, and stepping outside, "I will be back in a couple of hours. See you later," Sanna closing the front door, walking down the deck steps, and starting her jogging down the street. Roselyn watch from one of the side windows by the front door. Roselyn just sigh at Sanna, and going back downstairs to the basement.

Sanna jogging along the trail to the waterfalls, Sanna just listen to her music from her I-pod, and trying to forget what she heard that morning on the news about the two children gone missing. Sanna jog up to the second waterfall on top of the bottom fall, and stopping in front the waterfall. Sanna took breather for a minute, then looking straight up the flat rock wall, and whisper to herself, “Up there is were I need to go.” Sanna ran along the flat rock wall to slop part a few feet into the trees, and running up the slop to the top of the waterfall. Sanna stop at the top of the waterfall, walking over to the cliff, and looking out at the scene, the top of the trees, town in the distance, lake in the distance, and many more. Sanna took a deep breathe, and letting it out slowly. Sanna turn around away from the cliff, walking along the riverbed to a few rocks in the river water. Sanna jump across the rocks with no problems to the other side, looking over her right shoulder to see if anyone follows her. Sanna turn off her music, taking out her earphones out of her ears, and putting the earphones on her tank top. Sanna put her hood up on her head, and walk through the thick brushes to a small clearing where the tree branches cover the area, letting in very little light.

In the distancing of the thick trees, the ground with a few rocks around them, two swords, one with a blue handle and the other with a pink handle. Sanna pulled of her hood off her head, walking up to the swords, and sitting down on the ground in front of the swords. Sanna pulled her knees up to her chest, putting her arms around her legs, and her chin down on her knees. Sanna stared at the swords for a while, and softly speaking to the swords, “How it been? Good... Me? I have been better... Yeah, I know I do not look well, but I am getting better. I just have to stop worrying about everything, and force on myself then I will be getting better.” Sanna started to tear up, and tears fell from her eyes. Sanna spoke in a whisper-upset voice, “I wish you two were here with me.” Tears fell from Sanna eyes down her face, and hitting the dirt ground. Sanna keep on talking to the swords, “I like you two to know is that I have a boyfriend now... Yes again, but I am not letting this one go from me... His name is Adam, and he such a sweetheart to me. Very caring, helpful person, and give me so much love. I wish of you could meet Adam.” Sanna started to get angry, Sanna raise her head to the swords, and spoke in angry voice, “I will revenge you two to the max, and Donovan will die for taking you two away from me for good.” Sanna start to cry, tears rolling down her face to the ground. “I have to keep my promise to you two. I have come to visit you two graves. I miss you two so much.” Sanna sat there on the ground crying, looking at the swords with red-eyes, Sanna sniff a bit. Sanna could listen to the sound of the water running in the distance over the falls, the wind blowing through the trees rusting leafs in the trees, and the colors of the leafs falling to the ground.

Chapter Fourteen

Donovan Move & Anilea Hurt!

Sounds of two hands slowly clapping behind Sanna, Sanna turn her body around to the sound of the clapping. Sanna saw Donovan standing behind her in the distance by the tree line, looking at Sanna in his black clothes. "Bravo, Anilea, bravo, you should not be spirit, but an actor, that was awesome acting," Donovan walking closer to Sanna. "Aw... together with your two died friends. So cute, are you saying that you will be joining them next year?" Sanna stood up from the ground quickly, and Donovan walks around Sanna, "I will enjoy getting rid of you for good next year... and that guy, Adam, will be your downfall for good. I will use Adam to get to you the best way." Donovan looks over Sanna body, "My dear sister was right about you being weak." Donovan whisper in Sanna right ear, "You will never win; you will die by my hands," Donovan walks away from Sanna, a few steps.

Sanna tighten her hands into fists, and try not to punch Donovan in the face. Sanna narrowing her eyes at Donovan, and in a piss-off voice, "Piss-off Donovan, I want you go now!"

Donovan stops in front of Sanna, and looking at Sanna, "No, I will not piss-off. Beside you look so pale in your face, and thin you should be the one died along with your two friends there," Donovan pointing over Sanna shoulders at the two swords in the ground.

Sanna look over her right shoulder at the two swords in the ground, "So you know what happen after the Dark Ages?"

Donovan walks closer to Sanna, and looking Sanna in the face, "Yes, I know what you did for your two died friends. Hobbling up here to this area, two sword in your arms, sticking the swords in the ground, putting the rocks around the blades, and casting that spell to seal those swords there that only spirit eyes can see them, not humans eyes. Moreover, you using your own blood to seal the spell by lying down on the ground as your blood pour from your wounds. You had a chose to stay on earth as a puny human for a short time or come back to your spirit world. You choose to stay on earth, well I choose to back to my spirit world and rests up a bit to come after you again."

Sanna clench her teeth together at Donovan, "I said 'PISS-OFF!' or you can't hear me because you're getting older that your hearing going," Sanna told Donovan through her teeth; tighten her hands more into a tight fist to dig her fingernails into the palms of her hands.

Donovan looks at Sanna with narrow eyes, walking closer to Sanna face, and spoke through his teeth, "Come on hit me in the face Anilea... I know you want too." Donovan step back from Sanna, and watching Sanna body language knowing she was very mad at him.

Sanna lower her head to the ground, teeth clench together, waiting a few minutes, then punch Donovan across his face with her right fist. Sanna started to breathe heavily, moving her right arm back to her right side of her body, and spoke to Donovan, "You ask for it." Sanna raise her head up to see Donovan holding the right side of his face with his right hand.

Donovan stood up straight, fixing his black jacket, and looking at Sanna. Donovan quickly ran up to Sanna, grabbing Sanna by the neck with his right hand, and slamming Sanna against a large tree. Donovan looking at Sanna in the face to face, and spoke to Sanna in a piss-off voice, "Smart move Anilea, you have the guts to do that, but you're still weak. It was so easy to grab you by your skinny neck." Donovan looking into Sanna eyes, "I know your weakness..." Donovan whisper into Sanna right ear, "It is your boyfriend Adam, and I will enjoy using him to get to you," Donovan move back from Sanna face.

Sanna putting both hands on Donovan right hand to get Donovan hands away from her neck. "You leave Adam alone. Adam is not the one you want... I am the one you want... Don't you dare hurt Adam, along with your group?" Sanna could feel Donovan grip tighten around her neck.

"You're a weak now, I will use Adam if I want too... I'm tired of you now," Donovan took his hand, unzipping Sanna hoodie, and held his left hand on the left side of Sanna chest by the heart.

Sanna could feel Donovan nails digging through her shirt to her skin, Donovan quickly grab the collar of the shirt with his left hand, and ripping down the front of the shirt. Donovan smile evilly at Sanna, putting his left hand back where Sanna heart is, and keep on digging his fingers through Sanna skin slowly to her heart. Sanna could feel every movement Donovan did, and beg Donovan to stop in pain, "If you kill me now, there will be no one to fight later, plus you don't want an easy kill from me, I know you want to fight me to the death." Sanna could feel her blood drizzling from the wounds down her body. Sanna was trying to breathe through the pain, Sanna lend her head back against the tree wide mouth, and gasping for air, and her eyes widen open looking up at the sky.

Donovan through for a moment on what Sanna told him, pulling his left fingers out of Sanna chest, cover in Sanna blood, looking eye to eye with Sanna, and spoke in a slyly voice, "You win this time, but when we fight next year there no begging for life," Donovan let go of Sanna neck in his right hand.

Sanna slid down the tree to the ground, Sanna sat on the ground coughing, holding her neck with her left hand, and looking up at Donovan with narrow eyes. "You son of a bastard," Sanna quietly spoke to Donovan trying to force herself sitting on the ground. Taking her right hand from beside her, Sanna putting her right hand on her chest were her heart is, feeling the blood drizzling from the wounds, and looking down at her right hand at the blood drizzling down her body. "I will get you, Donovan, for this," Sanna started to feel pain in her chest where the wounds were.

Donovan stood over top Sanna, looking down at Sanna sitting on the ground looking up at him, and say, "I will win and there nothing you will do about it… You will died like your two past friends there, and your past lover and family. I will enjoy getting rid of your new lover next year. It has been almost 400 years since I have done that to you… There nothing you can do… I will win." Donovan knelt down to Sanna level and punching Sanna in the left eye with his right fist. Donovan stood up from the ground, and told Sanna, "That for punching me in the face earlier." Donovan walks away a few steps, turn back around to looks at Sanna, and spoke in an evil tone voice, "The next time we will meet will be on May 20, 2065. Be ready to die then," Donovan laughs evilly walking away through the trees.

Sanna could hear Donovan evil laughing slowly fading away to nothing. Sanna sat there on the ground with her rip shirt, open hoodie, and blood stains on her body from the blood drizzling from the wounds. Sanna look down at the wound and saw five bloody red marks from Donovan fingers. The wounds heal over quickly, but the marks take a while to heal complete. Sanna took off her hoodie for a moment, and looking at the scar on her upper right arm. "You will pay for everything you have done to me… Every scar I get from you will do nothing, but piss-me-off more," Sanna whisper, lowering her head to the ground, and keep on whispering to an uproar, "No Donovan… I will not die next year… You will be the one!" Sanna quickly raise her head to looks at the two swords in front of her. Sanna got to feet slowly, and stood in front of the swords, "I will promise to you that I will kill Donovan for good." Sanna tighten her right hand into a fist, raising her hand to her face level, and looking at the little bit of blood from the wound falls to the ground. Sanna clench her teeth together, and try not letting herself glow. Sanna throw her head back, arms out to the side, and screaming at the top of her voice in rage. Sanna calm down at the end, breathing heavily, looking at herself for a moment, zipping-up her hoodie, looking at the swords on last time, and left the area walking slowly.

Sanna stumble all the way home, trying not let the pain, and what Donovan told her in the woods get to her. Sanna stumble up to the backdoor, up the stairs to the deck, and to the back door. Sanna stood in front of the backdoor, trying not the pain in her chest be showed before she enter the house. Sanna took a deep breathe, putting her right hand on the doorknob, slowly opening the backdoor, and quietly entering into the sunroom. Sanna quietly closed the backdoor behind her, trying not to make a sound or looking up to see if anyone was in the sunroom. Sanna turn around to see Roselyn and Tiffany lounging on the couches, each reading a book in their hands. Sanna try to sneak by them to the kitchen, when Roselyn called Sanna without looking up from her book, "Come here little missy," Roselyn keep on reading her book. Sanna slowly walks up to Roselyn on the south wall couch, feeling in the guts that she could be in trouble with Roselyn, Sanna stop in front of Roselyn. Roslyn put her bookmark in her book, closing her book and sitting up on the couch looking at Sanna. Roselyn looks at the blood stained on Sanna right hand, and looking up at Sanna, "How was your jog?" Roslyn ask Sanna.

Sanna looks down at Roslyn, and say, "It was good, I went up to the falls, and around there." Sanna trying not let Roselyn and Tiffany know what happen at the falls between Donovan and her.

Tiffany marks her spot in her book with the bookmark, closing her book, and sat up on the couch. Roselyn look at Sanna with a raise-eyebrow, and ask a question that struck fear in Sanna eyes. "That good... Where did you get the blood stained on your right hand?" Roselyn and Tiffany, both looks at Sanna right hand with the blood stained.

Sanna started slowly backing up to the kitchen with her right hand behind her back. "What blood stained on my right hand?" Sanna try to throw off Roselyn and Tiffany while backing up.

Roselyn and Tiffany stood up from the couches, staring at Sanna slowly backing up, and Roselyn ask Sanna again with a piss-off voice, "Anilea answer me... Where did you get that blood stained on your right hand?" Roslyn and Tiffany started to step forward toward Sanna.

Sanna keep on backing up to the kitchen and right into Andrew and Aaron in the doorway. Sanna felt backing up into Andrew chest, Sanna turn around to see Andrew and Aaron standing in the doorway. "What up sport?" Andrew says to Sanna, looking down at Sanna. Sanna back away from Andrew, with fear in her eyes, and try to find away of the room, without breaking any windows. Sanna stood in the middle of the room, not saying anything to anyone. Sanna eyes were wide with fear, and her breathing was fast. Andrew walks up to Sanna with Aaron beside him. "What going on here? We can hear yelling," Andrew asks Roselyn walking up behind Sanna.

Roselyn looks at Andrew, and say with her arms cross in front of her body, "Just looks at Anilea right hand, and you will find out why I yelled at Anilea," Roselyn keep her eyes and Sanna.

Andrew and Aaron look down at Sanna right hand at the blood stained on her right hand, and Andrew ask Sanna nicely, "where did you that blood stained?'

Sanna did not say a word, fear fill her body that she could just run away, but she was block in a circle of her friend, there was no way out the sunroom. "That what I been try to get out of Anilea mouth. She has not said a word when we ask her that question," Roselyn told Andrew unfolding her arms, and looking at Sanna standing there in fear.

Sanna quickly try to run through Andrew and Aaron. Andrew quickly grabs Sanna by both arms, and held Sanna upper arms back. "Let me out now!" Sanna scream loudly, and try to get out of Andrew grip.

Andrew turns around to Roselyn with Sanna in his hands. "There now you can find out what Anilea was hiding from you, Roselyn," Andrew says to Roselyn holding Sanna in his hands.

Roselyn walks up to Sanna, took Sanna right hand in her hands, and ask again to Sanna, "Tell us where you got this blood stained?" looking down at the blood stained on Sanna right hand.

Sanna try not to look at Roselyn in the face, "I'm not telling you or anyone else," Sanna spoke rudely to Roselyn.

Roselyn let go of Sanna right hand, looking at Sanna seeing a piece of Sanna shirt hanging under the hoodie rip up. Roselyn took her hands; put her right hand on the hoodie zipper, and un-zip the hoodie from Sanna. Roselyn move the hoodie, and saw five small red marks on Sanna chest around the heart. Roselyn step back from Sanna with wide eyes, "What happen? Who did that to you?"

Sanna look down to the floor, Sanna felt wrong about the whole thing. Sanna slowly spoke to Roselyn in Andrew hands, "Donovan." Sanna look up to Roselyn with piss-off eyes and her teeth clench together.

Roselyn look at Sanna in shock, Roselyn look at Andrew, and told Andrew, "Let Anilea go, Andrew please."

Andrew let go of Sanna arms, and step back from Sanna. "Good luck sport," Andrew whisper to Sanna.

Roselyn walk up to Sanna, moving the piece of shirt, looking at the marks, and gross out look came to Roselyn face, "Anilea why did Donovan do this to you?" Roselyn question Sanna still holding the piece of shirt in her hand, and looking at the marks and bloodstain down Sanna body.

Sanna could not speak with rage coming over her body. Sanna try to calm down to try speaking to Roselyn and everyone else. "I stop to catch my breaths at the falls, when Donovan shows up behind me. We had argument between us, he grab me by my neck with his right hand, and slam me against a tree. Donovan rips open my shirt, grab my chest with his left hand, and start to dig into my chest with his fingers." Sanna could still feel Donovan hands on her body, and pain started to show in her face.

Tiffany looks at Sanna left eyes, and seeing the black eye. "I see that Donovan gave you a black eye," Tiffany says to Sanna looking at Sanna left eye.

Sanna shrug her shoulders, and told Tiffany, "Yeah Donovan did punch me in the face, after I punch him in the face first," Sanna pointing to her left eyes with left finger. "Now can I please have the rest of the day to myself, please don't disturbed me." Sanna walk pass everyone to the kitchen, and slowly stumbling upstairs to her bedroom.

Roselyn and Tiffany walks to Andrew and Aaron, "Aaron, will Sanna be okay?" Tiffany asks Aaron, as Aaron wraps his arms around Tiffany body.

"I have no idea, but I never seen Anilea act so scared before," Aaron says to Tiffany looking down at Tiffany.

Roselyn spoke up to everyone, "Anilea is afraid of Donovan, but Anilea is strong for that... Anilea does not want to lose anyone of us or anyone in the town."

Andrew wrapping his arms around Roselyn body, and told Roselyn, "We know about that, it is up to Anilea to pick her only path for next year. I think Anilea need sometime to think and calm down."

Roselyn nodded her head to Andrew, "I agree with you." Roselyn turn to everyone else, "It thinks it is for lunch." Roselyn move out of Andrew arms, and walking into the kitchen thinking about Sanna.

The sunset on fall day, the sky changing from a blue sky to an orange-red sky, Sanna enters the balcony wearing her two-piece PJS that a long pant and t-shirt. Sanna had a shower early that day, wrapping up the wound on her chest with a bandage-aid, and letting her hair down. Sanna hop up on the railing, sitting on the railing, lending her back against the sliding of the house. Sanna watch the sun setting over the trees and lake. Sanna thought about what happen that day between Donovan and her up at the falls in the area. Sanna pulled her knees up to her chest, wrapping her arms around her knees, and putting her chin on top of her knees. Sanna look at the sun finishing setting in the distance to the dark night sky. The stars shine like diamonds in the night sky, and Sanna sigh at the thought.

Roselyn, Tiffany, Aaron, and Andrew peek outside the door, looking at Sanna sitting on the railing. "Hey Anilea, how are you feeling now?" Roselyn ask Sanna walking outside onto the balcony with everyone else behind her, and a cup of hot chocolate in her hands.

Sanna looks over at Roselyn, and spoke softly to Roselyn, "Hey, I am doing kind of good... I still feel like a loser from early today. I should tell you people what happen to me, instead of being mean to you people. I should not try to run away from you, and being so afraid of what Donovan say to me. I have not been myself, where I lost myself many years ago." Sanna explain to everyone still sitting on the railing.

Roselyn held out the cup of hot chocolate to Sanna, and say, "Here a nice cup of hot chocolate for you. We know how much you love hot chocolate." Roselyn smiled at Sanna still holding out the cup to Sanna.

Sanna took the cup of hot chocolate from Roselyn hands, holding the cup in her hands, taking a slip of hot chocolate, and say to Roselyn and everyone else sadly, "Thank-you guys for everything," tears fill Sanna eyes, and a few tears ran down her face.

Roselyn walks up closer to Sanna, and wiping the tears from Sanna face with her hands. "Your welcome Anilea," Roselyn smiled at Sanna. "Hey Anilea, smile at lest, and if anything you have on your chest that you need to tell us. This is the time to tell us," Roselyn told Sanna putting her right hand on Sanna left shoulder.

Sanna keep on drinking her hot chocolate in her hands, thinking on what Roselyn told her a few minutes ago. Sanna handed an empty cup to Roselyn, Roselyn take the cup in her hands, and held the cup in her hands. Sanna sigh a bit, looking down in front for her, Sanna hair falls in front of her face, and spoke softly, "Roselyn, there is something I need tell you guys that I been hiding from you for years." Sanna hop off the railing onto the floor, and slowly walk pass everyone to her bedroom.

Roselyn stop Sanna before Sanna enter the bedroom, "What is it that you been hiding from us?" Roselyn ask Sanna watching Sanna walking by her.

Sanna stop in front of the French doors, putting her hands on the doorframe, lower her head, and spoke to Roselyn, "I will tell you guys in due time." Sanna drop her hands to her side and walking into her bedroom. Roselyn, Tiffany, Andrew, and Aaron look at each other with a confused look on their faces. What is that Sanna hiding from them? Time will only tell what ahead for everyone.

CHAPTER FIFTEEN

More Trouble & Christmas!

All through the month of November, trouble growing in the town, people went missing all over the place. Children and adult went missing during the night, Sanna started to be piss-off more ever time she heard or read in the newspaper about another person gone missing. Sanna started to realize that Donovan was making this battle personal, by doing any thing to get into Sanna mind. Sanna was not letting Donovan get to her to weaken her for the battle.

On November 20/ 2014 at night, Sanna was sitting down on the loveseat in front of the fireplace. Sanna sat there on the couch lending forward toward the fireplace with the newspaper in her hands. The light from the flames in the fireplace lit the small area around Sanna. Sanna look down at the newspaper reading the headline on the front page. Sanna started to get angry, her body started to glow white, and looking at the countdown in the upper right corner. "The time is counting down to our battle, and when that day comes you will die for good," Sanna told herself with rage coming all over her body. Sanna stood up quickly from the loveseat with a white glow around her body. Sanna rage built inside of her, that Sanna throw the newspaper in the fireplace with one quick swipe. Sanna throw her head back, arms out to the side, and scream loudly that the white light explored outwards from Sanna. The windows in the living room and dinning room lighting up quickly with the white light, and slowly disappear to nothing. Sanna put her hands on the fireplace shelf, looking down at the flames of the fire flicking, and Sanna started to breath heavily.

Roselyn enter the living and dinning room, staring at Sanna actions, and started to worry about Sanna health. Roselyn slowly walks up behind Sanna, lending against the back of the love seat, and stared at the back of Sanna, "How it going?" Roselyn ask Sanna trying to keep Sanna calm down.

Sanna keep on looking down at the flames of the fire dancing slowly. "I feel like I fail already..." Sanna bang her right fist against the shelf with rage. "I just want to die now, so I don't have to fight Donovan later on next year," Sanna started to weep with tears filling her eyes, and falling to the floor. "I am a failed," Sanna whisper looking down still at the fire.

Roselyn shook her head slowly at Sanna, and spoke to Sanna hoping that it will help Sanna get out of the hole, "Anilea, you're not a failed... You never fail at anything, and you are not starting now... You are Anilea, the best warrior spirit to set foot in the human world, and a damn good one too... In addition, Donovan knows that he going to piss you off good, just to get in your mind. Therefore, you will be weak for him at then time... You are stronger then Donovan," Roselyn stood up straight from the loveseat.

Sanna lifted her head up, took her hands off the shelf, and stood up straight. "Your right Roselyn... I am Anilea, the white warrior spirit, that going to kick Donovan ass for good," Sanna spoke turning around to looks at Roselyn.

Roselyn walks around the loveseat, stood in front of Sanna, putting both of her hands on Sanna shoulders, looking into Sanna eyes, and say in a proud voice, "Don't forget who you are, and you still have us, your friends... Moreover, whatever you been hiding from us, you need to tell us before that battle next year, so you can force against Donovan."

Sanna took a deep breath through her nose, letting it out through her nose, and move away Roselyn, Sanna sat down on the loveseat, looking at the fire, and keeping her mouth shut. Roselyn sat down beside Sanna on the left side on the loveseat, and looking at Sanna. Sanna slowly speech to Roselyn, "Roselyn, the truth is..." Sanna had a flashback to her past of the final battle during the Dark Ages. Sanna could hear the screams of children, men, women, and the cries of babies in their mother's arms running away. The town swallow by huge flames of fire, and human blood all over the place. Then image of die bodies lying all over the place with their blood dripping to the ground. Sanna could see her two past friends been killed in front of her by Donovan hands. Sanna quickly cover her ears with her hands, and rocking back and forward on the loveseat, "Make it stop! MAKE IT STOP!" Sanna yelled in fear.

Roselyn put her right hand on Sanna back, her left hand on Sanna left lower arm, and spoke to Sanna in a worry voice, "What wrong Anilea? What going on?" Roselyn try to calm Sanna down, before Sanna can hurt herself.

Sanna tilt her head back, screaming loudly in the air and calm down slowly. Sanna lower her hands onto her lap, and try to breathe normal. Sanna look at Roselyn for a moment with wide-eyes and sadly spoke to Roselyn, "I do not want to lose you guys like them." Sanna calm down for Roselyn, but had a bad feeling about she has to tell Roselyn next.

"What do you mean like them? Do you mean your family, friends, and lover almost 400 years ago?" Roselyn ask Sanna, a raise eyebrow to Sanna.

Sanna took a deep breathe, signal Roselyn closer to her, and told Roselyn in a whisper, "You need to promise me that you would not tell anyone, once I tell you?" Roselyn nodded her head to Sanna. "Good… Here we go then," Sanna started to talk to Roselyn, snow started to fall outside the windows, making a light cover of snow on the ground.

~~*~*~*~*~*~*~*~*

December month came around, and Christmas was around the corner. Sanna was shovelling the sidewalks and driveway in a warm winter coat, two pairs of mittens, serf, ski pants, and winter hat that cover her ears. Sanna almost finish the last bit of shovelling on the driveway, when a snowball hit her behind her head. Sanna turn around to see who throw the snowball, and saw no one around. Sanna went back to shovelling the rest of the driveway, when another snowball hit her in the back, Sanna turn around to see, and again no one there. Sanna finish shovelling when she peak around the snow pile to see Adam crouching down by the snow pile, with a snowball in his hands. Sanna had an idea, she sneak to where Adam was with the shovel, putting the shovel on top of the snow pile, and push the snow down pile onto Adam.

Adam jump up quickly trying to get the snow out of his coat. "Oh cold… Cold," Adam say dancing on the spot. Sanna giggle at the sight of Adam funny dancing, Adam got the rest of the snow out of his coat, and turn around to Sanna, "You think that was funny?" Adam says to Sanna, fixing his coat.

Sanna just laughing at Adam, and nod her head. "Yes," Sanna say through her laughing.

Adam walks over the snow pile to Sanna, stood in front of Sanna, and say to Sanna in a slid voice, "Once Christmas is over, I will have my revenge on you for that trick."

Sanna chuckled at Adam, and told Adam the truth, "You know, you start it by throwing those snowballs at me first, we are even," Sanna stood there in the driveway, shovel in her right hand.

Adam nodded his head to agree with Sanna, "Your right, but it was funny trick to do on you." Adam walk closer to Sanna, taking the shovel from Sanna right hand, putting the shovel in the snow pile, and putting his arms around Sanna. "I love you so much, I could not wait for Christmas," Adam told Sanna in his arms.

Sanna look up at Adam, and smile at Adam, "I love you so much too, and I cannot wait for Christmas too," Sanna told Adam in his arms.

"I know my parents are coming down to visit, and to meet to you finally, my mom cannot wait to meet you. I been telling them about you, and they are so happy to meet you," Adam told Sanna with a big smile on his face.

"Yeah," Sanna say sadly to Adam. Sanna move out of Adam arms, turning her back on Adam, and starting to sob.

Adam walks up behind Sanna, and asks in a worry voice, "What wrong?"

Sanna turn around to Adam, and sadly say to Adam, "Your parents are coming down to meet me."

"Yeah, they want too," Adam told Sanna in a confused voice.

"That why I am sad, because I have no parents, and what if your parents want to meet my parents. My parents are died," Sanna started to cry with tears flowing from her eyes.

Adam wipes up the tears from Sanna face, and looks into Sanna eyes, "Don't cry, you will freeze that pretty face of yours, and don't worry about that. I told my parents want happen to you three years ago. They understand what you went through, and they would not bring it up around you." Adam hugs Sanna, and held Sanna closer to his chest. Adam look down at Sanna, Sanna look up at Adam, and Adam ask Sanna, "Do you want to go inside to have some hot chocolate?" Sanna nodded her head in Adam arms, moving out of Adam arms, and walks to the house with Adam behind her with the shovel in Adam hands.

~~*~*~*~*~*~*~*~*~*

Christmas day arrives, the ground was cover with a white blanket of snow, the top of the trees was cover with snow, and the lake frozen over with a thick ice. Sanna look out from her French door at the scenery, and sigh at a thought she had. It was in the late afternoon, everyone was getting ready for some guests and getting dress up in their nice clothes. Sanna stood in the front of her French doors wearing a dark red full-length dress with green lace over top the dress and down Sanna arms creating sleeves. A red belt with a couple holiday berries on the right side separated the dress. Sanna hair was down with her curls doing down her back, the bangs was pull back, and clip in the back of her head with a clip with white Christmas flowers on it. Sanna walk over to the end of her bed, and slipping on her black flat shoes. Sanna walk over to her window seat, sitting down on the seat, moving the curtain away a bit, and looking outside. Sanna could see Adam and his parents walking up to the house with a few gifts in their hands. Sanna move the curtain back in front of the window, got off the seat, and walking up to mirror over the make-up table. Sanna fix her hair a bit more, she heard the doorbell rang from downstairs, and looking at herself in the mirror, "Show time," Sanna told herself, walking out of her room, and down the stairs.

Outside Adam was talking to his parents, "Remember what I told you two about Sanna," Adam told his parents ring the doorbell.

"We know not to bring up anything about her parents or the scar on her arm. We know, we know," Adam dad, Tommy, holding a few gifts in his arms.

"Honey calm down, Adam is only worry about Sanna feelings that all, and I think it is cute that he worry about her," say Adam mom, Tess, holding a couple of gifts in her arms.

"Okay then," say Tommy passing Adam a couple of gifts.

The front door open, and Andrew stood there in the doorway wearing a red long sleeve shirt with black pants and shoes, and a green tie. "Welcome to our home, come inside," Andrew greeted Adam family. Adam parents and Adam walks inside the house, and Andrew closed the door behind them. "I can take those gifts from you," Andrew says taking the gifts from Tess arms.

"Thank-you," say Tess to Andrew taking off her coat, and holding her coat in her hands.

Aaron wearing a green long sleeve shirt with black pants and shoes, and a red tie, walks up to Tommy, and say nicely, "I can take those gifts from you." Aaron took the gifts from Tommy and Adam arms. Andrew and Aaron walks into the living room with gifts in their arms.

"Thank-you," Tommy says to Andrew taking off his coat. Adam and his parents hang their coats on the hanger by the door, and walking off the mat by the door with clean shoes on.

Roselyn and Tiffany stood by the stairs in their Christmas dresses; Roselyn wearing a red knee-length dress with short sleeves and a green belt around her waist. Tiffany wearing a green knee-length dresses with short sleeves and a red belt around her waist. Both wore black shoes, and their hairs was done up nice. "Welcome to our home," Roselyn greeted nicely to Adam family.

"Thank-you, I am mother, Tess," Tess greeted Roselyn and Tiffany, wearing a Christmas flower pattern dress knee-length with black shoes. Tess hair was blonde with a few grey hairs in-between, and shoulder length that pull back into a bun.

"Thank-you, I'm Adam dad, Tommy," Tommy greeted Roselyn and Tiffany, wearing a green and red long sleeve shirt with black pants and shoes. Tommy hair was blonde with a few grey hairs in-between, and short length.

Adam look at his parents, and spoke nicely to them, "Mom, dad, this Roselyn and Tiffany," Adam introduction his parents to Roselyn and Tiffany.

"Nice to meet you both," say Tommy to the girls shaking Roselyn and Tiffany hands. Tess follows behind Tommy shaking hands with Roselyn and Tiffany.

Andrew and Aaron came into the entryway, empty arms. Adam introduction them to his parents, "Mom, dad, this is Aaron and Andrew; Roselyn and Tiffany husbands."

"Nice to meet you both," Tommy say shaking Aaron and Andrew hands. Tess follows behind Tommy shaking hands with Andrew and Aaron.

Sanna slowly came downstairs in her dress, and looking at Adam parents shaking everyone hands. Sanna try to stay calm, but she was so nervous to meet Adam parents for the first time. Sanna was a few steps away, when Adam saw Sanna coming downstairs, Adam tips both his parents on their shoulders with his finger, and pointing to Sanna. "Mom, dad, this is Sanna, my beautiful girlfriend," Adam say to his parents walking to the stairs, and holding out his left hand to Sanna.

Sanna took Adam left hand in her right hand, and walking down the last few stairs with a smile on her face. Sanna stood in front of Adam parents with her right hand in Adam left hand. "Hello," Sanna greeted Adam parents.

Tommy and Tess looks over Sanna, and Tess spoke to Sanna, "Hello Sanna, I am Tess and this is my husband Tommy. We are Adam parents, and we are so happy to meet you in person. Adam been telling us all about you, and we had to meet you." Tess hugs Sanna, and Tommy hug Sanna too.

Sanna stood there quietly for a moment, and spoke sweetly to Adam parents, "I am so happy to meet you too. Adam has been telling me about you two a lot. It is so nice to meet you, welcome to our house," Sanna smile at Adam parents.

Roselyn say to the rest of them, "Let's go into the living room, and talks some more," Roselyn signal everyone into the living room.

Everyone enter the living room chatting, and found a place to sit down. The living room decorated with Christmas stuff, the large pine tree was along the wall in front of the fireplace. The fireplace lit as the smell of wood burning fill the air. The stereo was playing Christmas songs on low, and the tree lit with white lights. Decorations on the tree tickled and shine was they slowly move with the air moving around the room. The angel holding a small gold rose in her hands, and she look closely to Sanna in looks. Roselyn getting up from a chair, and ask everyone in the room if they would like anything to drink, "Would you like anything to drinks?"

Tommy looks at Roselyn, and says nicely, "Sure some punch for my lovely wife and I. Adam, Sanna, what will you like to drink?"

"Some water sound nice for us," Adam says to Roselyn nicely.

"Some punch sound nice my dear for the three of us," Andrew say to Roselyn nicely.

Sanna got up from the couch slowly, "Roselyn, I can give you a hand with those drinks," Sanna say walking up to Roselyn.

"Sure Sanna," Roselyn say to Sanna heading to the kitchen to get the drink for everyone.

In the kitchen, Sanna and Roselyn were getting the drinks together for everyone. Sanna was pouring the punch in some glasses, when Roselyn whisper, "What do you think of Adam parents?"

Sanna finish pouring the punch in the glasses, and whisper, "I like them a lot, and I think they like me too, but the night is early to tell. Right now, I am trying to stay calm around them, and not let my nervous get to me," Sanna grabbing a few glasses in her hands.

"Will be easy on those nervous, I don't want to be the one picking you off the floor," Roselyn say to Sanna grabbing a few glasses in her hands. Sanna laugh at Roselyn entering through the dinning room archway to the living room. Roselyn laugh at Sanna, following Sanna into the living room.

When Roselyn and Sanna arrive back into the living room, everyone was walking around the room, and talking about a few things. Roselyn walks up to the men by the fireplace, passing out the glasses to them, went back to the kitchen to grab her glass of punch. Sanna walks up to Tess and Tiffany with the glasses in her hands, passing the glasses to them, by the Christmas tree. Sanna stood there holding her glass of water, and seeing Roselyn walking up to them. Sanna took a slip from her glass, and listen to the chatting between Tiffany and Tess. "This is the most beautiful Christmas trees, I have ever seen, so shiny and elegant, where did you pick up the ornaments?" Tess asks Tiffany looking over the ornaments on the tree closely.

Tiffany smile at Tess, and proudly told Tess where the ornaments came from, "They are hand-made by Sanna, she very creative on this stuff. In addition, Sanna love to decorate for Christmas, mostly the Christmas tree."

Tess looks at Sanna with a surprise look on her face, and spoke with a smile on her face, "You made all of these ornaments by hand. Wow, very creative, and they must take a lot of time to make each one by hand?"

"Thank-you and yes they took along time, about a day to three days to do. The angel took me a month to do, she was hard to make by hand. So many detail to put on, but in the end she turn out beautiful," Sanna looking up at the angel on top of the tree, looking down at Tess and Tiffany.

Adam walks up to the women, putting his arms around Sanna waist, and his head on Sanna left shoulder. "What are you, ladies, chatting about?" Adam asks Sanna looking at the tree, and all the ornaments on the tree too.

Sanna looks up at the angel keeping her eyes on the angel, and say to Adam, "Your mom was asking us where we got our ornaments from."

Adam spoke to Sanna, looking over Sanna left shoulder, "Yeah, where did you get them?" Adam keeps his arms around Sanna waist, and laying his chin on her shoulder.

Sanna looks at Adam, and spoke nicely, "I made them, include the angel on top of the tree," giving Adam a kiss on the right cheek.

Adam smile at Sanna, kiss Sanna on the left cheek, lifted his head off Sanna shoulder, and stood there with Sanna in his arms. "Your so creative, they look so beautiful, but not as beautiful as you look this evening," Adam told Sanna, and looking up at the angel. Adam raise an eyebrow with a thought in his mind, then ask Sanna a question about the angel, "The angel look so much like you. Did you mean to do that?"

Sanna looks back at Adam, and say, "Maybe, she took a month to make. She so beautiful that way I made her," Sanna looks back at the angel, knowing why she made that angel that way.

Around 6 o'clock in the evening, Roselyn and Tiffany started to set the dinning table with food. Everyone walks up to the table and sitting down on the chairs around the table. Sanna and Adam sat next to each other with their backs to the window, Adam parents sat across from Sanna and Adam. Aaron sat down next to Adam on the left side; Tiffany sat at the head of the table between Aaron and Tommy. Andrew sat down beside Tess on the left side, and Roselyn sat down at the other head of the table between Andrew and Sanna. Everyone looks over the food on the table. The turkey was cook to a golden-brown, potatoes was bake prefect, vegetates was cook very nicely with butter mix in, and stuffing was so good looking. Tommy mouth was watering at the sight of all the food on the table. "Let's dig in, before everything get too cold," Roselyn say to everyone, and start to pass the food around the table.

Andrew craved the turkey, passing out the meat to everyone, and sat down after the last person was service. "Roselyn, everything is great my dear. You're the master of cooking," Andrew says to Roselyn scooping a spoon full of vegetates, and putting the spoon full on his plate.

"Why thank-you Andrew, but I had help Tiffany and Sanna. You have to see what Sanna made for dessert, it looks so good," Roselyn say to Andrew starting to eat.

Andrew looks over at Tiffany and Sanna, and spoke happy, "Thank-you two for helping making supper. Everything is awesome," Andrew took a bite of food, and smile happy.

Everyone enjoy eating the food, talking about his or her jobs, and a few things. Tess looks over at Sanna, and asks Sanna a question, "So Sanna, do you have a job?" picking up a bit of food on her fork, and about to eat it slowly.

Sanna shallow the food in her mouth, and spoke nicely, "No, I don't have a job, but I do sell a few of my artworks for some cash." Sanna felt wrong about telling Adam parents the truth about her not having a job, but more what her real job and who she is really as a white spirit.

Tess sat back in her chair, looking at Sanna, and spoke to Sanna, "I see, you don't want a job in this town."

Sanna shook her head, and spoke nicely to Tess, "I am saving my money to open as artwork shop in town, but the time is not right. In addition, I do not have very much money to opened, also it depend on my friends jobs. I like to travel with them, we stick together like family, and I like to stick with my family. My friends here helping me through the hardest parts of life, and I cannot abandon them."

Tess was surprise of Sanna, and what Sanna saying to her, and says to Sanna nicely, "I see, I think this town need a shop like that. In addition, if you decide to open that store maybe Adam can sell some of his music there too. I think that will be cute of you two working together in one build," Tess pointing to Sanna and Adam together.

Adam and Sanna looks at each other, blushing in the cheeks, and quickly looking away from each other. Sanna mind was going wild, *'Anilea what are you thinking telling Adam mom that... opening an artwork store... Yeah right... how can you open a store once you leave the town for good...Yeah maybe in another 100 years I will open one, but now not a good time or maybe never... It depends on this battle next year, and if I will survive the fight... I want to be with Adam forever, but it will hurt to his heart. When the time comes, I wish that I can tell truth to Adam to end this hurt inside of me,'* Sanna finish eating her food, along with everyone, and sitting there quietly now.

Roselyn, Tiffany, Tess, and Sanna cleaning up the table, and get everything ready for dessert. Roselyn and Tiffany bought in the small plates out to the dinning area, Tess went back to her spot at the dinning table, and Sanna brought in the dessert of chocolate Christmas cake. Sanna put the cake down on the table, started to cutting the cake, and service the cake around the table. Sanna grab her piece of cake and sitting down in her spot beside Adam. Tommy took a bite of the cake, and surprise at the taste of the cake. "Sanna this is the best Christmas cake I have ever have in my years, "Tommy told Sanna smiling.

Tess was surprise at the taste too, and asking Sanna, "I must have this recipe for this cake. The favours are so good well blend into the chocolate and moist too. Sanna, you need to tell me your secret to this great cake," Tess holding a fork full of cake.

Sanna nodded her head to Tess, and say nicely, "Sure I can type-up the recipe for you, but I am going to warn you it take along time, and whole a lot of calm to make this cake." Sanna taking a bite of her cake piece, sitting there in her chair quietly, and try to keep herself calm around Adam parents.

After dessert was over, the cake was all gone. Tommy, Aaron, Andrew, and Adam land back in their chairs rubbing their stomach with their hands. "Sanna, my dear, which was the best food I have ever tasted. I am so stuff, that I can go have a small nap before gift time," Tommy told Sanna with a smile on his face.

Roselyn look over at Tommy, and say nicely, "Tommy if you want a nap. You can have one, there no problem with that, beside us girls need to clean up the kitchen. So if you men want a nap, you can," Roselyn stood up from the table with a small pile of plates in her hands.

Everyone stood up from the table, the men whet to the couches to have a nap, and the women headed to the kitchen to clean up from supper. Sanna grabbing the dishes from the table, headed into the kitchen with hands full of dirty dishes, and set the dirty dishes by the sink. Roselyn had her hands in the dishwater, Tess drying the dishes, and Tiffany put the clean dishes away in their places. Sanna walk over to the front of inland, lend against the inland watching everyone clean up, and start to worry about next year after the battle. *'What will life be like after May 20? Will there still be a Christmas or any holidays? What about life after the fight next year? Will everyone be able to survivor after the fight? I still wish I had all the answers for once... Why my real lives have to stay hiding from everyone? I wonder what will happen if I tell Adam the truth? He will proudly be angry at me for not telling the truth,'* Sanna thought to herself.

Once the women done cleaning the kitchen, they headed back into the living room to meet up with the men. The women arrive into the living room to see the men sleeping on the couches and chairs. Aaron and Andrew was sleeping on the chairs, Tommy on the north wall couch, and Adam on the east wall couch. Roselyn and Tiffany walks up to Andrew and Aaron, lend over the men, and kiss them on the lips. Tess walks over to Tommy, lend over Tommy, and kiss him on the lips. Sanna walks over to Adam, looking down at Adam with love in her eyes, lend down over Adam, and kiss Adam on the right cheek. The men eyes start to stir slowly open up to see the women over top of them, and return the kiss to their woman. Adam looks at Sanna with a smile on his face, and spoke sweetly to Sanna, "Hey is it gift time?" Adam rubs his eyes with his hands.

Sanna spoke sweetly back to Adam, "Of course Adam," Sanna slowly walk to the Christmas tree, and sat down on the floor by the tree.

Everyone walks over to the tree, taking a seat in the spots in front of the tree/ Sanna start passing out the gifts to everyone, and watch everyone starting to open their gifts. Joy fills the room with smile, laughter, and talking. People thanking other people for the gifts, Sanna thanks Roselyn for a glass fingering of a young woman riding a white horse. Adam handles Sanna the last gift, a small box with a gold bow on top, Sanna look and whisper, "What is it?"

Adam whisper in Sanna right ear, "You have to opened it?' Adam lend back from Sanna for a bit. Sanna open the box, the hinges move, the top swing opened, and Sanna eyes grow big at the sight of the gift.

Chapter Sixteen

Christmas, New Year, and V-Day Surprise!

"Sanna, what is it?" Tiffany asks Sanna wondering what Adam gave Sanna that made Sanna eyes grow bigger.

Sanna looks down at the gift, taking her right hand, and slowly taking out a white and yellow gold necklace with two hearts twisted together in the middle with two small diamonds in the hearts. Sanna looks over at Adam, and happy spoke to Adam, "Adam, this pretty awesome necklace, I love it," she looking at the two hearts, a yellow gold and a white gold. "Can you help me put the necklace on?" Sanna handled the necklace out to Adam, turn her back to Adam, and lifting up her hair. Adam unclips the necklace hooks, putting the neck around Sanna neck, and hooking the hooks back up. Sanna turn around to Adam, putting her left hand on the hearts, and looks at Adam. "I love it Adam, thank-you so much," Sanna hug Adam.

Adam whisper in Sanna left ear in his arms, "Your welcome sweetheart," Adam held Sanna longer in his arms.

Sanna move out of Adam arms, sat there on the floor looking at Roselyn, Tiffany, Aaron, Andrew, Tess, and Tommy, sigh with relief. Tommy stood up from the chair with a glass in his right hand, raising his glass up in the air, and say, "I will like to make a toast." Everyone grab their glasses, and raise the glasses up in the air. Tommy keep on speaking, "I like to make a toast to new friends, and family. To all those people who have missing family, that those people will return home safe and sound. Cheers to that," everyone touch each other glasses together.

Sanna sat on the floor by the tree thinking, *'I want those missing people home ... In addition, I want Donovan die for doing that to this town... Donovan, you better is ready to take me on in May, because I am piss-off big time.'* Sanna curling her fingers together into a tight fist, and lower her head to the floor.

Roselyn watch Sanna actions, lend over to Sanna, and whisper in Sanna right ear, "Calm down Anilea... You do not want Adam and his parents to find out that you are a spirit if you glow white... Calm down."

Sanna turn her head to Roselyn, and whisper to Roselyn, "Sorry, I am just piss-off, because of the whole missing people around town... I just want to go after Donovan now," she trying to calm down around everyone.

"Not right now... You need to keep your strength for the battle in May... We do not want you to die... You need to keep your angry under control for a bit, then in May you can go full force on Donovan," Roselyn spoke to Sanna in a whisper, trying to keep Sanna calm down enough.

Sanna took a few deep breathes, and slowly calm down for Roselyn. "Thanks Roselyn, I own you one," Sanna say to Roselyn after calming down.

"You're welcome Anilea," Roselyn say to Sanna sitting back in her chair.

Sanna stood up from the floor, fixing her dress, and looking at Tess and Tommy. "Tess, Tommy, I will like you to choose one ornament each from the tree," Sanna say to Adam parents in a nice voice.

Tess and Tommy stood up from their spots, looking at Sanna, and Tess asks Sanna with a confused voice, "Are you sure Sanna? They look lovely and we don't want to take away from the beautifulness of the tree."

"It is okay, I can always make new once next year," Sanna told Tess nicely with a smile on her face.

Tommy and Tess walks up to the tree, looking over the ornaments, and picking one each. Tess chose a little teddy bear holding a small doll in it paws, and Tommy chose a little drummer boy playing it small drum. They both look down at the ornaments in their hands, and looks over at Sanna. "Thank-you Sanna for these wonderful gifts," Tess says to Sanna with a big smile on her face, Sanna smile at Tess nicely.

Tommy spoke kindly to Sanna, "Thanks Sanna for letting us choosing one of these beautiful ornaments," Tommy looking down a small drummer boy on in his hands.

Sanna smile at Tommy, and spoke sweetly to them, "Thank-you both for coming here, and spending time with my friends and me."

Everyone got up from theirs spots around the tree, moving over the couches, and starting to talk. Adam and Sanna sat down on the loveseat in front of the fireplace; Adam put his arm around Sanna shoulders, and pulling Sanna closer to him. Sanna put her head down on Adam right shoulder, and looks at the fire in the fireplace. Adam kisses Sanna on top of her head, and spoke softly to Sanna, "I love you Sanna, and thanks for doing that for my parents."

"Your welcome Adam and I love you too," Sanna, say to Adam, looking up at Adam into his eyes. Sanna heart started to beating faster, her body start to shake with nervous, and Sanna feeling want crazy. Something inside Sanna say to kiss Adam on the lips, Sanna kiss Adam right cheek, sitting back in Adam arms, and watches the flames dancing in the fireplace.

Sanna watch the flame moving around the wood, an image came in the flames that scare Sanna. Sanna saw blood all over the town, bodies laying along the streets, Donovan group killing people, and Donovan laughing loudly over a died body. Sanna looking closer into the flames, and seeing died body was her. Her blood on Donovan hands, and pouring out of her body from the wounds in her chest. Sanna quickly flick with terror in her eyes, her face went white quickly. Fear came over Sanna; she could not believe the image that came to her in the flames. Sanna did not scream, but sat there on the loveseat in Adam arms with terror running through her blood. Adam looks over at Sanna, and spoke in a worry voice, "What wrong sweetheart? Are you feeling all right? You look so pale looking," Adam put both arms around Sanna shoulders, and held Sanna close to his body.

Sanna did not say a single word to Adam at first; she could not shake that image out of her head. "The blood," Sanna spoke softly, keeping her eyes on the image in the flames of the fireplace.

"What are you talking about… the blood?" Adam was confused with what Sanna was saying.

"The blood… my blood… All over the place," Sanna spoke again with fear in her voice, and her eyes widened.

Adam put both hands on Sanna shoulders, turn Sanna around to face him, and again ask Sanna with a stun voice, "What do you mean the blood? Why you're own blood?" Adam looks into Sanna eyes to find out what going on with Sanna. Why Sanna was acting this way?

Roselyn, Andrew, Tiffany, and Aaron watching Sanna actions in front of Adam, and stand up quietly from their spots from the couches. Roselyn and Tiffany walk quietly to Sanna by the fireplace, and put their hands on Sanna shoulders. "Excess us Adam, we know how to deal with this," Roselyn say to Adam. Adam took his hands off Sanna shoulders, stood up from the loveseat, and walks quietly to the couches under the east window. Adam walks pass Sanna slowly, could not take his eyes off Sanna as he walking by Sanna.

Roselyn waited for Adam to sit down on the couch before dealing with Sanna. Roselyn turn her attention back to Sanna. Roselyn sat down on the loveseat, looking at Sanna sitting there on the seat with a blank look on her face. Roselyn spoke in a whisper to Sanna, "Anilea what wrong? Why are you acting this way?"

Sanna slowly move her mouth, and spoke quietly to Roselyn, "I don't want to talk about it right now. Not with Adam and his parents here… I had an image… I will tell you two later," Sanna started to calm down around Roselyn and Tiffany, and taking a few deep breaths to help calm down.

Adam sat there on the couch with his parents beside him, just staring at Sanna with Roselyn and Tiffany talking on the loveseat. Tommy lends over to Adam, and asks in a whisper, "What happen over there?"

Adam shaking his head slowly, and says quietly, "I have no idea. I never have seen Sanna act this way before… I think it was something from her past that is still bugging her. Maybe from her wedding day three years ago, that is the only thing I can think of that will cause Sanna to act like that." Adam just watches Roselyn and Tiffany talking to Sanna, Adam heart sunk in his chest for Sanna feelings.

Sanna nodded to Roselyn and Tiffany, got up from her spot on the loveseat, walks up to Adam and the rest of them, and apologize to them for her actions, "I am sorry for the way, I was acting. It was something that came to me that scares me, I am sorry."

Tommy stood up from his spot on the couch, and spoke fro everyone, "We understand you, Sanna. It is proudly something from your past that is still haunting you, maybe something from your wedding day," Tommy nodded his head to Sanna.

Sanna stood there in shock that Tommy say that, and did not knowing the truth about her. Sanna started to calm down quickly, in front of everyone, and spoke kindly to him or her, "Your right Tommy about my wedding day, it been haunting me for a long time that I cannot let it goes. Thanks for that Tommy," Sanna walks to Tommy, and gave him a hug.

The rest of the night went off without any more problems. They play some games, and have a few good laughs at the way Aaron and Andrew trying to play 'Twister'. Aaron and Andrew were so twist together, that they could not reach any more, and end up falling on top each other. Roselyn and Tiffany laugh the loudly at the sight of the boys on top each other, and helping the boys off the floor. The best game of 'Twister' was Sanna, who change into a jeans and t-shirt, and Adam. Adam looks up at Sanna with his body twisted up good, and spoke with a chuckled, "Are you going to give up Sanna?"

Sanna looks at Adam right in his face, and say with a challenge in her voice, "Nope, you?" Sanna was twist up around Adam.

"Nope, I was wondering," Adam try to hold his body up, but could not hold on very longer, and fell slowly to the floor.

Sanna stood up quickly on her feet, arms in the air in victory, and held out her right hand to Adam. "Champ of Twister," Sanna say to everyone, and look at Adam, "Want to play again?"

Adam grab Sanna right hand with his left hand, Sanna pulled Adam to his feet, and Adam say to Sanna nicely, "Not right now, maybe later." Adam held Sanna hand longer, and stared into her eyes, "You look so lovely this evening," Adam whisper to Sanna, and moving in for a kiss on the lips.

Sanna turn her head to the right, Adam kiss Sanna on the right cheek, and sigh. "Adam, please not now. I don't want to kiss on my lips yet," Sanna whisper to Adam still having her head turn to the right side.

Adam looks at Sanna with a worry look on his face, "Are you okay sweetly?"

Sanna nodded her head to Adam, and spoke in whisper, "Yeah, it was just..."

"You're not ready to kiss on lips, that okay then I don't mind waiting," Adam spoke to Sanna in a whisper.

Sanna turn her head back to Adam, and smile at Adam, "Thanks Adam," Sanna say to Adam, and giving Adam a hug.

"You're welcome," Adam says to Sanna, hugging Sanna.

Sanna laid her head on Adam chest, Sanna can hear Adam heart beating, and a thought came to her mind, *'What will I do now?... Adam heart is beating for me. What will happen if Donovan use Adam against me or worse killed Adam in front me? I wish there something I can do to keep Adam safe from Donovan and his group... I wish.'* Sanna listen to Adam heart beating more for her love.

It came time for Adam and his parents to leave for the evening. Adam let go of Sanna, kiss Sanna on top of her head, saying his good-bye to Sanna, and left he house with his parents. Sanna watch from the living room window on the east wall, Adam and his parents walking away, and Sanna heart sunk in her chest. Roselyn, Tiffany, Aaron, and Andrew walks up behind Sanna and Andrew ask Sanna, "Hey sport, are you alright?"

Sanna took a deep breathe, and spoke to her friends with her back to them, "Yeah I am okay, it just that I heard Adam heart beating for me, and it may me think on a few things."

"Like what?" Aaron asks Sanna.

Sanna lower her head for a moment, lifting her head up straight with narrow eyes, and spoke in a ragging voice, "That if Donovan or his group hurt Adam, I will kill them on the spot, but…" Sanna calm down to speak normal, "How keep Adam safe from Donovan, and there one way. It is the only way I know to do to keep Adam safe from Donovan without hurting him."

Roselyn and Tiffany know what Sanna was thinking. "Sanna, you're not thinking of?" Tiffany says to Sanna with a shock voice.

Sanna turn around to her friends, and slowly answer Tiffany question, "Break-up with Adam. Not right now, but later."

~~*~*~*~*~*~*~*~*~*

New Year eve, Sanna was over at Adam place for New Year party with Adam friend and her friends. It was a fun time playing games for hours, watching movies, listening to music, and throwing a few pranks on each other, just small pranks and playing nice with each other all night. Adam was arm-wrestling Jay over the last piece of cake. They were eyeing each other over the table, and putting everything they got in their arms. Jay looks at Adam, and say to Adam, "Your not going to win, that piece of cake is my," Jay pushing against Adam arm.

Adam laughs a bit, and told Jay, "Nope, that piece of cake is my," Adam pushing against Jay arm.

Adam and Jay was arm-wrestling for the last piece of cake, Jay girlfriend came up the cake, and took the last piece of the cake without the boys knowing that it was gone. Jay slam Adam arm down onto the table, "Winner!" Jay jump up in victory, and look at the empty cake plate. "Hey where the last pieces of cake go?" Jay was confused where the cake piece went.

Sanna walking up to the table, and told Jay, "Your girlfriend took the cake along time ago." Sanna walks up to Adam and start to rub Adam shoulders with her hands.

Jay turns to his girlfriend, who was sitting on the couch eating the piece of cake. "Aw man, I was looking forward for that piece of cake," Jay says with a pouting look on his face.

"How many pieces of cake did you have?" Sanna ask Jay, still rubbing Adam shoulders with her hands.

"Three," Jay told Sanna holding up three fingers to Sanna face.

Sanna stop rubbing Adam shoulders, looking down at Adam head, and asking Adam, "How many pieces of cake did you have?"

Adam tilts his head back to see Sanna, and say, "Two pieces, and that it."

"Then why were you two arm wrestling for the last piece then, if you two have enough," Sanna ask Adam and Jay with a raise eyebrow to them.

"Because you made it sweetheart," Adam says to Sanna with a smiled on his face.

Sanna tap Adam right cheek with her right hand, and spoke, "Your such a tit, Adam, but I still love you," Sanna kiss Adam forehead, and left Adam and Jay for a bit.

A few minute to midnight, Dave called everyone downstairs in the basement to watch the countdown on the big screen TV. Everyone enter the basement and stand in front of the TV to watch the countdown. "Ready everyone," Dave say to everyone getting ready for the countdown.

"Ten!" Sanna stood by Adam watching the countdown.

"Nine!" Sanna watch the ball on the TV slowly moving down.

"Eight!" Sanna felt Adam arm around her shoulders.

"Seven!" Sanna took a deep breathe.

"Six!" Sanna let out her breathe.

"Five!" Sanna know it was half-way there to the New Year.

"Four!" The battle date is coming soon.

"Three!" Sanna tighten her body.

"Two!" Nervousness set in with Sanna.

"One!" Sanna closed her eyes.

"HAPPY NEW YEAR!" Everyone cheer loudly, hugging each other, and kissing their girlfriends.

Adam lends over to Sanna, kissing her on the right cheeks, and whisper in Sanna right ear, "Happy New Year Sanna, I hope this year will go good for you." Adam let go of Sanna, and walking away.

Sanna stood there quietly, and spoke in a whisper, "Happy New Year to you too, Adam... I hope this year will be good too... I hope the chose I have to make here soon will not hurt our friendship." Sanna keep her eyes on Adam walking around the room, hugging, and talking to his friends. Sanna heart felt heavy inside of her chest knowing there no way Adam and she can be together.

February 14 came around and love was in the air, Aaron and Andrew surprise Roselyn and Tiffany with breakfast in bed and a lovely evening for two anywhere in town. Sanna woke to the sound of her alarm clock going off, she turn over, hitting the off button, and turn back over to sleep again. Sanna bedroom door open, Adam enter the room, Adam closed the door quietly behind him, and walking up to Sanna bed. Adam climb onto the right side of the bed, laying there looking at Sanna sleeping away peacefully, and move a piece of hair away from Sanna face with his hand. Sanna mourn a bit and slowly opening her eyes to see Adam lay beside her. "Morning," Sanna say in her sleepy voice.

"Morning my sweetheart, today is a lovely day to be in love with the most beautiful girl ever,"

Adam spoke to Sanna in a sweet voice.

"Aw, you're so sweet and handsome too, I love you," Sanna say to Adam stretching in her bed.

Adam sat up in the bed, looking down at Sanna laying in her bed, and spoke to Sanna, "You better get up, and ready for a big day today. I made plans for us," Adam got off the bed.

"What is it?" Sanna ask Adam getting out of the bed, and walking to her closet to get dress.

"I am not going to tell you anything. It is a surprise, just get dress normally for now, and later you need to put a dress on," Adam told Sanna lending against the door of the closet with his back.

"Is that hint for this evening?" Sanna ask Adam putting on a pair of jeans and pink t-shirt. Sanna exit the closet to see Adam standing there. "So is this alright for now?" Sanna turning around to show what she wearing to Adam.

Adam watches Sanna turning around in a circle, "You looks lovely always, and yes that prefect for now," Adam told Sanna leaving Sanna bedroom. Sanna quickly brush her hair, throwing it back into a ponytail, and leaving her room to follow Adam downstairs. Adam was putting on his coat, when Sanna came downstairs. "Grab your coat, we are going out for breakfast," Adam spoke to Sanna, watching her putting on her coat and shoes. Adam opened the door for Sanna, and let Sanna exit the house first closing the door behind him.

They walk to Adam car, Sanna got into the passenger side, and Adam got into the driver side. Adam started the car and drove to the little café, where they had lunch one time. "Adam this so nice of you," Sanna say to Adam as the car stop in front of the café.

"I know you would like it, beside the memories we had here after the museum trip," Adam say to Sanna shutting off the car. Sanna and Adam exit the car, walking up to the café, Adam held the door opened for Sanna, and Sanna enter the café. There were no other people in the café, just Sanna and Adam. They sat down at a small wooden table by the window, as an old grey hair woman came up to them. "Hello you two, it is nice to see you two lovebirds again," she spoke to Sanna and Adam in her sweet old voice.

"Hey granny, how it's going?" Adam asks the older woman. Everyone in town calls her granny, because she likes a grandma to everyone.

"Good Adam, so what can I get you two?" Granny asks them kindly.

"Ladies first," Adam say to Sanna nicely.

Sanna look over the menus and say to Granny, "I will have the waffle special with raspberries, banana, and whipping cream topping." Sanna smiled at Granny, "Plus a glass of water too, please."

Granny wrote down Sanna order, then looking at Adam. Adam spoke to Granny, "I will have the special too with the same toppings, and a glass of water too," Adam smiled at Granny.

Granny took down Adam order, and left the table. "Okay I will be back with your orders," Granny says to them.

Sanna looks at Adam, and whisper to him, "Copy cat," Sanna had a smiled on her face.

Adam shrugs his shoulders at Sanna, and smiling at Sanna. "Why did someone created Valentine day? I don't need a day to remind me that I love you very much with all my heart," Adam say to Sanna, holding Sanna right hand in his hand.

They stared into each other eyes and their hearts beating for each other. Granny came back with two glass of water, and their breakfast. "Enjoy you two," Granny say to them handing out the waffles to them, and left the table.

"Thanks Granny," Sanna and Adam yelled nicely to Granny.

Sanna look down at her waffles to see two-heart shape waffles with raspberries, banana, and whipping topping. Sanna shook her head at the plate, and starting to eat her food. "These are good," Sanna say to Adam after taking a bite of the waffles.

"I know that why I brought you here, to have some good food," Adam told Sanna eating his breakfast.

After they finish eating, Adam went to pay the bill, and Sanna looks over the bakery treats in the glass case. Granny looks at Sanna closely, and says to Sanna, "You look like someone I have seen you somewhere before in some pictures from my mother." Granny move closer to Sanna face over the countertop, and keep on talking, "You look so close to someone powerful... like a white spirit." Granny tries to finger out Sanna, "You look like Anilea the white spirit."

Sanna face went white, and her eyes widen, *'How did Granny find out that I am Anilea?'* Sanna thought to herself just staring at Granny.

Adam snap Sanna out of her thought by saying to Granny, "Granny, Sanna is not a spirit, expertly Anilea. Sanna may look like Anilea, but she not Anilea at all. You know the tales of the two spirits, Anilea and Donovan only show up on May 20 every 100 years, and this year they are coming. I still do not understand why it is 400 years now?" Adam crocks an eyebrow trying to think about the question.

Sanna grab Adam left hand with her right hand, "Come on Adam, I thought you made plans for today?" Sanna ask Adam in a hurry, trying to get Adam out of the café. Adam shook his head to clear his mind, say his good-byes to Granny, and left the café with Sanna.

Adam drove to the go-kart place in town, stopping outside the build, looks over at Sanna, and says with a smile on his face, "Surprise Sanna, what do you think?"

Sanna looks at the go-kart build, and say happy, "You got to be kidding me. We are going go-kart on V-day, no way," Sanna had a huge smile on her face. Adam laugh at Sanna actions for a second, then exit the car with Sanna right behind him.

They walk inside the go-kart place, up to the front desk. A young middle age woman came from the back office to the front desk, and asks in a friendly voice, "Hi, how can I help you two today?"

Adam spoke to her nicely, "We are here to do some go-carting."

"Okay then, lets get you two ready to go," she say to Adam and Sanna, walking around the desk, and lead Adam and Sanna to the go-kart area. "Okay here are the rules on the track; no hard hitting, no bad words, no dirty playing, and no donuts after the last lap," she say to Adam and Sanna handing out the helmets to them.

Sanna and Adam climb into two go-karts; Adam got a green one and Sanna a blue one. The woman started the karts up, and let Sanna and Adam go on the track racing around for 20 laps. Adam was leading in the first five laps, until Sanna came up right behind him, and passing Adam on the straightaway. Sanna laugh at Adam passing by him, and keep the lead for 15 laps. Adam keep on bumping Sanna back bumper, and trying pass to Sanna, but it was too late the fun had to end for now. Sanna and Adam pulling the karts parking place, and getting out of the karts onto the floor. "Champ!" Sanna say to Adam exiting the go-kart.

Adam chuckled at Sanna, and say, "I let you win," exiting the go-cart area.

Sanna look at Adam with a 'yeah right' look on her face, "Yeah right, you don't want to tell the truth that I won fair and square," Sanna say to Adam walking from the track to the lunch area.

Adam follow Sanna to the lunch area, laughing at what Sanna say to him about that he lose honestly to Sanna. "How about a re-match after lunch then?" Adam asks Sanna.

Sanna looks at Adam, "It is so on."

Adam put his right arm around Sanna, walking to the café area to have lunch. Adam pay for the food for both of them, setting the tray on the table, and pulling out a chair for Sanna. Sanna sat down in the chair, letting Adam push her in nicely to the table, and sitting down on the other side. "Thanks Adam," Sanna say nicely to Adam looking down at her plate of chicken fingers and fries.

"Your welcome," Adam says to Sanna looking down at his plate of cheeseburger and fries.

After lunch, Adam challenge Sanna to another 20 laps racing. Sanna and Adam suit up for the race, sitting down in the go-karts, and start their engines. The flag person got them line up on the line, and gave them the sign to go. Sanna took off first the line around the go-cart track, until Adam pass her after a few laps. They were neck to neck on the lap's couple of laps, bumping each other side to side, and in the back. Sanna speeded up her engine on the last lap, and won the race again. Sanna spin around to see Adam crossing the finish line last place. "Champ again," Sanna say to Adam taking off her helmet, and shaking her hair out.

"You're the winner, this time," Adam says to Sanna taking off his helmet, and stared at Sanna with love in his eyes.

Sanna got out of the go-kart, staring back at Adam. "What?" Sanna say to Adam throwing her arms out to the side, and wondering what going through Adam mind right now. Sanna fix her hair with her hands back into a ponytail.

Adam got out of go-kart, walk up to Sanna, and spoke sweetly to Sanna, "Nothing, but looking at the most beautiful angel that steals my heart away." Adam stood in front of Sanna, looking down at Sanna with smiled on his face.

Sanna looking at Adam, and say to him, "Aw, that so sweet, but I still win the race."

Adam chuckled at Sanna, and say, "Of course you did. I was thinking that we should get home to get ready for supper tonight."

"Of course, I still wondering what you have plan for me tonight," Sanna ask Adam with a raise eyebrow. Adam wrap his right arm around Sanna shoulders, walking out of the building with Sanna to the car, and getting into the car, and Adam drove away from the go-kart place.

Adam drop Sanna at her place, and told Sanna that he will be picking her up around 6 o'clock that night. Sanna nodded her head at Adam leaving the car, walking up to her place, and hearing the car taking off down the street. Sanna walks up the steps to the front door, opening the door, and entering the house. Sanna closed the front door behind her, taking off her coat and shoes, hanging up her coat, and heading upstairs to her bedroom to get ready for her date with Adam. Sanna mind could not off the fact that Adam has a surprise for her. Sanna got to the second floor to see Roselyn, Tiffany, Andrew, and Aaron getting ready for their date tonight. Sanna smiled at them, and went upstairs to her bedroom.

Sanna enter her room, closing the door behind her, and lending her back against the door, looking up at the ceiling. Sanna sigh moving away from the door to the bathroom. Sanna enter the bathroom, closing the door behind her, getting undress to her underwear, and washing her long hair in the tub. Sanna finish washing her hair, wrapping it up in a towel, stood up straight, and walking to the mirror to brush out her hair. Sanna un-wrap the towel from her head and start to brush out her hair with a brush. Sanna looks at herself in the mirror at her long wet hair, pale face, skinny body, and scars that Donovan gave her. Sanna felt a slight bit of pain in her chest around her heart, Sanna held her chest with her right hand. "Damn-it over did today at the go-kart place," Sanna held onto the sink edge with her left hand trying to breathe through the pain, and the pain slowly went away on it own.

Sanna stood up straight in front of the sink, grabbing the hair cream, opening the lid, squeezing some cream on her left hand fingertips, closing the lid, putting her finger tips together, lend over letting her hang down in front of her, and running her finger tips through her hair. Sanna stood back up straight, ruffling her hair more with her fingers more, looking at herself in the mirror again, and leaving the bathroom to the closet to get dress. Sanna look through her closet for the right dress, and finding a full-length light pink dress with thin straps. Sanna looks at herself in the full-length mirror holding the dress in front of her body. "Prefect," Sanna told herself taking the dress off the hanger, and putting the dress on. Sanna straighten out the dress on her body, and going to do her hair and make-up.

Around 6 o'clock, Sanna just finish getting ready, when Andrew called from the main floor. "Showtime," Sanna say to herself in the mirror with a smile on her face, and exiting her room.

Adam was waiting downstairs in the entryway with a nervously look on his face. Adam was nervously about what he wants to do tonight with Sanna. Andrew and Roselyn look over at Adam by the stairs. "Adam, are you so nervous?" Roselyn ask Adam waiting for Sanna. Adam nodded his head, "Just calm down, and whatever happens between you two. You will always be a friend forever, so be happy and smiled," Roselyn heard Sanna footsteps coming down the stairs. "Sanna is coming now, so smile, calm down, and everything will be fine."

Sanna walks down the stairs with a smile on her face. Adam mouth drop at the sight of Sanna in her dress, her hair pull back from her face, and her pretty face. Sanna reach the bottom step, and look at Adam. "Good evening Adam," Sanna spoke in a sweet voice. "I am looking forward to our date tonight." Sanna stood in front of Adam looking into his eyes.

Adam snap himself back to normal, and spoke nicely, "Good evening Sanna, you look... wow... lovely this evening." Adam helps Sanna putting on her coat, and looks over Sanna lovely body.

Roselyn and Andrew looks at Sanna and Adam standing there in the entryway getting ready for the biggest date of their lives. "Have fun you two," Andrew say to Sanna and Adam watching them leaving the house.

"Thanks, and see you guys later," Sanna say to Andrew and Roselyn exiting the house to Adam car. Adam open the car door for Sanna, Sanna got into the car, Adam closed the door once Sanna inside, going around to the drive side, entering the car, starting the car, and driving away to the restaurant.

Adam pulls into the parking lot of the restaurant, but a different place from the first date. It was a small restaurant by the lake and in the big park. Adam exits the car, walking around to Sanna side, opening the door for her, Sanna exit the car. Adam closed the car door behind Sanna, and heading to the restaurant holding hands with Sanna. They arrive at the restaurant doors, and Adam opens the doors for Sanna. "Thank-you Adam," Sanna say to Adam entering the building, and Adam follow Sanna inside. They wait to be seat, and right way the waiter came to seat them at a table over looking the lake. Sanna looks around at the restaurant to see candle lit tables with pretty flowers, and young and old couples in love. Sanna look down at Adam, smiling at him.

Adam took his right hand, placing it on top of Sanna left hand, and looking into her eyes. "I love you very much," Adam told Sanna with love in his voice.

Sanna looks into Adam eyes, speaking sweetly to Adam, "I love you too, Adam, very much. There nothing that will change that," Sanna held Adam right hand in her left hand.

The waiter came over to the table, taking Sanna and Adam orders, and left them alone for a while. They sat there looking into each other eyes, and Sanna ask Adam a question, "Adam, what on your mind?"

Adam looks at Sanna with a surprising look on his face, and say nicely, "Nothing much, but how much I love you, that all." Adam held Sanna left hand in his right hand, "There one thing on my mind that been on for awhile, and I hope you like it."

"What is it?" Sanna smile at Adam, hoping that Adam gift was going to be nice, holding his hand in hers.

"I cannot tell you, I want it to be a surprise for later," Adam told Sanna, looking into Sanna eyes and a smile on his face.

"Then I will wait nicely then," Sanna told Adam smiling back at Adam.

The waiter came back with their food and setting the plates of food in front of them. "Enjoy," the waiter told them leaving the table.

"This looks great Adam," Sanna say to Adam starting to eat her meal.

"Not a great you look tonight," Adam says to Sanna. Sanna smiled at Adam, and keep on eating her meal.

Rest of the evening went off without a hitch; there was no sign of Donovan or his group the whole night. The music plays softly through out the build with old and young couples in love with each other. Sanna and Adam sat there at their table, finishing their dessert, Adam look over at Sanna, and smile at her. Sanna look back at Adam with a smile of her face, and thinking on what Adam surprise was for her. Adam pays the bill with a tip, helping Sanna with her coat, and left the building with Sanna on his right arm. They walk down a pathway to a gazebo over looking the lake. Adam and Sanna stop in gazebo, Sanna lend on the railing looking at the lake, and smile at her that nothing bugging them all night. Adam lend on the railing beside Sanna on the right side, and looks out on the lake. "This night has been the greatest night of my life. Thanks a lot

Adam for everything you have done for me, I love you so much," Sanna say to Adam looking over at Adam with a huge smile on her face.

"This evening has been great, and there nothing will ruin this evening," Adam say to Sanna looking over at Sanna with a smile on his face.

They look out the lake, holding their hands together, and enjoying the beautiful scenery in front of them. Adam looks over at Sanna to say nicely to her, "Sanna, I have something I want to ask you, and I want to know your answer to this question."

Sanna look at Adam, and ask nicely, "What is your question that you want to know from me?"

Adam and Sanna look into each other faces; Adam took Sanna left hand, held her left hand in his hands. Adam try to find the right words to ask Sanna, "Sanna, we been know each other for a while, and I felt that what I am going to tell you will not hurt our friendship." Adam let go of Sanna left hand, turning his back to Sanna, reaching into his coat pocket, pulling out a little box, and holding it in his hands.

Sanna place her right hand on Adam left shoulder, and say in a worry voice, "Adam, whatever you got to tell me, it will not hurt our friendship. I love you from the bottom on my heart." In the back of her mind, *'Please do not let Adam break-up with me. I do not want to lose him. I love him very much.'*

Adam turn around to face Sanna, got down on one knee with the small box in his hands, opening the top of the box to show Sanna. A white and yellow gold heart sharp with a small diamond ring, and pop the question to her. "Sanna, will you marry me?" Adam had a smiled on his face. Sanna stood there looking down at Adam holding the ring box in his hands, and waiting for Sanna to answer the question of marriage.

Chapter Seventeen

Desdemona vs. Anilea & Anilea Hurting!

Sanna look down at Adam, and spoke to Adam kindly, "Adam, I love you very much from the bottom of my heart, but my answer for now is no. I am not ready for marriage after, well you know." Sanna felt sorry about telling Adam that, but she want to stay force on what she here on Earth for to defect Donovan and his group.

Adam closed the box, got off the ground to his feet, placing the ring box back in his coat pocket, looking at Sanna. Adam wrapping his arms around Sanna shoulders, and spoke to her nicely, "I know about what happen to you on your wedding day many years ago. That is okay, I should not rush you into this, but you know how much I love you. Maybe I should wait for the right time, and the signs for you to be ready for marriage." Adam lend down kissing Sanna on the right cheek, and looking into Sanna eyes.

Sanna look up into Adam eyes, and whisper, "I love you very much, and I am getting cold now," Sanna shiver in Adam arms and her teeth chatter.

Adam nods his head to Sanna, and says nicely, "Okay then, and let's go home before you get sick." Adam walks along the pathway with Sanna in his arms. Adam drove Sanna home, and talking about stuff. They had a good laugh all the way home, and saying their goodnight with a kissing each other on the cheeks.

~~*~*~*~*~*~*~*~*

Through out the two months into April 9, trouble grew through out the town with business been broken into, people fighting everywhere, and more people going missing here and there. Sanna stood on her balcony on the night of April 9, 2065 with the newspaper in her hands, and reading about the troubles going on in town. Sanna was raging at the fact Donovan was making this battle, the last one ever. Sanna look up to see the night sky changing into the morning light. Sanna sigh headed inside to her room to get ready for the day. Sanna thought that she would go up by the falls to practice her fighting skills, without her sword, that at the museum still, and need to finger out how to get her sword back from the museum. Sanna got dress into her workout clothing, throwing her hair into a ponytail, and leaving her room for the day.

Sanna walk downstairs to hear Andrew and Aaron yelling in rage. Sanna walk into the living room to see Andrew and Aaron yelling at the top of their voices, and Roslyn and Tiffany sitting on the couches covering their ears with their hands. Sanna had enough of it, "WHAT GOING ON HERE?" Sanna yelled at the top of her voice.

Andrew and Aaron stop yelling at each other and looking over at Sanna standing in the living room archway. Roselyn and Tiffany uncover their ears, looking at Sanna, Roselyn stood up for the couch, walking over to Sanna, and spoke to Sanna, "Sanna, Andrew and Aaron are arguing about the trouble going on around town and your safely from Donovan group. Andrew wants you to stay home with us, Aaron wants you to be free and go out around town without us." Roselyn place her hands on Sanna shoulders, looking into Sanna eyes, and speaking to Sanna, "The chose is yours, what you want to do? Make the right chose for you."

Sanna look around the room at everyone, and spoke to them. "I'm going to practice my fighting skills at the falls. See you later," Sanna left the house, and jog to the falls. Everyone watch Sanna leaving the house to go practice her fighting skills at the falls.

Sanna ran up to top of the first waterfall and in front of the second one. Sanna stood on top of the first waterfall looking out at the trees in the distance and trying to forget what Andrew and Aaron was yelling about this morning. Sanna practice her fighting skills in the opening around the falls, and forcing her powers. Sanna jump onto a huge rock in front of the fall without any problems, taking a deep breathe in through her nose, closing her eyes, and slowly letting out her breath through her mouth. Sanna slowly move her body to tai-chi movement, forcing on what she needs to do on May 20 this year. Sanna stay calm and relax, listening to the roar of the falls behind her, and sounds of nature around her. Sanna body started to glow white and felt more powerful then before. Sanna stop moving her body, titling her head back, opening her eyes to the sky, and breathing normal. "I am now more powerful Donovan. This year you will died, along with your group too," Sanna told herself with no one around her.

Sanna heard someone clapping his or her hands slowly to the left side along the edge of the water. Sanna turn her head to the sound to see Desdemona standing there along the edge of the water, clapping her hands. "Desdemona, what are you doing here?" Sanna rudely say to Desdemona, stop glowing white.

Desdemona looks at Sanna, standing there on the rock looking at her with narrow eyes, and spoke in her evil tone voice, "I say you looking great this time. How Adam doing?"

Sanna jump from the rock to the ground, and looking at Desdemona to say through her teeth, "Leave Adam alone, he is none of yours or your big brother business. I am the one Donovan wants to get rid of for good, just leave Adam out of this fight, I don't want to lose other lover to your brother and your doing." Sanna started to tear up at the thought of losing Adam for good to Donovan or Desdemona doing.

Desdemona looks at Sanna face to see a tear rolling down Sanna face. Desdemona smile evilly at Sanna, and spoke in a mean voice, "Did I hit an old wound in your heart and memories? Adam will be fun to torment him on May 20 this year... His screams and yelling for help will make me wet around my pussy. I will enjoy getting rid of Adam in front of you, and my big brother will enjoy spilling your blood all over the place. Once you're gone for good, the human race will be under Donovan control forever, and your little friends will be salves to Donovan." Desdemona laugh evilly in the air at Sanna thought of Sanna dieing.

Sanna lower her head for a moment, letting the tears fall to the ground, and spoke through her teeth, "Piss-off Desdemona... Tell your stupid ass big brother that his blood will be the one spill and he will be the one gone forever. I was sent here to earth to save the human race from the darkness, and there nothing your big brother or you will do about it."

Desdemona stood there in front of Sanna with her left hand in her hip, and spoke in a rude voice, "In your fucking dreams Anilea. My brother defect two spirits, remember them. You're..."

"Enough!" Sanna yelled at Desdemona in a mad voice. "Don't say may more to me. Let's end this argument now!" Sanna stood there in rage that Desdemona brought up her two fallen friends.

Desdemona lend closer to Sanna face, spoke to Sanna in a piss-off tone, "Are you afraid that you will joining them... Gone forever... Not being here or in the spirit world." Desdemona laugh in Sanna face. Sanna tighten her hands into fist, taking her right fist, hitting Desdemona across the face, and stood there mad. Desdemona held her right side of her face with her right hand, narrowing her eyes at Sanna, and say in a piss-off voice, "Nice Anilea, that smart of you to do that. You got guts to do that, but you're not that smart." Desdemona fly right at Sanna, slamming Sanna against the rock wall of the waterfall, and looking into Sanna face. "But your still weak Anilea and your weakness is Adam. He will be your downfall, and Adam will die with you. There nothing you will do about it," Desdemona told Sanna, keeping her hands on Sanna shoulders, and looking into Sanna hazel eyes with green eyes changing red. "You die by my brother hands, and he will enjoy your screaming of pain and watching you die in front of him," Desdemona laugh evilly at Sanna.

Sanna struggle in Desdemona hands, lifting her feet up to Desdemona chest, placing her feet onto the chest, and quickly pushing Desdemona away from her, "Piss-off Desdemona!" Sanna say pushing Desdemona away from her with everything, she got. Sanna landing on her feet in front of the rock wall.

Throw Desdemona let go of Sanna back from Sanna kick, sliding on her feet across the ground. Desdemona looks at Sanna with wide eyes, surprise at the strength that Sanna haves, and poke to Sanna, "You are stronger now, but still your weakness is Adam still... Enough talking lets fight," Desdemona got ready to fight Sanna.

Sanna stood her ground and got ready to fight Desdemona. "Bring it fat bitch," Sanna say to Desdemona moving away from the wall.

Desdemona made the first move running up to Sanna, and swing with her right fist. Sanna move to the left side avoiding the hit by Desdemona, taking her right fist, and hitting Desdemona in the stomach. Sanna quickly move away closer to the water edge. Desdemona hunch over from the punch to her stomach, getting mad at Sanna, and standing up straight. "That smart Anilea, but you're a bitch for doing that to me. A cheap shot that it was, but you will never defect Donovan on May 20 this year," Desdemona told Sanna walking slowly up to Sanna, quickly picking up speed, and hitting Sanna in the face with her right fist.

Sanna flow back hitting the big rock in the water on her back, "AAAA!" Sanna scream as her back hit the rock, lay there on the rock for a moment, and slowly moving but the pain all over her body. Sanna scream in pain loudly, sitting up on the rock, and trying to get her feet. "That fucking hurts!" Sanna looks straight at Desdemona with narrow eyes, and keep on yelling at Desdemona, "YOU BITCH!" Sanna felt her face with her right hand, felt blood dripping her nose. Sanna looks at the blood on her right hand, chuckling to herself as her hair fell out of her ponytail, and blowing in the wind. Sanna stood up on the rock looking at Desdemona, and getting ready to fight. "Bring it bitch!" Sanna signal Desdemona with her left hand.

Desdemona jump across the water onto the rock edge, and running up to Sanna with rage running through her blood. Sanna and Desdemona hands collided together as the water explored around them on the rock, and the water rain down on them making everything wet. Desdemona use her body weight pushing against Sanna hands, and growling at Sanna through her teeth. "You maybe strong now, but your strength will not last for very long. I can feel your strength slowly going now. You are so easy to push on, and beat up now... Donovan wants me to make sure that your strength will never return," Desdemona say to Sanna in her evil voice.

Sanna try to push back on Desdemona, and spoke to Desdemona, "You don't know me very well and never does your brother... My strength never will leave me," Sanna use her strength to throw Desdemona off the rock into the water below. Sanna looks over the rock edge, and laughing at Desdemona hitting the water.

Desdemona pop her head out of the water, her long black-red hair hanging down in front of her face, and her make-up running down her face. "ARG! Your BITCH will pay for this! These clothes are dry-cleaned only, now they are ruined!" Desdemona yelled at Sanna looking up at the rock to see Sanna laughing at her. "You will pay for this Anilea!" Desdemona jumping out of the water, and flow towards Sanna. Sanna eyes whet wide, and she knows she was in trouble with a piss-off Desdemona. Sanna felt the hit of Desdemona body hitting her body, and flying through the air slamming into a big tree. Desdemona slam Sanna against the tree, and looking at Sanna in the face. "Your still weak Anilea," Desdemona spoke to Sanna with rage and letting go of Sanna.

Sanna slip down the tree, sitting on the ground for a moment, and coughing up some blood from her mouth. "You bitch," Sanna say to Desdemona getting off the ground using the tree for support. Sanna stood on her feet, and stumble toward Desdemona. Sanna picking up speed and ran toward Desdemona in rage. Desdemona step to the right side, Sanna ran by Desdemona. Desdemona grab the back of Sanna shirt by the neck, slamming Sanna down on the ground in one quick move. Sanna body slam on the hard ground, and groan in pain shooting through out her body. Sanna know that she will fail here soon, but she never give up on fighting. She closed her eyes as she lay on the ground in pain.

Desdemona knelt over Sanna body, looking at Sanna lying on the ground, and spoke in a mean voice, "Some white powerful spirit, I did not have to use full strength to take you down... Your fail... You will never win at anything." Desdemona heard Adam calling for Sanna on the bottom of the second falls. Desdemona turned her head to Adam voice, grinning evilly, and spoke to Sanna, "I see Adam here... Adam does not know that you are a spirit. I wondered how he would react to the big secret that you are keeping from him... I should go tell him, maybe."

Sanna pushing Desdemona off her using her feet on Desdemona chest and speaking to Desdemona, "Leave Adam alone!" Sanna use a bit of her strength to make Desdemona flying through the air into the rock wall by the falls. Sanna slowly got to her feet, standing her ground, and running toward Desdemona.

Desdemona move away from the wall, once Sanna came closer, letting Sanna run by her, using her long fingernails, and racking them down Sanna back in one quick move. Sanna felt Desdemona long fingernails digging into her back, moving down her back slowly, it felt like, and her blood drizzling down her back. Sanna stop an inch from the wall, and trying to force her eyes, but everything was blurry. Sanna shook her head, turning around to face Desdemona, wiping the blood off her face, and spoke through her out of breathe voice, "You're a dirty player, that was not cool... Bitch." Sanna try to stay on her feet, could hear Adam voice coming through the trees from below, and started to worry about Adam seeing her like this. Moreover, showing that she not human, but a spirit.

Desdemona looks at Sanna by the wall, smiling evil at Sanna, and say to Sanna, "I would what will you do if I go hurt Adam now?" Desdemona walks into the tress.

Sanna ran up to Desdemona from behind, "Leave Adam out of this," Sanna called out to Desdemona from behind. Desdemona turn around to see Sanna running up to her. Once Sanna was close enough, Desdemona taking her right arm, hooking under Sanna right arm, and flipping Sanna over the cliff edge. Desdemona watches Sanna rolling down the steep slop, through the trees, smiling evil, and left the area slowly from the area.

Sanna rolled down the slop hitting rocks, trees, and brushes, before hitting the bottom face first. Adam saw Sanna rolling down the slop, and seeing Sanna hitting the bottom face first. "Sanna!" Adam called out running up to Sanna, and turning Sanna over in his arms. "Sanna, are you okay?" Adam ask Sanna in his arms, taking his right hand, placing it on Sanna chest to feel if Sanna was still alive, and could not feel anything at all. Adam started to panic, "Come on Sanna, breathe," Adam laid Sanna on the ground on her back to start CPR.

Before Adam could start CPR on Sanna. Sanna eyeshot opened, sitting up from the ground, and yelled in rage, "THAT BITCH!" Sanna realize that Adam was sitting beside her. Sanna turn her head to Adam with a shock look on face, quickly getting to her feet, and running into the trees along the trail.

Adam could not believe what just happen, getting to his feet quickly, and running after Sanna along the trail. Adam could not see or find Sanna in the trees, "Where did she go?" Adam asks himself under a huge tree, scratching his head with his right hand, and walking away from the tree.

Up in the tree, Sanna stood on a big branch, looking down at Adam below her, holding the tree with her left hand, and spoke in a whisper, "Sorry Adam, but it is too early for you to know who I am really... Sorry my love." Sanna watch Adam walking away from under the tree. Once Adam was far away, Sanna jump down from the tree, and slowly walking home in pain.

Sanna stumble up the back steps to the back door, opening the door, slowly enter the house, and closing the door behind her. Sanna slowly walk into the kitchen to find Roselyn and Tiffany in the kitchen doing some baking. Roselyn turn around with a big bowel of cake batter in her hands from the countertop by the sink, seeing Sanna all mess up and cover in blood, and dropping the bowel to the floor as cake batter slip all over the floor. Roselyn looks at Sanna with a scared look on her face, and ask Sanna in her worry voice, "Anilea, what happen to you?" Tiffany turn around from the oven to see Sanna cover in blood, a shock look came to her face, and she walk closer to Roselyn.

Sanna stood in front of the inland, blood drizzling down her body to the floor below, and looking at Roselyn and Tiffany to say, "Desdemona did this to me. I was practicing by the second upper fall, when she shows up. We ague a bit, we started to fight, and next minute I know I was rolling down the steep slop to the bottom." Sanna held in the screams of pain, and keep on telling them more, "The weirdest thing was Adam show up, when I was laying on the ground. I snap out of being knock-out to see Adam there beside me, I ran away from him into the trees, climbing a tall tree to hide, waited for Adam to leave, jumping down from the tree, and slowly walking home with pain shooting through out my body. Now I want to be alone," Sanna slowly walks to the stairs.

Roselyn and Tiffany looks at each other for a moment, then went to help Sanna up the stairs to Sanna bedroom. "Here Anilea, we will help you up to your room," Roselyn told Sanna taking Sanna right arm, Tiffany taking Sanna left arm, and helping Sanna up the stairs.

"Thank-you," Sanna say to them slowly, walking up the stairs with pain shooting through her body with every step, Sanna took on the stairs, without letting out a scream from her mouth, just mourns and groans.

Once Roselyn and Tiffany got to Sanna bedroom, Roselyn told Tiffany to go get the first-aid kit from the second floor, and took Sanna into the bathroom to clean Sanna up. Roselyn sat Sanna down on the toilet lid, ran a tub full of warm water, helping Sanna undress to Sanna blood-beat-up body, and helping

Sanna into the tub full of warm water. Sanna felt the warm water hitting her wounds, and screaming loudly in the air. "Roselyn, it fucking hurts!" Sanna scream trying to get more into the tub, Sanna finally got fully into the tub, and trying to relax in the water.

Roselyn starts to clean the blood off Sanna, and worry about Sanna health. "Anilea are you scared? You know if the same thing will happen to you as you're..." Roselyn say to Sanna, washing Sanna back with a cloth.

"Don't say it!" Sanna stop Roselyn from talking. Sanna lending forwards more in the tub, and tries to stay calm, "Please Roselyn no more talking about my past time." Tears fell from Sanna eyes hitting the water, Roselyn felt wrong about saying that to Sanna. Roselyn just sigh, and keep on washing the blood off Sanna body.

After an hour, Roselyn finally got off all blood off Sanna body. "There feeling better a bit?" Roselyn ask Sanna, putting the cloth down on the side of the tub, and looks at Sanna with worry eyes. "What are you thinking about Anilea?" Roselyn stared at Sanna for a bit, getting up from the floor, grabbing a big towel from the hanger from the door, and returning beside the tub. Sanna lay there in the tub, the water over her shoulders, her wet hair floating in the water, looking up at the ceiling, sighed, and slowly got out the tub.

Roselyn wrap the big towel around Sanna body, getting some underwear on Sanna, helping Sanna to her bed, and having Sanna lay down on her stomach with Sanna head down at the end of the bed. "Easy Anilea," Roselyn say to Sanna helping lay down on the bed, un-wrapping the towel from Sanna body. Roslyn looks down at Sanna half-naked beating body, and seeing the fingernail marks from Sanna shoulders to her butt. Roselyn saw the first-aid kit on the bed, and Tiffany ready to help.

Both Roselyn and Tiffany sigh, and worry about Sanna health. Sanna lay there facing the bedroom door with a pillow under her chest, her hands under the pillow, and trying to forget what happen at the falls with Desdemona and having Adam seeing her coming back from the death. Sanna felt a sharp pain from her back, "OW!" Sanna scream slamming her head down on the pillow, and screaming.

"Sorry Anilea, I put too much rubbing alcohol on the pad. Just breathe, and the string will be done soon," Roselyn told Sanna touching Sanna back with the pad again.

Sanna breathe until the pain was gone. Sanna lay there on the stomach thinking on a few things, and then spoke softly to Roselyn and Tiffany, "I will fail at the battle on May 20... I know that I will surely die on that date, and well never return to earth or the spirit world." Sanna lay her head down on the pillow, closing her eyes for a bit, and relaxing for a bit.

Tiffany look down at Sanna, and ask a question, "Anilea, what are you afraid of that or something else?"

Sanna lift her head up off the pillow, and spoke to Tiffany in a worry voice, "Roselyn, Tiffany, I have to tell Adam that I am a white spirit before he start asking questions about thing that he been seeing around me."

Roselyn and Tiffany mouths drop to the floor, and Roselyn drop the wet pad with the rubbing alcohol onto Sanna back. Sanna scream in pain as the pad hit her back, and slamming her head down on the pillow again. Roselyn quickly remove the pad from Sanna back, and spoke to Sanna in a shocking voice, "Anilea, you cannot do that… You cannot tell Adam that you are a white spirit; it will put Adam in shock… In addition, remember the rule that you set up for yourself years ago to keep yourself safe… 'Not to tell any human that we are spirits.' Remember that rule…You can't break it… unless that what's holding you back from your being at full strength and force." Roselyn cover Sanna back with band-aid pad.

Sanna nodded her head to Roselyn and Tiffany, "That what holding me back… I cannot keep this secret from Adam anymore. I have to tell him here soon, but now I need some rest." Sanna lay her head down on the pillow, and felling a sleep quickly. Tiffany and Roselyn clean their mess up, Roselyn cover Sanna with a blanket, and they left the Sanna room to let Sanna sleep the rest of the day.

Chapter Eighteen

Anilea Gets Her Sword Back!

May came around the corner; ten days until the battle between Anilea and Donovan was coming soon.

May 10, 2065; Sanna woke up that morning, got dress, looking at herself in the closet mirror, knowing that she need to get her sword back, and have to tell Adam the truth about her being a spirit. She left her bedroom, heading straight out of the house to the museum. Roselyn saw Sanna running down the stairs to the second floor. "Where are you going Anilea?" Roselyn ask Sanna seeing, her turning the corner to the staircase.

"Going to the museum to get my sword back now, and don't stop me," Sanna say running down the staircase to the front door, getting her shoes on, and heading out of the front door. Sanna was on her way to the museum to get her sword back. Sanna walk pass Adam place, seeing Adam washing his car in the driveway, and Sanna did not stop to talk to Adam. Ever since the innocent on April 9, down at the falls, Sanna never forgot that, and trying to keep Adam safe from Donovan group by not get Adam involve with anything going on. Adam watches Sanna walk by quickly, and did not say a word to her. Adam felt that Sanna was hiding something from him, and he want to know tonight.

Sanna walk all the way to the museum went inside, up to the front desk, and asking Molly, "Hey is Prof. Jeff in today?"

"Yes he is in, do want me to call for him for you?" ask Molly behind the front desk, looking up from her computer, and smiling at Sanna.

Sanna putting her hands on the deck, smiling at Molly, and quickly told Molly, "Just tells Jeff that I want to talk to him about something important in the exhibit about the two spirits." Sanna ran from the front desk, up the stairs to the second floor, and heading to the exhibit to meet Jeff.

Jeff waits at the entryway of the exhibit seeing Sanna coming up to him. "Good morning Sanna, what do you want to talk to me about that so important?" Jeff asks Sanna, seeing her stopping in front of him with a huge smile on his face.

"I need to tell you something about me that you need to know, and I also here for the sword too," Sanna say to Jeff entering the exhibit with Jeff behind her, walking up to the display case that has the dagger in.

Jeff follows Sanna to the display, stop with Sanna in front of the display case, and ask Sanna a question, "What is that you want to tell me Sanna?"

Sanna took a deep breathe, letting out the breath to say to Jeff in a worry voice, "Jeff, what I am going to tell you promise me that you will not freak-out or go tell anyone in the town too."

Jeff nodded his head to Sanna, "I promise you, Sanna. Whatever your going to tell me I would not freak-out or tell anyone," Jeff promise Sanna that he would not freak-out or tell anyone about whatever Sanna going to say to him, and raising his left hand in the air and right hand on his chest.

Sanna lower her head for a second, took a deep breathe to calm down, and lift her head to face Jeff to speak, "Jeff, my real name is not Sanna, but... Anilea the white spirit, sent to earth 1314 years ago to defect the leader of the dark spirits Donovan."

Jeff did not believe Sanna at first, and started to quiz Sanna to see if Sanna was really Anilea, "I got some questions for you, Anilea, if that real name. To see if your telling the truth about yourself.

"Ask away," Sanna say to Jeff getting ready to for Jeff questions, throwing her arms to the side.

"Question one: What year did Anilea came to earth?" Jeff started ask his questions to Sanna.

"The year 750, half-way through the Dark Ages, but after the Dark Ages went to rest as a human. Born and die as a human for 400 years after the Dark Ages, until June 9, 1640. I was born again, and taking the name Sanna, until May 20, 1665. My spirit side was reborn by losing my love ones to Donovan evil ways," Sanna answer Jeff, and start to get upset for a second then straight herself out.

"Okay that right, question two: Did you have partners during the Dark Ages?" Jeff asks Sanna again.

Sanna bite her bottom lip for a second question, running her fingers through her hair, lowering her head for a moment to calm down, looking back up to Jeff in the eyes, and answer Jeff in an upset voice, "Yes, I did, but please don't ask anymore about them. My heart is still broken effect, I don't want to remember what happen to them that one fight. What happens to them is horror enough to my heart, and it hurt to remember that last battle at the end of the Dark ages."

Jeff was surprise that Sanna answer that question very well. "Okay then I won't ask about them, but here a question about your new friends. What year did they show up, and how?"

Sanna answer the question straight out to Jeff, "May 10, 1412, they came to earth to find me. It was not until May 20, 1665 they came to me on my wedding day to my fiancé. When Donovan and his group start killing my family and friends right in front of me at my wedding their screams of terror and pain echoing in my ears, their blood spilling all over the forest floor, and their bodies were lying lifeless as I seen Donovan and his group standing there. Red evil eyes as blood staring at me, they grinning at me, seeing the terror on my face, Donovan laughing at me as he watching my suffering watching everyone that I love die... My friends show up to protect me from Donovan and his group, until I was reborn back to my real self."

Jeff mouth drop for a second, shaking his head, and ask the last few question to Sanna. "Here multiple questions for you, Question three: What did Donovan leave on Anilea body, when she was still a human? Question four: How does the dagger works?" Jeff hoping to throw off Sanna or she was really in person.

Sanna answer Jeff questions right, "Donovan left a scar across my right upper arm, as I try to keep my lover safe as he was dieing on the ground, but my lover try to save me from Donovan and he was stab in the chest." Sanna took off her hoodie to show the scar on her right arm, and trying not to cry at the old memory hitting her in the mind and heart. "The answer to your last question is the dagger only works in my hands, and it turn into a really cool sword that can kill Donovan only, if I can get it right through the his dark evil heart," Sanna told Jeff without stopping to think about anything, plus keep her eyes in Jeff eyes the whole time.

Jeff mouth drops for a second, then ask Sanna another question, "Do you have anymore proof that you're really Anilea?"

Sanna reach into her back pocket of her jeans, pulling out an old black and white photo, and showing the photo to Jeff. "Do you know who this little girl with me?" Sanna ask Jeff and question holding out the photo in her hands.

Jeff looks closely at the photo of the little girl, who was 10 years old, and realizes who it was that with Sanna. "That my grandma, when she was little girl. How do you know my grandma?" Jeff asks Sanna with wide eyes and a shocking look on his face, and his mouth dropping a bit more.

"I save her life that day; it was right before the fight between Donovan and me. She always talking about it to her family all the time, when the date shows up," Sanna say to Jeff handing the photo to Jeff, and smiling at him.

Jeff took the photo in his hands, looking over the photo in his hands, and thinking about his grandma. "Anilea, I never know the stories were true. I thought at first grandma was going crazy the older she got before she pass away 15 years ago. Her parents was the one that opened this exhibit a 100 years ago after the last battle, and my grandma found the sword in the ground smoking," Jeff told Sanna with a shock in his voice, and thinking about all the stories that his grandma told him growing up.

"How did she get her hands on the sword without a burn mark on her hands, unless the sword power die off a bit like me," Sanna look down at the dagger in the display for a moment. "Jeff, did anyone touch this dagger once it was in the case for the last 100 years?" Sanna ask Jeff in worry voice and knowing what will happen to a human if they touch the sword.

"No one has touched the dagger in the display, why?" Jeff asks Sanna with a confused voice, looking at the dagger himself, and trying to finger out what Sanna was telling him about the dagger.

"Because the dagger works with my powers, when my power grows the sword powers grows too. If anyone who not a spirit with be shock to death, in addition when the power low the person can handling the sword will get a burn mark on their hands, and trouble will start for them... Still how did your grandma not get a burn mark on her hands, unless I was that weak for the power to be use," Sanna explain to Jeff looking down at the dagger, thinking on how weak she could have been after the last fight that happen between Donovan and her in that town.

Jeff mouth drop with shock, shook his head, and spoke to Sanna, "I did not know about that about the sword power. I should have known that was something about you, Sanna, that was not right... I should know that you were a spirit when you put Robbie and Cookie in their place that day I met you, and all the info you had about Anilea and Donovan. I should have known that you are Anilea; there were signs when I was watching you walking around the exhibit looking over the stuff. Your reactions to a few things in the exhibit may me wonder, but now to know that you are really Anilea." Jeff took his keys to the display case out of his coat pocket, unlocking the case, lifting up the glass lid, and looking at Sanna. "Take the dagger to prove that you're really Anilea," Jeff say to Sanna holding opened the glass lid to the case.

Sanna walks closer to the display case, looking down at the dagger for a moment, taking her right hand, placing it on the handle of the dagger, lifting the dagger out of the case, looking down at the dagger in her hand. Forcing her powers on the dagger, and in a second the dagger turn into a long sword. Sanna started to glow, and her normal clothes slowly turn into her spirit clothes.

T-shirt and jeans turn into a white flowing, full-length dress with thin straps, and running shoes turning into white low-heel strap shoes. Sanna sunshine blonde with light brown highlights hair unravel from her ponytail, the hat disappear, letting the waves and curls show themselves down her back, and gold-chain headpiece hang along her forehead with a light blue heart-sharp jewel hanging in the middle of her forehead. Sanna stop glowing, standing in front of Jeff holding her sword in her right hand. "I am complete now," Sanna whisper, looking down at her sword for a moment, then back up at Jeff. "Thank-you Jeff for everything," Sanna say to Jeff with a smile on her face.

Jeff mouth drop to the floor, and Jeff was speechless for a minute. "I... I... cannot believe you're really real, and that mean this year is?" Jeff spoke to Sanna for a moment, then his eyes when wide realizing that if Anilea here in person that mean that Donovan was also in town, and their battle will started here soon.

"The battle will start in ten days, during the party downtown on May 20, 2065... The party must stop before people will be killing by Donovan and his group... Jeff, you need to stop the partying downtown that day. I trusting on you to do that for me and for everyone in this town," Sanna told Jeff standing there still in her spirit clothes, placing her sword in the sheath turning back into a dagger. "I need to go Jeff... Please try to stop that party downtown on May 20 this year." Sanna change back into her normal human clothes, got out of the exhibit, and exiting the museum with her dagger under her hoodie.

Jeff stood there watching Sanna leaving the museum, "Good-luck Anilea," Jeff whisper to Sanna leaving; he went to try to stop the party downtown this year or people will died during the fight.

Sanna got back home with her dagger under her hoodie, she open the front door, closing the door behind her, and running upstairs to her bedroom. Sanna quickly open the bedroom door, entering the room quickly to close the door behind her. Sanna lend against the door with her back, breathing deeply, looking door at the dagger in her right hand, narrowing her eyes, and tighten her grip around the dagger gold handle. Sanna throw her head back against the door, and just want to scream in the air with rage, but she stay calm. "This year only one will be standing after the battle," Sanna spoke to herself with her head still against the door. Sanna took a deep breath, letting it out, taking off her hat, throwing it to the side, clipping her stealth on her left hip, and walking away from the door to the French doors. Sanna open the French doors to the balcony, and walking outside onto the balcony with the dagger on her left hip.

Sanna was watching the sun setting over the lake, when Roselyn and Tiffany came outside on the balcony to see Sanna standing there looking out at the lake with the dagger hook to her jeans, on the left side. Tiffany says to Sanna, "I see that you got your sword back."

Sanna nodded her head, turning around to face Roselyn and Tiffany, and speaking to them, "Yes, and now I have a decision to make now."

Roselyn looks at Sanna with a confusing look on her face, "What decision do you have to make now?"

Sanna sigh at Roselyn and Tiffany, and spoke again in a worry voice, "I have to decide that I should or not tell Adam the truth about me being a spirit. The only way I can force on the battle with Donovan. I have to be force during this battle, and having Adam knowing who I am really... I can force big time on fighting Donovan."

Roselyn and Tiffany mouths drop to the floor at what Sanna just said them. Tiffany spoke to Sanna in a shock voice, "What do you mean that you are going tell Adam the truth about that you're a spirit. Are you crazy?" Tiffany started to freak out at Sanna actions, and thinking what could happen if Sanna tells Adam the truth about her being a spirit.

Roselyn looks at Sanna with a smile at Sanna, and spoke to Sanna kindly, "The chose is up to you if you want to do that, but be careful telling the truth to Adam. He might not take the truth very well as you think... Just be preparing what Adam might tell you. I have funny feeling that Adam will be in shock, and that will make you hurt your feelings like that, but it is up to you now. Your our strong leader and that the only thing that you need to know."

Sanna nodded her head to Roselyn and Tiffany, "I know; I'll be ready for whatever Adam reaction to what I tell the truth about me being a spirit. Now I going for a walk down by the lake for a while, I will like to be alone," Sanna told Roselyn and Tiffany walking back inside the house, downstairs to the back door, exiting to the backyard, and heading down to the lake for a bit to be alone. Roselyn and Tiffany watch Sanna walking away from the balcony, and hope that everything will all right between Sanna and Adam.

Sanna walk along the tree line that by the water edge, finding a stone bench, and sitting down on the bench. Sanna took out her hair out of the ponytail, letting her long hair fall around her head and looking out at the last bit of sunset over the lake. Sanna sigh to herself for the thought she had at home. "What am I thinking? Tell Adam the truth about the real me... I am nothing but an idiot," Sanna whisper to herself lowering her head to the ground, placing her hands on the side of her head, and trying not to get mad at herself.

"You're not an idiot," a familiar kind male voice says from behind her.

Sanna lifted her head up, looking over her right shoulder to see Adam standing there behind her, and Sanna wondered how much Adam heard just now. "How long have you been there?" Sanna ask Adam in a wondering voice, and wide eyes.

Adam walk around to the front of the bench, sitting down on the bench beside Sanna on her right side, and looking at Sanna to say, "All I heard is you calling yourself an idiot. What that all about?" Adam took Sanna right hand in his left hand, holding her hand getting a weird feeling all over his body, and raising an eyebrow at Sanna. "There something that your not telling me about you." Adam look down at Sanna body to see the dagger handle poking out from her hoodie, had a worry look on his face, and whisper to Sanna, "Sanna is that the dagger from the museum?... Why do you have it? Did you steal it?" Adam let go of Sanna right hand, and sat there staring at Sanna with a weird look on his face.

Sanna cover the dagger handle with her hoodie, lowering her head letting her hair fall in front of her face, and letting out a sigh, and looking at Adam in the face to say, "Adam, the truth is my name is not Sanna, it's my human name. My real name is Anilea the white spirit."

Adam sat there with a shock look on his face, "The real Anilea, the white spirit, which going fight against dark lord Donovan?" Adam asks Sanna about her real name with huge wide eyes on Sanna telling the truth to him.

Sanna sigh as she lower her head, then raising her head, looking into Adam eyes, and then spoke in a worry voice, "Yes."

Chapter Nineteen

The Truth Comes Out!

"Come with me, Adam," Sanna say to Adam, getting up from the bench, grabbing Adam right hand in her left hand, and leading Adam back to her place. Adam follows Sanna back to her place and trying to putting a few things together about Sanna or Anilea was holding his hand. Adam wondering whom he fall in love with many months ago was it Sanna or Anilea that he in love with all the bottom of his heart. Adam was so confused about the whole thing that Sanna told him about being the real Anilea.

They arrive at Sanna place, entering through the back door, closing the door behind them, and walking quietly to the living room. Tiffany, Roselyn, Aaron, and Andrew were sitting on the couches under the windows talking about stuff. When Sanna and Adam came into the living room from the kitchen, walking up to them, Sanna let go of Adam hand, walking over to the living room archway, and lending against it looking at Adam with a worry look on her face. Adams sat down in one of the chairs in front of the couches, looking at Sanna friends, and wondering if they know that Sanna is really Anilea.

Everyone stop talking, turning their heads to Adam, and staring at Adam with blanket looks on their face. After ten minutes of quiet, Roselyn spoke through the silent to Adam, "So Sanna have told you the truth about her being the real Anilea, and it is 100o/o true about that. Also you know that all of us are also white spirits, more like warrior spirits." Roselyn pointed to Andrew, Aaron, and Tiffany with her right index finger. "Do you have any questions or concerns Adam?" Roselyn ask Adam hoping that Adam will understand about everything that Sanna and they have gone through the last 400 years, and more for Sanna.

Adam sat there in the chair with a shock look on his face at what Roselyn say to him. Adam shook his head for a second, then spoke in a shock voice, "So lets me get this straight all of you are all spirits that been on earth for how long?"

He could not believe what he was hearing right now, all this time he thought they were just normal human, and not spirits.

"655 for the four of us, and 1315 years for Anilea," Andrew says to Adam with a smiled on his face, sitting beside Roselyn on the couch.

Adam turned to Sanna in the archway, and spoke to her, "So Anilea, you been on earth for 1315 years, that means you been on earth since the year 750. That half-way through the Dark Ages, you have been on earth for along time alone, before these four show up... This I need proof that you are really spirits." Adam still could not believe that his girlfriend and her friends are really spirits.

Sanna with a straight face took off the dagger with the sheath on, throwing it onto the coffee table in front of Adam, and looking at Adam. "If you how the dagger works, I dare you to touch it," Sanna told Adam watching Adam body language after she throw the dagger onto the table.

Adam looks at the dagger, then to Sanna standing into the archway, and back to the dagger. Adam took his right hand to reach out to the dagger, but quickly pulled away from the dagger. "I know about the dagger powers, and what it could do to a human who touch it. I heard about it from my great grandpa, many years ago. No, I am not going to touch that dagger. I need more proof that you guys are what you are telling me," Adam say to Sanna, looking at her more, and seeing she not giving up on spilling the real truth about being Anilea or faking everything that she been telling him.

Sanna rolled her eyes at Adam, walking up to the coffee table, quickly grabbing the dagger off the table, and hooking the stealth back to her jean on the left side. "There one way to prove that we are white spirits," Sanna say Adam, looking over at Roselyn giving the signal, and knowing it has to be this way to reveal the real truth to Adam.

Roselyn, Tiffany, Andrew, and Aaron got up from their spots on the couches, and walk around the house closing curtains. Once they done closing the curtains tight around the house, they went back to the living room standing by the fireplace. Adam stood up from the chair, turning around to see them standing there, and amazons what he saw next. Roselyn, Tiffany, Andrew, and Aaron starting to glowing white, and their normal clothes started to change in front of him.

Roselyn and Tiffany shirts and jeans change into white knee-length dresses. Roselyn with long sleeve, Tiffany with short sleeves, both white low heel shoes, and white flowers in their hairs.

Andrew and Aaron shirts and jeans change into white dress pants, white long sleeves shirts, and white dress shoes.

Adam mouth drop at what he saw in front of him. Adam felt a white glowing beside him. Adam turned to the archway to see Sanna standing there in her spirit clothes. Adam eyes widen and his mouth drops more. "It is truth… your really Anilea, and the rest of them, wow!" Adam sat back down on the chair in shock, and could not believe Sanna was really telling him the truth.

Roselyn, Tiffany, Andrew, and Aaron sat back down on the couches. Sanna walk over the fireplace looking at Adam, and worry about the whole thing telling Adam the truth about her being a spirit. Adam snaps out of for a bit to speak, "Anilea," Adam turn around to face Sanna, "You have been here for years before meeting your four friends here."

Sanna spoke to Adam, "The truth is Adam, and Roselyn is the only one who knows from the others. I was never alone during the Dark Age; I had two other spirits with me. Matthew looks 20 years old, and Melissa, look 18 year old… My younger brother and sister," Sanna took a breath, and keep on speaking, "Before you wonder why they are not here, because they were killed at the end of the Dark Ages by Donovan evil hands." A tear was sled from Sanna right eye, rolling down her cheek, falling to the floor, and hitting the floor slowly.

Adam looks at Sanna with a wondering look on his face, and spoke kindly to Sanna, "How can spirit be killed? I thought they live forever, and what happens to them once they die? Do they go somewhere or not?"

Sanna looks at Adam, and spoke through her upset voice, "Adam, the only way a spirit can die is by other spirit stabbing with a sword or dagger in the heart or exploring the heart in the hands. The spirit body once die turn into dust and disappear forever. They are gone forever the only thing is left is their memories… The only thing I have of my brother and sister is their swords on top of the second waterfall in a very heavy brush area, and only spirit eyes can see them."

Adam keeps on looking at Sanna for a second, and asks a question to her, "How come spirit eyes can see them, but not human eyes?"

Sanna walks over to Adam, standing in front of Adam, and spoke to him, "Spirits can cast a spell with by using their own blood to seal the spell. I place rocks around the swords blade, once they were in the ground, and I lay down on the ground letting my blood spill onto the ground as I cast the spell. I vow to be a human until the day Donovan return with his group to Earth, and I get my revenge for their deaths."

"Wooh! Hold it! Donovan, the leader of the dark spirits, and his group is for real… I should have known there was something about you, after we went to the museum trip almost a year ago. When you told Robbie and Cookies off about the two spirits, and the info you had about them. Now I get it, so the battle is truth too," Adam says to Sanna, putting the pieces together in his mind.

Sanna lower her head and spoke sadly, "In ten days, and after this one. Only one will survive between Donovan and me after this battle." Sanna felt wrong about telling Adam that, but she wanted Adam to know about it.

Adam looks up at Sanna, and spoke, "You mean between Donovan and you, only one will be the last one standing." Adam thought for a moment, and then it came to him. "You mean that you will proudly die during this battle for good."

Sanna nodded her head slowly, and spoke, "This is the last time the battle Donovan and I will ever happen. I am worry about everyone else life in town, mostly my own after the last battle." Sanna walk away to the fireplace area and walking to her friends feeling the pit hit her stomach on the last time she fought Donovan.

Adam thought for a second, then stood up in a hurry, and spoke in a shocking voice, "You mean you nearly die last time you fought Donovan a 100 years ago. Now you are going to fight again to do what die during it. I do not want you to do that; I cannot live my life without you. Please don't do it for me," Adam tries to beg Sanna not to go fight with Donovan in ten days. Adam walk up to Sanna, wrapping her arms around Sanna body, looking into her eyes, and speaking to her in a worry voice, "I love you very much, and don't care that you're really a spirit. I love you Anilea or Sanna, whatever you want to be call. Just please don't go fight Donovan, I want you to live for me, please." Adam lends down for a kiss on the lips, but Sanna move her head to the left side as Adam kiss her right cheek.

"Adam, I have something to say to you," Sanna spoke to Adam, trying hard not to let her heart break under the thought coming to her mind now.

"What is it?" Adam asks Sanna in a worry voice, looking down at Sanna, and seeing something was on her mind now. More then the battle yet to come for her, but something personal now.

Sanna move away from Adam arms, and taking a deep breath to say, "I am sorry Adam, but I cannot see you anymore... I am sorry my love." Sanna lower her head to the ground, felt her heartbreaking into two, and tears getting ready to form in her eyes, but she held them back now.

Adam mouth hitting the floor, and speaking through the shock, "You're breaking up with me, why? Was it something I did? I can keep this a very good secret from everyone... Why?"

Sanna lifted up her head to face Adam, and spoke to him, "Because you're my weakness, and Donovan knows it. He will use you to get to me in any means, and I do not want you ending up died… I already lost lover once 400 years ago, I am not going to lose other again. I am sorry, but this is the only way I can force on the battle with Donovan." Sanna move away from Adam to the living room archway, stood there with a sad look on her face, as a small tear started to roll slowly down her cheek, and falling to the floor slowly as it hit the hardwood flooring.

Adam walk up to Sanna, looking at her in the eyes, and spoke to her, "I will be careful when the time comes. I will disappear from the town for the fight, and return after it to be with you. I really love you to be your weakness here, and I will find away to keep myself safe so you can forces on the fight here soon."

Sanna looks at Adam, shaking her head slowly, and spoke to him, "No Adam, they will find you any where, just to bring you back to this town just to kill you in front of me. I have to break up with you to keep you safe from them and my feelings too."

"No, I want to be with you forever… I do not want to lose the love of my life… I cannot let you slip through my fingers. I want to hold you forever in my arms. Please don't break up my heart into two," Adam says to Sanna in worry voice, as he try to step forward to Sanna, but stop close to her by seeing her left hand raising in front of him.

Sanna lower her hand, curling both hands into fists, getting mad at Adam, and yelled at him with rage in her voice, "Adam! You do not get it! Donovan or anyone in his group will kill you! I am trying to keep you unharmed! I do not want you die! So please just listen to me!" Sanna calm down a bit to speak more to Adam with tears slowly streaming from the corners of her eyes, "Adam, I will be okay and I will return to be with you. I just want to force on the fight with Donovan. I promise that I will be okay."

Adam walking up to Sanna, wrapping his arms around Sanna body, holding Sanna close to his body, and spoke to her in a whisper, "I will always love you my Anilea." Adam kisses Sanna on top of her head, and leaving the house. "Your secret is safe with me," Adam says to everyone standing by the front door, closing the door behind him, and exiting the house.

Once the front door was close shut tight, Sana looks at the front door with reddish in the whites of her eyes from tearing up, and collapsing to her knees on the floor. "Anilea!" Roselyn and everyone say to Sanna running to her sides. "Are you okay?" Roselyn ask Sanna, touching Sanna shoulders with her hands, and hoping Sanna feeling alright, but had a funny feeling Sanna emotions was taking care for a bit.

Sanna was wide eyes and in shock came out of her mouth, "Yeah, I am okay it just that... I still have feels for Adam, and now I feel like such a fucking loser. How can I break Adam heart, when he still has feels for me," Sanna told everyone around her, getting off the floor to her feet, and walking upstairs to her room. "I am going to lie down now," the last thing Sanna, say to her friends before going upstairs to her room to lie down on her bed.

For the rest of the day Sanna stay in her bedroom, wearing her normal clothes. Sanna had to force on the battle with Donovan in ten days, but her heart still beat for Adam. Adam feelings for Sanna keep her mind out of the game. It was nothing but distraction her from forcing. "Why? Did I do that?" Sanna whisper with her head lower, looking down at the bed covers, and a tear was sled from the corners of her eyes.

Chapter Twenty

Preparing of Battle!

May 19, 2065 came around; the town was getting ready for the big party downtown. The town people were decorations Main Street with streamers and balloons. People were putting the final touches on their parade floats and costumes for the party. Everyone in town was very happy and enjoying themselves as they help their friends with stuff.

In a dark alleyway, Donovan and his group watch the town people working away with things for the party the next day. "I see the town is making this more fun for us tomorrow night. When we destroyed the town, I will defect Anilea for the last time. That little bitch will not return to this world or the spirit word. I will enjoy watching Anilea skinny body slowly turn into dust," Donovan told his group laughing evilly, as the rest of them join in. "Enough! Now my dear sister, you take care of Anilea boyfriend, Adam. For the rest of you, if Anilea friends get involve with this fight, keep them away from Anilea and me. Now let's go home and rest up for the next day," Donovan told his group walking down the dark alleyway to his home with his group following him.

~~*~*~*~*~*~*~*~*~*

At Sanna place, Sanna was sitting down on the balcony railing, shaping her sword in her hands with a sharper stone and looking out at the large inland in the middle of the lake. Sanna pointed to the inland with her sword tip, and spoke to herself, "That were you will die, Donovan. I do not want to fight in the town anymore to destroy this place and many lives. This will be the last time we will meet forever." Sanna lower her sword to her right side, and sigh. Sanna look over at Adam place to see Adam standing on his balcony looking out at the lake.

Sanna sigh at Adam, and placing her sword back into the sheath. Sanna stood up on the railing, jumping into the air over to Adam place, and landing on the railing at Adam place. Sanna stood there on the railing looking at Adam, "I am sorry Adam," Sanna say to Adam keeping her eyes on Adam.

"What are you sorry for? What for… Keeping a huge secret from me or breaking my heart into two? Your chose Anilea or Sanna or whoever you are now to me," Adam says to Sanna not even looking at her, he keep his eyes on the lake, and watching the movement of the water.

Sanna sat down on the railing, and told Adam how she felt about everything, "I am sorry for everything that I did. I do love you still, but if Donovan finds out that, we are still together. He will kill you in front of me. I need to force on the battle with Donovan, and do not have to worry about you being killed. I do still love you very much, but there something about you that making me thinking about, and I cannot put my finger on it. Like we are meant to be together forever."

"We are meant to be together forever, and then I don't want to lose you." Adam turn around to face Sanna, and keep on talking to Sanna, "I do love you love very much, but you broke my heart into two, and now we might never be together forever," Adam lower his head trying hard not to get angry with Sanna right that moment.

Sanna lower her head, and keep on talking to Adam, "I know, but I have to fight Donovan. Then we can together forever, if I survive the battle first." She felt wrong about if she lose her life to Donovan how will Adam feel about losing her forever.

Adam lifted up his head, walking up to Sanna on the railing, and spoke to her looking into her eyes, "I know about that, but don't want you to fight. If you have to then I would not hold you back. Not until you give me a kiss good-bye at lest on the lips." Adam closed his eyes; slowly move in for a kiss from Sanna on the lips.

Sanna stood up quickly on the railing, stopping Adam from kissing her lips, and saying to Adam, "Sorry, but not now," jumping back to her place, landing on her railing for a moment. Adam opened his eyes to see Sanna back at her place, sighing Adam entering his place, and closing his bedroom doors. Sanna lower her head, jumping down from the railing, went back inside her room feeling wrong about not letting Adam kiss her on the lips, but there was something about Adam that Sanna had no clue, but her heart was thinking of one thing that Sanna lost a long time ago.

~~*~*~*~*~*~*~*~*

Donovan place: Donovan, Crevan, and Ryu were practicing fighting outside in the back yard. Desdemona and Eris were watching from the back deck in two chairs. "Oh the boys are getting rip with big muscles. It makes me wet down below," Eris say to Desdemona licking her lips seeing her husband working-out, and her mind was thinking dirty big time.

"I know me too, but they cannot be bug with their training. We got a big day tomorrow with the battle for life with Anilea and her bitching group. I cannot wait to put my brother plan into action," Desdemona say to Eris with an evil grin on her face.

"What is the plan?" Eris asks Desdemona with a raise eyebrow, and trying to think about the plan Donovan had planned to end Sanna life.

Desdemona looks at Eris, and told Eris the planned, "To use Anilea lover, Adam, to weaken her. So my brother can take care of her finally." Desdemona gave Eris the 'dud' look, and turn back to watch the boys practicing.

"What are we going to do about Roselyn and Tiffany? They will interfere with Donovan plan for Adam," Eris says to Desdemona raising an eyebrow, and thinking about if Sanna friends get involved.

"We will have to weaken those two enough that they cannot bug me with my work. You have to make sure those two bitches do not stop me working with Adam. Once they are weak enough for you to keep them down, but let them watch at lest. I want them to see my handling work," Desdemona say to Eris rubbing her hand together, thinking about her part of the plan with Adam, and cannot stop grinning evilly.

The boys was done practicing their fighting skills, Crevan and Ryu walks up to their wives, and Crevan spoke to them, "We want your two sweet asses upstairs in the bedrooms in the bed, naked. We want sex with you two now." Desdemona and Eris got up from their spot in a sexy matter, walking into the house, and upstairs to their bedrooms. Crevan and Ryu follow the wives to the bedrooms to have sex with them.

Donovan watches them entering the house. Donovan looks up at orange-red sky, and chuckling evil. "Tomorrow will be a big day for us, my dear Anilea. One will stand and one will fall. This will be a biggest battle in history, and I don't care how many lives get lost this year, as long one of us will died. Anilea, you will be the one died." Donovan throwing his arms out to the side, and laughing evil in the air.

~~*~*~*~*~*~*~*~*~*

Donovan evil laugh echo through the town, Sanna watch the sun setting over the lake in her spirit clothes, outside on her balcony. When she heard Donovan evil laughing echoing through the tress, Sanna felt an evil chill down her spine, that make her shiver in fear, "What am I doing?" Sanna whisper to herself, "How can I defect Donovan tomorrow? I am not strong enough... What am I saying? Snap out of it Anilea! You will defect Donovan just not in town limits, but out the inland in the middle of the lake. That were the battle will end once and for all." Sanna looks over at Adam place, "I do feel sorry for hurting your feeling Adam, but I need to force on the battle. I love you from the bottom of my heart," Sanna keep on talking to herself, turning her head back to the lake, and stood there listening to Donovan evil laughing slowly fading into nothing.

Roselyn came outside in her spirit clothes with Tiffany, Andrew, and Aaron, behind her "Hey Anilea, how are you feeling?" Roselyn ask Sanna in a worry voice, seeing Sanna standing looking out at the lake.

"Scared and worry," Sanna say to Roselyn turning around, walking pass Roselyn and everyone else into her bedroom.

"Why?" Roselyn ask Sanna closing the French doors behind her, once Tiffany, Andrew, and Aaron enter.

Sanna stop by the window seat, turning around to face Roselyn to speaking to her, "Because this will be the last battle forever, and only one of us will still be stand between Donovan and me. I am scared and worry about anyone one in this town and you guys to be losing to Donovan group. I lost too many people that I care about to Donovan evil ways of dieing. I do not want to lose anymore to them... So please be careful for me, I don't want watch anyone dieing in front of me."

Roselyn looks at Tiffany, Andrew, and Aaron for a moment, and back to Sanna. "Anilea do not worry us, we will be alright. You worry about yourself, and force on the final battle with Donovan. We will make sure we got your back during the fight," Roselyn say to Sanna. "Anilea, I have faith in you, that you will win this battle for good," Roselyn gave Sanna a hug.

"We all have faith in you, Anilea," Tiffany says to Sanna with a smile on face, and knowing Sanna will defect Donavan for good.

"Me too, you're the only one can beat Donovan ass," Aaron say to Sanna with a smiled on his face, and believing Sanna can do what she need to do to end this battle forever.

"Sport, you will win the battle with Donovan. You know Donovan moves and evil ways, you will win the battle, and we will there to help. When need, beside

I want a piece of Crevan," Andrew say to Sanna with smile on his face, knowing Sanna has the strength to end Donovan life forever, and need to finish up some unfinished business with Crevan from last time they met.

"I have bone to pick with Ryu," Aaron says to everyone with a smile on his face, and knows Ryu ways of fighting.

"Eris and I need to finish off our little fight from last time," Tiffany says to everyone with a smile on her face, and knowing Eris movements in a fight.

"Desdemona and I need to finish our fight too." Roselyn say to everyone with a smile on her face, and going to make sure Desdemona will try anything to play in Sanna mind in any way.

Sanna took a deep breath, letting it out slowly, and speaking to everyone, "Donovan is my, we need to finish this off once and all. I do not want ever fight him ever again. He will die this time for good." Sanna looks around at everyone, "We are strong family and family stick together. I have the best family ever here. Let's get ready to finish this battle for good." She knew that her friends have her back during this battle with Donovan.

The sunset on a quiet and peacefully night, rising on a new day, and the battle of lifetime will start. Two will fight, but one will fall and one will stay standing forever.

Chapter Twenty One

The Big Town Party!

May 20/2065, the sun rose to a new day, Sanna and Donovan stood outside their places watching the sun rising in the distance. Sanna stood on the front deck in her normal clothes, "Today the day...The battle for life will begin and end forever. One will fall and one will stay standing forever," Sanna say to herself watching the orange-red sky changing into a blue sky thinking of everything that about to happen that day, mostly will happen at night. She lowers her head with her hair falling around her head, and thinking what could happen at the end of the battle.

Donovan stood outside his house, watching the sun fully rising into the sky. An evil grin came to his face as he chuckled to himself. Donovan held up a glass of red wine to the sky, letting the wine glisten in the sunlight. "Today the day... Anilea and I will fight for human lives, and that young man, Adam. It will be the last time he will breathe and his heart beating. I will enjoy seeing Adam and your last breath of life. This is your last day on this earth and spirit world. I will enjoy seeing your skinny body turning into dust, and blowing away in the wind. The human race will be under my control forever," Donovan say to himself lowering the glass of red wine, taking a slip of wine, and looking down at the red wine in the glass. Donavan started to chuckled to himself and slowly turning into a huge evil laugh.

The evil laughing echoes through the tress, hills, and around the lake catching Sanna ears. Sanna raised her head from looking down, looking straight in front of her to see rolls of house down the street, and seeing image of her past flashing through out her mind. Seeing what every battle with Donovan looks like, seeing the people running through the streets, blood everywhere. Hearing the sheiks of women, men, children, and babies slowly dieing, seeing fire blazing through out the town, Sanna looks down at her hands to seeing human blood them, and her sword cover in human blood. *'Why should this happen every time? I do not want humans losing their lives because of me, and mostly Donovan, he going down tonight. One the sun is cover by darkness, that when everything will start, once all over only one of us will stay standing forever,'* Sanna thought to herself standing there on her front deck looking out at cars passing by the house. Sanna sighing and went back into the house with a sad look on her face.

~~*~*~*~*~*~*~*~*~*

The afternoon hit; the town people of Spirit-villa putting the last final additions on everything for the party of the 400 years old fight between the two spirits for human lives. Sanna stood out on her balcony wearing her spirit clothes, and hair down. Sanna looks out the big inland in the middle of the lake. Sanna breathe in through her nose, out through her mouth, and trying to stay calm. Sanna let a sigh out, and turn her head to Adam place to see Adam standing there looking at her.

Adam signal Sanna over to his place, Adam wanted to know a few more things about the real Sanna, before she goes and fight Donovan. Sanna jump over to Adam place, and landing in front of Adam on the floor. "What do you want Adam?" Sanna ask Adam looking into Adam blue eyes, and feeling her heart beating quickly in his chest.

Adam looking at Sanna in her spirit clothes, he blush a bit in his cheek, then ask his questions to Sanna, "I have a few questions for you, Anilea."

"Okay ask away then Adam," Sanna say to Adam, lending against the sliding of the house with her back.

Adam fool around a bit to find the right questions to ask Sanna, "Okay then Sanna, when you were reborn back into your spirit, the year and date too?"

Sanna looks at Adam, and answer him back with a chucked in her voice, "You don't know your history Adam. What is today date?"

"May 20/2065?" Adam says to Sanna with a confusing in his voice, knowing the date on the day, and looking at her with a weird look on his face.

"May 20/1665 on my wedding day, remember last year I told you what happen to my family, friend, and lover. That what really happen to me 400 years ago by Donovan and his group. Plus Donovan gave me this scare on my right upper arm." Sanna show Adam the scare across her right arm, from where Donovan left on her, when she was still a human, and before she was reborn back into her spirit self. "He did this before my spirit side came out. Then we fought each other for the first time since the Dark Ages. My friends show up fighting along side of me. After that, Donovan and his groups ran away in fear. For the first 100 years, I went after Donovan, and found back him in this town where I was born June 9/1642, any other questions?" Sanna ask Adam, crossing her arms in front of her body, and sighing at the old memory coming to her mind now.

Adam looks at Sanna with wide mouth and eyes, "I cannot believe that how this all started 400 years ago, on your wedding day... Okay then, how did you met you last lover?"

Sanna try out get upset about the question Adam ask her, but held it together, then spoke to Adam, "We were living beside each other on a farm land. We grow up together, along with our six younger siblings each, 3 boys and 3 girls. We were friends as children into our early teens, and then we fell in love in our last teens. I was 24 years old, him 25 year old, when he pops the question to me around here. One year later, we were getting marry around here, that when Donovan attack me, right before sunset over the lake. That all I am going to tell you, my heart cannot take the bearing of old that old memory right now."

"I see then, and I am sorry for your loses of your family, friends, and lover," Adam says to Sanna. There was quiet for a while between Adam and Sanna, and then Adam spoke up for a bit, "Anilea."

"Yes Adam," Sanna say to Adam looking at him with a blank look on her face, as her eyes met with his eyes, and she can feel her heart beating quickly in her chest still.

"Please be careful for me, and kick Donovan ass," Adam say to Sanna with a smile on his face, and knowing she can and will defect Donovan and his group this time around for good.

Sanna smile at Adam, and say to him, "I will be careful, and I will beat Donovan ass... Please be careful for me." Sanna looks into Adam eyes, and smiling a bit now.

"I will, see you later," Adam says to Sanna, giving Sanna a hug. Sanna hug Adam and left Adam place jumping back to her place. Sanna looks back at Adam place with a smiled on her face, she look up at the blue sky slowly turning orange-red. Sanna enter her bedroom to get ready for the battle between Donovan and her, the last battle ever.

~~*~*~*~*~*~*~*~*~*

That evening the downtown was booming with games, rides, food, and everyone dress up in their costumes. The noise of the party carry all the way to Sanna place, Sanna stood outside her place on the front deck listening to the noises coming from downtown, and looking at her friends standing in the yard, all of them wearing their spirit clothes. "Are you sure we going through that party wearing our spirit clothes? Donovan will be watching out for us, and might attack us early," Aaron says to Sanna in a worry voice.

"He would not attack until the sky is cover with darkness and the sun is cover that went Donovan will attack. We need to make sure we are watching out for them in the crowd, and keep a good eye on them if you spot them anywhere. Now let's go and make this the last battle ever, I don't want to do this never again," Sanna told everyone, walking down the steps, and keep on walking down the street to the party downtown. Sanna was force on the final battle with Donovan, but in her heart, she could not forget Adam love for her.

Will Adam love hurt Sanna force on the battle with Donovan or make her stronger?

~~*~*~*~*~*~*~*~*

Party was going strong downtown; everyone in town was enjoying themselves, and having the time of their lives. Everyone dress up in the coolest costumes, and the children playing with fake swords in their hands imaging that they are white or dark spirit running around the streets. Adults dress up too, having fun watching their family and friends having fun, and enjoying the party.

In the shadows on an alleyway, Donovan and his group watching every town people have fun. Donovan chuckled a bit, "Those fools have no idea what really going today. They will soon find out what this day is really about, as they slowly dieing in front of me. Poor Anilea will not be strong enough to defect me. I know her weakness, and I will use it against her big time. She will not live after this battle," Donovan told his group, then looks at Desdemona to say to her, "My dear little sister, you know what today to that Adam guy, and make sure Anilea witness Adam dieing in front of her. Then I will attack Anilea, and kill her for the last time with my sword. I will be the last one standing and the human kind will be my forever." Donovan started too chuckled at the thought he got, and slowly his chuckled growing into an uproar, throwing his head back laughing evil. Everyone in his group join in with Donovan laughing evilly. "Enough now remember to stay lower for now. Once the sun is cover with darkness that when we attack," Donovan told his group, looking out at the town people having their fun one last time, and his mind was on the plans to kill off Anilea once and for all.

"Can I please hurt one person now?" Ryu beg to Donovan with his body twitching, itching to hurt someone very badly right now, and wanting to see some blood right away.

Eris smacks Ryu in the back of the head with her left hand, and spoke to him in a commanding voice, "Not until the sky is cover with darkness." Eris and Desdemona stood there in black leather pants, red tank top, and black boots. Instead of skits, and everyone had weapons behind them.

"Okay my dear sexy wife," Ryu say in a sorry voice to everyone, rubbing the back of his head with his right hand, but still itching to hurt a human really badly.

"Lets get going, and stay lower in shadows. If you see, Anilea or her friends keep a close eye on them. When the time come, as the sun is cover by compete darkness, we attack on this little town," Donovan says to his group, walks along the street keeping his eyes out for Aniela, he wants to get her this year, and finishing off her life this day forever.

Sanna and her friends arrive at the party downtown, standing there at the entryway of the party, looking at everything going on downtown. "Remember to keep your eyes open for any Donovan group, and make sure your ready to fight, when the time comes," Sanna told her friends looking at the party going on in front of them. "Be careful too, I don't want to lose any of you guys. We are family and family stick together."

"We will be Anilea, and you are careful too," Roselyn say to Sanna placing her right hand on Sanna left shoulder, and knowing Sanna mind was on the main part of this battle to finish off Donovan forever.

"I will Rose," Sanna told Roselyn placing her right hand on Roselyn right hand, and nodding her head now at her friends. Sanna let go of Roselyn hand, feeling Roselyn hand lifting off her shoulder, and Sanna mind was force on the fight now.

They went their separate ways around the party to keep an eye out for Donovan group, Sanna keeping her eyes open for Donovan. Sanna was walking around the party in her spirit clothes watching out for Donovan. When she bumping into someone, "I am so sorry sir," Sanna say to the person, not looking up for a second as she keep her eyes down at the ground, and looking up to face the person back now.

The person turns around to face Sanna, and looking at her with a smile on his face. "That okay madam," he told Sanna wearing white clothes and a mask along his eyes.

Sanna realize the male voice talking to her, "Adam? What are you doing here? I told you to stay lower," Sanna whisper to Adam through her teeth, after she told him to stay lower and out of Donovan sight.

"What for and miss this fun downtown. In addition, they would not find me, I am wearing a mask. Do not worry about me, I will be fine. You need to force on the battle and taking care of Donovan forever," Adam told Sanna with a smile on his face, and happy she was standing in front of him for that moment.

"I will, take care of yourself, Adam," Sanna say to Adam walking pass Adam, and not getting too close to Adam if Donovan group is watching being together.

Adam quickly grab Sanna left wrist with his right hand as she pass by her, "Please one slow dance for one last time, for me," Adam ask Sanna with a sad voice, and wanting one more thing from Sanna before the battle begins.

Sanna looks at Adam with a shock look first, them calming down to say to Adam, "Okay one slow dance, then I have to keep my eyes opened for Donovan Just one slow down, and not funny business. No kissing or grabbing my butt, I will hurt you if you decide to do that to me."

"Okay then," Adam say to Sanna with a huge smile on his face, and taking Sanna to the dance floor to slow dance that was playing.

Adam held Sanna close to his body, and Sanna blush bright red in her cheeks. "Adam, this is too close for comforter. Please no more of this," Sanna told Adam dancing in Adam arms, and keeping her eyes out for Donovan or his group.

"Please let me do this for this moment together. This might be the last time we will together, after this night you will be gone. Andrew and Aaron told me, that they always take you away from this town for along time. Please enjoy our last dance together," Adam say to Sanna, dancing with Sanna slowly in his arms. Sanna gave into Adam request and enjoying the slow dance in each other arms, as they were the last ones on the dance floor as everyone left the dance floor slowly.

The darkness slowly covers the sky, as the sun set over the lake, and dark clouds cover the stars and moon. Donovan emerges from the shadows seeing Sanna dancing in Adam arms with an evil smiled on his face. "This will be so easy," Donovan say walking closer to the dance floor slowly, drawing his sword from its sheath with his right hand, and smirking evilly the whole time.

A drunken man stops Donovan in his track, right in front of Donovan, and smelling like he had a bit too much to drink, "Hey buddy, who are you dress up as?" The drunken man spoke to Donovan looking over Donovan clothes, and he cannot stand still at all as his body swing side to side.

"I am Donovan, ruler of the darkness and its dark spirits. Now get of my way human, I have business with a bitch ass spirit, who due to be put to death tonight," Donovan rudely spoke to the man, trying to get around the drunken person, but nothing was working now.

"Your not Donovan, he will never wear those clothes. He too old to wear the new style, you're a liar," the man spoke to Donovan with bad beer breath, red drunken eyes, his clothes hanging off his body, and his body swinging side to side still.

Donovan was getting tired of this drunken man nonsense, and badly drunk breath from all the beers this man had now. Donovan quickly draws his long sword from the sheath, from the left side of his body with his right hand, with one quick move stabbing the drunken man through his stomach. The drunken man started to coughing up blood from his mouth, and lending forward on Donovan sword with wide eyes. Donovan whisper to the man left ear, "Now you believe me for who I am really. Now you are died to me, burn in hell because you smell very badly." Donovan pulled his long sword out of the drunken man stomach, letting the man fall to the ground with his blood all around body, and watching the man taking his final breath lying on the ground.

A young woman saw Donovan killing the man, and screaming at the top of her voice for everyone to hear around her. Desdemona, Eris, Crevan, and Ryu emerge from the shadows with swords in their hands, and evil grins on their faces as they walk closer to Sanna friends. Sanna friends know what was going on with the screams of terror coming from the middle of the town square, and quickly change into their warrior clothes, the white t-shirts, white pants for the men and white leggings for the women, and white shoe. Sliver wrist covers, leg covers, swords in their hands, they turn around in the time to block the evil spirits sword with their own swords. "Ah Roselyn nice to you again," Desdemona say evil to Roselyn face to face, snapping her teeth close to Roselyn face, and growling a bit.

"Nice to meet you again, Desdemona, how Crevan doing ever since Andrew beat his ass, from the last fight we had 100 years ago," Roselyn say to Desdemona face to face with narrow eyes. Desdemona got very angry, starting to swing her sword at Roselyn, Roselyn draw her sword quickly, and standing they getting ready to fight now.

"Andrew, nice to see you again, and how that beautiful wife of your?" Crevan say to Andrew face to face, using his strength against Andrew sword lightly against each other, and snapping his teeth in front of Andrew face.

"She is fine, and so is I, Crevan," Andrew say to Crevan face to face with narrow eyes, keeping his sword closed to his chest, and pushing Crevan slowly away from his body with his sword.

“Tiffany, how are you doing?” Eris says to Tiffany evil tone in her voice with her sword across her body, and looking Tiffany getting ready fight between each other.

“Fine Eris, now enough of this small chatting lets do this,” Tiffany say to Eris, looking at Eris with narrow eyes, and cannot wait for start this fight with Eris.

“Aaron, how nice to see you again,” Ryu say to Aaron face to face with narrow eyes and his right hands hovering over his swords handles.

“I am doing great, how you doing, Ryu?” Aaron says to Ryu face to face with narrow eyes, and his right hands hovering over his swords handles.

They all stood their ground across from each other in the town square, as they staring each other down with swords across their chest, and all the humans running around them in terror.

The final battle for human life had started, who will be one reminder standing, and who will fall.

CHAPTER TWENTY TWO

The Battle Begins & Down fall to Humans!

Sanna heard the screams of people, looking over her right shoulder to see Donovan standing there in the distance, died body at his feet and blood on his sword. "Adam, get out here now!" Sanna yelled at Adam quickly pushing Adam always from her, and keeping her eyes on Donovan as she still looking over her shoulder at him.

"Why?" Adam asks Sanna with a confused voice, but he could not believe what he saw next. Adam back away from Savanna a few steps and seeing someone dress in all black glaring at them both from a far.

Donovan came quickly running up to Sanna, his sword at his right side, the blade ready to go, and an evil grin on his face. Sanna turn around quickly drawing her dagger from the small sheath with her right hand, turning the dagger into a sword, and blocking Donovan attack with her sword. Sanna spirit dress blasted off her body revealing her warrior clothes; white tank top, white leggings, white shoes, gold wrist covers, gold leg covers, and hair long hair pulled back into a ponytail. "Ah Anilea, you finally unveil who you are really to the humans. It is too bad that this will be your last battle, and the last time we will meet. I will enjoy getting rid of you once and for all," Donovan told Sanna face to face, as his eyes the color blood red, and pushing against Sanna sword with his sword.

"Donovan, you will be the one gone forever, I will win this battle between us. This end this year forever," Sanna told Donovan face to face, keeping her eyes on Donovan, and keeping her sword against his sword.

Donovan laughs evilly in the air, and spoke to Sanna evilly, "You will never win, and I know your weakness." Donovan look over Sanna, eyeing Adam with his red eyes, and an evil grin came to his face. Donovan knows his plans to use Adam to finish off Sanna for good, and it might cost Adam life too.

Sanna looks over her right shoulders at Adam, and yelling at him, "Get out of here now! GO!" Sanna keeping her grounds with Donovan strength, feeling his strength against her sword, and using her own strength to keep herself safe now.

Adam got the hint from Sanna taking off running through the crowd, *'Be careful Anilea,'* Adam thought to himself as he ran through the crowd of terror people, and feeling his heart sinking deeply in his chest knowing this could be the last time he seen Sanna forever.

Sanna saw Adam running away Donovan and her. Donovan pisses-off seeing Adam getting away from him. "NO!" Donovan cries out at the top of his voice, punching Sanna in the face with his left fist, feeling Sanna strength letting go of his sword, putting his sword away in his sheath on the right side of his hip, and took off running through the crowd to get Adam on foot.

Sanna re-force herself by giving her head a shake, putting her sword in her sheath, and taking off after Donovan quickly as she can on foot. She needs to keep Donovan and his group away from Adam for good, and she needs Adam to be safe for her love. Sanna got closer to Donovan from the behind, jumping into the air to tackle Donovan to the ground, pinning him face down on the ground. Sanna had Donovan pin on the ground with her hands on his back, looking at Adam, who stops moving, and yelled at him, "Get going now! Hide from the dark spirits now!" Adam nodded his head, and ran to hide. Sanna try to keep Donovan down on the ground with her body still, feeling Donovan struggling under her body.

Donovan uses his strength to get Sanna off his back as he was piss off big time. "Get off me now, bitch!" Donovan yelled in rage at Sanna, pushing off the ground on all fours, and sending Sanna flying backwards in a side of a building.

Sanna screams flying into the side of a building, hitting the building her back against the brick siding. Sanna stood there with her back against the building. "Ouch that hurts big time," Sanna told herself trying to stay force. Sanna looks up to see Donovan flying toward her at high speed with sword ready to killed Sanna. Sanna quickly drove to the left to dodge Donovan attack, Donovan flow into the building, crashing through the brick siding, making a huge hole in the building. Sanna got to her feet slowly to see her friends in the distance fighting Donovan group, but her mind was on where Adam was now. Sanna look around to see if Adam left the party along with everyone else in town or hiding in a good spot from the evil spirits.

Sanna could not see Adam anywhere, until she felt warming touch on her left shoulder. Sanna turn around quickly, sword ready in her right hand, pointing the blade tip at whoever was behind her. Sanna was surprise who was standing behind her, "Adam? I told you to go hide, this is not hiding," Sanna told Adam in a shock voice, lowering her sword to her right side, and could not believe that Adam did not listen to her.

Adam looks at Sanna to say, "I don't want to hide. I want to help you to defect Donovan forever." Adam took off his mask from his face, throwing it to the ground. Adam looks into Sanna eyes with his eyes, and his heart beating quickly for Sanna love.

Sanna looks at Adam quickly, "You can help me by getting your butt hidden somewhere safe from Donovan," Sanna say to Adam pointing over Adam right shoulder. Sanna keeping her eyes on Adam, and trying to get Adam away from there before anything bad happens to Adam.

"No, not until you kiss me on the lips," Adam say to Sanna lending closer to Sanna lips. Sanna try not giving in to Adam request, and closing her eyes to receive Adam kiss on the lips, but she turn her head to the side to feel the kiss on her cheek. Sanna keep her eyes on hole where Donovan created hitting the build, Sanna grab Adam left hand in her right hand, and trying to get Adam away from there before anything bad happens to Adam by running through the empty town square.

A huge blast of flames came out from the build, and fire started to burn through out downtown. Donovan came walking out from among the flames to see Adam and Sanna standing there close together. "Ah Anilea, your still going to make this so easy to get rid of Adam now," Donovan spoke to Sanna holding his sword tight in his right hand, eyeing Adam with the glaring of the flames in his red eyes.

"Adam runs now!" Sanna say to Adam pushing him away from her with her hands. Adam took off running to find a hiding spot away from Donovan.

Donovan swing at Sanna with his sword, hitting the scar across her right upper arm with the blade, and reopening the scar again. "First one to draw blood, and you know I will win the final round here," Donovan say to Sanna seeing her blood running down the sword blade with an evil grin on his face. Donovan closed his eyes to the smell of Sanna blood on his sword, and enjoying the smell of any blood, growling softly under his voice, and opening his eyes at Sanna.

Sanna stumble back from the building, holding her right arm with her left hand. "Fuck, not again!" Sanna say to herself with pain hitting her body, but she never show the pain in front of Donovan. Her mind has now been on this battle with Donovan, but she was worry about Adam, where he was hiding now.

Donovan walks closer to Sanna with his sword ready to kill her, and one big evil grin on his face. "Any last wishes Anilea before I get rid of you forever, like your spirit family, your human family, friends, and last lover. I enjoy spilling their body blood all over the place, and now it is your turn," Donovan told Sanna pointing the sword tips in Sanna face, and waiting for her attacks any moment.

Sanna stood her ground in front of Donovan, looking around to see multiple died bodies laying in the street, women, men, and children with their blood around their lifeless body. Sanna remember the one nightmare she had when she move here over a year ago, and know what could happen. Sanna swing her sword at Donovan with rage. "No Donovan, I will not died this year or ever. You have ruined enough human lives every time, and this end now!" Sanna yelled at Donovan in rage, and attacking Donovan with her sword.

Their swords clashing together as they dance around downtown area, sparks from the metal of the swords shown. Donovan and Sanna were face-to-face, bearing their teeth at each other. "Give up Anilea, and I may spare you worthless life. If you coming my bride forever?" Donovan says to Sanna through his teeth evilly, looking down into her eyes with his evil eyes, and knowing that there was only one chose for Sanna to choose beside death to keep everyone alive.

Sanna thought for a second in her mind, and saying through her teeth in mean voice, "I will never give up that easy or become your bride forever. I will die first before I will be yours forever. Now enough of this chat lets finish this battle once and for all." Sanna use her sword to push against Donovan away from her, placing her sword back in its stealth, and ran down to the beach. Donovan took off running after Sanna, following her down to the beach, jumping into the air.

Sanna reach the beach, stopping along the water edge, turning around to see Donovan flying toward her, "Oh no!" Sanna say to herself feeling Donovan impact around her body, flying across the water, and right a tree into a large inland struggling in Donovan grip.

Donovan grabs Sanna face with his left hand, and looking into Sanna eyes. "My dear Anilea, you have been a worthy fighter all these years, it's a shame you must died now by my hand," Donovan told Sanna reaching back with his right hand, and quickly moving his hand toward Sanna chest.

Sanna quickly move out of Donovan grip to the right side, seeing Donovan right hand hitting the tree, and seeing his right fingers sticking into the tree. *'That was too closing comfortable,'* Sanna thought to herself. Sanna kick Donovan in the back of his head with right her foot and landing back on her feet.

Donovan fell to his knees slowly; his right fingers still in the trees, and try to re-force himself. "You bitch! That smart-ass move, but that will be your last move," Donovan says to Sanna ripping a huge hole in the tree, breaking the bark in his hand, and standing up straight. Donovan draw his sword out if the sheath, and pointing the tip of the blade at Sanna. Sanna drawing her sword of the sheath, and standing her ground waiting for Donovan move.

Ten minutes of silent's, nothing but the wind blowing through the leaves, the lake water crashing against the rocks. Everything was quite until Donovan made his move first running toward Sanna swords ready, Sanna block Donovan move with her sword across her body. The swords clash together as they move around the inland with their swords clashing together. Donovan tries to catch Sanna off guard, but nothing was working to weak Sanna. Donovan keeps up his attacks on Sanna, until he looks over Sanna to see Desdemona coming through the trees with Adam in her hands. "Will Anilea, what you do if something happens to your boyfriend, Adam?" Donovan says to Sanna with an evil grin on his face, stopping for the moment across from her, and pointing over Sanna right shoulder.

Sanna looks over her right shoulder to see Adam in Desdemona creepy hands, seeing Adam beaten face from Desdemona, and his blood drizzling down his face from a cut on his forehead, "Adam!" Sanna shouted to Adam pushing Donovan away from her body with her hands. "Unhand Adam now, Desdemona," Sanna say to Desdemona turning around to face Desdemona, closing her hands into a fist, and wanting Desdemona to unhand Adam right now.

Desdemona stood there along there along the tree line with Adam beside her. "Nope, Adam here is enjoying my company. Oh, by the way Roselyn is not going to be here to help you. She busy is picking herself off the ground, and maybe never coming to save Adam or you. I gave her the best knock-out I have ever given to her in a fight," Desdemona say to Sanna holding Adam closer to her body, snuggling into Adam right arm with the side of her face, and licking her lips sexy like to Sanna.

Sanna looks at Desdemona with narrow eyes, and a mean look on her face, "I say unhand Adam, now!" Sanna yelled at Desdemona, showing her teeth to Desdemona, and cringe her fists tighter now.

"Nope, he my new sex toy, and there nothing you can do about it, Anilea," Desdemona say to Sanna in a slid voice, and looking at Adam in his face, then asking Sanna. "Anilea have you ever kiss Adam on the lips?" Sanna shook her head to Desdemona. "Will then, maybe I should kiss Adam here to see what it is like then." Desdemona turned to Adam with her left hand, grabbing Adam face in her hands, and locking lips with Adam. Desdemona leaking her poison from her lips into Adam body as they kiss, and Adam trying to pull away from her but could not.

Desdemona let go of Adam, Adam stood there for a bit, then collapsing to the ground with wide eyes and mouths. Gasping for air, and holding onto life the best he can. Sanna stood there in shock for a bit, and then spoke in rage, "Desdemona how could you? Adam never deserve that, you bitch!"

Desdemona laugh evilly in the air, and spoke to Sanna, "I know he was your weakness, now you will died by my brother hands." Desdemona pointed over Sanna shoulders to Donovan with an evil grin on her face.

Sanna turn around quickly to see Donovan swinging his sword straight across, slicing Sanna across her lower stomach, making her blood drizzling down her lower body with a deep wound. Donovan look at Sanna to say evilly, "Adam is you downfall now, this now going to be so easy to get rid of you," Donovan raising his sword in the air over his head, letting the blade glisten in the moonlight.

Sanna watch Donovan sword being rising in the air, Sanna hunch over in pain with her left arms around the wound, and trying to force on Donovan. *'This is it, I'm a goner forever,'* Sanna thought to herself watching Donovan sword, and if Adam was going to die then she will die too.

Donovan was ready to lower his sword down to Sanna body, when a huge light ball came out of nowhere, hitting Donovan on the left side, and making Donovan flying through the trees. Sanna look to see her friends, standing there along the tree line. "Andrew! Aaron! Tiffany! Roselyn! Thanks goodness you guys are here now," Sanna say to her friends seeing them running up to her sides, and happy they are alive.

"Anilea are you okay?" Roselyn ask Sanna seeing the sword wound across Sanna lower stomach. Touching Sanna body with her hands, making Sanna cling in pain, and worry about Sanna health and fighting skills.

"I'm fine, but it's Adam. Desdemona poison him with her lips. I need to help him now, before it's too late," Sanna say to her friends, stumbling closer to Adam by the tree line with her arm across the wound, and trying not to cry that she seeing Adam dieing now.

"Anilea, you cannot do that, Desdemona poison will kill you too," Roselyn say to Sanna stopping in her tracks in front of Sanna, and knowing that Sanna will proudly die by the poison.

"I will not die; I can destroy the poison with my own lips. I will be in pain for a bit, but at lest Adam will be safe and alive if I do that. Please let me do this for Adam life," Sanna say to Roselyn stumbling away from her friends close to Adam slowly dieing body.

Donovan show up standing in among the trees with his group, laughing evilly with his group standing beside him. "Anilea, you think you friends little light show will not stop me from finishing you worthless life. Think again Anilea, you and your friends will disappear forever. Boys, girls take care of Anilea group, and Anilea is all my," Donovan told Sanna signalling his group to attack Sanna friends. Donovan group attack Anilea group, and Donovan attack Sanna by flying into her, slamming into her body, slamming her body against a tree, and snapping his teeth close to Sanna face.

Sanna try to move out of Donovan grip, and looking Donovan in the face with narrow eyes. Sanna got her feet up to Donovan chest, and quickly pushing Donovan away fro her. "Back the fucking off Donovan," Sanna yelled at Donovan as she pushing him away from her with her feet, sending Donovan through the trees. Sanna landed on her feet still holding her waist with her left hand, and pain shooting through out her body. Sanna remove her left hand from the wound, lifting her left hand up to her face, seeing her blood on her left hand, and slowly running down her arm. Sanna lower her left hand to her side, Sanna looks over at Adam slowly dieing on the ground. "I am not going let you die, Adam," Sanna say to herself stumbling toward Adam. Sanna knelt down beside Adam body on his left side. Sanna touching Adam face with her right hand, "I am so sorry Adam," Sanna spoke quietly to Adam, a small tear forming in the corner of her eyes.

Adam looks up at Sanna kneeling there beside him with a smile on his face, "Anilea," Adam quietly spoke to Sanna. "I... love... you, and I am sorry." Tears fell from Adam eyes, he felt so stupid for being involve with this battle, and being Sanna weakness.

Sanna looks at Adam to say to him, "Please Adam don't speak, save your strength for me. I am the one who sorry, I should not drag you into this mess of me, I should have keeping you out of it. Then you will not be like this, I love you Adam very much," tears starting to fall from her eyes hitting Adam cheeks.

Adam touches the wound on Sanna waist with his left hand, and spoke to Sanna through the pain from the poison, "You're badly hurt," seeing her blood on his hand, looking at Sanna with worry eyes.

Sanna took Adam left hand, holding it in her hands, and spoke to Adam with tears in her eyes, "It is nothing, I will heal, but you are dieing. I cannot have that, Adam. I love you very much from the bottom of my heart, and I will so happy to marry you." Sanna lower her head, closing her eyes for a moment, then opening them at Adam.

Adam looks at Sanna with pain in his eyes, and say to Sanna in a quiet happy voice, "So that a yes then." Adam smiled at Sanna, and thinking about the future, they could have together if he does not die.

Sanna nodded her head to Adam, and say to Adam in an upset voice, "It's a yes." Adam touch the left side of Sanna face with his left hand, smiled at her sweetly, slowly closed his eyes, and let out his final breathe. Sanna felt Adam left hand slipping down her face, and seeing Adam letting out his final breathe, "No! Please no!" Sanna shouting out loudly touching Adam face with her right hand, "I can at lest give you a kiss on the lips," Sanna softly spoke to Adam, lending down to kiss him on the lips, feeling Desdemona poison leaving Adam lifeless body, and entering her own body.

Pain set in quickly in Sanna body, Sanna let go of Adam lips, and feeling the burning feeling on the poison inside of her body. Sanna curled up into a ball on her knees, she was in pain from her body but in her heart, but Adam was gone forever. Sanna starting to deeply crying that she lost another lover, who she loves with all her heart and soul.

Chapter Twenty Three

A Spirit Reborn!

Donovan saw what Sanna did to Adam by kissing Adam on then lips, and seeing her pain from the poison, "You foolish girl Anilea. Desdemona poison is stronger then ever, and you think that you can get rid of it with own body. HA! I will die no matter what," Donovan says to Sanna walking up to her, grading Sanna ponytail with his left hand, and picking Sanna off the ground to face him. "Say it Anilea, you will die forever. Just like everyone in your past lives that I have killed," Donovan laughs evilly in the air that he have weaken her enough to end her life very soon.

Sanna closed hr eyes seeing people she know throughout the years and her family and lover that Donovan has killed. Sanna tighten her hands into a fist, and looking at Donovan with narrow eyes to say loudly, "You may get rid of my past friend, family, and lover, but you will never break me that easy. I will fight until my dieing breathe," Sanna turning around quickly in his grip, punch Donovan across the face with her right hand, feeling Donovan letting go of her hair, and standing there on the ground. Sanna draw her sword from the sheath, and pointing the tip at Donovan.

Donovan looks at Sanna in the face, drawing his sword too, and pointed the tip at Sanna. "You want to fight, let's fight to the death… One will remind standing after this battle," Donovan told Sanna being ready to fight to the death.

Donovan ran toward Sanna sword right-to-right, and yelling at the top of his voice. Their swords clash in the middle of the fighting. Sanna push against Donovan sword with her sword, and keep on fighting against Donovan with rage in her blood. The poison and the wound slowly got to Sanna; Sanna was slowing down in her fighting. Sanna try not let pain get to her as she keep on fighting with Donovan. Donovan saw how weak Sanna was getting with every blow she was giving against his sword with her sword. "You're still a fool Anilea.

You surly die by my hand. You're so weak that you cannot even stand up straight, and hold your sword tight in your hand," Donovan told Sanna looking at her in the face, quickly hooking his sword under Sanna sword, throwing Sanna sword in the air, and having it landing beside Adam on the right side. Donovan knocks Sanna down onto the ground with his right elbow on her back, and pointing his sword at Sanna face. "You will lose, called off your friends and I will call off my group. I want to do this alone, and if they think of doing anything stupid to save your worthless life, I want to know."

Sanna knelt there on the ground, nodded her head to Donovan to agree with him, looking at her friends fighting, and calling out to them, "Roselyn! Tiffany! Andrew! Aaron! Get out of here now!" Her friends stop fighting with Donovan group, and staring at her with wide eyes.

Donovan looks at his group to yell at them, "Ryu! Crevan! Eris! Desdemona! Get out Now! Back to the main land now, and wait for me!" His groups stop fighting with Sanna group, and looking at him with wide eyes.

Roselyn looks at Sanna to yell at her, "Why do you want us to leave?" Roselyn and the rest of them was surprise at Donovan and Sanna commands to them.

Sanna looks at Roselyn to say, "Because we want to finish the right way, one on one. Get back to the main land now, and wait for me. I will be fine my friends, this fight has always been between Donovan and me." Sanna looking up at Donovan hoping she had the strength to finish off Donovan forever.

Sanna friends and Donovan group left the inland back to the main land, and watching to see who will win the final battle between Donovan and Sanna. They stood there on the beach watching as the town people slowly show up to see what going on the inland. Sanna looks up at Donovan from the ground to say to him rudely, "Come on finish me now. I know that what you want do! Finish me off for once and for all! I have nothing to life for, you killed off the man of my love life," Looking into Donovan red eyes with her hazel eyes, showing no fear at all toward Donovan.

Donovan looks at Sanna, and saying to her, "You been a great fighter through out the years, now that is your final dieing wish I will grant you, good-bye forever Anilea." Donovan raises his sword above his head keeping his eyes on Sanna, giving up to him, and will enjoy finishing her off for good.

Adam right hand move a bit, slowly moving closer to the handle of Sanna sword, curling his fingers around the handle of the sword, and holding the sword tight in his hand. Sanna wait for her fault by Donovan lowering her head, "Good-bye everyone," Sanna closed her eyes as Donovan sword slowly coming down to finish Sanna off for good. She would never know that she going to died any second now.

The sound of metal colliding a few inches from Sanna body, "How could this be? You should be death by Desdemona poison… Unless you're a…" Donovan say to whomever his was talking too with shock in his voice.

Sanna open her eyes to see Adam standing there in white jeans, white jean jacket with white shirt underneath, white cowboy boots, and holding Sanna sword in his right hand. "A spirit," Sanna says to Donovan with a smiled on her face. "I know there was something about you, Adam, that I had a feeling about." Sanna could not believe that Adam a spirit, but also her past lover from 400 years ago on that date.

"Donovan! Your rain of darkness is over forever!" Adam spoke to Donovan in rage in his voice, holding Sanna sword tight in his right hand, looking at Donovan with narrow eyes.

"Now a new member to my game, this is will be the last time we will meet," Donavon say to Adam with an evil smirk on his face. Donovan held his sword in his hand, pushing against Sana sword in Adam hands.

Sanna struggle to her feet, and stood there behind Adam hunching over in pain with her left arm around her waist. "Adam gives me my sword," Sanna say to Adam holding out her right hand to Adam, trying out let the pain get her, and re-force her eyes.

Adam looks at Sanna over his left shoulder to say to her, "Are you crazy? You're badly hurt, if you try anything with your powers, you will die." Adam keeps his strength against Donovan sword, and keeping Donovan away from Sanna.

"Adam trust me, I will live after. Trust me," Sanna say to Adam still holding out her right hand to Adam for her sword. Adam rolling his eyes at Sanna was saying, pushing Donovan sword away from Donovan hands into the air, taking his right foot, kicking Donovan away from him, and throwing Sanna sword to her. Sanna grab the sword out of the air with her right hand, yelling at Adam, "Move Adam!" Adam move to the left side, running behind Sanna, placing his hands on Sanna shoulders, and transfer some of his powers to Sanna.

Sanna body started to glow white down to the sword tip. Adam body started glowing white with Sanna. Sanna rising her sword over her head, eyeing Donovan coming closer to her with his sword ready to strike Sanna with rage. Sanna in one quick swipe downwards to the ground, hitting the ground with the blade of her sword, and letting her powers spread along the ground. Donovan stop in his tracks away from Sanna and Adam, feeling the white light from Sanna sword hitting his body, dropping his sword to the ground as his body slowly burning up in the white light.

A huge fire started on the inland where Donovan stood; the glowing light from the fire lit the night sky, and everyone on the main land watch the inland slowly in glop in flames. Everyone was wondering about what going on with the battle. Sanna friends worry about Sanna life and hoping she okay and alive still.

Sanna stood there sword blade on the ground, breathing heavily, and Adam hands still on her shoulders. Sanna look down to see that she was in her dress, and her hair down. She moves out of Adam hands, turning around to face Adam, and spoke to him, "You're a spirit too," Sanna smiled at Adam.

Adam looks down at Sanna, and spoke to her with a smiled on his face, "Yes I am, and also you're past lover from 400 years ago too. I told you at our wedding day as I was dieing breathe that I will be back to take you as my wife fro real." Taking Sanna left hand in his hands, holding it nicely, and worry about Sanna health now from her wound across her body.

Sanna closed her eyes, thinking back 400 years ago to her wedding day, when Donovan group attack her past lover, and opening her eyes to say, "I remember those words that you say to me on your dieing breathe. Still I want to know how old is your spirit?"

Adam looks at Sanna, and laugh at her to say, "My spirit is the same age as yours, 1315 year old. I was the mystery spirit that helps you fight with Donovan during the Dark Ages, I try to save your family from him, but I fail at my mission to protract your family and you. I told myself to live a human life until you kiss me on the lips and be my wife or you save me from anyone of Donovan group doing. You have release my spirit with your kiss, and we defect Donovan together." Adam touching Sanna faces with his left hand, seeing her smiling a bit, happy her doing fine right now.

Sanna nodded her head to Adam to agree with him, '*That why my past memories was playing so strong this time around being in this town, because of Adam,*' Sanna thought to herself, looking into Adam eyes, feeling her heart beating quickly in her chest, and letting go of Adam right hand.

Sanna walks closer to the wall of the flames looking at the huge wall of fire with her sword in her right hand. Her drizzling to the ground from her wounds across her upper right arm and waist. She lower head to the ground, and spoke in a whisper, "The deal is done. It is over… finally." Sanna long hair glow by the fire as the moon glistening off the lake water. Sanna drop her sword to the ground, looking up at the flames, and letting out a sigh as she turns her back away from the fire. Sanna looks at Adam with a small smiled on her face.

Adam looks at Sanna to say with a smiled on her face, "You did it, Donovan is gone forever, and now you can live your life normal now. I love you." Adam looking at the way Sanna was standing by the wall of fire with a bloodstain on her clothes.

Sanna looks at Adam to say to him with a bit of pain in her voice, "I know, my life will not be complete without you my love," Sanna took a step forward from the fire.

A dark male shadow appears in the flames, its eyes glowing in the fire. His right hand reaches out from the flames, and grabbing Sanna by the back of her shirt. Fear hit in Sanna eyes with the hand on her back of her shirt. "It cannot be?" Sanna spoke in a stun voice turning her head to the shadow. The shadow started dragging Sanna back into the fire, Sanna shrieks loudly in the air, that echo through the valley as she keep on be dragging backward into the fire.

"Anilea!" Adam shouted to Sanna seeing her being drag into the fire by the dark shadow. Adam ran closer to the fire with his right hand out of Sanna to grab, but it was too late as the flames burning brighter and hotter, "No!" Adam shouted falling to his knees, slamming his fist on the ground in angry that he never got the chances to save Sanna.

Chapter Twenty Four

Anilea vs. Donovan!

Sanna pass through the flames of the fire to a wide-open area in the middle of the fire. The dark male shadow places both hands on top of her shoulders, it lend closer to her right ear, and whisper evilly in her ear, "You will never defect me Anilea. I will never die that easy from your ways. I will win this battle once and all." Tighten the grip on her shoulders with his evil hands, as he clinches his teeth together as he squeezes Sanna shoulders.

Sanna fell to her knees from the pain of the grip on her shoulders. "How could you still be a live Donovan? I use everything I have inside of me to kill you... How are you still standing?" Sanna say to Donovan in pain, thinking about the attack with the white light, and hoping Donovan will be gone forever now.

"I told you, Anilea. I am not that easy to kill by your stupid white light. You're also missing your sword, so you are going to be an easy target to kill now," Donovan says to Sanna looking down at the back of Sanna "Does this looks so formerly... You like this... When was the last time you were in the position?" Donovan thought back in his memories to the end of the Dark Ages. "Oh yes, when I was about to kill you at the end of the Dark Ages. Your family got involved between us that time, but now you have no one to help you this time, you will died." Donovan taking his left hand off Sanna shoulder, raising his hand back, and looking down at Sanna back with evil in his eyes.

Sanna closed her eyes get ready for Donovan attack, and she was ready to give up on fighting him. *'This is it, the end for me... Good-bye everyone,'* Sanna thought to herself waiting for Donovan attack on her. *'I hope it is quick,'* Sanna know that she was going die by Donovan hands, and lower her head with her eyes closed.

Donovan laughs evil looking at Sanna back with his eyes, quickly sending his left hand straight toward Sanna back, to her heart. "Good-bye Anilea, we will never meet again," Donovan says to Sanna as he takes his actions quickly. Out of nowhere, Sanna sword come flying through the flames hitting Donovan left hand with the blade, and stopping in the tree. "Who did that?" Donovan says loudly looking around the flames burning bright, stopping his attack on Sanna, and feeling his blood bleeding out of his left hand.

"I told you Donovan, your rain of darkness is over for good," Adam says to Donovan walking through the flames into the opened, stopping no that far from Sanna and Donovan.

"You're a fool Adam; you think you will save this little bitch from my actions. She will died by my hands, and there nothing you could do about it," Donovan say to Adam in rage, seeing Adam standing there, and that Adam was involve with his plans for Sanna.

Sanna quickly move out of Donovan grip, twisting her body in his right hand, running up to her sword, grabbing the handle of the sword, holding the sword in her hands looking at Donovan with narrow eyes. "Donovan this end now, Adam gets out of here now!" Sanna yelled in rage standing there with her sword ready to fight.

Adam understood Sanna requests, moving off to the side, and not being involved with this fight anymore between Sanna and Donovan. "Be careful my love," Adam whisper to Sanna watching from the sidelines.

Sanna stood her grounds in front of Donovan, holding her sword tighten in her hands, pointing the tip of the blade at Donovan chest, and narrow her eyes at Donovan. Sanna was not joking around anymore, and feeling her wounds healing up slowly to be more strengthening now. Donovan sticks out his right arm to the side with his palm wide open. Sanna saw Donovan sword flying through the flames of the fire, and into Donovan right hand. Donovan curled his fingers around the handle of his sword, slowly moving the blade toward Sanna chest, and smiled evil at Sanna. "You think that you are strong enough to defeat me. Think again, your still have the wound across your waist from early attack. You losing your strength, your blood, and your life slowly," Donovan say to Sanna evilly looking at the red bloodstain on Sanna clothes. Sanna would not let Donovan get to her, even if she could not keep her footing. Sanna know that she will died one way or another, but she will never gave up on her propose to end Donovan rain of darkness once and all.

The fire crackles and snaps moving around the inland, burning everything in sight from full of life to ashes and death. Donovan and Sanna stared each other down with narrow eyes, and clench teeth. Donovan made his first move toward Sanna, but Sanna dodging Donovan moves. Sanna swing her sword at Donovan, clinging with Donovan sword, and keep on fighting with Donovan. Even if Sanna strength was slowly disappearing from her body, her mind was force on the fight with Donovan. *'Keep your mind on the prize Anilea... End off Donovan evil life for good,'* Sanna thinking to herself, keeping her eyes on Donovan attacks, and keeping herself on blocking his shots now.

They dance around the opened of the fire, collide their sword together, and getting a few good hits in-between with sword fight. Sanna body was cover in her own blood with small cuts all over her body. Donovan body was cover in his own blood with many small cuts all over his body. They keep on fighting each other the best they can sword on sword attack, pushing against each other. Adam could only do is watch the fighting from the sideline, and hoping Sanna will win. "Come on Anilea, everyone is counting on you. Roselyn, Tiffany, Andrew, Aaron, and everyone in town all your friends you have made over the years. They are counting on you Anilea... I'm counting on you," Adam shouted to Sanna seeing Donovan getting the upper hand on Sanna, by hitting Sanna back with his elbow, and knocking Sanna to the ground.

Sanna hitting the ground face first, feeling more pain on her body. "Ouch!" Sanna scream hitting the hard ground. *'I cannot give up, everyone is counting on me,'* Sanna closed her eyes, seeing the faces of her friends she meet over the years, and seeing Adam face too. *'They are all counting on me to win,'* Sanna thought to herself lying on the ground face down, knowing all of her friends new and old is counting on her to finish off Donovan.

Donovan stood to the left of Sanna, raising his sword in the air the blade down. Donovan red eyes glowing with the fire light, an evil grin came to his face. Donovan quickly lower his sword down to Sanna back, but Sanna rolled quickly onto her back, and laying her sword across her chest to catch Donovan sword. "How do you have enough strength? Your weak," Donovan say to Sanna in a shock voice.

"I will never give up for my friends in this town. Their hopes and dreams is all I need to defeat you once and for all," Sanna say to Donovan starting to a bright white that blinded Donovan, slowly getting off the ground to her feet.

Donovan stumbles back from Sanna white light, coving his eye with his left arm, and trying to see straight. "You will never win Anilea. This battle is my win," Donovan shouting to Sanna running closer to Sanna, his sword ready to kill.

Sanna closed her eyes, listening to Donovan scream, and got ready to fight. Sanna sword slowly changes into dagger form in her right hand. Donovan sword got quickly hot in his right hand that he throw his sword to the ground, and keep on running toward with his right hand ready. Donovan yelling his warrior screams at the top of his voice, hitting Sanna body, and sending his right fingers through left side of chest of Sanna. "Yes, this is you last time we will meet Anilea.

You are going to die by hands," Donovan says to Sanna face to face with a crazy look on his face, and chuckling evilly to Sanna.

Sanna never stop glowing white, "Think again Donovan," Sanna say to Donovan with a crooked smiled on her face, still having her eyes closed.

Donovan looked down to see Sanna dagger in his chest right in his heart, and Sanna right hand on the handle. "This cannot be I will kill you first, before you got a chance to kill me first." Donovan slowly squeezes Sanna heart with his hand slowly, hoping he will end Sanna life before she ends his life.

Sanna was not in pain, all she did was keep her force on defeating Donovan. Sanna chuckled a bit at Donovan, then say to him with a smiled on her face, "I will never stop glowing or give up of defeating you. I am more powerful then you." Sanna quickly open her eyes, sending her powers down her right arm, right hand, the dagger, and straight into Donovan heart.

Donovan body slowly got hot quickly. Donovan let go of Sanna heart with his right hand, slipping his fingers out of Sanna chest, cover in Sanna blood. He gasps for air with wide eyes and mouth, and his blood drizzling down from the corners of his mouth and his chest. "You will never defeat me. I will be back to get my revenge on you, Anilea," Donovan crust as his body blast into flames.

Sanna held on a bit longer, giving everything she has to make sure Donovan was gone forever. Sanna let out aloud warrior scream as the white got brighter, swallowing the two of them, and blasting outwards throughout the inland.

Adam covers his eyes with his left arm, seeing what just happen between Sanna and Donovan, and hoping this is it... The end of Donovan rain forever.

Chapter Twenty Five

The Afterward Mass!

Sanna friends and everyone in town watches from the beach seeing the inland in the middle of the lake glow a bright white. Andrew and Aaron comfort Roselyn and Tiffany from behind in their arms. Roselyn watch the inland glowing, *'Please make it Anilea. We need you, everyone is counting on you to defect Donovan,'* Roselyn thought in Andrew arms, everyone on the beach watching, and hoping that Sanna will win the battle.

On the inland, Sanna still having her dagger in Donovan heart, and still sending everything she got to her dagger into Donovan heart. "Goodbye forever," Sanna shouted to Donovan giving her dagger a quick twist to the left in Donovan heart, and quickly pulling out the dagger from Donovan chest with his blood on her dagger blade.

Donovan falling to his knees with a hole in his chest, wide eyes and mouth, "I will have my revenge on you, Anilea and your friends too. This will not be the last time we will meet, mark my words we will meet again," Donovan say to Sanna falling to the ground on his face, his blood pooled around his lifeless body, and drawing out his last breath from his body.

Adam step up to Sanna from behind and spoke to her kindly, "It is finally over. Donovan is gone forever. Now you can rest, and live a normal life, plus I love you." Adam wraps his arms around Sanna waist, trying not to hurt Sanna.

Sanna look down at her dagger in her right hand, seeing Donovan blood dripping off the end of the blade, hitting the ground. Sanna let out a sigh in Adam arms, "I did it, and it is over finally. Now I can rest." Sanna say to Adam lending back in Adam arms, closing her eyes, and breathing normally.

Sanna slowly stop glowing, and the inland went back to the fire flames around slowly burning. Sanna put her dagger in the sheath, turning around in Adam arms, and looking into Adam eyes. They lend in close for a kiss on the lips, but the inland started to shake under their feet. "Let's get out of here, Anilea," Adam says to Sanna grabbing her right hand, running to a cliff on the right side of the inland. They stop on the edge of the cliff, looking back to see a huge fireball coming toward them. They jump into the air, hitting the water 50 feet down from the cliff. The fireball miss them shooting outwards from the trees into the air, and setting down back on the inland with fire burning.

Everyone watch from the mainland seeing the explored of fire on the inland hitting the air, and setting back down glowing a little orange light in the night air, Roselyn and Tiffany lend forward in Andrew and Aaron arms trying to see if Sanna got off the inland safe. "Can you see her?" Tiffany asks Roselyn looking out at the lake water to see if Sanna was in the water somewhere.

"No sign of her, I hope Anilea is okay," Roselyn say to Tiffany looking out of water to be she could see Sanna.

Tiffany started to get worry about Sanna, "You don't think Anilea is..." Tiffany started to tell Roselyn in a worry voice.

"Don't say it, Anilea made it. She finally defect Donovan forever. Anilea is proudly very weak, we need to have faith that she alright," Roselyn say to Tiffany still looking out at the water. Then something catches Roselyn eyes, Roselyn saw something slowly coming out of the water, and toward them.

Adam helps Sanna out of the water with his right arm around Sanna waist, and his left hand on her left shoulder. "Be careful Anilea, take small steps. We are all most on the mainland," Adam says to Sanna helping her out of the water, dripping wet from the water, and they where soaking wet now.

Sanna was hunch over, holding her waistline with her left arm, "Thanks Adam," Sanna say to Adam with a bit of pain in her voice, every step she took was very painful that she could scream loudly in the air. Both of them were all wet from the lake water and blood drizzling from her wound on her waist.

Roselyn poke Tiffany in the arm, and pointing to Sanna and Adam exiting the water together. "Anilea!...Adam?" Roselyn yelled running out of Andrew arms, up to Sanna and Adam. Tiffany, Aaron, and Andrew follow Roselyn down to the water edge.

Sanna and Adam stood on the beach at the water edge, Sanna still hunch over in pain, and trying to force her eyes. "Adam is my friends coming?" Sanna ask Adam seeing white four white blurs coming toward them, trying to stand up straight with pain shooting through her body.

Adam can see Andrew, Aaron, Tiffany, and Roselyn running toward them. "Yes Anilea, they are coming. You stay with me for a bit longer. They must know what happen on the inland after they left, and then you can rest," Adam told Sanna looking down at her in his arms, he was worry to see the color gone from her face now.

Sanna friends stop in front Sanna and Adam with smiles on their face. Roselyn step forward closer to Sanna and Adam, and spoke to Sanna, "Thanks goodness you're a live Aniela. Is Donovan?"

Sanna look up at Roselyn and the rest of her friends to speak to them, "Donovan is gone forever, he died, and I am so weak now." Sanna lend in closer to Adam body for support, and trying not to die in front of her friends.

Andrew step forward closer to Adam, and spoke to Adam, "So you're like us, a spirit and it look like the same age as Anilea. Sanna had a weird feeling about you that drove her up the wall trying to finger out what it was; now we know why." Andrew looking over Adam spirit clothes, and smiled at Adam.

Adam looks at Andrew to say to him, "Also her past lover that was killed by Donovan 400 years ago. I will explain more lately, now Anilea need her rest. It was a very close battles to the end it once and for all." Adam look down at Sanna in his arms, "Too close for comforter," Adam whisper to Sanna kissing the top of her head.

Tiffany looks at Sanna to ask her, "What do you want to do Anilea?" Sanna never anything, she turned her head to the right, seeing something great, and a smiled came to her face. Everyone was wondering what Sanna was looking at with a smile on her face. They turned their heads to the distance that Sanna was looking to the greatest thing ever.

There coming along the beach was the people that Donovan had kidnapped over the year. In front of the group were the two children that Sanna met on Halloween, "Mommy! Daddy!" They yelled running up to their parent's arms, and giving a big hug with tears of joy running down their faces. All the lost ones were rejoining with their family and friends, and everyone was so happy to be together. The little girl looks over at Sanna with a smile on her face, 'Thank-you,' she mouth to Sanna hugging her mother.

Sanna smile at the little girl, and mouth back, 'Your welcome.' Sanna looks at her friends to say to them, "We all did great during the battle; you all help me defeat Donovan. We defeated Donovan together as a family, like we are." Sanna gave her friends a hug together, feeling her body ready to collapse, but held it together for a bit longer.

Donovan group slowly sneak away from everything into the tree line, Aaron and Andrew saw Donovan group sneaking away. "Should we go after them?" Aaron asks Sanna keeping his eyes on the group going into the trees.

Sanna took one look at Donovan group sneaking away from the beach then she spoke to her group, "Don't worry about them. They are nothing without Donovan; they will not try anything bad anymore. They are powerless now, let them go."

"Aw, I wanted one more round with Ryu," Aaron wined to Sanna, seeing Ryu waling away with Eris in the tress.

"I know brother, I wanted Crevan one more time, but now it is over," Andrew says to Aaron wrapping his right arm around Aaron shoulders.

"You boys enough of the winning about it, the battle is over, but if they try anything bad in the town, then you two can go at it," Tiffany say to Aaron and Andrew, then looking at Sanna. "Will that be okay?" Tiffany asks Sanna nicely, looking at Sanna to find out if that was okay.

Sanna nodded her head to her friends, then spoke to them, "If they cause troubled then go at it, but take it out of town." Sanna seeing Donovan group fully gone into the trees, and sighing a bit on the thought if Donovan group try anything in the town again.

Sanna try to hold in her pain, but her face was showing the pain big time. Sanna looks around at the town people celebrating the happiness of everything were okay, and a new beginning. Sanna smiled at them, and looking out at them say to her friends, "They are okay now. I am done with my deal, now I can rest." Sanna eyes started to rolling back in her head, and slowly falling to the sand ground.

"Anilea! Stay with us!" Adam says to Sanna in a panic voice, catching Sanna in his arms, and scooping Sanna up in his arms. "We need to go now!" Adam says to Sanna friend's running back to Sanna place. "Hold on my love, we are almost home. I love you very much," Adam whisper to Sanna while running back to Sanna place. The town people saw what happen to Sanna, and worry hits them inside quickly. They worry that Sanna will not make it; she did save their lives from Donovan and his group. They following Sanna group back to the house, and everyone talking among themselves in whispers.

Sanna friends and Adam still holding Sanna in his arms arrive back to Sanna place. Tiffany open the back door of the house, holding the door open for Adam to entering the house with Sanna, the rest of Sanna friends enter the house behind Adam, and Tiffany closed the door tight. Roselyn looks at Adam to say, "Let's get Anilea upstairs to her bedroom. Tiffany and I will wrap her wounds up, and take care of her for you."

Adam nodded her head to Roselyn, and following Tiffany and Roselyn upstairs, carrying Sanna all the way in his arms. Andrew and Aaron follow Adam up the stairs to Sanna bedroom. Sanna mourn a bit in pain in Adam arms, her eyes closed shut. Adam looks down at Sanna to whisper to her softly, "Hang on sweetheart. You are almost in your own bed. I am here for you, please stay with me, my love." Adam hit the top steps on the third floor, walking to Sanna bedroom, and entering the room.

Roselyn looks at Adam to speak, "Just lay Anilea down on her bed, and don't worry about her. Tiffany and I will take great care of Anilea for you. Just wait outside the room with Andrew and Aaron. I will come get you when we are done cleaning and wrapping up Anilea with bandages. Just go and try to rest, you had a big day today; being reborn back into a spirit you need your rest. Now go so Tiffany and I can start." Roselyn push Adam out of the bedroom, after he lay Sanna down on the bed, and closing the door tight.

Adam turn around looking at the bedroom door with a sad look on his face. Andrew looks at Adam to say nicely, "Hey Adam, do not worry about Anilea. Roselyn and Tiffany are great with Anilea, she in great care. At lest this time we are home, last time we where down at the waterfall trying to clean Anilea up. Anilea is strong, she will make it, because there one thing she need live for." Hoping what he will tell Adam next will cheer Adam out of the dump feeling now.

Adam sat down on the floor with his back against the railing, cross legs, looking at the bedroom door, and having a sad look on his face. "What is the one thing she needs to live for?" Adam asks Andrew looking up at Andrew from the floor.

Andrew knelt down to Adam level, placing his hands on Adam shoulders, and saying to Adam looking into Adam eyes, "You are the one thing that Anilea need to live for. You are past lover and mystery partner back in the Dark Ages... In addition, you need to have faith in Anilea will be okay, and that you two will be marry. Have faith Adam; also we need to move you in us here soon, because you are one of us, a spirit." Andrew sat down beside Adam in the left side, Aaron sat down on the right side, and all of them hoping Sanna will be all right.

In the bathroom, Roselyn and Tiffany were cleaning the blood off Sanna skin with a few washcloths and a couple big bowels full with warm water. Sanna lay there on her bed in her underwear and her long hair down around the pillows. Tiffany was cleaning Sanna right arms, and letting out a huge sigh. Roselyn look up at Tiffany from cleaning Sanna waistline to ask in a worry voice, "What wrong Tiffany? You're never this down, what's up?" Roselyn can see a sad look on Tiffany face.

Tiffany looks at Roselyn and spoke, "I am worry about Anilea. I never seen her badly wounded in all the years we have been together. What if she does not make it, what will we do then?" Tears fill Tiffany eyes, and slowly rolling down her cheeks at the thought of losing Sanna forever.

Roselyn looks at Tiffany with a small smile on her face, and saying to her sister, "If Anilea does not make it, and we will live a normal life now. Donovan is gone forever and his group will not try anything bad now. They are powerless now, so we do not have to worry about them very much. Anilea will make it, because she has Adam in her life now, and they are planning a wedding, plus a life together later on. She will make it; we need to have hope now." Roselyn went back to work cleaning up Sanna wound, and Tiffany went back to work too with the thought of hope now in her mind.

Sanna lay there on her bed, her eyes closed and shallow breathing through her nose into her lungs. Roselyn and Tiffany stitch up a few deep wounds on Sanna body mostly the waistline, wrap up Sanna wounds with bandages wraps, covers Sanna body up with a sheet, and letting in the boys into the room. Adam walk up to Sanna right side of the bed, taking her right in his right, holding her hand, and spoke softly to Sanna, "I am sorry my love." Lending down to give her, a soft kiss on her lips, sitting down in a chair beside her bed, and holding her right hand in his hands with hope that she pull through now.

The sun slowly raised over the mountains on a brand new day in the town Spirit-villa, and the town people waited outside the house to know what's going on inside.

Chapter Twenty Six

Awaking Again!

Spring turn into summer, summer into fall, fall into winter, and winter back into spring. Sanna with in a coma state, in her bed with Adam stay by her side throughout the year. The only time Adam left Sanna side was when Andrew and Aaron were training Adam to help him get use to being a spirit, and try to make Adam happy. Alternatively, when Tiffany and Roselyn was checking and changing Sanna bandage wraps. Adam tries to be happy that Sanna does not have to fight anymore, and they can be together as a couple, but he did not like the way Sanna was looking. One night Adam lying beside Sanna left side of the bed took Sanna left hand, pulling out a small ring that he tries to give to her on February 14, 2065, slipping the ring on Sanna ring finger of her left hand, and kissing Sanna on the lips. "I wish you were still awake now, I miss hearing your voice Anilea. I got everything we need for own wedding, the only thing I need now is you in your wedding dress, and awake too," Adam whisper to Sanna rubbing her forehead with his right hand, and tears slowly fell from his eyes. "I love you very much," Adam softly spoke to Sanna, giving her a small kiss on the lips, and trying hard not to cry on the way Sanna was right now.

~~*~*~*~*~*~*~*~*~*

May 10, 2066, Adam wearing his normal clothes, went upstairs to check on Sanna, he opened the bedroom door, and a fear look came to his face. Adam saw Sanna bed empty and the curtains blowing in the wind from the French doors. Adam saw the walk-in closet door open wide, Adam ran to the French doors to see is Sanna was out on the balcony, but Sanna was not out there.

'Where are you, Anilea?' Adam thought with fear on his face. Adam enters back into the room, looking at the empty bed to see a small folded piece of paper on the pillow. Adam walks up to the bed, picking up the note, opening it, and reading the words on the paper. Adam knew where Sanna was now; Adam left

the room, running downstairs, told Sanna friends what happen, and left the house to the area where Sanna was right away.

Adam ran all the way up to the top of the second falls, going across the big rocks, and entering the thick bushes in front of him. Adam enters the small open area with the trees branches making a small ceiling above. Adam saw Sanna sitting down on the ground in front of the two swords with a blank look her face, and wearing normal clothes. Adam step closer to Sanna, and Sanna spoke to Adam, "You miss my voice, and my life. I am okay for now, I am still weak and in pain. Thank-you for the ring too, I love you Adam." Sanna never looks at Adam once as she spoke to Adam, then looking down at the ring on her finger.

Adam walk closer to Sanna, sitting down on the ground beside Sanna left side, and looking out at the two swords in front of them. "You really do miss them do you?" Sanna nodded her head to Adam looking out the swords. Adam keeps on speaking to Sanna, "You know they maybe gone in person, but their memories live on forever in your heart, and don't forget it." Adam wrap his right arm around Sanna shoulders and Sanna lend her head down on Adam right shoulder.

Sanna spoke to Adam softly, "You have everything ready for the wedding?" looking out at the swords still, and frowning a bit of the thoughts in her mind of her younger siblings.

"Not everything I am missing the most important thing ever," Adam say to Sanna looking down at Sanna left hand, taking her left hand in his right hand, and looking at the ring on her ring finger.

"What is that?" Sanna ask looking up at Adam with a raise eyebrow, and cannot finger it out for a moment.

Adam lend his forehead on top of Sanna forehead, looking into her eyes, and spoke sweetly to her, "You my love. I am missing you my Aniela, my wife-to-be. I love you very much from the bottom of my heart." Adam kisses Sanna on the lips and closing his eyes for a second to be happy that she still alive.

"I love you too, my love," Sanna looks at Adam in the eyes, and then seeing a dagger sheath clip to Adam left side. "I see you got your sword back," Sanna say to Adam seeing that Adam got his own sword back to him.

Adam looks down at the dagger on his left side of his hip, and saying to Sanna nicely, "Yeah it came back to me, I found it in the back of the museum, Jeff was happy to give it back to me, and I am sorry for using your sword last year it was beside me."

"That okay, I am happy that I don't have to fight anymore. I can live a normal life with you and my friends. I cannot wait to take you as my husband here soon," Sanna say to Adam looking into his eyes, and keep on talking, "I see the town people are living a normal life, and they must been worry about me for all I see in the front of the house. They know that I can leave without them knowing, and will never return at all." Sanna was thinking about leaving the town and everyone behind without them knowing that she really gone.

Adam eyes went wide quickly, and he spoke to Sanna in a shocking voice, "You would not leave the town now and never return? Yeah at first, they were in front of the house all the time to know when you would wake up, but now they know that you are okay. They love you as a friend you cannot leave them now. What about Roselyn, Tiffany, Aaron, Andrew, and me? You cannot leave us now." Adam started to panic that Sanna would do that, leave the town forever, and he was thinking about their future together.

Sanna smiled at Adam, and spoke to him nicely, "I am not going to leave this town. This is own home you know, and we are staying here forever. I was only joking to you," Sanna laugh at Adam a bit holding her stomach in her arms as she felt a bit of pain from the scar across her waistline.

Adam got what Sanna did to him, and felt so stupid about freaking out a moment ago. "I feel so dumb now. You got me good Anilea; I never know that you can do that to anyone. You have loose up a bit more now, and I love the new you." Adam laugh with Sanna, keeping his right arm around Sanna shoulders.

Sanna and Adam sat there on the ground talking about the past, present, and future. Sanna looks up at the sky to see the blue sky slowly changing into an orange-red color. "We better get home now, before everyone get worry about us," Sanna say standing up from the ground slowly and trying not to show her pain that shooting through her body. Sanna hunch over in pain a bit, wrapping her arms around her waist, and trying to take a step without any pain.

Adam stood up from the ground, looking at Sanna, and speaking to her in a worry voice, "Are you okay, Anilea? Your still in pain, you should stay home instead of being here." Adam places his right hand on her back and rubbing back gently with his hand.

Sanna looks at Adam with pain in her eyes, "Yes, I am still in pain, but had to come up here to tell my family that Donovan is gone forever. Let's get home before dark," Sanna say to Adam walking pass Adam to the tree line.

Adam stop Sanna in her tracks by asking her a question, "How did you the out of the house without anyone knowing that you left?" raising an eyebrow at how Sanna left the house without anyone knowing she was gone.

Sanna looks at Adam and spoke to him with a smile on her face, "I turn myself invisible, and walk right pass you... No, I jump from my balcony down to the ground, walk slowly up here, I was been careful. I wanted some time alone, but now I just want to go home to be with my friends. They are proudly worried about us now. The sun is setting, and the sky is changing." Sanna walks through the brushed to the top of the falls with Adam behind her.

Adam step up behind Sanna, looking out at the scene in front of them, and spoke to Sanna nicely, "Do you want to race home?" Adam saw the sun slowly setting over the town and lake.

Sanna looking at Adam, and told the truth, "No I am a bit weak now. I do not think a race will not work for me right now, but later when I am all better; it is so on between us. It is so on beating you in a race on foot." Knowing her own risk level, even if she really wants to race Adam home so badly, but she could do a face plant on the ground in front of Adam.

Adam wrap his arms around Sanna body, and spoke to Sanna caring, "What about a piggyback ride? I will carry you home, and everything will be great." Adam lends Sanna against his chest, rocking side to side with Sanna, and stop rocking after a bit.

Sanna turn around in Adam arms, and say nicely, "That will be great." Looking into Adam eyes, and nodded her head to Adam.

Adam let's go of Sanna, turning around to have his back to Sanna, Sanna jump onto Adam back, and Adam say to Sanna looking over his left shoulder at her, "Hold on sweetheart," Sanna held onto Adam shirt with both hands. Adam walks to the edge of the cliff of the second waterfall, jumping into the air with Sanna on his back, landing on the top of the waterfall below, running to the cliff to jump into the air again, and landing on the mainland. Adam and Sanna laugh all the way home as Adam ran with Sanna on his back.

They arrive back home, Adam let Sanna get off his back, they held each other hands walking up to the back door, Adam open the back door for Sanna, and Sanna enter the house with Adam behind her. Sanna walks to the living room to see her friends sitting on the couches reading a book each, "Hey you four, nice to see you again," Sanna say stopping behind the chairs with a huge smile on her face.

Sanna friends closed their books together, looking up at Sanna and Adam. Andrew spoke to first, "Hey sport, nice to see you fully awake." Andrew got up from his spot, walking up to Sanna, and giving Sanna a hug.

Aaron got up from his spot, walks up to Sanna, giving Sanna a hug, "I am so happy to see you awake. Trying to make Adam smile all the time was a mess.

Now he got the biggest smile on his face ever," Aaron says to Sanna, looking at Adam face with a smile on it, and overall just happy that Sanna is awake.

Tiffany got up from her spot, walking up to Sanna, giving her a hug, and saying happy, "I am so happy to see you a wake Anilea. We been worry about you all year, but we knew that you will pull through it, now you are awake."

Sanna looks at Roselyn, who was sitting on the couch, and spoke to her first, "I know, I should not left my bedroom, but I was being very careful," rolling her eyes at Roselyn, knowing Roselyn will say something about her leaving the house.

Roselyn walks up to Sanna, looking into Sanna eyes to say, "I know, I saw you jumping down from your balcony into the backyard from the dinning room window. Your always been a little sneaker, trying to get under our radar all the time. You are still in pain a bit and weak a bit, but it is nice to see you awake now." Roselyn gave Sanna a big hug, then saying to Sanna nicely, "So have you two pick a date to get marry?"

Sanna and Adam looks at each other, then Sanna say to her friends, "We were thinking on a date that we really wanted."

"What date is that?" Roselyn ask Sanna letting go of Sanna and walking up to Andrew.

"May 20," Adam says to Sanna friends with a smile on his face. "It was the original date that we wanted to be marrying on 401 years ago. Now this this year is the prefect for a wedding, with all the wonderful around this town."

Sanna smile at Adam, then it hit her, "What about my wedding dress? I don't think I will have time to a dress in ten days." Sanna started to panic that there no time to get a dress for the wedding.

Adam looks at Sanna, then say to her kindly, "Roselyn and Tiffany had that cover for you. They say they did not have to look very far to find your wedding dress, and they told me that you will love it."

Sanna looks at Roselyn and Tiffany to see them having a huge smile on their faces. Roselyn walks up to Sanna, take Sanna left hand in her hand, leading Sanna upstairs to Sanna bedroom. Tiffany follow them upstairs, arriving into Sanna bedroom, taking Sanna into the walk-in closet, and Tiffany saying to Sanna, "Okay Sanna closed your eyes, so Roselyn and I can get you into the dress." Sanna closed her eyes, Roselyn and Tiffany got Sanna undress to her underwear, then slipping the white dress over Sanna head. Roselyn lace the back of the dress, and tying a bow at the end of the ribbon. "Okay Sanna open your eyes and see your wedding dress," Tiffany says to Sanna standing behind Sanna with Roselyn.

Sanna slowly open her eyes to see in the long mirror what she was wearing, Sanna mouth drop at the sight of her wedding dress. The dress was white flowing full-length dress with thin straps, beadwork along the top of the sweetheart top. A lace train flow from around Sanna waist to the ground, split down the front of the dress, and lay a few feet behind the dress. A light blue ribbon belt around the waistline, hang down the back on the dress. Sanna stood there in shock that she was wearing her old wedding dress with a few changes to it. "I thought I will never wear this dress again. You fix it up more beautiful then before, and the rips are all fix up. Thank-you Roselyn and Tiffany for doing this for me and everything," Sanna say to Roselyn and Tiffany with tears of joy filling her eyes, and slowly rolling down her cheeks.

Roselyn and Tiffany hug Sanna, and Roselyn say to Sanna happy, "Your welcome Anilea and we are not done yet, there one more thing that you're missing." Roselyn look into Sanna eyes with a smiled on her face.

Sanna raised an eyebrow at Roselyn and Tiffany, "What that?" Sanna was confused at the girls got for her now.

Tiffany ran out of the closet to come back a minute later with a box in her hands. Roselyn opened the box in Tiffany hands, grabbing whatever in there and say to Sanna nicely, and "You cannot get marry without one important thing." Roselyn setting a long veil with silk flower crown along the top of the veil, a small heart shaped crown in middle of the flowers. The flowers was small white roses with white ribbon down along the side of veil, and the veil touch the floor with a small veil hanging over the face. Roselyn place the veil on top of Sanna head, making sure the veil is straight on Sanna head. "There now you're ready to get marry in ten days," Roselyn say to Sanna stepping back from Sanna for a moment.

Sanna stood there looking at herself in the mirror in her wedding dress with the veil. A tear came to her eyes of joy, and a smile on her face. "This look awesome, and now I am ready to get marry in ten days," Sanna say to Roselyn and Tiffany, trying not letting the tears roll down her face by wiping them away with her fingers.

The girls laugh in the walk-in closet at a few things, Sanna change back into her normal clothes, but stop for a moment to see the big scar from the final battle with Donovan. Sanna touch the scar across her waistline with her right hand with a sad look came over her face quickly. Roselyn and Tiffany saw Sanna sad look on the face, and Tiffany looks at Sanna, "You look great, the scar is almost gone. You cannot tell that you have that scar with your clothes on," Tiffany says to Sanna hoping to cheer up Sanna a bit more.

Sanna finish getting dress, and spoke to Roselyn and Tiffany with mild tone voice, "Have Adam seen my scar body?" Roselyn and Tiffany nodded their heads to Sanna. Sanna spoke to them, again "How did Adam take it, when he saw the scars?" Sanna stared into the mirror with a blank look on her face.

Roselyn spoke to Sanna in a calm voice, "Adam took it very hard at first, but now he is okay with the scars. He might not show very much that he reminded about that you almost lost your life in the final battle. Just stay calm and everything will be fine. He loves you very much that he going to marry you in ten days." Roselyn gave Sanna a hug, and Tiffany joins in the hug.

Sanna smiled at her friends and say to them happy, "Thank-you two fro everything." The girl carry on with the rest of their normal day by having fun with Sanna, and going over the plans for the wedding in ten days. Sanna was in shock at everything Adam had planned and done for their wedding, it was coming true, they were about to get marry for real this time around.

That evening Sanna was sitting sideway with her knees up to her chest on her balcony front railing looking out at the lake, seeing the moonlight shining off the lake water. Sanna let out a huge sigh; something was bugging her big time. Adam stood in the French door way, lending back against the doorway, looking at Sanna sitting on the railing, and spoke nice to her, "Penny for your thoughts."

Sanna turn her head to the left to see Adam in the French doorway, and say to Adam nicely, "I was wondering about something that all." Sanna turn her head back looking out at the night scene in front of her, and cannot get one think out of her mind now.

Adam walks up to Sanna, "What are you thinking Anilea?" wrapping his arms around Sanna shoulders, and held Sanna close to his body.

Sanna lend her head down on Adam chest, and spoke to him quietly, "I was thinking about your family, Adam. Do they know that you're a spirit now?" Sanna wonder if her husband-to-be family knowing anything about Adam being a white spirit now.

Adam looks down at Sanna, and spoke to her, "They know, and they are okay about me being spirit. My mom knew there was something about me from birth, now she knows about it. They know that I will live forever, and do great things now. They are happy that I am going to marry you, and they know that your friends and you are spirits too." Adam lifts Sanna face up to looks her eyes, and smiled at her sweetly.

Sanna looks into Adam eyes, and saying to him nicely, "Now I know that we can live together in harmony. I love you," Sanna kiss Adam on the lips, and lending against Adam chest again. Adam comfort Sanna in his arms looking out at the night scene with Sanna, thinking about their lives together forever, and finally getting marry her true love after many years.

Chapter Twenty Seven

The Wedding Day!

The big day came for Sanna and Adam wedding finally together after years of being apart. Sanna woke to the sun shining through the window, making Sanna stir in her bed, throwing the blankets over top of her head as she groaning a bit, and uncovering her head to show off her mess hair. Sanna eyes slowly opened looking up at the ceiling, slowly sitting up in her bed to see Roselyn and Tiffany sitting at end of the bed. Sanna scream at them, as she was surprise to see them sitting here. "Morning Aniela," Roselyn say to Sanna with a smile on her face. "Are you ready for today?" standing up from the bed with Tiffany.

Sanna rub her eyes with her hands and stretching in the air with a yawn. "Yeah I am, today is a day to celebrate something great," Sanna say to Roselyn and Tiffany getting out of her bed wearing her light blue nightgown with a huge smile on her face.

Roselyn and Tiffany walks up to Sanna placing their arms around Sanna shoulders, and looking at Sanna. Tiffany looks at Sanna to say kindly, "Anilea, you look way healthier then you did last year before the battle."

Sanna looks down at her body to see a big change with her body. She had color in her face and not skinny anymore. Sanna smile at herself, and then say to her friends, "I don't have to worry anything big anymore. I can live a normal life with my new husband and my family." Sanna walks out of her friend's arms to her closet. "Come on you two, we got to get ready for a wedding today."

Roselyn and Tiffany laugh at Sanna, walking up to Sanna, and Roselyn saying to Sanna, "I know, I heard the bride is such a bitch."

Sanna looks at Roselyn quickly, "Hey!" Sanna say to Roselyn, knowing Roselyn was only kidding with her.

"Sorry, you know I was only joking," Roselyn say to Sanna, giving Sanna a hug, and entering the closet with Tiffany and Sanna to get ready for the wedding with laugher echoing around the room.

Downstairs in Roselyn and Andrew bedroom, Andrew, Aaron, and Adam was getting ready for the wedding. "It sound like the girls got Anilea up, and is getting ready," Aaron says to Adam and Andrew entering into the bedroom with a smile on his, listening to the noise coming from Sanna bedroom.

Adam stood by the French door, looking outside at everything being setting up in the backyard for Sanna and his wedding. Adam stomach was getting butterflies, and Adam try to stay calm. Andrew walk up to Adam, wrapping his left arms around Adam shoulder, and spoke to Adam nicely, "What up Adam? Getting cold feet about your wedding, just calm down, and everything will be great. Anilea is a wonderful and lucky woman to have a great guy like you."

Adam nodded his head to Andrew, and say to Aaron and Andrew. "I know about that, I'm not worry about the wedding and living the rest of eternal with Anilea. I am so happy about that, it just something just bugging me, and I am not letting it get to me. Don't ask what it is, I have no clue about it, but something will happen over time, just don't know when it will happen."

Andrew and Aaron look at each other, back of Adam, and Aaron spoke up, "Well enough of this talking like girls. We better get ready for a wedding." Andrew, Aaron, and Adam got ready for the wedding in the bedroom.

Upstairs, Roselyn and Tiffany finish getting ready in their dresses. Sanna stood by the French doors looking out at the spring scene with worry look on her face. Wearing a long white rob, her long hair pulled back from her face, and hanging down her back in ringlets. Tiffany looks over at Sanna, and says to Sanna, "Anilea are you okay?"

Sanna turn around to see Roselyn and Tiffany in their light-blue bridesmaid dresses with thin straps, and long flowing floor length. Sanna spoke to them calmly, "I am just worry about something that all," looking back outside the doors to see the wedding stuff getting setup in the backyard.

Tiffany and Roselyn looks at each other then back at Sanna. Tiffany keeps on speaking to Sanna, "What is it that got you worried? Is it about the wedding? Or something else?"

Sanna let out a sigh, looking at Roselyn and Tiffany to say to them, "It feels like I am not done with something. That battle last year was only a warm up for something bigger. I am not let that feeling get to me today, I am getting marry to a great guy," a smile came to Sanna face slowly, but in the back of her mind, that feeling was bugging her.

Roselyn looks at Sanna to say kindly, "That great that you're not letting that feeling get to you today. After you are marrying Adam, then you can finger out what that feeling is all about, when you got time. Now the bride need to get ready fro her wedding." Roselyn watch Sanna walking into walk-in closet to get dress with Tiffany behind Sanna. Roselyn and Tiffany help Sanna finish getting ready in her wedding dress and veil. Roselyn and Tiffany stood back a bit to look Sanna over in her wedding dress. "Anilea, you look so beautiful. We are so proud of you for everything you have done over the years. Now you getting the one thing you always wanted to marry your lover." Roselyn and Tiffany started to tear up in their eyes, and trying not to rid their make-up.

Roselyn and Tiffany gave Sanna a hug, when they heard a knocking noise on Sanna bedroom door. Tiffany went to check to see who it was at Sanna bedroom door. Tiffany opens the door to see Andrew and Aaron standing there. "Hey you two, what bring you two up here?" Tiffany asks Andrew and Aaron seeing in their black tuxedos with blues ties and blues shirts.

"We come to see the bride is ready and her bridesmaids too," Andrew say to Tiffany nicely, and entering the bedroom. Sanna step out of the closet to show Andrew and Aaron that she was ready. Andrew and Aaron mouths drop to the floor on how beautiful Sanna was looking in her wedding dress, "Anilea, you look so gorgeous. Adam will love you, when he sees you coming down the aisle," Andrew says to Sanna in a shock voice, and wide eyes still at Sanna.

Sanna looks at Andrew and Aaron to say to them sweetly, "I am almost done then we can leave."

"What that sport?" Andrew ask Sanna in a confuse voice.

Sanna closed her eyes forcing on her forehead to have her gold headpiece with blue jewel hang down in front of her forehead showing up. Sanna open her eyes to say to her friends, "Now I am ready." Sanna friends smiled at Sanna, giving Sanna a big group hug, and left the bedroom.

Andrew and Aaron went first to get Adam out of the house first. Therefore, Adam does not see Sanna coming down the stairs. The boys left the house to get ready to walk down the aisle. The boy music started to play, and the boys starting to walk down the aisle one at the time. Aaron went first, then Andrew next, and last Adam with his parents. The boys stood front of everyone in town that came to the wedding. Adam waited for Sanna to come down the aisle to him. Adam was smiling ear to ear after so many years he was going to marrying his true love at last. Adam stood there in his black tuxedo and white shirt with light blue tie.

The girl's music starting up and everyone turn their head to see Tiffany and Roslyn walking down the aisle holding red silk roses in their hands, and huge smiles on their faces as they walks slowly down the aisle. They got to the front of everyone stood where they had too, a waiting for Sanna to come down the aisle. "Everyone please stand from the bride," the pastor says to everyone in his or her seats, everyone stood from his or her seats, waiting for Sanna walk down the aisle.

Sanna music start up, everyone eyes stared at the back down to see Sanna walk. Sanna took a deep calming breath, letting it out slowly, stepping out into the deck with a bunch of red and white silk roses with a few small light blue flowers in-between in her hands. A small veil hangs down in front of her face, and Sanna smiling under the veil. Sanna slowly started her walk to the front, her eyes was on Adam the whole time. After along time she was going to marry her lover at last and her heartbeat for Adam. Sanna step up to the front of everyone, handing her flowers off to Roselyn, placing her hands in Adam hands, and smile on her face. "I love you," Sanna whisper to Adam hearing everyone sitting back down in his or her chairs.

"I love you too, my Aniela," Adam whisper to her, with a smile on his face, holding her hands in his hands.

The pastor started to speak to everyone about marriage and to love one another forever, no matter what happen. Then the pastor turn to Adam to say, "Adam, do you take Anilea to be your wife forever, lover, and protract for all eternal, even through the darkness that surround the both of you?"

Adam looks into Sanna eyes sweetly, and spoke "I do and I will forever, no matter."

The pastor turn to Sanna to speak to her, "Anilea, do you take Adam to be your husband forever, lover, and protract for all eternal, even through the darkness that surround the both of you?"

Sanna look into Adam eyes sweetly, and say to Adam, "I do, and I will forever, no mater what."

Pastor had Sanna and Adam say their vows to each other. Adam had the sweetest and funny vows to say to Sanna. He will always love her forever, even when she win at the games and pranks. That he will always be the shoulder for her to cry on, and the warmth through her darkness days. He will love her to his dieing breathe, and will protract her forever. Adam slip on a small wedding band on Sanna left ring finger after saying his vows to her, and whispering, "I love you always from the bottom of my heart forever."

Sanna started to tear up, calming down after letting out a huge breath, and then say her vows to Adam without tearing up. That she will love Adam forever, taking him as her husband at last is the best thing ever. That she love you him forever, and when the darkness surround them, she knows that her back is cover. Adam tearing up a bit wipes a tear away from his eyes, and force on the wedding. Sanna slip on a wedding band on Adam left ring finger, and whispering, "I love you forever from the bottom my heart forever."

After they signing the papers that say that they were marry. The pastor say to the rest of the people that Adam and Sanna are husband and wife, and Adam can kiss the bride. Adam lifts up the small veil from Sanna face, looking into her eyes, and gives Sanna a big kiss on the lips. Sanna lips meet Adam lips, and it was cool. Adam finish kissing Sanna, waited for Sanna to get her flowers from Roselyn hands, scoop Sanna up in his arms, and carrying her down the aisle. Sanna laugh at Adam actions, Sanna friends ran down the aisle together, and enjoy the rest of the day with their family and friends.

Once pictures were finish, they went to the reception in the backyard in a huge tent. They enter the tent to see all the tables, chairs, and everything else set up for their party time. People sitting down in the chairs, watching Adam and Sanna entering the tent, having great food, a few laughing mostly the cake smashing, and some sweet moments. Adam and Sanna had their first dance on the dance floor in each other arms. "I love you my Anilea, my wife," Adam whisper in Sanna right ear.

Sanna lay her forehead down on Adam chest, and whisper back to Adam, "I love you too my Adam, my husband." They dance in each other arms for the rest of the song, then kissing each other on the lips at the end. The party really started on the dance floor, and the rest of the night went off without any problems at all.

Sanna friends saw Donovan group in the shadows of the trees. They got Adam and Sanna showing them were Donovan group was in the trees. Sanna walks up to the tress, and speaking to Desdemona nicely, "Hey, what bring you guys and girls here?" Sanna friends and Adam stood behind Sanna with narrow eyes at Donovan group.

Desdemona looks at Sanna to say, "You have a wonderful wedding, you two are a great couple. We are here to see the wedding, and not doing anything wrong. We have change we want to live a normal life without Donovan. We want to be friends with your friends and you, Anilea." Desdemona show that everyone in the group had change for the better, and does not want to cause any more trouble among the groups anymore.

Sanna friends were getting ready to fight with Donovan group, but Sanna and Adam stop them by raising their left hands. Sanna spoke to them, "We will like to be friends with you. The battle is over between us, now we can live together as friends. Welcome our new friends," Sanna gave Desdemona a hug and everyone join in hugging the group and talking to each other.

"Be careful Anilea, Donovan is tougher to defeat, then he was during the Dark Ages, please watch yourself and your family," Desdemona whisper into Sanna right ear. Sanna nod her head to Desdemona, and invite them to come to the party. Desdemona and the rest of them thanking Sanna and her friends, and went to party in the tent.

Sanna watch her friends and Donovan group walking away from her. Adam walks up to Sanna, wrapping his arms around Sanna shoulders, and say to her, "You don't think the battle is over or only starting?"

Sanna nodded her head to Adam, looking out at the lake at the inland, and speaking to Adam, "That what I am afraid of that, we are not done with Donovan at all," Adam kiss Sanna on the right cheek, and stood there looking out of the lake with Sanna in his arms. Sanna lend back in Adam arms thinking that the battle is only the beginning between Donovan and her; the war will begin here soon. Fear hits Sanna body with the thought she got of her losing her live-forever to Donovan doing. *'Please don't let this feeling be true... Please do not let Donovan be alive at all... I destroy Donovan for good last year. I stab him in the heart with my dagger. His heart explored in his chest; I saw his blood on the blade of my dagger, and his blood all over the ground,' the only thing that was going through the mind.* Sanna stared at the inland on the lake in Adam arms, and try to calm down after thinking that Donovan had survive her attack last year.

Adam held Sanna in his arms, kissing her cheek, and whisper to her, "How about we worry about this later? Let's go enjoy this night together without any worries, and start our lives together as husband and wife like it should have been 401 years ago." Adam lends Sanna back to the party in the backyard, and Sanna agree with Adam that she should enjoy tonight without any worries. In the back of both their minds, they were worry on what will happen in the future and if Donovan is really died or not.

Chapter Twenty Eight

The End?

On the inland, new life starting to re-growing from the battle a year ago from the ashes of the fire, as the moon shine down on the inland, hitting the black dirt ground, and off the little green plants. Everything was calm and peaceful. No worries or evil at all, on or off the inland.

A male right hand cover in ashes and dirt, shot straight out of the ground, reaching for the night sky, closing the hand into a fist, and saying one name with rage in its voice from under the dirt, "Anilea!"

The end or is it?

'I can hear their shrieks, their cries of torment carried by the wind and their howls for help; cries from babies, screams from children, men and women. I can see the people running through the streets screaming in terror. I can see the flames razing the houses and scorching the roads, corpses littering the streets; the smell of blood filling the air as it flows down the streets - the blood on my hands again. I love being truly evil.'

~Donovan thoughts

CPSIA information can be obtained
at www.ICGtesting.com
Printed in the USA
LVOW11s0512150317
527232LV00001B/39/P